MORE THAN A CONVENIENT BRIDE

BY
MICHELLE CELMER

Published in Great Britain 2015
by Mills & Boon, an imprint of Harlequin (UK) Limited,
Eton House, 18-24 Paradise Road, Richmond, Surrey, TW9 1SR

© 2015 Harlequin Books S.A.

Special thanks and acknowledgement are given to Michelle Celmer for her contribution to the TEXAS CATTLEMAN'S CLUB: AFTER THE STORM series.

ISBN: 978-0-263-25252-1

51-0315

Harlequin (UK) Limited's policy is to use papers that are natural, renewable and recyclable products and made from wood grown in sustainable forests. The logging and manufacturing processes conform to the legal environmental regulations of the country of origin.

Printed and bound in Spain
by CPI, Barcelona

Michelle Celmer is a bestselling author of more than thirty books. When she's not writing, she likes to spend time with her husband, kids, grandchildren and a menagerie of animals.

Michelle loves to hear from readers. Visit her website, michellecelmer.com, like her on Facebook or write her at PO Box 300, Clawson, MI 48017, USA.

To Best Friends

One

Julie Kingston stood and waited in the crowd, her heart overflowing with pride as her best friend and colleague, Lucas Wakefield, prepared to cut the ribbon marking the opening of the new, state-of-the-art Wakefield Clinic. It seemed as though the entire town of Royal, Texas, had shown up to mark the occasion.

The town's original free clinic once stood directly in the path of the F5 tornado that had ripped through Royal last October. In the blink of an eye, all that had remained of the structure was the concrete foundation. Patients from all over the surrounding counties had lost an important lifeline in the community.

Lucas, who had been a regular volunteer there despite his duties as chief of surgery at Royal Memorial Hospital, hadn't hesitated to donate the money to rebuild, using some of the proceeds from the sales and licensing of surgical equipment he'd invented several years ago.

Humble as he was for a multimillionaire, he'd intended to keep his identity as the donor a secret, but someone leaked the truth, and the news spread through Royal like wildfire. The town council had immediately wanted to rename the clinic in his honor. But of course

Luc had protested when he'd heard about plans for the Lucas Wakefield Clinic.

"This clinic doesn't belong to me," he'd told Julie when she'd tried to convince him that he was being ridiculous. "It belongs to the people."

"This is a huge deal," she'd argued time and again. "You donated millions of dollars."

He gave her his usual, what's-your-point shrug, as if he truly didn't understand the scope of his own good will. For a man of his wealth and breeding he lived a fairly simple life. "It was the right thing to do."

And that was Luc in a nutshell. He always did the right thing, constantly putting the well-being of others first. But finally, after much debate, and a whole lot of coercing from his mother, Elizabeth, Julie and his colleagues in the Texas Cattleman's Club, he relented, allowing the use of his last name only.

Julie smiled and shook her head as she thought back on it. Lucas was the most philanthropic, humble man she had ever known. And at times, the most stubborn, as well.

Luc looked out over the crowd, and when his eyes snagged on hers she flashed him a reassuring smile. Despite his dynamic presence, and easy way with his patients and coworkers, he despised being the center of attention.

To his left stood Stella Daniels, the town's acting mayor. To his right, Stella's new husband, Aaron Nichols, whose company R&N Builders rebuilt the clinic. In the six months since the storm, the town's recovery had been slow but steady, and now it seemed as if every week a new business would reopen or a family would move back into their home.

"I'm so proud," Elizabeth Wakefield said, dabbing away a tear with the corner of a handkerchief. Julie knelt beside the wheelchair Elizabeth had been forced to use since a botched surgery a decade ago left her paralyzed from the waist down. In the months since Julie came to Royal last October, Elizabeth had contracted a multitude of infections that led to numerous hospital stays, and she now required permanent, round-the-clock care from a registered nurse. Though she was a beautiful and proud woman, she looked every one of her sixty-eight years, and a recent hospital stay for viral pneumonia had left her weak and vulnerable. Originally Luc forbade her from attending the ribbon cutting, but she insisted she be there. After much debate, he eventually caved, and it was more than clear to Julie where he inherited his stubborn streak.

"You have every reason to be proud," Julie said, patting Elizabeth's frail arm. "You've raised your son to be an amazing man."

"I wish his father could be here. From the day Luc was born he insisted that his son was destined for great things. It still breaks my heart that he didn't live to see how right he was."

Julie took her trembling hand and gave it a gentle squeeze. "He knows."

The mayor completed her brief speech and handed Luc a pair of gold-plated scissors. With a quick swish of the blades the ribbon drifted to the freshly laid grass, and a round of applause erupted from the crowd. Luc's club brothers crowded around him to congratulate him and shake his hand, but Julie hung back, still clutching his mother's hand. Elizabeth looked proud but tired. The simplest of activities exhausted her.

"We should get you home," her nurse, Theresa, said.

Too sleepy to argue, Elizabeth nodded.

"Shall I call Luc over?" Julie asked. "So you can say goodbye?"

"Oh no, don't bother him. I'll see him at home later tonight."

Julie kissed her papery cheek and said goodbye, then joined her friends Beth Andrews and Megan Maguire several feet away.

"She doesn't look so good," Beth said as Theresa wheeled Luc's mother toward the parking lot to the van Luc had custom-built for her. When it came to taking care of his mother, he spared no expense.

A stab of sadness pierced Julie's heart. In the six months since she'd moved to Royal, Julie had come to consider Elizabeth a dear friend. She was the closest thing Julie had had to a mother since her own mother died giving birth to her sister, Jennifer. Her father waited to remarry until after she and her sister had left home, and though he dated, he'd never brought a woman home to meet his daughters. He traveled extensively, so they were raised by nannies and the other house staff. Homeschooled by tutors.

And when he was home? Well, she didn't like to think about that.

"I don't suppose you'll have any free time to volunteer this week," Megan said. "Just an hour or two? Someone left a cardboard box of three-week-old puppies on the doorstep. They need to be bottle-fed every hour or so and I'm ridiculously understaffed this week." Manager of the local animal shelter, she was known for taking in strays. Animals and humans alike. She had certainly gone out of her way to make Julie feel welcome when she arrived in Royal. Her significant other, as well as Beth's, were members of the Cattleman's Club with Luc.

It was shaping up to be a very busy week, but Julie could always make time to help a friend. And sadly, this would probably be the last time. "Of course," Julie said. "Just let me know when you need me."

Megan sighed with relief. "You're a lifesaver!"

They stood chatting for several minutes, before Julie heard a familiar voice say, "Good afternoon, ladies."

She turned as Luc joined them, smiling brightly to hide the deep feeling of sadness that seemed to radiate from the center of her bones. She could tell by the way he tugged at his tie that he was already irritable. No sense in making him feel even worse.

"It's a wonderful thing you've done," Megan told him, and Beth nodded in agreement.

"Thank you, ma'am," he said, pouring on the Texas charm. Though he was her boss, and they had never been more than friends—best friends, but just friends—that drawl sometimes gave her a warm feeling inside her bones.

"Can I give you a lift home?" he asked Julie. Her apartment was within walking distance from the clinic, and it was a sunny and pleasant day for a stroll, but she suspected he was looking for any excuse to leave.

"If you wouldn't mind," she said, playing along, noticing a look pass between Megan and Beth, as if they knew Luc was eager to escape.

"Good to see you ladies," he said, nodding cordially, that hint of Texas twang boosting his charm somewhere into the stratosphere.

Julie followed him to his car, his stride so much longer than hers she practically had to run to keep up.

"What's your rush," she said, though she already knew the answer.

"Damn," Luc muttered, pulling at his tie as if it were a noose. "Why does everyone have to make such a big deal about it?"

Seriously? "Because it *is* a big deal, doofus. You're a hero."

"It's not as if I built it with my own two hands," he said, using his key fob to unlock his Mercedes. "I just wrote out a check."

"A ridiculously enormous check," she reminded him as he opened the door for her. He'd also remained involved through the design stage and the construction process, to be sure that everything was built to his exact specifications. Whether he wanted to admit it or not, this was, in many ways, *his* clinic.

As they drove through town, sadness and regret leaked from every pore. In the six months she'd been here, Royal had become her haven. The US felt like more of a home to her now than her native South Africa, and now she had to leave. She had no idea where she would go, or what she would do, and she had little time to figure it out.

Silence filled the car, and as they pulled into the gated community where she was currently staying, Luc said, "You're awfully quiet. Would you like to talk about it?"

"Talk about what?" she asked, dreading the inevitable conversation. But Luc could always tell when she was upset. She could swear that sometimes he knew her better than she knew herself.

"Whatever is bothering you." He parked outside her condo and turned to her. "Did I do something to upset you?"

"No, of course not." She'd hoped to put this off a little while longer, so as not to dampen his special day, but there was so much concern in the depths of his eyes, it seemed only fair to tell him now.

"So, what is it?"

As her brain worked to find the appropriate words, tears burned the backs of her eyes. Maybe the parking lot wasn't the best place to do this.

"Can you come inside for a few minutes? We need to talk."

His brow furrowed, he killed the engine. "Of course. Is everything okay?"

No, not at all. "Let's talk inside."

Gentleman that he was, Luc took her keys as they reached her door and unlocked it for her. He didn't even do it consciously. It was just his way. His mother, born and bred in Georgia, was old-fashioned when it came to matters of social grace. He claimed that from the day he was born, she'd drilled him with proper Southern manners.

Whatever she'd done, it had worked. He was one of the most courteous men Julie had ever known. In all the time they had been friends and worked together, he'd never said a harsh word, or once raised his voice to her. Or to anyone else, for that matter. He had such a commanding presence, he never had to. People took one look at those piercing hazel eyes and that *GQ*-worthy physique, heard the deep baritone voice, and spontaneously bent to his will. Women especially.

As they stepped inside the apartment, afternoon sunshine and fresh spring air poured in through the partially open window in the living room. Luc shrugged out of his suit jacket and dropped like a lead weight onto the sofa, looking far too masculine for the floral printed chintz. The furniture, which was too formal and froofy for her taste, and not all that comfortable, either, came with the apartment. Expecting good news when she'd filed to renew her visa, she'd been tentatively window-shopping in her spare time for furniture more suited to her. She wouldn't be needing it now. Not here, anyway.

She wasn't even sure where she would live. Other than a few distant aunts and uncles, she had no family left in her hometown. And when her father had passed away, his wife, whom Julie never had the pleasure of meeting, sold off the entire estate before the body was cold.

Julie had so much to plan, and so little time to do it.

She set her purse on the coffee table and sat beside Luc, fisting her hands in her lap. There was nothing she hated more than giving good people bad news.

Luc unknotted his tie, tugged it off and tossed it over the sofa arm on top of his jacket. Relaxing back against the cushions he undid the top two buttons of his dress shirt. "Okay, let's hear it."

She took a deep breath, working up the nerve to tell him. "I heard back from immigration yesterday."

One brow rose in anticipation. "And?"

Just say it, Jules. "My application to renew my visa again was denied."

In a blur of navy blue Italian silk and white Egyptian cotton, Luc was on his feet. "*Denied*? You can't be serious."

Tears pricked the corners of her eyes. Now was not the time for a messy emotional display. She'd learned years ago that crying only made things worse. "According to your government I've overstayed my welcome. I have two weeks to pack up my things and get out of the US."

"How is that possible? You're on a humanitarian mission."

"Technically I'm on a work visa."

"I still don't see the problem. You're still my research assistant. Gainfully employed. What changed?"

"Remember how I told you that in college I attended several protests."

"I remember."

"Well, what I didn't tell you is that I was arrested a few times."

"Were you convicted?"

"No, but I was afraid that if I put it down on my application I would be denied."

"So you left it out?"

She bit her lip and nodded, feeling juvenile and ashamed for having lied in the first place. But she would have done almost anything to come to the US and help her best friend. Now that one serious lapse in judgment was coming back to bite her in the rear. "I screwed up. I thought that because the charges were dropped, and it was a peaceful political protest, it wouldn't matter anyway. I was wrong."

"There has to be something we can do," he said, pacing the oriental rug, brow deeply furrowed. "Maybe I could talk to someone. Pull some strings."

"The decision is final."

His chin tilted upward. "I can't accept that."

She rose from the sofa, touching his arm, stopping him in his tracks. "You don't have a choice. It's done."

He muttered a curse, one he wouldn't normally use in the presence of a female, and wrapped his arms around her, pulling her close. She rested her head against his chest, breathed in the scent of his aftershave. It wasn't often that they embraced this way, and she found herself dreading the moment he let go.

The stubble on his chin brushed her forehead as he spoke. "There has to be something we can do."

There was one thing, but it was too much to ask. Even of him. *Especially* of him. "At this point all I can do is accept it. And move on."

He held her at arm's length, and she could see the wheels in his head spinning. But this was one situation all his money and influence couldn't fix. "Where will you go?"

"South Africa for a while, until I can find another research assistant position. Maybe in Europe, or even Asia."

"I'll do whatever I can to help. I'll write such a glowing recommendation people will be clamoring to hire you."

The problem was, she didn't want to work for anyone else. She used to love moving from place to place, meeting new people and learning new cultures and customs. Now the only place she could imagine living was right here in Royal. It was the first place in her travels that had genuinely felt like home. The first place in her life really.

There had to be something she could do.

Two

Luc sat at the bar at the Cattleman's Club swirling a double Scotch, watching the amber liquid tornado along the sides of a crystal tumbler, still reeling from Julie's news. And wracking his brain for a way to fix this, to keep her here in Royal where she belonged. Where she wanted to be.

She was the only person in his life—aside from his mother—who truly understood him. Who knew what made him tick. In fact, there were times when he wondered if she knew him better than he knew himself. These past few months, with the stress of seeing his hometown devastated, she was the anchor that had kept him grounded. She had been there to support him during his mother's past two hospital stays, which seemed to stretch longer each time she was admitted. Julie sat with her on her breaks, read to her when she was too weak to hold a book in her own two hands. He never even had to ask for her help. She just seemed to sense when he needed her, and she was there.

Drew Farrell, a fellow club member, and the owner of Willowbrook Farms, slid onto the stool beside him at the bar. In blue jeans, worn boots and a dusty cowboy hat, he looked more like a ranch hand than a man responsible for breeding multiple Triple Crown–winning horses. And though he dealt regularly with an elite and prestigious clientele, he couldn't be more down-to-earth. He was that guy in town everyone liked. Well, everyone but his neighbor Beth Andrews, who, up until the storm, had it in for Drew. But now, by some strange twist of fate, they were engaged to be married.

The complicated nature of relationships never ceased to amaze Luc.

Drew gestured to the bartender for a drink, and within seconds a bottle of his favorite brew sat on the bar in front of him. "What's the score?" he asked Luc.

It took Luc a few seconds to realize Drew was referring to the game playing on the television behind the bar. He'd been so lost in thought he hadn't even noticed it was on. "No idea," he said, taking a sip of his drink.

"I'm sorry I missed the ribbon cutting at the clinic. I had a client in town looking to buy one of my mares."

"No apology necessary. If there was any way *I* could have gotten out of it, I would have."

"Is that why you look so down?"

Luc ran his thumb around the brim of his glass. "Nope."

"Anything I can do to help?"

He shook his head. "Nope."

"Maybe it would be better if I left you alone," his friend said, grabbing his beer and making a move to get up.

"No," Luc said, realizing that he was being unnecessarily rude. And frankly, he could use the company. "I'm sorry. I just got some bad news today."

"It must have been pretty bad to put you in such a foul mood."

"Julie's request to extend her visa was denied."

Drew's eyes went wide with disbelief. "No way."

"I couldn't believe it, either." Nor was he willing to accept it. But when it came to plausible ideas to stop this from happening, he was coming up short.

Drew shook his head, expression solemn. "After all she's done for this town since the storm, they should be giving her a medal, not kickin' her to the curb."

Luc's thoughts exactly.

"What are you going to do?" Drew asked.

At this point there wasn't much Luc could do. Despite her objection he'd made a call to his lawyer, who had confirmed what Julie had told him. It was a done deal. "Let her go, I guess."

"Dude, you can't do that. You can't give up on her."

"I'm out of options."

"I'll bet there's one thing you haven't considered," Drew said.

"What's that?"

"You could marry her."

Marry Julie? His best friend? Drew was right, he hadn't considered that, because it was a ridiculous notion.

"Julie is like me," he told Drew. "She's very focused on her work. Neither of us has any plans to marry."

Drew rolled his eyes, as if Luc was a moron. "It wouldn't have to be a real marriage, genius. But it would be enough to keep her in the country."

A pretend marriage? "Not only is that a preposterous idea, it's illegal. We could both get in serious trouble. We could go to prison."

Drew grinned. "Only if you get caught."

Luc could hardly believe that Drew of all people

was suggesting he break the law. "And if we do get caught, what then?"

He shrugged. "Volunteer in the prison infirmary?"

Luc glared at him and Drew laughed.

"I'm kidding. Besides, it would never come to that. No one in this town would ever question the validity of your marriage."

Confused, Luc asked, "Why is that?"

"Are you kidding? You two are inseparable. Or at least, as inseparable as two workaholics can be. Most married couples don't spend as much time together as you two do."

"We're colleagues. It's part of the job description."

"It's more than that. You just...I don't know, *fit*."

"Fit?"

"People have been waiting for you guys to hook up. And there are others who think that you must already be knocking boots."

Annoyed that anyone would make that assumption, Luc said, "People should mind their own damn business."

Drew shrugged. "Small towns."

That didn't make it any less irritating. He and Julie didn't have that kind of relationship, nor would they ever. Yeah, he may have had the hots for her when they first met, but he had been reeling from his ex-fiancée, Amelia, abruptly calling off their engagement, and Julie had just come out of an emotionally rocky relationship herself. Before they'd had a chance to get over their former significant others and explore a physical relationship together, they had become pals instead. She was his buddy, his confidante. He would never do anything to jeopardize that. "We're just friends, and that's all we'll ever be."

Looking exasperated, Drew said, "Dude, it doesn't matter. You would be married in name only. Consider the alternative."

He had, a million times since she'd hit him with the bad news. Although the term *bad news* didn't quite measure the depth of his feelings when he imagined her leaving. Living thousands of miles away. Who would he talk to? Who would remind him to pick up his dry cleaning, or share late-night Indian takeout with him in the break room on those evenings when they were both too jammed to leave the hospital?

There had been nights like that for weeks after the storm, performing surgery after surgery. Some successful, some not. While volunteering for Doctors Without Borders, he had seen his share of heartbreaking situations and managed to stay detached and objective for the most part. A disaster in his hometown was a completely different story. Without Julie to lean on, to keep him grounded, he would have been a wreck. She was his anchor, his voice of reason.

Did he love her? Absolutely. But that was very different from being *in* love. And finding a new research assistant would be a nightmare. Julie knew his work inside and out. Training someone new would take more time and energy than he cared to expend.

"I obviously don't want her to leave," Luc said. "But if we were caught and something happened to her, I would never forgive myself."

After she was gone they could keep in touch through email and social media. They could even video chat on their computers or phones, though it wouldn't be the same as having her there. But was defrauding the government and risking both her freedom and his the answer?

"I'm telling you, no one is ever going to know," Drew insisted. "Even if the truth comes out, you're a local hero. Can you name one person in town who would turn you in?"

He made a good point. And even if there was an investigation, he and Julie knew each other as well as any married couple. He had no doubt they would pass any test with flying colors. The question was: How would Julie feel about it? She was the one with the most to lose.

"I guess it couldn't hurt to bring it up and see what she thinks," he told Drew.

"Great. I suggest a small- to moderate-sized ceremony and reception at the club and a long relaxing honeymoon somewhere tropical."

A wedding was one thing, but leaving Royal? That was out of the question. "I wouldn't have time for a honeymoon. I'm needed here."

Drew laughed and slapped him on the back. "Dude, you're a brilliant and devoted physician and, yes, this town needs you, but *everyone* needs a break now and then. No one will blame you for wanting a honeymoon. When was the last time you took time off? And I mean *real* time."

Luc tried to recall, and came up blank. It had definitely been before the storm. And probably quite some time before that. A year, maybe two. Or three. He'd traveled all over the world volunteering with Doctors Without Borders. That was how he'd met Julie. Their duties had taken them to many exotic and unfamiliar destinations, but it had been no vacation. Maybe they could use a break…

Luc shook his head. He and Julie married and taking a honeymoon? Until today the thought had never even crossed his mind. And it wasn't that he didn't find her appealing, both mentally and physically. Any man would be lucky to win her heart. He'd found her so appealing when they first met, it had been a little difficult to be objective. Practicing medicine in a developing country, the accommodations weren't exactly lavish. It wasn't uncommon for all the volunteers, male and female alike, to share living quarters, where modesty took a backseat to practicality. He was used to seeing his colleagues in various stages of undress. But in the case of Julie, he would often find his gaze lingering just a little longer than most would consider appropriate. But if she'd noticed, or cared, she'd never called him out on it. The issue was exacerbated by the fact that Julie didn't have a bashful bone in her body. In his first week working with her he'd seen more skin than the first two months he'd been dating Amelia, his college sweetheart and ex-fiancée. She'd had enough body hang-ups for half a dozen women.

But he would never forget the day he'd met Julie. He had just arrived at the camp and was directed to the tent where he would sleep and store his gear. He stepped inside and there she was, sitting on her cot, wearing only panties and her bra, a sheen of sweat glistening on her golden skin, her long, reddish-brown hair pulled into a ponytail. He froze, unsure of what to do or say, thinking that his presence there would offend her. But Julie hadn't batted an eyelash.

"You must be Lucas," she said, unfazed, rising from

her cot to shake his hand while he stood there, caught somewhere between embarrassment and arousal. It was the first of many times he'd seen her without her clothes on, but that particular memory stood out in his mind.

He and Julie had seen each other at their best, inventing surgical tools and techniques that they knew would change the face of modern surgery, and at their worst, unwashed and unshaven for weeks on end covered in bug bites from every critter imaginable. They had been to hell and back together, and they always, under any circumstance, had each other's back. Was this situation any different? Didn't he owe it to her?

It was becoming less of a question of why, and more of a question of why not. "You really think this could work?" he asked Drew, feeling a glimmer of hope.

"You would have to make it convincing," Drew said.

"Convincing how?"

"Well, she would have to move in with you."

Of course as a married couple they would have to live together. He and his mother had more than enough space, and four spare bedrooms for her to choose from. "What else?"

"In public you would have to look as if you're in love. You know, hold hands, kiss…stuff like that."

There was a time when he'd wondered what it would be like to kiss Julie. A real kiss, not her usual peck on the cheek when she hugged him goodbye. How would her lips feel pressed against his? How would she taste?

The tug of lust in his boxers caught him completely off guard. What the hell was wrong with him?

He cleared his throat and took a deep swallow of Scotch. "I could do that."

"No one else can know it's not real. We keep it

right here, between us," Drew said. "You know you can trust me."

Trusting Drew wasn't the issue. He knew that any one of his club brothers would lay down their life for him. The whole idea hinged on Julie's willingness to break the law and play house with him for heaven only knew how long. And her willingness to play the part convincingly.

It was something he would have to investigate thoroughly on his own before bringing it up to her. Talk to his attorney about the legalities. Make a list of the pros and cons.

"I'll talk to her," he told Drew.

"Who knows," Drew said with a sly grin, "you two might actually fall in love."

That's where Drew was wrong. If Luc and Julie were meant to fall in love, meant to be a couple, it would have happened a long time ago.

Julie sat in her office the next day, eyes darting nervously from the work on her desk to the clock on the wall. She was due to meet Luc in the atrium for a late lunch in fifteen minutes. Seeing her best friend had never been cause for a case of the jitters, but this was different: this had her heart thumping, her hands trembling and her stomach tied in knots. She was planning to ask Luc a favor, the biggest and most important favor she had ever asked him. Ever asked *anyone*. But if there was a single person on the planet she could count on to come through for her, it was Luc. More so than her own sister, who could be flighty at best. It sometimes took her days or even a week to answer a text or email. Sometimes she didn't answer at all.

Luc was truly the only person in her life who she could count on unconditionally. And if everything went as she hoped, she would be able to stay in the country indefinitely. Worst case, Luc would laugh in her face, and she would be on her way back to her native home, where she had only distant family left and no friends to speak of.

In the event that Luc said no, she would spend the rest of her time in the US tying up loose ends regarding the research on Luc's latest invention. She had reports to file and interviews to transcribe so that the switch to his new assistant would be a smooth one. Though the idea of someone else finishing her work left an empty feeling in the pit of her stomach.

The sudden rap on her office door startled her out of her musings. She looked up and was surprised to see Luc standing there. She checked the clock. She still had ten minutes to spare.

"Can I come in?" he asked. He wore scrubs under his lab coat, meaning he must have had a surgery scheduled that morning.

"Of course," she said, gesturing him in. "I thought we were meeting in the atrium. Did I get the time wrong?"

"Nope." He stepped into her office, which wasn't much larger than a small walk-in closet, and as he did, she felt as if all the breathable air disappeared from the room. It would explain the dizzy feeling in her head, the frantic beat of her heart.

What was wrong with her? She'd never been nervous around Luc. The truth is, she never got nervous about much of anything. Especially Luc. Everything about him, from his slow, easy grin and low, patient voice to his dark, compassionate eyes, naturally put people at ease. He could be intimidating as hell when he wanted to be. She'd seen it. But unless the situation warranted it, he chose not to be.

"I wanted a minute to talk in private," he said, snapping the door closed behind him. He crossed the two steps to her desk and sat on the edge. She could be mistaken, but he looked a little uneasy, which wasn't like him at all.

"There's something I need to ask you," he said.

What a coincidence. "There's something I need to ask you, too."

"Why don't I go first," he said.

Now that she'd worked up the nerve, she couldn't back down. "I think I should go first."

"What I have to say might impact what you have to say."

All the more reason to say it right now. The last thing she wanted was to make a huge deal about this. If she made a fool of herself, so be it.

It sure wouldn't be the first time.

Three

Luc was watching her expectantly, and she knew that the longer she dragged this out, the harder it would be. What she was about to ask him was no small favor. She wouldn't blame him at all if he said no.

Okay, Jules, you can do this.

Hoping he didn't hear the slight quiver in her voice, notice her unsteady hands or the erratic flutter of her pulse, she said, "I may have come up with a way to stay in the country. But I need your help."

His brow rose expectantly. "What kind of help?"

Her heart lodged in her throat, so when she opened her mouth to speak, nothing came out. For several seconds she sat there like a fool, the words frozen in her vocal cords.

Wearing a quirky smile, Luc asked, "Are you okay?"

Yes and no.

She was being silly. He was her best friend. Even if he said no, it wouldn't change anything. Hopefully it would only be slightly humiliating.

Come on, Jules, just say it.

Gathering her courage, she said, "You know that I really don't want to leave the US."

"And I don't want you to leave," he said.

"Royal has become my home. I feel like I belong here."

"You do belong here." He said it as if there were no question in his mind. "And you know that I'll do anything I can to help. As a matter of fact—"

"Please, let me finish." Earnest as he appeared, he might want to take that back when she told him her plan. "I've looked into every possible avenue, but there's only one way I've come up with that will assure I can stay."

She paused taking a deep, empowering breath. Then another.

"Are you going to tell me," he asked, looking mildly amused. "Or do you want me to guess?"

Oh, for Pete's sake, just say it, Jules. "We could get married. Temporarily of course," she added swiftly. "Just until I can earn my citizenship. Then we can get a quickie divorce and pretend it never happened. I'll sign a contract or a prenup. Whatever makes you most comfortable."

Luc blinked, then blinked again, and then he burst out laughing.

Wow. There it was. Her worst nightmare realized.

"You're right," she said, quickly backtracking. "It was a ridiculous idea. I don't know what I was thinking." She shot to her feet, when what she really wanted to do was curl up in the fetal position and wallow in shame. "Let's forget I said anything and go have lunch."

She tried to duck past him, and he wrapped a very large but gentle hand around the upper part of her left arm.

"Just hold on a minute," he said in that firm but patient way of his. From anyone else it would have come off as condescending. "It is *not* ridiculous. Not at all. I'm laughing because I came here to suggest the exact same thing."

It was her turn to blink in surprise. Did he mean that, or was he just trying to make her feel less stupid. "Seriously?"

"But it is a legally and morally gray area. I wasn't sure if you would be willing to risk breaking the law."

Desperate times required desperate measures. "I'm willing if you are."

"We can't risk anyone else knowing the truth."

"I won't tell if you don't."

"Drew knows. He's the one who suggested it. But we can trust him. And I won't lie to my mother."

Julie had never known Drew to be anything but a stand-up guy. If Luc trusted him, so would she. And she would never expect Luc to lie to Elizabeth, nor would she want him to.

Julie had no one else to tell, except her sister, Jennifer, who probably wouldn't care anyway. When she married her husband, an older, wealthy man she'd met on a trip to New York, he became the center of her life. She quit college and set her sights on being the perfect trophy wife. Between charity balls and country club brunches with the other trophy wives in her elite social circle, she had little time for her nomadic, unsophisticated sister.

Though she had never actually met Jennifer's husband—nor did she care to—her sister's description of him gave Julie a bad feeling. He sounded very controlling, like their father. But now was not the time to dredge up those old memories. She had promised herself a long time ago that she would never look back in regret, but instead learn from her past and always move forward. Always strive to better herself. Marrying Luc, though completely unexpected, would be just another leg of her journey.

"Having second thoughts already?" Luc asked, and she realized she was frowning.

"No, of course not. Just wondering what happens next."

"Drew suggested we have the ceremony and reception at the club and we have to do it soon."

"How soon?"

"How's this Saturday afternoon looking for you?"

This Saturday? That was only five days away. She knew absolutely zero about planning a wedding, but less than a week sounded ridiculously fast. "Is it even possible to put a wedding together that quickly? And what about immigration? Don't we have to have an interview or something?"

"My attorney is taking care of all of that. And as for the wedding, we'll keep it simple. Close friends only. Very informal."

"I don't even know where to start."

"All you need to do is find a dress. And a maid of honor. I'll take care of the rest."

Of all her friends in Royal, Lark Taylor was the closest. They'd met during the first few weeks of the cleanup efforts and became fast friends. She was a nurse in the intensive care unit at the hospital. They often took coffee breaks together, and sometimes went out for drinks after work. She was planning her own wedding to Keaton Holt, a longtime Cattleman's Club member, so perhaps she could give Julie a few pointers.

"We'll have to kiss," she heard Luc say, and it took her brain a second to catch up with her ears.

"Kiss?"

"During the ceremony," he said.

"Oh…right." She hadn't considered that. She thought about kissing Luc and a peculiar little shiver cascaded down the length of her spine. Back when she first met him, she used to think about the two of them doing a lot more than just kissing, but he had been too hung up on Amelia and their recently broken engagement to even think about another woman. So hung up that he left his life in Royal behind and traveled halfway around the world with Doctors Without Borders.

A recent dumpee herself, she'd been just as confused and vulnerable at the time, and she knew there was nothing worse for the ego than a rebound relationship. They were, and always would be, better off as friends. In her experience, it was usually one or the other. Mixing sex and friendship would only end in disaster.

"Is that a problem?" Luc asked.

She blinked. "Problem?"

"Us kissing. You got an odd look on your face."

Had she? "It's no problem at all," she assured him, but if that was true, why did her stomach bottom out when she imagined his lips on hers. It had been a long time since she'd been kissed by anyone. Maybe too long.

"We'll have to start acting like a married couple," he said.

"In what way?"

"You'll have to move in with me."

She hadn't really considered that, but of course a married couple would live together. Having separate residences would raise a very bright red flag. Since Julie left home, when she wasn't volunteering abroad, she'd lived alone. She liked the freedom of answering to no one but herself, of doing what she wanted to do, when she wanted to do it. That would be hard to give up.

As if Luc read her mind, he added, "Nothing in our relationship is going to change. We only have to make it look as if it has."

But by pretending that it changed, by making it look that way to everyone else, wasn't that in itself a change?

Ugh. She never realized how complicated this could be. She could already feel the walls closing in on her.

"Look," he said, and this time he was the one frowning. "If any of this makes you uncomfortable, we don't have to do it. I want you to stay in the US, and I'll do whatever I can to help make that happen, but if it's going to cause a rift in our friendship, maybe it's not worth it."

"I'm just used to living on my own. The idea of changing that is a little intimidating. But it is worth it. And I don't want you to think that I'm not grateful. I am."

"I know you are." He smiled and laid a hand on her forearm, and the feel of his skin against hers gave her that little shiver again. What the heck was going on? She never used to shiver like that when he touched her. She was sure it was due only to the stress of her situation.

What else could it possibly be?

"It's bad, isn't it?" Julie looked up at Lark, her maid of honor, in the dressing room mirror at the Cattleman's

Club. Julie was on her third attempt of giving herself "smoky eyes." But she looked more like a cheap street walker than a bride.

"When it comes to eyeliner and shadow, especially for someone as naturally pretty as you, I think less is more," Lark said, which was her kind way of telling Julie to give it up.

"Oh my God, what a mess," Julie said, swiping at her eyes with a damp cloth. It had looked pretty simple in the instructional video she'd found online, but her technique lacked a certain…finesse. Which is why she never wore the stuff.

Her father had lived by very traditional values and as teens, Julie and her sister had been forbidden to use makeup of any kind. Or wear pants. Dresses and skirts were the only acceptable attire for a female in her father's home, and Julie had played the role of obedient daughter very well. It was easier not to make waves. She concentrated on her studies and getting into a good college. She never did develop the desire to wear makeup, but after eighteen years of wearing only skirts and dresses, she swore she would never wear anything but pants. Yet here she was now in a newly purchased, off-white, silk shift dress, which she had to admit hung nicely on her athletic frame. But with her raccoon eyes Luc was going to take one look at her and run in the opposite direction.

Her sister, the queen of all things girly and impractical, would have been a big help right about now but she wasn't answering calls or texts. If it was anyone but Jennifer, Julie might have worried, but that was typical for her sister. She was either completely distant and unreliable, or smothering Julie with her sisterly love. There was no middle ground.

"I suck at this," she said.

"Maybe just a little mascara and liner," Lark suggested, with a sympathetic smile. "Would you like me to help?"

Julie looked up at her with pleading, raccoon eyes. "Yes, please."

Lark worked her magic and she was right. Julie was lucky to have been blessed with smooth, clear skin, and just a touch of liner and mascara and a little clear gloss on her lips subtly enhanced her features.

"You're a genius," she told Lark.

"And you look beautiful," Lark said, smiling and stepping back to admire her work. "Lucas is a lucky man. And forgive me for saying, but it's about darned time you two tied the knot."

Julie had heard that same remark from a dozen people since she and Luc made the announcement earlier that week. "It doesn't seem...*sudden*?"

"I always suspected you and Luc had something going—I think everyone has—but you're a very private person, so I didn't want to ask. I figured that if you wanted me to know, or needed to talk about it, you would tell me."

If there had been anything to tell, Julie probably would have.

There was a rap on the dressing room door and Lark's sister Skye stepped into the dressing room. She looked surprisingly healthy for someone still recovering from a near-fatal car crash during the tornado. Luc had performed an emergency cesarean to save her unborn child, and her injuries had been so severe she'd been in a coma for four months. Until Skye was well enough to care for her daughter, Lark had taken responsibility for Baby Grace, who was the sweetest most adorable infant Julie had ever seen.

"It's time," Skye said, then sighed wistfully. "You look beautiful. Luc is a lucky guy."

Julie took a good look at herself in the mirror, spinning in a circle to get every angle. Not half-bad.

Though she usually kept her hair pulled up into a ponytail, she'd worn it down today, in loose, soft curls that tumbled across her shoulders. She'd even put on her mother's diamond earrings. It was the only thing of her mother's that she had left. In his grief after she died, Julie's father had removed every trace of his wife from their home. Photos, personal items, anything that reminded him of her. Julie had only been four at the time, but she remembered sitting on her parents' bed, crying as she watched their housekeeper clear out her mother's closet, shoving her clothes into black trash bags.

Between his wife's death and having a newborn infant to care for, her father seemed to forget that he had another child who was mixed up and lonely and desperate for the unconditional love and affection her mother had always given so freely. Within weeks of her death he'd hired a nanny and began traveling extensively. He had never been what anyone would consider an attentive father, but after her mother's death he had become virtually nonexistent.

Julie breathed deep to ease the knot of sadness in her chest, the burn of tears behind her eyes. Now was not the time to think about her less than ideal childhood. God forbid she start crying and ruin her makeup.

"How are you doing?" Lark asked. "You nervous?"

Julie shook her head. This wasn't going to be a real marriage, so what reason did she have to be nervous?

Though they wouldn't be married for long, she had insisted on a prenup. To protect not just his interests, but her own, as well. She'd never been the type to flaunt her wealth, but with the inheritance her father had left her and her sister, and a little savvy investing, Julie was pretty much set for life. A simple, no frills life, but that was fine with her. She didn't need much.

"So, are you ready?" Lark asked, and Julie turned to find her and Skye watching her expectantly.

After one more quick glance in the mirror, she nodded and told her friends, "Let's do this."

Four

With so little time to plan the wedding, Drew had volunteered to put a guest list together for Luc. But now, as Luc stood with Drew at his side, waiting for the ceremony to begin, scanning row upon row of guests idly chatting, he was beginning to think that had been a bad idea. It seemed as if half the town was there.

He leaned in close to Drew and said in a harsh whisper, "This is your idea of small and intimate?"

"Just helping to make it convincing," Drew said with a wry smile. It was obvious to Luc that he was thoroughly enjoying himself. "Are you nervous?"

"Of course not." What reason did he have to be? This was nothing more than a business arrangement between friends. In fact, he felt exceedingly calm. A little bored even.

"All grooms get nervous," Drew persisted.

"But I'm not a real groom, am I?"

"Look around you. This sure looks real to me. Besides, you can't argue with a marriage license."

Okay, so maybe he was a real groom, but not in the traditional sense. They would be married, but not really married. Together, but not really together.

Luc glanced over at his mother, who sat in her

wheelchair in the front row, an encouraging smile on her face. When he told her about the marriage she was beside herself excited, even when he explained the true nature of the situation.

"It's just a way to keep Julie in the States," he'd explained.

"Of course it is," she'd said with a twinkle in her eyes, as if she knew something he didn't. If she believed it to be anything more than a friend helping out another friend, if she had her heart set on Luc and Julie falling in love, she would be sorely disappointed.

Stella Daniels, who was officiating, touched Luc's shoulder and said softly, "Words cannot express how happy I am for the two of you. And forgive me for saying this, but it's about damned time."

He kept a smile planted firmly on his lips, but he felt a distinct twinge of guilt. He'd heard many similar remarks this past week, and as much as he hated the idea of lying to everyone, he and Julie had no choice.

The music started and everyone turned to the doorway where Lark stood, carrying a small bouquet of miniature yellow roses—Julie's favorite color.

Here we go, Luc thought, his stomach bottoming out.

Okay, so, maybe he was a *little* nervous.

Lark made her trip down the aisle, but Luc's attention remained fixed on the doorway, anticipation tying his stomach into knots. Then the "Wedding March" started and Julie appeared in the doorway, and all Luc could think was *wow*.

Rarely did he see Julie with her hair down, and in all the time he'd known her he couldn't recall ever seeing her in a dress. Cut several inches above the knee, it was just long enough to be tasteful, but short enough to showcase her toned, suntanned calves and a little bit of thigh…

Whoa, he thought, as his pulse picked up speed. This was Julie he was gawking at, his best friend. But damn, who could blame him? She looked stunning and sexy and as his eyes met and locked on hers, he experienced a distinct tug of sexual attraction. Bordering on red-hot lust.

Talk about getting caught up in the moment. If this kept up he was going to need a serious attitude adjustment.

Everyone stood and she started down the aisle, walking alone, holding a single long-stemmed yellow rose, looking cool and composed, as if she did this sort of thing all the time. This may have been a "pretend" wedding, but in that moment it couldn't have felt more real to him, and despite her cool exterior, when Julie faced him and he took her hands, they were trembling.

Stella began the ceremony, but he was so focused on Julie, the mayor's words all seemed to run together. It was almost as if he was really seeing Julie for the first time. And though he'd been to more weddings than he could count, as they recited their vows, he realized he'd never really grasped the gravity of the words. Real marriage or not, as he slid the platinum band on her ring finger—she'd balked at the idea of a diamond—he pledged to himself that as long as they were married, he would honor those vows.

Then came the part he'd been most anticipating. The kiss to seal the deal. They had to make it look convincing. Too chaste or formal and it might make people suspicious; too passionate and Julie might crack him one. Probably not here at the wedding, but later, when they were alone.

There was another possibility. One he hadn't truly considered until just now. What if he kissed her, and he liked it? So much so that he wanted to do it again. And even more intriguing was the possibility that she might like it, too.

"You may kiss the bride," Stella said, and Julie's pulse jumped as Luc, seemingly in ultra slow motion, bent his head. The entire ceremony had been a bit surreal, as if she were standing outside of her body watching herself. But this? This was very real.

Her chin lifted in anticipation, and she began to wonder if this was something they should have rehearsed ahead of time. No one's first kiss should have an audience, yet here they stood with dozens of pairs of eyes planted firmly on them.

Oh boy, what had they gotten themselves into?

Luc reached up, his hand gently cupping her cheek, and her knees went weak. His lips brushed softly across hers, seeming to linger undecidedly between obligation and curiosity, and a sound, like a soft moan, slipped unexpectedly from her lips. Without realizing she'd even moved, her hands were on his chest and curling into the lapels of his suit jacket, pulling him closer. If it hadn't been for the sudden round of applause, and the hoots and howls from their guests, she would have gone right on kissing him. As their lips parted and she looked up into his eyes, she could see that he was equally perplexed. And as lame and juvenile as it sounded, she heard herself saying softly, "Wow, you're really good at that."

A wry grin tipped up the corners of his lips. "So are you."

Her kissing skills, and his, were irrelevant. So why the shiver of pleasure? The weak-kneed feeling of anticipation? There was nothing to anticipate. They were married and she was a legal resident. As devious plans go, this one was playing out exactly as they'd expected. The hard part was over.

With all the handshaking and hugs, the walk back down the aisle took so long that when they finally made it to the room where the reception was being held, people were already sipping very expensive champagne and nibbling on the appetizers catered by a restaurant in town that had reopened its doors just last week. Though she distinctly remembered Luc saying it would be small and intimate, it looked to Julie as if nearly every member of the Cattleman's Club and their significant others were in attendance.

She looked up at Luc. "Small and intimate, huh?"

"I put Drew in charge of the guest list," he said, nabbing two glasses of champagne from a passing waiter and handing one to her. "So if you have a bone to pick, it's with him. And forgive me for saying it, but you look positively stunning."

Forgive him? His words made her feel dizzy with pleasure. "If it wasn't for Lark's help, you would have married a raccoon."

He regarded her with a curious expression.

She laughed and shook her head. "Never mind."

Somewhere behind her Julie heard the sharp tink of metal on glass and turned to see Skye tapping her champagne flute with the tines of her fork. Her husband, Jake, mirrored her actions, then several other guests joined in, all turning to look at Julie and Luc as if they were waiting for them to do or say something.

She heard Luc mumble something under his breath, and asked him in a hushed voice, "What are they doing?"

"They want us to kiss."

Julie blinked. "Kiss?"

Luc shrugged. "It's tradition."

And he couldn't have warned her about this? So she could at least prepare herself. "I've never been to an American wedding. You're saying we have to kiss? Right now? In front of all these people?"

"If we want them to stop."

Considering the rising decibel level, if she and Luc didn't kiss, someone was bound to shatter something. Besides, it had been so nice kissing him the first time. One more time wouldn't hurt, right? Who was she to question the tradition.

"Well, if we have to," she said.

Luc bent his head and brushed a very brief and chaste kiss across her lips, but the tinking didn't stop.

"You can do better than that," someone shouted.

Her heart did a back-and-forth shimmy in her chest. Oh boy, this could wind up being a very long evening.

Luc gazed at her questioningly, his eyes saying it would be best if they appeased the crowd. Julie shrugged, whispering, "We have to make it look real, I guess."

She tried to play it cool, but on the inside she was trembling as Luc cupped the back of her head, his hand sliding through her hair, fingers tangling in the curls. And if that didn't feel nice enough, his kiss nearly did her in. When his tongue swept across her lower lip she felt it like an electrical charge, as if every cell in her body came alive all at once. But then it was over and she had to fight the urge to toss her champagne glass aside, grab the lapels of his jacket and pull him in for more.

It must have been sufficient for the guests, because the tinking faded out, only to start up again a few minutes later, instigated this time by Paige Richardson, who stood beside her brother-in-law Colby.

Colby was Aaron Nichols's partner in R&N Builders, which was almost single-handedly responsible for rebuilding the town after the tornado. And though Julie knew him to be a friendly and outgoing, all-around nice guy, the deep furrow in Colby's brow said something was troubling him.

The tinking rose to an unreasonable level and Julie could swear that every single guest had joined in.

She looked up at Luc, who appeared as amused as he was apologetic. "I have the feeling we're going to be doing a lot of kissing today."

"So do I." And what a hardship that would be. *Not.* And even if he was the worst kisser on the planet, her citizenship depended on it. It was her obligation to make this marriage look as real as possible. Because if she were to be discovered, and someone proved the marriage was a sham, she would go down hard and take Luc with her. That was not an option.

Before he could make a move, to change things up a bit, she set her empty champagne flute down, slid her arms around his neck and kissed him first. A no-holds-barred, knock-him-on-his-butt kiss that jump-started her pulse and made her tingle in places she didn't even know she could tingle. His arms went around her and he tugged her against him. He cupped her behind and rocked his pelvis against her stomach. She gasped against his lips when she felt the thick ridge behind his zipper. Obviously he was just as into this as she was, and not at all shy about letting her know it. If not for his suit jacket, everyone else would probably know, too.

This time when they parted he was wearing a wry, sexy smile, and whispered, without a trace of contrition, "What can I say. I'm a guy."

This was a side of him she'd never seen before. Playfully sexy and a little risqué. She wanted nothing more than to be alone with him, and at the same time felt thankful for their guests. Until they both had time to settle down, being alone together might be a bad idea.

No, not *might*, it *would* be.

As the evening progressed, each subsequent kiss was more brazen and more ardent than the last, his touch as bold as it was scandalous.

It went on like that for a good hour before, to Julie's disappointment, the kiss requests finally began to taper off until they stopped altogether. People began to leave, until only their core group of friends remained.

Though Julie had already had far too much champagne, she headed to the bar for another drink and Beth followed her. "This has been so much fun," she told Julie.

"I think so, too."

"Your sister couldn't make it?"

Julie had texted her, called her and sent her a detailed email about the situation, but still no reply. Her husband traveled extensively for business and Jennifer often accompanied him, occasionally for weeks at a time. "I couldn't get ahold of her. They're probably out of the country."

"That's too bad."

Julie shrugged. "It was awfully last-minute."

"It certainly was. Which brings me to my next question. What was it like making out with your best friend?"

Julie just stood there, mouth agape. Did she mean—?

"Drew told me. We don't keep secrets from each other."

Now Drew, Beth, Luc's mother and her sister all knew the truth?

"Don't worry, I won't tell a soul," Beth assured her. "And for what it's worth, you gave a very convincing performance."

And Julie had relished every moment. Much more than she meant to, or should have. "He's a good kisser."

Beth grinned. "So I gathered. I'll bet he's good at a lot of things."

Her suggestive grin left no question as to what she was implying. And Julie knew she was probably right. She was dying to know how it would feel, their bodies intertwined, his weight pushing her into the mattress...

A ripple of heat coursed through her veins and she could feel her cheeks growing hot. Definitely not something she should be thinking about. "I'm sure he is," she told Beth. "But I'll never find out."

"The way Luc looks at you, I get the feeling you won't have a choice."

No choice? "What is it you think he'll do? Tie me down and make passionate love to me?"

Beth's smile widened. "One can hope."

Oh God, she was right. If Luc wanted Julie in his bed, restraining her wouldn't be necessary.

Ugh, *no*. She was not going to sleep with him. The combination of champagne and all that kissing was screwing with her brain, flooding it with hormones, or pheromones, or some other kind of mones. They were friends and that's all they would ever be.

"Where are you two going for your honeymoon?" Beth asked.

"Nowhere. Luc has a new patient to evaluate this week. A little boy who needs spinal surgery. Besides, you know how he is about leaving the hospital for any extended amount of time. Or his mother. She's still weak from her last hospital stay."

"Most new brides would expect to be put first."

Julie shrugged. "I guess I'm not like most new brides. I can't expect him to rearrange his whole life just because we're married. I wouldn't want him to."

Luc's ex-fiancée had been one of those women. Like any young resident, Luc had been required to work insane hours. It was part of the job. Amelia demanded more attention than he was able to give, which was what ultimately caused their split. The way Luc described her, she was spoiled and snotty, always wanting things her way. Even if she had married him, Julie doubted it would have lasted.

"A lot of women go into a marriage thinking they can change their spouse," Beth said.

"That's ridiculous. If you don't love the person for who they are, why marry them in the first place?"

Beth grinned. "Luc is a lucky man."

Julie wasn't sure what she meant by that, and she didn't ask. Drinks in hand, they rejoined the others.

Luc, Colby and Whit Daltry, owner of Daltry Property Management, were discussing the hospital, and how much money it would take to rebuild the damaged portion. Stella and her husband, Aaron, were discussing baby formula options with Lark and Skye, who both had plenty of information on all things baby. Paige, who Julie noticed had been avoiding her brother-in-law like the plague all evening and pretending not to see the looks he kept shooting her way, sat silently.

Beth took her seat at the table where they had all congregated, and for a minute Julie stood there watching everyone, soaking it all in, a feeling of peace and happiness warming her heart. The town, the people... they were so familiar to her now and so accepting. This was, without question, home.

"Come sit down," Luc said, holding out his hand for her to take. She twined her fingers through his, intending to sit in the empty chair beside him, but Luc had other ideas. He tugged her down onto his lap instead, and up went her heart, right into her throat. He slipped one arm around her and settled his palm against her stomach, his thumb grazing the underside of her breast as he did, and the other hand came to rest on her bare knee. What if that hand were to slide up the inside of her thigh under her dress? Would she stop him? *Could* she?

She glanced over at Beth, whose smile seemed to say, *I told you so.*

She realized just then, with no small amount of anticipation, that if Luc decided he wanted her, there wasn't a damned thing she could do about it.

Five

They didn't get home until eleven—it was a little weird to think of Luc's house as home—and they were both bushed. It had been a long and exhausting evening spent in a near-constant state of arousal, but now it was time to shut it down. The wedding was over and they were back to being friends.

Luc walked her to her bedroom door, which was directly across the hall from his own. She expected a hug and a kiss, even if it was just on her cheek, but she got neither.

"Well, good night," he said, shutting the door to his room firmly behind him.

She stood in the hallway alone, wondering what just happened. After having his hands on her all evening, that was the best he could do? He could just walk away without even acknowledging it?

What if he was having second thoughts? What if he realized he didn't want to be married? He'd been exceedingly quiet on the drive home—there was that word again...*home*. He could be in his room right now, pacing the floor in a panic, thinking that maybe they should get the marriage annulled.

There was no way she could fall asleep with this

hanging over her. She had to know what was going on in his head, before she let herself get too comfortable.

Was she really home, or wasn't she?

Taking a minute or two to think it over, she devised a genius plan to engage him in a conversation. Once she got him talking, she could spring her suspicions on him and see how he reacted.

Feeling confident that she was doing the right thing, she rapped softly on his door. He opened it several seconds later wearing silk pajama bottoms slung low on his hips, his chest bare.

Oh good Lord.

She had seen him bare chested plenty of times in the past, but it occurred to her that she had never actually *seen* him. Only now did she really notice and appreciate the lean muscles of his torso. The sprinkling of dark hair that circled his navel and disappeared under his waistband. Wide chest, above average pecs. He was beautiful.

He hadn't even touched her and she was feeling all tingly again.

He leaned against the doorjamb. "Everything okay?"

"I'm sorry to bother you, but I wondered if you could unzip me. My dress, I mean."

His brow rose. "Seriously?"

Was that such an odd request? "Yes, seriously. I can't reach it."

He folded his arms, looking amused. And sexy as hell. How had she not noticed before how insanely gorgeous he was? Had she been wearing blinders all these years?

"So what you're telling me is that if I weren't here

to unzip you, you would be stuck in your dress indefinitely?"

She blinked. "Well...no, but—"

"If you're going to make up an excuse to come to my room, you could be a little more imaginative, don't you think?"

Boy, did he have her number.

"You were so quiet on the way home I was afraid something was wrong," she said. "I thought that maybe you were having second thoughts about this."

"Then, why didn't you just say that?"

Because...well, she didn't exactly know why. She'd never had a problem being totally honest with him before they were married. Maybe this time she was afraid of the answer she might get. But she had to know.

"So, are you?" she asked him.

"Am I what?"

"Having second thoughts?"

He shook his head and said, "Nope."

She waited for more, for some sort of assurance everything was fine, but he just stood there looking at her. *Oooookay.*

"You were very distant on the ride home. Then we got here and, well..." Why was this so hard to say? He wasn't helping matters, standing there all sexy and gorgeous, his eyes locked on hers.

"We got here and what?"

"We're married now. I figured you would at least hug me good night or something. Maybe a kiss on the cheek?"

"You don't want me to do that."

"I don't?"

"Nope."

"Why not?"

"Suffice it to say, I'm a little...overstimulated."

Oh, this was interesting. Now they were getting somewhere. "So, you're turned on."

He trained his eyes on her and...*whoa*. The heat smoldering in their dark depths could have burned a hole through her dress. That was a definite yes. Her heart flip-flopped, making her pulse race and her mouth go dry.

"You want the truth?" he said.

She nodded.

He leaned in just a little closer. "I wanted everyone to leave the reception so I could lock the door, strip you naked, spread you on the table and lick wedding cake off every inch of your body."

"*Every* inch?"

He grinned. "*Every* inch."

She knew there was a reason she should have wrapped up the leftover cake and brought it home.

"However," he added, "friends don't do that."

"Some friends do. And I'm pretty sure I read somewhere that we have to consummate the marriage to make it official and legally binding."

"And I'm pretty sure you just made that up."

Yes, she had made it up. But she needed to kiss him again, feel his hands on her. Right now. Without her clothes getting in the way. It was their wedding night for heaven's sake. Hadn't she earned the right to jump his bones? Just this once? Would that really be such a terrible thing? Their friendship was solid. It would take a lot more than one night of sex to come between them. Or even two or three nights.

His pajama bottoms did little to hide the erection

pushing outward as if it was reaching for her touch. And oh, did she want to touch him.

One strategically placed hand and he would be toast. Not to toot her own horn, but she knew her way around the male body. He wouldn't be able to resist her, and he damn sure would walk away thoroughly satisfied. "So, you don't think we should sleep together?"

"I didn't say that."

What did he want her to do? Get down on her knees and beg? "You didn't *not* say it, either."

"It's been an emotional day, and we've had a lot to drink—"

"Oh, I get it. Say no more. I would never want you to, you know, embarrass yourself."

His brows jumped upward. He knew she was up to something, and clearly he was enjoying the game just as much as she was. Verbal foreplay was highly underrated.

"Embarrass myself how?"

"You're worried about your performance. Alcohol can make things a little, well, limp."

He glanced down to his crotch, then back up to her. "That's obviously not the case."

No, it wasn't. *And enough playing around already.* She was ready to get to the good stuff.

"Are you sure?" She reached out and wrapped her hand around his hard-on through his pajamas, giving it a firm squeeze. Holy cow, he was *big*.

Luc groaned and leaned into her hand, clutching the doorjamb in a white-knuckled grip, his eyes never leaving her face. He was hers, no question.

"I guess you're right—everything seems to be in working order. But just to be sure…" She slipped her hand under his waistband and around his erection, skin against skin, giving it a couple of slow strokes, teasing the tip with the pad of her thumb. "Feels good to me."

His eyes turned black with desire. She almost had him. Most men would have caved by now, but Luc had a steel will.

"You're positively sure you want to do this?" he said.

At this point, how could he even ask her that? Wasn't it obvious that she wanted him? "Without a doubt."

"You're not worried that it will change things between us?"

"One time? It's not as if we're going to make a habit of this." She squeezed and felt him pulse against her palm. "Besides, we spent half the day making out and now I'm standing here with my hand in your pants. If something was going to change, wouldn't it have already?"

"So what you're saying is, the damage is already done?"

"In a manner of speaking." He was making a bigger deal out of this than was warranted. But he was a planner. He liked to think ahead, plot out his every move. Which, she supposed, was why he was such an accomplished surgeon. She, on the other hand, was more of a live-in-the-moment, fly-by-the-seat-of-her-pants girl. They sat on opposite ends of the spectrum. He was all about duty and honor and doing the right thing. She believed in trying new things and taking chances. Living life to the fullest and going where the wind took her.

Tonight, the wind was blowing her in the direction of his bed.

Knowing Luc the way she did, she knew exactly

how this would play out. He would caress her as he slowly removed her clothes, taking his time. Her pleasure would be his main priority because that's the kind of man he was. Always putting the needs of others before his own. She would let him take his time, and when they were both good and worked up, she would take over. If this was going to be the only time they slept together, she planned to give him a night that he would never forget. And if they decided to do it again, well, that was okay, too.

That was her plan at least, but Luc was playing by a totally different set of rules. He looked at her as if he were a hunter stalking its prey, and then he lunged and went all caveman on her. One second her feet were on the ground, and the next, she was hanging over his shoulder, which was more than wide enough to accommodate her. She gasped and clutched his back, dizzy with desire and a little disoriented as he kicked the door closed and carried her across the room to his bed. And there was nothing gentle about the way he tossed her down on the comforter.

Who was this man and why was she just now meeting him? And how, after all these years of friendship, could she have pegged him so wrong?

He knelt on the mattress beside her, his hand resting on her inner thigh, and all she could think was *more*. He slid the hand up under the hem of her dress. His fingertips grazed the crotch of her panties, no more than a tickle. She sucked in a breath and her thighs parted, straining against the skirt of her dress.

He pulled his hand away and her back arched, her body seeking out his touch. "Did I mention how sexy you look in this dress?"

"Thanks. I don't usually wear them," she said, the words coming out all breathy and uneven. She couldn't seem to pull enough air into her lungs. What happened to all the oxygen?

"I'm going to buy you a dozen more."

If this was the reaction she got when she wore a dress, maybe that would be a bad idea. Or a good one. She wasn't sure. Suddenly everything felt backward and upside down.

He was back under her dress, tugging her panties down. There was nothing slow about the way he undressed her. Or gentle. Then he took his pajama bottoms off...

Yikes. He wouldn't be the only one walking away satisfied. This was going to be fun.

She tried to push him onto his back but it was like trying to move a brick wall. She wound up on her back instead, and when she reached out to touch him, he pinned her arms over her head, a move that would normally trigger a sense of panic. He wouldn't let her take control, which both frustrated and aroused her. But she knew deep in her heart that she was safe with him. She usually felt threatened by sexually aggressive men, but she *wanted* him to dominate her. She trusted Luc, so she did something she had never done before. She dropped her guard and let go, let him be the one in charge.

It was as cathartic as it was exciting. And Luc held nothing back, stroking here, kissing there. Licking and biting and flipping her around until she felt like a pretzel, so he could explore every inch of her body. He knew exactly what she liked, what she needed, without her having to say a thing. Besides, she was too busy gasping and moaning to form intelligible words. He teased her relentlessly. And every time she thought she was getting the upper hand, he turned the tables on her again. She'd orgasmed twice, and was headlong into number three when he rolled her onto her back and settled over her.

He didn't ask her if she was ready, or if she was having second thoughts. They were both too far gone for that. He parted her thighs with his knee and thrust inside her. She savored the sweet stretch of her body accepting him, his weight pressing her into the mattress as he eased back, then thrust again. And again, picking up speed, but with more hip action this time. Pretty much all she could do was wrap her legs around his hips and hang on for the ride. Pleasure rippled through her in hot waves, her body clenching down around him like a vise as orgasm number three took hold.

After that things got very fuzzy. And rowdy. And a little loud. He asked a lot of questions, too. "Do you like this?" "Does this feel good?" He must have told her a dozen times that she was beautiful, that she was the sexiest woman he'd ever seen. "By leaps and bounds," he said. And he wasn't shy about telling her what he wanted, and exactly how she should do it. "Touch me here, lick me there. Faster. Slower. Just like that." She'd never been with a man so chatty during sex. Or bossy. But the best part by far was watching him reach his peak, seeing him completely let go, knowing that she was the one making him feel that way.

When it was over, and they lay there in a sweaty tangle, she couldn't seem to wipe the smile from her face, until she realized, with considerable horror, that she hadn't given a single freaking thought to birth control.

Luc lay with Julie, his leg resting between hers, one arm under her neck, the other draped across her stomach. "I guess an annulment is out of the question now," he joked, and without warning Julie shot up in bed, nearly dumping him over the edge onto the floor—the *hardwood* floor—and spewed a string of expletives.

Luc sat up beside her. He put a hand on her shoulder and she jumped, as if she'd forgotten he was there. "It was a joke, Julie."

"Oh my God," she said, looking panicked, the color leaching from her face. "I can't believe we did this. How could I be so stupid?"

But it had been some of the best sex he'd ever had, and she had seemed to enjoy herself, too. "Don't you think it's a little late to be having second thoughts?"

She looked puzzled, then said, "I'm not having second thoughts. At least, not in the way you think."

"In what way, then?"

"This is probably a dumb question under the circumstances, but did we just have unprotected sex?"

Is that what this was about? "Relax, you're not going to catch anything from me."

"I know that," she said. "But unless you're sterile, we could have bigger problems."

Whoa, wait a minute. "I thought you were on the Pill. You told me you were."

Her eyes went wide with indignation. "When did I say that? I *never* said that."

"A couple of years ago. You were complaining that it made you nauseous."

"Which is why I *stopped* taking it."

Aw, hell. He should have asked. He was a doctor, after all. He knew better than to assume. Which is why he always kept condoms on hand. They were in the drawer in his bedside table, not two feet away. "This is my fault. I should have checked with you first."

"No, I'm just as much to blame. It never even crossed my mind." She dropped her head in her hands. "How could I be so careless? I don't want a baby. Definitely not now, maybe not ever."

"Before you get all panicked, stop and think about where you are in your cycle."

She took a deep breath, looking so tense she could have snapped like a twig. It took her several seconds to collect herself, then she said, "I'm due to start my period in a couple of days. A week tops."

"Then, we're probably fine. The odds are pretty slim that you would conceive so late in your cycle."

"Is that your official medical opinion?"

"It is." There was a sprinkle of optimism in his tone for good measure. And on the bright side, it wouldn't be long before they knew for sure.

"You're right," she said, sounding a little less freaked out. She rested her head on his shoulder. "I'm sorry I got so upset."

He put his arm around her shoulder, drawing her closer. "No apology required."

She was quiet for a moment, then said, "Just so you know, I don't usually sleep with men on the first date. But since our first date was our wedding, I thought I could make an exception."

"I understand."

She smiled up at him. "That was really good, by the way. The sex, I mean."

"Was?"

She looked confused.

"There is no 'was.'" He lay back and pulled her on top of him. "We're just getting started."

Six

Julie woke slowly the next morning to the sound of water running. Her first thought was that the leaky pipe under her bathroom sink had finally burst. Eyes too heavy to open, she reached over to grab her phone off the bedside table, but it was gone. Not just her phone, but the table itself wasn't there. She pried her eyes open only to realize that this was not her bedroom. Not even her apartment. She lived with Luc now, and the sound of the running water was coming from his bathroom. Then she recalled last night and a smile curled her lips.

Best. Sex. Ever.

She had always assumed, because Luc was so reserved and practical, that he would be the same way in bed. Boy, was she wrong. Hours later she still felt limp as a dishrag and sore in places she didn't know could get sore. If she knew he would be that good she would have jumped him years ago. Just thinking about it was getting her all worked up again. Then she remembered that they forgot to use a condom the first time and her heart sank a little. But Luc was right, the odds were low she would get pregnant. And if she had, they would deal with it. At least they were married. Right?

She sat up and looked around for her phone, finding it in her purse on the floor beside the bed. It was 8:00 a.m., which was early even for her. Sundays were the only days she allowed herself to sleep in. She typically dragged herself out of bed around ten, went for a run around the track at the high school, then showered and sometimes met Lark for brunch. But not today. She looked at the platinum band on the ring finger of her left hand. She was a newlywed. A married woman.

That was going to take some getting used to.

The water shut off, and a minute later she could hear Luc humming to himself—one of those country songs he loved so much—while he shaved. She'd only ever heard him hum when he was in a good mood. And why wouldn't he be after last night?

He would be out of the bathroom any minute now and she really should go to her own room, lest she be tempted to pounce on him. But she wanted to see him. She wrestled with her options, but before she could make a decision, the bathroom door opened and Luc stepped out. And boy was she glad that she stayed. He wore a towel slung low on his hips, his dark hair damp, his face cleanly shaven and smooth. Droplets of water clung to his chest, rolling down his pecs and over those wonderfully ripped abs.

She usually looked like a beast in the morning, her hair askew, pillow creases on her cheek, and she imagined the liner and mascara had smeared under her eyes for that charming raccoon effect, but he'd seen her looking worse.

"Good morning," he said, looking surprised to see her awake.

"G'morning. You're up early."

He shrugged. "Habit."

He was usually at the hospital by 7:00 a.m. to start his rounds, but this was Sunday, not to mention their honeymoon. Technically speaking.

He sat on the edge of the bed beside her and kissed her forehead. If he was put off by her appearance he didn't say so. "Sleep well?"

"Like the dead." When she had finally gotten to sleep, which hadn't been until 3:00 a.m. or so. In typical man style he'd fallen asleep before her, about a half an hour earlier. For a long time she'd lain there wrapped up in his arms, listening to his slow even breaths, wishing they could hit Rewind and relive the night all over again. "How about you? Sleep well?"

"Great. How are you feeling this morning?"

How was she feeling? "A little sore, actually. You gave me quite the workout."

"Jules, I don't mean physically."

She didn't think so. "I'm not having regrets, if that's what you mean. Are you?"

"Nope. I do feel a little guilty for not feeling guilty, if that makes any sense."

"I know exactly what you mean."

"Are you sorry that we can't have a honeymoon?" he asked.

"Not at all. You have responsibilities. We both do. In fact, I was thinking about going into work for a while today."

"You can't."

"Why not?"

"Because I read somewhere that a marriage isn't official unless the newlyweds spend the day after their wedding together."

Oh, so they were going to play this game again. "Did it say what we have to do?"

"We have to have sex again. Then lunch, and maybe a walk in the park. Or we could combine the two and have a picnic, weather permitting."

That sounded like fun. "What then?"

"More sex, of course."

Of course. "And after that?"

"A candlelight dinner."

"Then more sex?"

"Obviously." He shot her one of those steamy smiles. "And we should get started right away. You know, to make it official."

He hooked the edge of the covers and slowly eased them down, revealing her breasts, which were covered in love bites, then her stomach, then the tops of her thighs. *Here we go again*, she thought, struck by how natural it felt. How comfortable she was with him, as if they had been sleeping together all along. And at the same time it felt exciting and new.

His hand, which was still warm from his shower, came to rest on her thigh, then trailed slowly upward, his touch light, it was barely more than a tickle. Her legs parted, giving him space to play around, but they were interrupted by a firm rap on his bedroom door. He mumbled a curse, removed his hand and pulled the covers back up over her.

"I'll make it quick," he said.

He grabbed his robe from the foot of the bed and tugged it on as he walked to the door. Julie sat and held the blanket up to cover herself.

It was his mother's nurse. She glanced over, saw Julie in the bed and quickly averted her eyes. Julie was surprised Luc had opened the door wide enough to let her see inside.

"I'm sorry to bother you, Mr. Wakefield, but I thought you should know that your mother is running a low-grade fever."

A look of concern transformed his face. "How high?"

"Only 99.8. She said that she feels fine, and not to bother you, but I thought you should know."

For the average healthy person a temperature that low wouldn't have been a big deal, but Julie knew that any sign of systemic infection had to be addressed immediately. Elizabeth had barely gotten over the last illness and her body was still weak. Another infection this soon, even something as simple as the common cold could spiral out of control and become deadly.

"Did you check for sores or wounds?" he asked the nurse.

"She wouldn't let me."

Luc sighed and shook his head. "I'll be down there in a minute. And tell her that *I* told you to check her."

"Yes, sir," she said, and he closed the door, mumbling to himself about his mother being stubborn.

Ever look in a mirror? Julie wanted to say.

"You realize she saw me," she told him.

"I know she did." He stepped into his closet for clothes, seemingly unconcerned.

"What if she tells your mother?" Julie called after him.

"So what if she does?" he called back.

"Didn't you tell her that this isn't a real marriage? That we're still just friends."

"I seem to recall you telling me last night that to

make the marriage official we had to have sex." He stepped out wearing jeans and pulling a T-shirt over his head. "Didn't you?"

"You know damn well I made that up to get you into bed. You were being very...uncooperative."

His brows rose. "Is that what I was doing?"

"Don't change the subject. You don't think it will confuse your mother?"

"Her body may be failing her but as you know, her mind is sound."

That was putting it mildly. "I know. I just... I respect her and I don't want her to think I'm slutty."

"For having sex with your husband?"

She shot him a look. "You know what I mean. It might upset her."

"What is she going to do? Ground me? Besides, we're two consenting adults. Married or not, it's still not hers or anyone else's business what we do in bed."

"You know you're impossible."

"I have to go check on her," he said, but he was smiling.

"I'm going to take a shower."

"When I get back we're going to finish what we just started," he said, grinning suggestively as he walked out. If she hadn't already been aroused, that would have definitely done the trick.

She had been a little worried that this morning might be awkward, or involve misplaced guilt and needless justifications. There was nothing more depressing than to wake up with a man and hear why the fantastic sex you had the night before was a mistake. That had happened to her once, and was the precise reason she didn't sleep with men on the first date.

The only thing that seemed to have changed with Luc was that now they both knew what the other looked like naked. *Totally* naked. Up close and *very* personal.

And if he was okay with his mother realizing what was going on between them, who was Julie to question it?

Elizabeth, it turned out, had a small scratch on the back of her thigh that had become infected. Because she had no feeling below the waist, she'd had no idea it was there. Which is why daily physical exams, especially after she'd been moved in and out of her chair frequently, were so critical. With such poor circulation, the smallest scratch could become a festering wound overnight.

Knowing she was bound to get worse before she got better, Luc stayed with her, and they never did get to finish what they'd started. But as she told Beth last night, she didn't expect him to drop everything when she snapped her fingers. Besides, he had just done her an enormous favor; the last thing she had the right to do was demand his attention. In fact, without the threat of deportation looming in the future, this was the most content and happiest she'd felt in months. Any uncertainty she'd had about her future was gone.

She was confident that it would be smooth sailing from here on out.

Luc spent his first day as a husband not in bed having phenomenal sex with his new wife—sex he never planned on having—but instead carefully monitoring his mother's condition. He felt guilty that he'd had to cancel his and Julie's plans, but not only had she not complained, or acted the least bit perturbed, she spent most of the day with him at his mother's bedside. Her temperature continued to rise, slowly but steadily all day, even after the nurse cleaned and dressed her wound and administered ibuprofen and intravenous antibiotics. He was considering hospitalization when finally, around eight that evening, her fever broke. He checked on her several times during the night, and by Monday morning her temperature was holding steady in the normal range and her wound seemed to be healing well.

"I think I need to hire a new nurse," he told Julie that morning. She sat on the edge of his bed, looking adorably mussed, watching him get ready for work. She had offered, for his own peace of mind, to stay home from work and keep an eye on his mother and the nurse. Which was a bit like needing a babysitter to watch the babysitter. "This could have been prevented if she had only done her job. I've stressed to her, more than once, that the physical exams are critical. And my mother knows better. If the nurse can't handle her—"

"Your mother really likes this nurse."

"That isn't my concern." Her safety and physical well-being were the only things that mattered.

"It should be your concern," she said in a tone so sharp it nearly took him back a step. "How would you feel having some stranger inspect every inch of your body twice a day, day in and day out? And don't you think there would be times when you just wanted to say to hell with it and take a break? Maybe her nurse was being more compassionate than negligent. She made a mistake."

He tugged on his shirt and buttoned it, saying, "A mistake that could have cost my mother her life."

"And I'm sure she's learned her lesson."

She damn well better have.

Julie was quiet for a minute, then said, "I've mentioned my nanny Ginise, haven't I?"

"That was the nice one, right?"

"Did I ever tell you why my dad fired her?"

He shook his head, looking thoughtful. "I don't think so."

"I'm sure I told you how strict my father was."

He nodded. From all the stories Julie had told him, to say her father was strict was putting it mildly. She and her sister were practically prisoners in their own home.

"Nanny Ginise was hard-nosed when he was around, but when he was gone, she really loosened the leash. She let me and my sister go to friends' houses and use the phone. She let us go without tights on hot days. She let us drink soda and eat candy. Nanny Ginise gave us the freedom to be kids. Which is eventually what got her fired."

"What happened?"

"One of my friends from school was having a pool party. I begged my father to let me go. All of my friends were going to be there, including boys—though I didn't tell him that—but he still said it was out of the question. I cried and pleaded but he wouldn't budge. But the day of the party he was away on business and wasn't due back until the following night. Nanny Ginise let me go. She even bought me a two-piece bathing suit to wear, since all the other girls would be wearing them and I wanted to fit in. I mean, what thirteen-year-old girl doesn't?"

He flipped his collar up and looped his tie around his neck. "Naturally."

"Well, my father came home early, and Nanny Ginise had no choice but to tell him where I was. He charged over to my friend's house, which was just up the road. The fact that I defied him was bad enough, but when he saw what I was wearing, and that there were boys there, he went ballistic. I had never seen him so furious. He pulled me out of the pool by my hair."

Luc's eyes went wide. "In front of everyone?"

She nodded. "He wrapped me up in a towel and dragged me home. I was mortified, and as if that wasn't punishment enough, I wasn't allowed to leave my room for a month. I was a prisoner. He even made me eat my meals in there."

That wasn't strict, that was abuse. He knew her childhood was bad, but he hadn't realized just how bad. "How could he treat his own children that way?"

"Our mother's death really hit him hard. I'm still not sure if he was trying to shelter us, or if he just resented us."

"Why would he resent you?"

"For being alive, when she wasn't. It took years for me to accept that it wasn't my fault. That it was his problem, not mine."

The idea that she grew up so miserable made his chest ache. "And Nanny Ginise, what happened to her?"

"Fired on the spot. Two days later we had a new nanny. Ms. Fowler, a retired headmistress of a private girls school in Wales."

"What was she like?"

"Horrible. She'd followed our father's rules to the

letter. And came up with quite a few of her own. She believed that teenage girls all had lusty and indecent thoughts and therefore should not be left alone to their own devices. She forbade us from closing our bedroom doors, and walked right in without knocking whenever she felt like it. If she caught us doing something she considered inappropriate she gave us the switch."

"The switch?"

"Yeah, it was this stick she carried around with her all the time."

Luc blinked. "Are you saying that she used to hit you with it?"

"All the time. Damned thing hurt like a bitch and left nasty welts."

Jesus. Luc actually felt sick to his stomach. "Did your father know?"

"Of course. He was all for corporal punishment."

And it just kept getting worse. "Did he hit you?"

"Me *and* my sister. But she got the worst of it. I learned to drop my head, keep my mouth shut and be as invisible as possible. Jennifer was outspoken and defiant. I remember a time, not long before I left for college, when she snuck out of the house in the middle of the night to meet a boy. Our father caught her. There was hardly a spot on her that wasn't black and blue. He grounded her to her room for weeks."

Luc sat down on the bed beside her, at a loss for words. "I don't even know what to say. I knew your childhood wasn't ideal, but I had no idea it was that bad."

"I didn't tell you to make you feel sorry for me. I just want you to try to see things from your mother's point of view. She's a prisoner in a body that constantly betrays her. I think the nurse was just trying to cut her a little slack, like Nanny Ginise did for me and my sister. There was no malicious intent. And I know she feels horrible about it."

Wow, talk about a convincing argument, and she spoke of it so matter-of-factly, as if it had happened to someone else. And yes, sometimes he forgot what his mother must go through. How difficult and unpleasant her life could be. Years ago, before her surgery, she was active and independent. Now she relied on others for most of her needs. That couldn't be easy for her. "You're right," he told Julie. "She meant no harm. If my mother is happy with her, then I'm happy."

"Thank you. You're a good man. And an even better son."

"I don't know about that," he said.

She smiled. "I do."

He couldn't help himself. He had to kiss her. He leaned in and she met him halfway. He was enjoying this arrangement, and found himself thinking about her, far more than he should have.

The kiss didn't last long. Julie patted his shoulders and said, "You need to get to the hospital. You'll be late for rounds."

She was right. Typically he looked forward to work, but today staying home in bed with Julie sounded much more fun. "Maybe tonight, if all goes well—"

"Yes," she said with a saucy smile, knowing exactly what he was going to say before he said it. It looked as if he wasn't the only one with sex on the brain. And if he didn't finish getting dressed and get his ass out of there, he might not make it to the hospital at all. It had been a long time since he'd been so hot for a woman he wanted to play hooky from work.

He stood, knotting his tie, then pulled on his suit jacket. She sat on the bed watching him. "Are you sure you're okay with staying home today?"

"I have my laptop," she said. "I can work here. I have some numbers to crunch. And phone calls to make. And your mom mentioned something about a few rounds of poker."

"For God's sake don't let her talk you into playing for money."

Julie laughed. "She's a cardsharp, I know."

"And she's ruthless."

He grabbed his wallet and keys from the basket on the chest of drawers, hesitating another second. Damn, he really didn't want to go. If it weren't for the new patient he was seeing this morning, he just might stick around for a while, have one of his residents do rounds for him.

"I'll see you tonight," he said. He considered kissing her goodbye, but once he got started he wouldn't want to stop. "Call me if there's a problem."

"I will."

He was almost to the door when Julie said, "Hey, Luc."

He turned to find her kneeling on his bed. Then she dropped the covers to flash him.

Her breasts were full and firm. Not large by modern standards, but they fit her just right and he couldn't wait to get his hands on them again.

With that saucy smile, she said, "Have a nice day, dear."

Oh, he definitely would. And an even better night.

Seven

Luc made it to work with five minutes to spare, stopping in the cafeteria for a cup of coffee on his way up to his office.

"Cutting it close today," his secretary, Ruth, said, looking at the clock. She was used to him being on time, or most days, a little early.

"Busy weekend," he told her.

"I'll bet. It was a lovely wedding. You two looked so happy, and so in love."

It sounded as if they'd done a pretty good job fooling everyone. But the happy part? That was real. His best friend was here to stay. What more could he ask for?

"Tommy James was admitted last night," she said.

"No problems?"

"Not that I've heard."

"How is the rest of my day looking?" He was hoping to get home at a decent hour tonight. Maybe even a little early. One of his favorite upscale restaurants had reopened in the past week and he thought maybe he would take Julie for a nice dinner.

Oh hell, who was he kidding. To heck with dinner. He wanted to get her back in bed and finish what they'd started.

He shrugged out of his suit jacket. Ruth took it from him and handed him his lab coat. "You have a procedure at 9:15, and a staff meeting at 11:30. In the afternoon you have several consultations. And a meeting at 5:00."

He pulled it on and she clipped his ID onto the pocket. It had been their morning routine for as long as he'd been chief of surgery. A position that was as much about politics as it was medicine. Ruth, who had been in hospital administration for three decades, had been his saving grace.

"So how does it feel?" she asked him, straightening his collar.

Puzzled, he asked, "How does what feel?"

"Being *married*."

Better than he thought it would. In fact, it was pretty damned fantastic so far. Friendship and sex without the complications. Who wouldn't want that? And it was really good sex.

No, it was *fantastic* sex. And he couldn't wait to get home so they could do it again.

"It's good," he said, and left it at that. "If Julie calls, page me immediately. My mother had an infection over the weekend. Julie is staying with her today."

Ruth clucked and shook her head. "I'm so sorry. I noticed at the wedding that she looked tired. Poor Elizabeth, she's been through so much."

And every infection seemed to suck more of her strength, more of her spirit. As a physician, he knew her time was running out. Her body could handle only so much before it gave out for good. But as her son, he wanted her to live forever.

"She pushes herself too hard," Luc said.

"She's a proud woman."

More stubborn than proud if you asked him.

Luc left his office and checked on the five surgical patients in his care, each in different stages of recovery. Knowing the parents would have a million questions for him, as he would if his son were going in for major surgery, he saved Tommy James in the pediatrics ward for last.

The boy had come in as a referral from a colleague in Houston that Luc had known since med school.

"This is right up your alley," he'd told Luc when he called last week. The five-year-old had congenital lumbar spinal stenosis that had begun to cause him considerable pain, and in the past few weeks he had begun to lose feeling in his legs. It was a rare condition for a child but using techniques he'd perfected himself, with Julie's help of course, Luc could correct the problem by fusing the spine. The parents would be hard-pressed to find a physician more qualified than him to do the surgery.

Because it was congenital, this was quite possibly a temporary fix. As Tommy matured, the stenosis, which started in his lumbar spine, could gradually work its way upward into the thoracic, then cervical spine. This might be one of several surgeries he would need to stabilize his spine before adulthood. But other than his back being less flexible, he would live a long, productive life. Just not as a gymnast. And he would have the bonus of impeccable posture.

Luc stopped outside the patient's door, where a nurse stood updating his chart on her laptop.

"Is he all settled in?"

"Yes, Doctor. He was pretty uncomfortable so I gave

him pain meds. He's sleeping now and his vitals are good. He seems like a real trooper. He always has a smile on his face, even through the pain."

Kids were resilient. It was the parents who were typically the toughest to deal with. "Are the parents in there?"

"His mother stepped out to get coffee. She should be back in a minute."

"And his father?" Luc asked.

"Not here. And from the sound of it, he won't be coming to Royal."

"That's a shame." Luc knew that having a chronically ill child could devastate the soundest of marriages. He'd seen it all too often. But to not be there for your child who's having major surgery? What sort of man was this boy's father?

Though he had studied the chart thoroughly, he gave it another quick look to be sure that nothing had changed before he stepped into the boy's room.

He was indeed asleep, and though he looked small and fragile—all skin and bones—his color was good. Luc checked his vitals again, then he eased him onto his side to see his back, and checked his feet. Despite the loss of feeling in his legs, his circulation was still adequate. There wouldn't be any permanent damage.

He heard someone behind him and turned, his usual greeting on the tip of his tongue and ready to go...then froze when he saw the woman standing there.

The spark of recognition was instantaneous, but it took another ten seconds to determine that his mind wasn't playing tricks on him. That it really was his ex-fiancée, Amelia, standing there holding a cup of coffee and a gossip magazine. The woman who'd shredded his heart like confetti and ate it for breakfast without batting an eyelash.

"Amelia," he said, more a statement than a question, and regretted it the instant the words were out of his mouth. But it was too late now.

She flashed him a weak, tired smile. "Hello, Lucas. How have you been?"

Meeting new patients could be hit-or-miss, yet of the dozens of scenarios he might have imagined, this one didn't even come close to making the list.

She hadn't really changed all that much. She was a little thicker around the middle, and a little older. The stress of her son's condition showed in her face, in the fine lines at the corners of her eyes.

For a good ten seconds he was at a loss for words. *You're the physician*, he reminded himself. The one with the upper hand. And she was just the mother of the patient. Nothing more. He had to keep this professional. Yet he heard himself saying, "Should I assume this isn't a coincidence?"

"Yes and no. Tommy's doctor in Houston told me that he knew another doctor with more experience in this sort of surgery. I had already made the decision to come when he told me who and where the doctor was located. Of course then I knew it was you."

"And you came anyway?"

"It's not about me."

She was right. Nor was it about him. And he had no right to question her motives.

Keep it professional. "Why don't we talk about the surgery."

"Okay."

He went into surgeon mode, describing the procedure and recovery in layman's terms, feeling a bit like a robot. It was the same speech he'd used countless times before, but now it felt stilted and awkward.

"His doctor explained all of this in great detail," Amelia said. "He said permanent paralysis was a possibility."

"That is a possibility, but given your son's age, and the fact that he's in otherwise good health, I don't foresee any complications," he said.

Of course there were no guarantees. Complications could arise, but Luc was confident the surgery would go smoothly. Besides, she didn't have much choice at this point. "No surgery comes without risks. But without the procedure, the spinal column will continue to narrow. Then you'll be looking at paralysis, loss of bladder and bowel function. Excessive pain."

"I know all that," she said, looking conflicted. "I just needed to hear it from you. Of course he needs the surgery. And I trust that you'll take good care of him. How soon can you do it?" she asked.

"It would be next week at the soonest."

Her mouth fell open, eyes went wide. He knew that look as well as if he had seen it yesterday. *"Next week? But he's in pain! I assumed you would do it right away."*

He sighed quietly. That was Amelia, always expecting things to be done her way. "I'm already booked up this week and most of next. I have to check with my secretary, but I think I can squeeze it in either next Thursday or the following Tuesday."

"You can't do it *any* sooner?"

"Thursday or Tuesday. That's the best I can do."

She nodded slowly and said with a weak smile, "So, no special treatment for the ex-fiancée, huh?"

Is that what she'd expected? Special treatment? "I have a busy schedule," he told her. "Until the surgery we can control the pain and at this point there's no danger of permanent damage. But he will have to stay in the hospital so we can monitor him."

"If that's the case I'm staying here with him. In the room," she said, her chin lifting a notch, as if she were trying to challenge his authority, when there was really no need. This combative attitude was unnecessary. As her son's surgeon, his patient was his main priority.

"You'll have to talk to your son's nurse about hospital policy," he told her. "But I'm sure it won't be a problem."

"There is something else I wanted to ask you, that, uncomfortable as it is, I feel needs addressing."

He made a point of checking the time on his watch. He was already running late. "Okay."

"I need to be sure, because of our past, that you don't see this as a conflict of interest," she said.

Several years ago it might have been. But after getting over the initial shock of seeing her again, the only thing he felt was a medical obligation to care for his patient to the best of his ability. As he always did.

And she was nothing more to him than the mother of his patient.

"There's no conflict," he said, and he could see the instant she noticed the ring on his left hand.

"Oh. You're married," she said, sounding surprised.

"Yes, I am."

"Anyone I know?"

"No."

She paused, as if she was expecting him to give her

a name, or details, and when he didn't, her smile wavered. "I'm very happy for you.

"In case you're wondering, I'm divorced now. For almost two years. He traded me in for a younger model," she said, bitterness dripping from her words. "They moved to San Antonio and are expecting a baby. He sends Tommy gifts, and calls occasionally, but he never comes to see him."

None of Luc's business. He was her son's doctor, not a confidant.

He checked his watch. "Is there anything else—?"

"Leaving you was the biggest mistake I ever made," she blurted.

Oh, what he would have given to hear those words six years ago, but it was too late to turn back. He was happy with his life just the way it was. He didn't love her anymore. He hadn't for a long time. Maybe all along he'd only been in love with the idea of her, and deep down she had never been what he needed.

Julie was, though. And he did need her. More than he'd ever realized.

"I'll talk to my secretary and see about scheduling the surgery," he told Amelia. "In the meantime I'd like to run some tests."

She looked up at him with big blue eyes that used to melt him on the spot, and he felt nothing. Not a single damn thing. He was beginning to wonder what he had *ever* seen in her. Had he changed so much since then?

It was clear now that all these years he'd been wondering what-if had been a waste of time. Now he knew. Even if she hadn't dumped him, he seriously doubted they would have lasted very long. Her narcissism would have eventually driven him away.

"You don't want to talk about it," she said. "I get it. Just let me say that I'm really sorry for the way things turned out. I know I hurt you. I hope someday you can forgive me."

He might have laughed if he wasn't so appalled. Same old Amelia, thinking she was the center of the universe, and he refused to take the bait.

"I'm ordering tests today. I'll let you know when I get the results." Or more likely, he would tell one of his residents, who would then notify her. The less contact he had with her the better.

"I really am sorry," she said softly, looking genuinely apologetic, but she was six years too late. He turned and walked out without another word.

Julie set up a folding table and chair to make a small work space for herself at the foot of Elizabeth's bed where she could keep an eye on her while the nurse, who had been up most of the night, took a few hours to nap. Luc had spared no expense on his mother's home care. The room was as efficient and well equipped as any hospital room Julie had ever seen, yet it lacked that sterile atmosphere that was inevitable in a hospital setting. But if his mother's health continued to fail her, Luc would have to consider hiring another nurse for the overnight shift.

As fragile as Elizabeth was now, Julie was a little nervous being even temporarily in charge of her care. She was too emotionally invested in the relationship to be impartial. Elizabeth was her mother-in-law, but more than that, she was becoming a good friend. A bit like the mother that Julie never had.

When Julie and Luc first discussed their childhoods,

she had asked him about growing up without a father. Did he feel resentful or cheated? Had he ever wished his mother had remarried?

My mother gave me everything I could have possibly needed, he'd said. *We took care of each other.*

They still did. Julie wished she could have been so fortunate, that there had been someone in her life who always had her back, who loved her unconditionally. Wasn't that what everyone wanted? What everyone needed to feel whole? Luc had brought her closer to that feeling than anyone in her life ever had.

"Are you in love with my son?"

The sound of Elizabeth's voice startled her. She looked up from her laptop and saw that her mother-in-law was watching her. "You're awake. How do you feel?"

The older woman's shoulders lifted in a shrug and she smiled weakly. "Eh, I've been worse."

Her strength of character, her resilience, never ceased to amaze Julie. She could only hope that faced with similar circumstances, she would handle her condition with equal poise.

"So? Are you in love with my son?" she asked again.

"He's the most important person in my life."

"But that isn't what I asked, is it?"

Julie hesitated. Luc was right, his mother was sharp as a tack. "Elizabeth—"

She held a hand up to stop her. "No, no. You don't have to explain. You feel what you feel. I know how that is. But a mother can hope, can't she?"

Julie picked her chair up and moved it closer to Elizabeth's bed. "I'm honored that you feel that way, that you would want me in your son's life, and I wish things were different. I really do. What Luc and I have is very special, it's just not..." She struggled for the words to explain.

"Luc was my miracle baby," Elizabeth said. "Did I ever tell you that?"

Julie shook her head.

Elizabeth smiled wistfully. "His father and I had been trying for five years to have a child."

"Wow, that's a long time." For her and Luc's dad it must have felt like forever.

"Back then there weren't as many options as there are now, but we did everything we could. I was young enough to keep trying, but Luc's father was seventeen years older than me. He felt as if he was getting too old. I was his second wife and he had two grown boys when I met him, so he'd been through it all before. I couldn't blame him for his feelings. But, as these things sometimes happen, when we finally made the decision to give up, when I resigned myself to the fact that I would never have a child of my own, I got pregnant."

"Luc doesn't really talk about his father."

"He doesn't remember him. But they're so very much alike. My husband was a simple man. He believed in hard work and family, and giving back to the community."

"That does sound like Luc."

"We used to own one of the largest ranches in the county. He always hoped his boys from his first marriage would want to take over, but they had no interest in the family business. Or me for that matter. That ranch was his life and out of respect I wanted to keep it running, keep it in the family, but then I had my surgery and everything changed. I couldn't keep up with the day-to-day operations, and like Luc had no interest in ranching. I knew he was meant for greater things. The proceeds from the sale of the business paid for medical school."

"Luc said his dad had a heart attack."

"A massive coronary," she said, looking so sad, even all this time later. "They found him out in the field, his horse at his side. They told me that it was instantaneous, that he never suffered. I always took comfort in the fact that he died doing what he loved most.

"That's why I believe in seizing the moment. Living as though every day might be your last."

"I was in love once," she told Elizabeth. "I met him at university. I thought he was the love of my life."

"But he wasn't?"

She shook her head, the pain of that time still as real and sharp as a slap in the face.

Elizabeth frowned. "If you're uncomfortable talking about it…"

"It's not that," Julie said. It was just embarrassing to admit she had been so desperate for love. So gullible.

"You have to bear in mind how I was raised," she told Elizabeth. "I had no positive male influence in my life. My sister and I grew up believing that nothing we ever did was good enough."

"Oh, honey," Elizabeth said, patting her arm. "You've done amazing things with your life. You've dedicated yourself to helping people. You should be proud of your accomplishments. No matter what anyone else thinks."

That was easier said than done. "I try, but there's always that small part of me that says it's not enough.

That I could be doing more. That I'll never quite measure up."

"Inner demons," Elizabeth said with a sigh. "There's nothing more difficult to face than your own overinflated expectations. Believe me, I've been there."

Julie certainly had her share of those. "I found most men intimidating at that time, but there was something so different about him. He was so gentle and kind. He filled a place in my heart that had been empty for so long. I was able to set my fears aside. I was convinced he would never hurt me. At first."

"But he did."

She nodded. "Things started to gradually change. Little things at first. He became more critical and more demanding. He wanted all of my attention. He resented my friends, my professors, my homework. But I was so desperate for someone to love me, to accept me, I was blind to what was happening, to the way he was gradually tearing down my self-esteem, shrinking my world until I was totally dependent on him. By the end, he controlled nearly every aspect of my life."

"Love makes us do foolish things," Elizabeth said, and something in her eyes said she was speaking from experience. "Especially when we're vulnerable. The important thing is that you got away."

"It took every bit of courage I had to walk away from him. I was miserable for months. He had me convinced that I needed him. But as time passed and things moved into perspective, I was disgusted with myself, and embarrassed that I let it go as far as it did. I felt as if I should have known better. The first time he called me stupid I should have walked out the door." She paused, shaking her head. "No, not walked. I should have run for dear life."

"It's not your fault," Elizabeth said. "You were vulnerable and he took advantage of you. He was a predator."

"And he was damned good at it. I haven't been in a serious relationship since. I still don't trust my own instincts."

"Do you trust Lucas?"

"I do." With her life. He was the only person she trusted unconditionally

"You believe he would never hurt you?"

She could see where Elizabeth was going with this, and though Julie hated to disappoint her, there was no way around it. "Not purposely, no. But Luc and I will never be anything but friends. I love him. I can't imagine what I would do without him. Hands down he's the most important person in my life."

"I know he feels the same way about you."

That didn't change anything. "I'm sure as a mother, you want what's best for Luc," Julie said.

"Of course."

"Even if we were in love, he deserves someone without all the emotional baggage. It would be unfair to lay that all on him."

"Everyone has emotional baggage, Julie. *Everyone*. Even Luc."

Yes, well, some had more than others. Elizabeth didn't realize that Julie was doing both her and Luc a favor. She didn't know the first thing about being a wife. Or a daughter-in-law, for that matter.

"I wish things were different. I don't doubt that Luc would be an exceptional husband. In fact, I *know* he would be. It's my role as his wife that I'm not so confident about."

"Shouldn't Luc be the one to make that decision?"

As far as Julie was concerned, he already had. "I can't force myself to fall in love, and neither can he."

Eight

The nurse returned from her nap a few minutes later to check Elizabeth's vitals and gently suggested that it was time for her to rest. Julie gathered her things and went back to her bedroom, where she set up a work area at the small desk under the window overlooking the rolling green lawns and sprouting flower beds of the estate.

She opened the window and breathed in deeply. Spring was in the air. When she'd arrived in October, everywhere she looked there was devastation. It seemed as if now, slowly but surely, the town was waking up to the world, and life in Royal was returning to normal. Or what she perceived to be normal. Displaced families were back in their homes, and every week shops and restaurants had begun reopening.

She needed to get out more and explore the city. If this was to be her permanent home, she needed to get to know it better. And the people. That was the worst part of growing up so sheltered. The lack of community, missing that feeling of belonging somewhere. But things were different now. *She* was different.

She smiled to herself, thinking, *This is home*. This was exactly where she was meant to be.

Taking one last deep breath of cool fresh air, she closed the window, opened her laptop and got back to work. Sorting data took every bit of her attention and concentration, so it was no surprise that she didn't hear Luc walk in the room. When he spoke her name, she nearly jumped out of her skin.

"Didn't mean to startle you," he said, but he knew as well as she that when she was immersed in work, startling her was inevitable. "How's the research going?"

"Great." She looked over at the clock, surprised to see that it was barely after four. She couldn't remember the last time he'd left the hospital before seven in the evening.

Her first thought was that something must have been wrong. "Is everything okay?"

"Fine," he said, shrugging out of his jacket, which he then tossed over the footboard of her bed. "Why wouldn't it be?"

"The time, for one. You're home so early."

He loosened his tie and pulled it off, then started unfastening the buttons on his dress shirt. "I told Ruth to clear my afternoon. That I had something I needed to do."

Something that required he take his clothes off, because that's what he was doing. And why was her bedroom door closed? "What do you need to do?"

A sexy grin tipped up the corners of his lips. "You, of course."

What the advance lacked in creativity, he made up for with red-hot sex appeal. He unbuttoned his shirt, slowly exposing a band of smooth, defined chest with just a sprinkle of crisp black hair.

Nice.

"You know, I almost stopped to pick up Mardi Gras beads on the way home," he said.

Huh? Why would they need those?

Seeing her confused look, he said, "You don't recall flashing me this morning?"

Oh yes, she had done that, hadn't she. She never dreamed that a quick peek at her breasts in the morning would motivate him to cancel his afternoon appointments and rush home three hours early.

Damn. She must be doing something right.

"We never had our postwedding sex-a-thon. Unless you don't want to," he teased, his shirt halfway down his arms. Big, thick, delicious arms she wanted to feel wrapped around her.

"Oh, I want to," she said.

"Then, why are you sitting over there?" he asked, and the hunger in his eyes made her heart flutter.

"I'm enjoying the view."

"You'll enjoy it more on the bed."

She'd never known him to be impatient, but rather than wait for her to get up on her own, he walked over to her chair and scooped her up, then tossed her onto the bed.

He did seem to enjoy manhandling her, and weirdly enough, she liked it.

Bare chested and beautiful, Luc climbed up with her, kneeling on the mattress, straddling her thighs. "So, about this shirt."

She looked down at the totally unsexy but comfortable T-shirt she'd thrown on this morning. "What about it?"

"It needs to go."

No problem. She made a move to pull it over her head, but he said, "Allow me."

He grabbed the front of her shirt in his fists and gave it one good tug. She gasped as the fabric came apart in his hands.

"Better," he said, looking satisfied with himself. He was literally tearing her clothes off. And she *liked* it.

He unfastened her jeans and tugged them off, though she had the feeling that if he could have torn the denim, he probably would have ripped those off of her, too. But now he was eyeing her bra, and thank goodness for the front clasp or he may have tried to rip that off, too.

Of course the panties were the next to go. Had she been wearing socks he would no doubt rip those, as well.

Luc sat back to admire his work. "You're perfect," he said, his eyes raking over her. He cupped her breasts, rolling her nipple between his thumb and forefinger. He knew from their wedding night how crazy that made her.

"Tell me what you like," he said, pinching hard enough to make her gasp. "I'll do anything."

"Anything. Everything." *Just keep touching me.*

His brow lifted. *"Anything?"*

The look in her eyes must have said it all. She wasn't sure what she was getting herself into, but she didn't care. In the past she never would have suggested such a thing. She would never leave herself so exposed. The ramifications would have scared her to death. Amazing what trust could do.

And boy did he "do" her. And kept on doing her.

For two solid hours. Until he'd established an up-close-and-personal relationship with every inch of her body.

"I need to rest," she finally said, limp and draped across the bed, her head hanging over the side of the mattress. The comforter lay on the floor, the bottom sheet had come loose and was halfway off, and the top sheet was…well, she wasn't sure where that had gone.

"Finished *already*?" he asked, but his smile said he was teasing her.

"Aren't you supposed to roll over and go to sleep?" she said.

"You don't want me to do that."

She did and she didn't.

Her stomach rumbled and she realized that not only was it dinnertime, but she'd skipped lunch today.

"No more sex until you feed me," she said.

"We could go out. We never did get that candlelit dinner I promised you."

"Would I have to get up and get dressed?"

"I highly recommend it."

That sounded romantic and all, but putting on clothes and fixing her hair was just too darned much work. "Or we can make sandwiches and eat in bed."

"Are you sure you don't want to go out?" he asked, looking as if he was still raring to go. Did he ever get tired?

Her legs were so weak from being overextended—she hadn't realized her feet could go that far over her head—she wouldn't make it to the front door. "Some other time."

"Sandwiches it is," he said, hopping off the bed. *He actually hopped*. Then he pulled his slacks back on, walked to the door and, wiggling his eyebrows suggestively, said, "I'll be back. Don't start without me."

Not a chance.

She must have dozed off, because he was back in what seemed like seconds, a tray propped on one palm.

"Dinner is served," he said, setting it right on the bed.

She dragged herself into a sitting position, noticing that he was hiding something behind his back. "Whatcha got?"

"Let's call it dessert."

"Can I see what it is?"

He held up a squeeze bottle of chocolate syrup, wearing that lascivious grin, and all she could think was, *Oh boy, here we go again.*

The rest of the week flew by. Luc and Julie tried to make time for one another, but life kept getting in the way. Luc had hoped to spend Sunday with Julie, but she had already promised Megan she would volunteer for the pet adoption fair, to find homes for the animals displaced in the storm.

The following Monday Luc was sitting in the cafeteria catching up on his reading while he ate a late lunch, when someone sat down across the table from him. He glanced up from the medical journal, expecting to see a colleague sitting there.

It was Amelia.

He cursed silently. He had no other patients in Pediatric, and hadn't seen her since the consultation last Monday. To be honest, he hadn't given her much thought, either. But that hadn't stopped her from seeking him out. She'd come to his office several times hoping to "catch him" and he heard that she'd objected rather firmly when his resident came to check in on Tommy in Luc's place.

As careful as he'd been to avoid her, here she was anyway, invading his space. Other than information about her son's care, he had nothing to say to her.

"Someone has been avoiding me," she said in a sing-song tone. Her smile said she thought she was being cute, when in reality, it was just annoying.

"Is there something I can help you with?"

Her smile wavered. "I saw you sitting here so I thought I would stop and say hi."

"Hi," he replied, knowing that wouldn't be the end of it. He recognized that determined look on her face.

"It would be nice if we could talk."

Nice for her maybe. As far as he was concerned they had nothing to say to each other. "I have an extremely busy afternoon."

"You know you can't stay mad at me forever, Luc."

He wasn't mad, just disinterested in whatever she had to say. She seemed hell-bent on getting him to concede his feelings, but the truth was, he didn't have any. At least, not the kind she expected him to have. "As Tommy's surgeon, it's critical that I remain impartial. I'm sure you can understand."

"I just want to talk," she said. "I've missed you. Haven't you missed me even the tiniest little bit?"

His blank expression had her frowning.

"You're playing the tough guy. I get it."

"I'm not *playing* anything," he said. "I'm just trying to eat my lunch in peace."

"No need to get snippy," she said, in the voice one

might use while addressing an impatient child. "I'm just trying to be polite."

Had she used that tone with him six years ago? And if she had, how did he stand it?

He looked across the table at her. *Really looked.* He wondered what it was about her that he had found so appealing. She was attractive, in a debutante sort of way. Never a hair out of place, her makeup applied to perfection, her clothes designer and expensive. And he had been a penniless college student, working two jobs, struggling to keep up with her high expectations. Which seemed ridiculous now when he considered the generous weekly allowance her father provided. And if that wasn't enough, all she had to do was ask and he would supply her with yet another credit card.

Her parents thought that Luc, the lowly son of a rancher, wasn't good enough for their precious daughter. But Luc knew he was destined for great things, and he was proud of all that he'd accomplished. He wondered what her parents would think of him now, and realized he didn't really give a damn. But he sure had back then. Amelia wanted the prestigious role of a surgeon's wife, but not the work and sacrifice it would take to get there. But like any other young resident he'd had to pay his dues, and Amelia had no patience to wait around for him.

"So, how is your mother?" she asked him. "I heard that she's been ill."

"She's recovering."

"She must get lonely in that big house all by herself. Maybe I could come visit her someday."

Not a good idea. His mother never liked Amelia. *That girl is too big for her britches*, she used to say.

There was nothing his mother liked less than pretension, and Amelia's nose was—as his mother liked to say—locked in an upright position. His mother's wheelchair made Amelia feel awkward, as if by going anywhere near it she might catch something.

In all the time he'd dated her, he couldn't recall Amelia and his mother having any more than a five-minute conversation. So why the need to talk to her now? And what did she know about his "big house"? Had she been snooping into his personal life?

He wondered where he would be now if she hadn't run off with someone else. He'd been too proud to beg her to come back, but he'd wanted to. Those first few months afterward he'd been beside himself. It was only after he met Julie that he began to feel whole again. She was the one who filled the empty place in his heart. Just by being a good friend.

"My mother isn't well enough for visitors," he told Amelia. "Her immune system is too vulnerable."

"I'm sorry to hear that," Amelia said. "Maybe some other time."

Doubtful.

"Please send her my regards."

When he was away from work, Amelia was the furthest thing from his mind. And why would he think about her when he had Julie? Even though they weren't a real couple, she was everything he could ask for in a woman, and a wife. And especially a lover. Pleasing her, making her feel good, was by far his favorite part of the day. There was only one thing missing. After sex, she always went back to her own room to sleep. If he had his way, she would be sleeping in his bed. Even if it was only temporarily.

"Just the man I wanted to see," Luc heard someone say, and turned to see Drew walking toward him, swooping in like an angel of mercy to save him. He looked from Luc to Amelia, one brow raised slightly. "I hope I'm not interrupting."

"Not at all," Luc said, pushing to his feet, picking up the tray with his half-eaten lunch. "I'm finished."

With his lunch *and* with Amelia. He didn't introduce her to Drew, nor did he say goodbye when he walked away. Maybe now, after this chilly conversation, she would take the hint and leave him alone.

He dumped the contents of his tray in the trash on their way out of the cafeteria and asked Drew, "What brings you to the hospital?"

"I dropped off fresh flowers at the gift shop for Beth, then came in here for a soda. Then I saw you and, frankly, you looked like maybe you needed rescuing."

Now, that was a true friend. "Drew, you have no idea."

They stopped at the main bank of elevators. "Is that her?"

"Is that who?"

"Your ex."

Luc blinked. He'd made it a point not to say anything to anyone about Amelia's being in Royal. Not even Julie. "How did you know she was my ex?"

"Amelia...is that her name?"

Luc nodded.

"Well, she's been kinda broadcasting it all over town."

Disbelief stopped him in his tracks. "She's doing *what*?"

"Word is spreading fast."

Fantastic. Just what he needed. But was he surprised? Not really. Amelia loved to be the center of attention. And he'd bet anything she was pinning him as the bad guy. "What has she been saying?"

"She's making like you guys are getting chummy. At least, that's what I've heard."

He cursed and shook his head. "Nothing could be further from the truth. Today was the first I've seen of her in a week. And it wasn't by choice, believe me."

"Yeah, you looked pretty uncomfortable sitting there with her. What does Julie think about her being here?"

"Like I said, I haven't told anyone."

Drew looked pained. "Please, tell me you're joking."

"I prefer to leave work at work. Amelia is the mother of my patient, nothing more. She has nothing to do with my personal life."

Drew's expression said that Luc was a sad and pathetic man. "Dude, I hate to be the one to break it to you, but in a marriage, it doesn't really work that way."

"But we're not really married, are we?"

"No, but she is your best friend. I thought you guys told each other everything."

Well, almost everything. And he could see Drew's point. If Amelia was broadcasting the details of their past relationship, Julie was bound to hear it from someone. He didn't want it to appear as if he was hiding things from her. "I'll talk to her tonight."

"Smart move. The way it's spreading, it's only a matter of time before the entire town knows."

Luc cursed under his breath. He should have known that Amelia was up to something. He should have expected it.

Hadn't she done enough damage? Caused him enough pain. He was going to put an end to whatever she thought she was doing.

Nine

Julie met Megan and Lark for lunch at the Royal Diner. There was a real camaraderie among the three of them, a sense of genuine respect and friendship. Only recently, as she'd grown so close to these women, did Julie realize all that she'd missed out on being so sheltered as a child, and having that inherent lack of trust. But it was never too late to start living.

"The adoption fair seemed to go well," she told Megan after the waitress took their orders.

"And we're still bursting at the seams. It's like that every spring, plus we're still feeling the aftereffects of the tornado. We have a lot of animals coming in, but not so many getting adopted back out. I don't suppose you would be interested in a puppy or a kitten? Or better yet an older cat or dog?"

Julie had never had a pet before. Her father forbade animals of any kind in the house, and at university, with a full class-load, there hadn't been time. After that she'd moved around so frequently, spending months abroad, owning an animal, even something as benign as a goldfish, had been impractical.

Her condo in Royal had a no-pet policy, so adopting had never been an option. But she no longer had that obstacle, did she? She wondered how Luc would feel about adopting a small dog or even a cat. He spoke fondly of the various pets his family had owned in their ranching days, so she knew he liked animals.

"Maybe I'll come by and take a look," she said. "After I talk to Luc about it, of course."

"Speaking of," Megan said. "How is he holding up?"

"He's good." It had been touch and go with his mother all last week, but now she was infection free, eating better than she had in months and growing stronger every day. As they drew closer to April, and the days grew warmer, Elizabeth had been spending time outside in the gardens with her nurse.

"It must have been a shock for him," Lark said.

"Not really," Julie told her. "It's just a part of her condition."

"Condition?" Megan asked, looking confused. "I thought her son was the patient. Is Luc treating her, too? And wouldn't that be a conflict of interest?"

Julie frowned. *Her* who?

"Far as I heard he's only treating the boy," Lark said. "Which is bad enough if you ask me."

There were obviously some crossed wires here. "I'm a little confused."

"And that's perfectly natural," Megan said. "I would be, too, if Drew's ex showed up."

Drew's ex? *Wait, what?*

Before she could ask what the heck they were talking about, she noticed Stella approaching their table.

"Hello, ladies! Isn't this fantastic." She gazed around the diner. "It's so inspiring to see things getting back to normal in our little town."

"Are you here for lunch?" Lark asked her.

"Would you like to join us?" Megan chimed in. "We're giving Julie some much needed moral support."

They were? And what exactly did she need support for?

Stella sat in the empty chair next to Julie and with eyes full of sympathy said, "I heard she was in town. How are *you* holding up?"

She who? "Guys, I'm really confused."

"Of course you are," Stella said gently. "Who wouldn't be under the circumstances."

"No, I mean I'm confused right now, by this conversation. I must have missed something, because I'm lost. Who are we talking about?"

"Amelia," Stella said.

"Amelia who?" The only Amelia that she knew of was the one who'd broken Luc's heart. The one he was still hung up on all these years later. They couldn't possibly mean...

The three women exchanged a look, and Megan said, "I'm sorry. We just assumed Luc had told you."

Julie was beginning to get a very bad feeling. "Told me what?"

"His ex-fiancée, Amelia. Her son is Luc's patient."

Amelia was here, in Royal? Julie's stomach did an odd little flip-flop and a rush of heat flooded her cheeks.

As his wife, she should have known that. Even as his fake wife, a heads-up would have been nice. Weren't they supposed to make this marriage look legitimate?

"I guess it must have slipped his mind," Julie said. Though technically Luc was her boss, it wasn't often that their paths crossed at the hospital. On the average day, she rarely left her office. And though she had seen a picture of Amelia from six years ago, she had no clue what she would look like now. She could have passed her in the hall and not even known it. "We're both pretty busy. Some nights we don't even see each other."

Maybe Amelia and her son had just arrived and he'd forgotten to mention it. And maybe seeing her again, talking things over with her, would give him the closure he needed. So really, this could be a good thing. Right?

"When did she get here?" Julie asked them, forcing a smile, trying her best not to come off as the jilted wife.

The women exchanged another look and the bad feeling grew.

"Last Monday," Stella said.

For reasons that escaped her, Julie's heart plummeted to the pit of her belly and her appetite disappeared. She had been in Royal for more than a week?

"I'm so sorry you had to find out this way," Lark said. "We all just assumed you knew."

As Luc's wife, she should have known. But as his friend and employee, since that's all they really were, he was under no obligation to tell her anything. He had his life and she had hers. But he'd put her in a difficult situation.

She wracked her brain for a way to backpedal, to make herself look at least a little less pathetic, but trying to explain something she had no real answer for would only make things worse. Maybe Luc was trying to protect her feelings, or maybe he figured she wouldn't care either way.

You're rationalizing, and for no good reason, she told herself. It was what it was. An arrangement. After all that he'd done for her, how could she complain? If he wanted to talk about it with her he would in his own good time. And if he didn't, that was okay, too.

"He probably just didn't want to upset you," Megan said. "Her showing up so soon after the wedding. Maybe he felt hesitant to tell you."

"Or maybe he's so over her that he didn't feel the need to say anything," Lark added.

Julie appreciated their efforts, but they were only making things worse. "Can we maybe not talk about it anymore?"

"Of course," Stella said with manufactured cheer. "Hey, did you guys see in the paper that the coffee shop is set to reopen next week? And construction on the hospital will begin next month. I'm not sure if it's possible, but I'd like to have the new city hall building completed by the first anniversary of the tornado. We've come so far already in our rebuilding efforts."

"It's definitely starting to look like home again," Lark said.

The rest of the meal was awkward to say the least. No one brought Amelia up again, but considering the occasional sideways glances and sympathetic smiles from her friends, the subject was clearly on everyone's mind.

It would have been easy for her to make some sort of excuse and leave the diner, but Julie forced herself to sit there and pick at her salad, pretending to follow the conversation, when inside she was all jumbled up. She wondered how much time he'd been spending with Amelia. He'd come home very late from the hospital the past two nights. Could he have been with Amelia? Had they rekindled their romance? Was it possible that he was sleeping with her?

The thought made Julie sick to her stomach, though it shouldn't have. They never said they wouldn't see other people. Julie had just assumed, in the spirit of making their marriage look legitimate, and because they were intimately involved, that they wouldn't. And though she wanted to put it out of her mind and let it go, her brain went into overdrive instead.

She picked at her food and sipped her sweet iced tea, when what she really needed was something big and alcoholic. Anything to loosen the knots in her chest, to sooth her bruised pride.

The lunch seemed to go on forever, but Julie refused to be the first one to leave.

Claiming she had more establishments to visit, Stella left first, and then Lark got a call from the hospital and had to rush back to work, leaving just Julie and Megan.

"Julie, I am so sorry," Megan said the instant they were alone. "We never meant to embarrass you that way. We just…"

"Assumed that as his wife Luc would have told me. I would have thought so, too."

"I'm sure he had a good reason for not saying anything. And I'm sure nothing is going on between them."

"Are you sure? Really? If nothing was going on, why would he hide it from me?" She heard herself and shook her head with disgust.

"As your friend, husband and boss, he should have had the courtesy to tell you. You have every right to be angry with him."

At this point Julie wasn't sure what she was feeling. Or what she *should* feel. If the tables were turned, would she have done anything differently?

Yes, she would have. She would have told him the truth. She wondered how she could be so blind to what had been going on around her. Had she just been lulled into a false sense of security? And why hadn't anyone told her?

"What exactly have you heard about her?" Julie asked Megan.

Megan hesitated. "Maybe you should talk to Luc about it."

Oh, she would, but first she wanted the entire story, or as much as Megan could tell her. "I want to know what you've heard. I thought she was married."

"Divorced."

Swell. "What else?"

Looking pained, Megan said, "I heard they've been spending a considerable amount of time together. But that could just be talk."

She doubted it. "How much longer will she be here?"

"I really don't know. Her son is having spinal surgery, so as long as it takes him to recover I guess."

At least a week, maybe a little longer. That wasn't too bad. "Did Luc do the surgery yet?"

Megan shook her head. "And I have no idea when he's supposed to do it. Soon, I would imagine."

Not soon enough as far as Julie was concerned. The faster they left, the better. Unless it was already too late. Maybe he'd fallen back in love with her. Which would mean what for Julie? Divorce? Deportation? Or would she simply have to share him until she became a legal citizen?

What a horrifying thought.

For the rest of the day Julie walked around with a knot in her chest. And though she had no right to, she felt angry and betrayed. She went back to the hospital and tried to work, but she couldn't concentrate worth a damn. What she wanted to do was confront Luc, but she was still too hot under the collar. She needed time to cool off and put things into perspective. Convince herself that technically, Luc had done nothing wrong.

She left work early and headed for home, wondering how much longer she would actually be calling this grand place home. Would Luc move Julie out, and bring Amelia and her son in? Or would they all live there together as one big happy family? The idea made her shudder.

She wandered the house aimlessly for several minutes, confused and scared, her thoughts too jumbled to be rational, wondering what her next move should be. Should she confront Luc, or let him tell her in his own good time? And what if she didn't like what he had to say?

She wound up in the den, with its ceiling-high stone fireplace and panoramic windows, staring blankly into the afternoon sunshine, feeling as if the perfect life she'd had just this morning had completely fallen apart.

"You're home early," she heard Elizabeth say, and turned to see her wheeling her chair into the room. "How's my favorite daughter-in-law today?"

She said it with a smile so filled with love and genuine affection, Julie burst into tears.

An emergency surgery came in just as Luc was about to leave the hospital, so by the time he finally did get home it was after eleven. He went straight to Julie's room to tell her about Amelia, but she was already asleep.

"Julie," he called softly, but he didn't get an answer. He considered waking her, but he figured the news would be much better received after they both had a good night's sleep.

His stomach rumbled, reminding him that he'd skipped dinner, so he went down to the kitchen for a snack. He foraged though the fridge and found a pot of leftover stew.

"You're home late," he heard his mother say, and turned to see her wheeling herself into the kitchen. She was in her pajamas, but clearly hadn't been to bed yet.

"What are you doing up?" he asked her. "You know how important it is that you get your rest."

"Where have you been?" she asked.

"The hospital."

"Doing what?"

He frowned. What did she think he would be doing? "I had an emergency surgery. Why? Is something wrong?"

"Come here," she said, gesturing him to her.

He set the pot on the stove and walked over to her.

"Down here," she said, and he leaned over, thinking she wanted to give him a hug. Instead she whacked him upside the head.

Hard.

"Ow! Jesus," he said, seeing stars, rubbing the pain away. He could say with confidence that her strength was definitely coming back. "What the hell was that for?"

"Amelia is here," she said, and her tone said she wasn't at all pleased about it.

"Yes. Her son is my patient."

"And you didn't think this was something your wife might have liked to know?"

Aw, hell. "I was going to tell her tonight when I got home. I take it she already knows?"

"Of course she knows! The way people talk around here, how long did you think you could keep it a secret?"

"I wasn't keeping it a secret." He just hadn't brought it up.

"And the way she found out…" She pressed her lips together in a thin line, shaking her head. "What were you thinking?"

"I honestly didn't think it was a big deal—"

"Not a big deal?" she shrieked, her eyes wide, and he backed up a step, just in case she took another swing at him.

"—until today," he finished. "Drew warned me that Amelia has been all around town making noise like she and I have some sort of relationship, but it's not true."

"That's a little hard to believe, all things considered," his mother said.

Did she actually believe the lies Amelia had been spreading? And if she did, had Julie believed them, as well?

"How did Julie find out?"

His mother explained that she'd been out with her friends when the subject came up, and that everyone knew but her. "The poor thing was beyond humiliated."

He cursed under his breath. He never meant for it to go this far. He should have known Amelia would do something like this. "I intended to tell her tonight."

"Well, you're too late. And you owe her an apology."

"Of course I'll apologize."

"Not only are you a lousy excuse for a husband, you're not a very good friend, either."

Damn, she really was furious. "You don't think that's a little harsh?"

"Not in the least. Honesty and trust are the basis for any relationship. Platonic or romantic. You lied to her."

Technically, he hadn't, but he knew what his mother would say, because he'd heard it a million times growing up. A lie by omission was still a lie. "As I said, I didn't think it was relevant. I had no idea Amelia was spreading rumors."

"The poor thing sobbed on my shoulder."

He blinked. "Amelia?"

"No, you idiot. Julie."

Julie *cried*?

Julie?

In all the years he'd known her, through the worst conditions and situations, he'd never so much as seen her well up. She had tenacity, and nerves of steel. She really must have been humiliated to get that upset. And he felt like a louse for putting her in that position. His mother was right. He was an idiot. And a sad excuse for a spouse. And an even worse friend. Had he honestly believed that by avoiding Amelia, she would have no impact on his life? Or Julie's? This was Amelia they were talking about; he should have known better.

"Are you still in love with her?" his mother asked.

"Julie?"

She rolled her eyes. *"Amelia."*

The fact that she would even ask that question was a clear indication of just how far out of hand this had gotten. In retrospect, all this time later, he wasn't sure if he'd ever loved her. If it had instead been a case of extreme infatuation. "I do not love her. I have no feelings for her whatsoever. I didn't intend for any of this to happen."

"But it did happen, and you need to fix it."

He intended to. First thing tomorrow he would talk to Julie.

Ten

After tossing and turning most of the night, Julie dragged herself out of bed at the crack of dawn, relieved to discover that Luc was still sleeping. She'd heard him come in last night, but feigned sleep when he opened her bedroom door. Late as he was, it didn't take a genius to know where he'd been. And whom he'd been with.

She knew they needed to talk about it, but she needed to get her head on straight first. It was weird how quickly things could change. One minute everything was fine and going as planned, the next she didn't have a clue what to expect. But it wasn't Luc's fault, or hers. Neither of them could have anticipated this happening. But if he wanted Amelia, Julie wouldn't stand in his way.

If Luc were to divorce her so soon after the wedding, the immigration people would be suspicious to say the least. She needed to formulate a plan, an exit strategy that wouldn't involve deportation though the idea of staying Royal had lost its appeal. It would be too humiliating. There was nothing for her in South Africa. Maybe she could move closer to her sister, find a new job.

She sat in her office at the hospital, staring blankly at her laptop, her mind moving in so many directions at once, she couldn't make sense of anything. And she dreaded the moment Luc walked through her office door wanting to talk, because she had no idea what to say to him, or how she was even supposed to feel.

Several minutes had passed when she heard a knock on her door. Her heart raced up to her throat and her knees went all soft and squishy.

Here we go.

She took a deep breath and looked up, expecting to see Luc, but when she saw who was really standing there, her heart plummeted to the pit of her stomach. She'd seen that face before, in a photo Luc used to carry in his wallet. For all she knew it was still in there.

Amelia looked so harmless, her skin pale, her hair flat and lifeless and in need of washing, Julie almost felt sorry for her. Having a child with a chronic illness had obviously taken its toll on her.

"Hi, there," she said, looking nervously around the office. She spoke with one of those adorable Southern accents, and despite looking a little run-down and tired, she was still a very beautiful woman.

"Hello, Amelia, I'm Julie."

"You know who I am?"

Unfortunately.

Julie rose from her chair and crossed to the door, reaching out to shake her hand. It was small and delicate, just like the rest of her, but her grip was firm.

"I hope I'm not interrupting anything," Amelia said. "I just had to meet the woman who finally got a ring on Luc's finger."

The way Julie understood it, Luc had been more

than ready to settle down with Amelia. It was she who ran off with someone else. Which obviously hadn't worked out very well for her.

"Have you got a minute?" Amelia asked her. "Can we talk?"

"Come in." As much as Julie wasn't looking forward to this, she knew that it would be best to clear the air. Since Luc didn't seem inclined to talk to her about it, she could hear it straight from the source. At least here, in her office, she had the upper hand. Amelia was in her territory.

Amelia stepped inside. Julie shut the door and gestured to the chair across her desk. "Sit down."

Amelia hesitated, looking conflicted. "Are you sure? I know this is awkward…"

Not as awkward as it would be if they didn't talk. "I'm sure. Please, sit."

Amelia sat on the very edge of the seat, as if she might jump up at any second and bolt for the door. Julie returned to her chair and sat.

"I understand there's been talk," Amelia said. "I wanted to clear the air. I'm not sure what Luc has told you…"

Not a single damned thing, but she didn't tell Amelia that. When in doubt, change the subject. "First, how is your son?"

At the mere mention of her boy, her face lit. "Antsy. Ready for his surgery, but still a little scared. He knows his recovery will be slow and painful. But he can't wait to get on his feet again so he can play with his friends. He's crazy about baseball, and for a five-year-old he's really good, too.

"The last few months, as he's become more and

more limited physically, have been very hard for Tommy. Tommy's father, my ex-husband, rarely sees him. He never could forgive me for giving birth to a less than perfect child."

"I'm sorry to hear that," Julie said, feeling sympathy for the boy. She knew too well what it was like to grow up in a single parent home. Though her father, at best, was never more than half a parent. *At best.*

"He traded me in for a younger model," Amelia said with a weak smile. "I guess that's what happens when you marry for money and social standing."

The admission surprised Julie, and it must have shown.

"I don't deny that I've made many mistakes," Amelia said, head held up proudly. "My only regret is how it's affected my son. After all he's been through, he deserves better. He deserves a father who gives more than a monthly check."

"He has you," Julie said. "What more could he possibly need?" She would have given anything to have her mother back, for her parents to trade places. For her father to be the one who died.

Tears welled in Amelia's eyes. "My gosh," she said, dabbing at them. "You are just so sweet. I want you to know that when I came here I had no idea that Luc was married. He's a lucky man."

"I'm the lucky one," she said, and it was true. It was a wonderful thing he was doing for her and she couldn't lose sight of that. Even if he did fall back in love with this adorable woman. Who would blame him?

"I hear a bit of an accent there," Amelia said, cocking her head slightly. "Where are you from?"

"South Africa. But my parents were from Wales originally."

"Were from? They're not with you anymore?"

"No."

"Mine are alive and kicking," Amelia said with a sigh of exasperation. "And still trying to tell me how to run my life."

"I'm sure they mean well."

"No, they're just nosy and controlling. They always have been. I swore that when my Tommy was born, I would allow him to grow up to be whatever he wants to be. Play with the friends he likes regardless of their social standing, marry the girl he loves even if she's penniless. All of the things I never had. I'll even let him go to public school if that's what he decides he wants."

It sounded as if she and Amanda had quite a bit in common when it came to family. "My sister and I went to a private girl's school," Julie told her. "I hated it. I never felt as if I fit in."

"And I fit in too well. I was an entitled, spoiled brat. If not for my Tommy, I probably still would be, but having him has taught me so much about what really matters, you know?"

Julie could only imagine.

Amelia relaxed back into her seat, looking a bit less as if she might bolt. "How did you and Luc meet?"

"We were both volunteering for Doctors Without Borders."

"Oh, you're a doctor, too?"

"No. Currently I'm Luc's research assistant."

"Research for what?"

"Luc's medical inventions and surgical techniques.

They've made him quite famous in the medical community." And very wealthy.

"What is it that you do exactly?" Amelia said, looking genuinely interested.

"I conduct interviews, collect data and statistics."

"So you must see him a lot."

"Actually, no. As chief of surgery for the hospital, he's always on call. There are days when I barely see him."

Amelia scrunched up her nose. "Don't you hate that?"

"That's just the way it is," she said. "The way it's always been. But I work long hours as well, so I can't really complain." Nor would she ever feel the need.

"I used to hate that Luc's career meant more to him than I did. I was so jealous. At the time, I was used to getting what I wanted, and he did try to accommodate me. Looking back now, I have to wonder why he stuck around as long as he had. Why he wasn't the one who dumped me. I was such a bitch sometimes."

Julie had no answer for her. But she was guessing it was because he loved her, and he was willing to overlook the not-so-perfect stuff.

"He's still mad at me," Amelia said, eyes lowered. "I feel so bad for the way I treated him and I was really hoping we could put the past to rest, but that doesn't seem very likely. He won't even talk to me."

"Just give him time. I'm sure he'll come around."

"I appreciate the encouragement, but I think it's misplaced. And you're probably the last person I should be confiding in about this. To be honest, I'm not even sure why you're talking to me. If the situation were reversed, I wouldn't talk to me. Or if I did, I would tell me to stay the hell away from my husband. Why aren't you, by the way?"

Because he isn't really my husband. "You two clearly have unresolved issues. It's in both your best interests to deal with them so you can move on."

"That's all I want."

Julie wasn't sure she believed that. She didn't not believe it, either. Luc had always described Amelia as cold, heartless and manipulative. To Julie, she just seemed sort of...pathetic.

"How is his mom doing? I heard that she's been sick. It must be difficult for him, as close as they are."

"It is."

"Do you get along with her?"

Julie hesitated and Amelia cringed.

"Am I getting too personal? I'm sorry if I am. I'm just curious. Too curious for my own good, my daddy used to claim."

"Yes, we get along. I consider her one of my closest friends."

"She hated me—but I didn't like her, either. She and Luc were very close and I was threatened by that."

Elizabeth was as down-to-earth and easygoing as her son. It was hard to imagine her *hating* anyone. And Julie had always considered his close relationship with his mother a good thing. She'd certainly never felt threatened or jealous.

Amelia must have read her mind. "I don't blame her for not liking me. I was different back then. I was very much into appearances. Her disability made me uncomfortable and I'm sure it showed. I'd never known anyone in a wheelchair. I had no idea how to act around her. I realize now how ridiculous it was for me to let her disability define who she was as a person. The idea of someone judging my Tommy based on his physical capacities makes my heart hurt. I feel as if I owe her an apology. I asked Luc if I could visit her. He didn't seem to think that was a good idea."

"Her health is compromised, leaving her vulnerable to infection. I'm sure that's the reason." Though to be honest, she really wasn't sure.

"And I'm sure that you're just saying that to make me feel better," Amelia said with a sad smile. "But I appreciate the effort. I guess some things just aren't fixable."

She genuinely seemed to want to rectify her past mistakes. Luc should at least give her the chance to explain, for both their sakes. "I'll talk to Luc and see what I can do, but no promises."

"You know," Amelia said, "you're not at all what I expected."

When Julie smiled, she really meant it. "Neither are you."

That morning, the instant he stepped through the hospital doors an hour later than usual, Luc was ambushed by half a dozen people needing him for one thing or another. Sign this. Initial that. Should it be the red or the blue pill? It was the major drawback of being chief of surgery. When he did finally get to his office, Ruth greeted him with one brow raised, looking from him to her watch, then back to him again. "Working a half day, are we?"

"I know, I was up late and slept through my alarm." All night, Luc had been attuned to even the slightest noise coming from Julie's room across the hall. When she woke he wanted to talk to her, but he never got the chance. The last time he looked at the clock it had been four forty-five and still dark. When he opened his eyes again, sunlight was pouring through the blinds and the clock said 7:38 a.m. He'd gotten up and checked Julie's room, but of course she was gone.

He took off his suit jacket and waited for Ruth to get up and retrieve his lab coat, but she just sat there. "Lab coat?" he said, expecting her to jump to attention.

She didn't.

"I'm very busy," she said, but she just sat there, arms crossed, glaring. She didn't look busy to him. She did look pissed off though.

"Did I do something to upset you?" he asked her.

"Like what?"

"I have no idea. That's why I'm asking."

"It wouldn't have anything to do with the fact that a week after your wedding you're hooking up with ex-girlfriends?"

"Hooking up?" He'd never heard her use the vernacular of a much younger generation. "Do you even know what that means?"

"I know that what you're doing is wrong," she said, chin tilted stubbornly. "How do you think this will make Julie feel?"

Pretty lousy if what his mom said was true. "Cancel anything I have before noon," he told Ruth, getting the lab coat himself. He had a lot of explaining to do, and he had the feeling it might take a while. "And for the record, I am not hooking up with Amelia. I've barely spoken to her."

"That's not what I've heard."

And he didn't have the time to sit there and explain. Ruth's feelings on the matter were the least of his worries.

He headed to Julie's office three floors up. He knocked on the door, hoping she was there.

"Come in," she called, so he opened the door...and got the shock of his life when he realized Amelia was sitting there with Julie.

Talk about awkward.

Or was it? Julie and Amelia looked completely at ease with each other.

"What the hell is this?" he asked, his tone sharper than he intended, feeling like the odd man out.

Julie looked at Amelia, and Amelia looked at her, and then both women burst out laughing.

Eleven

"We weren't laughing *at* you," Julie insisted to Luc several minutes later after Amelia left her office and they were alone.

"You looked right at me and laughed," he said, not sure who irritated him more, Julie or Amelia. Or maybe it was how cozy the two of them had looked sitting there together. This was not supposed to happen. Julie was supposed to dislike Amelia as much as he did.

"Not ten seconds before you knocked we were talking about how you would react if you walked in and saw us together," Julie said. "It's the timing that had us laughing. Not you."

It sure hadn't felt that way. He sat on the corner of her desk. "We need to talk."

"About what?"

About what? Was she joking? "For starters, what Amelia was doing here."

Julie shrugged. "We were talking."

Thanks, Captain Obvious. "I could see that. What were you talking about?"

"You, mostly."

Swell. Did he even want to know what was being said? Probably not.

"I should have told you that she was here," he said. "And that her son is my patient. And I know the fact I didn't looks suspicious—"

"*Luc*, stop. You don't owe me an explanation."

Of course he did. "We're married, I should have said something about her being here."

"This marriage is only pretend, remember?"

He was getting a little tired of her reminding him of that. Who was she trying to convince, him or herself? "Then, as your friend, I should have told you."

"I'm sure you had your reasons not to. Besides, I think it's good that you're finally getting a chance to settle things with her. You should have done it a long time ago."

"There's nothing to settle."

"For her there is."

"That's not my problem. And despite what you've probably heard, I have not been spending time with her. She, on the other hand, has been stalking me."

"I know. She told me."

He blinked. "She did?"

"Well, she didn't use the term *stalking*, but I know she's been trying to see you. All she wants to do is talk."

"You believe that?"

"Unless I hear otherwise from you, what reason do I have not to?"

He could think of a couple dozen. "You don't know her the way I do."

"People do change."

Not people like her. "She's the same old Amelia, trust me."

"How can you know that if you won't talk to her?"

He knew Amelia was manipulative, but to coax Julie over to her camp with a single conversation? That was quite an accomplishment, even for her. "As I said, I have no need or desire to discuss or settle anything from our past. Period."

"She's been through a lot. I really think that she's different now. Who knows, she may still be the love of your life."

Oh, good God no, she wasn't. "She is not the love of my life."

"Either way, it's okay with me if you spend some time getting to know her again. And if you decide you need to end our marriage—"

"Absolutely not." Was she serious? What kind of friend would he be? Besides, he would choose Julie over Amelia any day of the week. The trouble was making her believe that. Julie had never had a man in her life who hadn't disappointed her deeply in one way or another. It was almost as if she expected it, planned for it even. He refused to let that happen to her again. He wouldn't let her down, no matter what he had to do. "Until you get your permanent citizenship you're stuck with me. As long as it takes. I don't go back on my promises." He took her hand and squeezed it hard, his eyes locked on hers. "I mean that. I don't want this to come between us. You're the most important person in my life."

"It won't come between us."

"You promise?"

She smiled. A *real* smile. "I promise."

Somehow that just didn't seem good enough. There was something else going on here that he just couldn't seem to put his finger on. "Are you sure you're okay? My mom said you cried. You never cry."

Her cheeks blushed a vivid shade of pink. She never cried, and she blushed even less often. "I wish she wouldn't have said anything to you. It was really, really embarrassing."

"She was concerned."

"It was PMS, that's all. Every now and then it makes me emotional. And for the record, I do cry occasionally. I just don't let anyone else see it. It was just bad timing."

"So, if you have PMS, I guess that means you're not..."

"I'm not pregnant."

He waited for the relief to flow over him, but weirdly enough, he felt a twinge of disappointment instead. He wasn't ready to be a parent, and neither was Julie, but knowing there had been a slight possibility, it had gotten him thinking. But the timing couldn't have been worse. And he was completely overlooking the fact that, as she liked to point out, he and Julie were married in name only.

"I was thinking, if you're going to be seeing Amelia—"

"I'm *not*. I'm married to *you*, and until that changes I'm not *seeing* anyone else."

"I was just going to say, you should try to keep it on the down low."

Was she giving him permission to cheat on her? Did she really believe he would put her citizenship in jeopardy? Not to mention her dignity. And his own. And their *friendship*. What sort of man did she think he was? "It's not going to happen. Not now, not ever. I don't find her even remotely attractive."

"You can't deny that she's beautiful."

On the outside maybe. "As far as I'm concerned, she's nothing more than the mother of my patient. That's as far as it goes now, or ever will go. Amelia and I had our shot and she blew it. She doesn't get a second chance."

"I think she's really changed."

Somehow he doubted that. Amelia liked to manipulate, and she was good at it. He didn't doubt that she was manipulating Julie. Julie's instincts when judging a person's character had never been stellar, but she'd had Luc around a good majority of the past six years to give her guidance. She'd always listened to him before. Why not now? "Are you that eager to get rid of me?"

"Of course not," she said, laying her hand on his arm. Her skin was soft and warm. Whenever she touched him, something happened, something deep down inside of him shifted. He'd never been with a woman who could excite him the way she did, or frustrate him, while at the same time making him feel more at peace than he ever had in his life.

"I just want you to be happy," she said.

"Then, please trust me when I say to stay away from her. *That* will make me happy."

"Why?"

"She's not the person you think she is." Julie was too trusting, too nice to see Amelia for what she really was. Amelia would chew her up and spit her back out without batting an eyelash.

"We'll see," Julie told him, as if she knew something he didn't. Some significant piece to the puzzle that hadn't yet fallen into place.

Chumming up to him was one thing, but why would

Amelia befriend Julie? What did she possibly stand to gain? Or was she just screwing with his head, hoping to cause chaos? Anything to make herself the center of attention.

"What do you think of cats?" Julie asked, and the abrupt change of subject threw him for a second.

"I think they're delicious. Why?"

She laughed, and it was truly like music to his ears. He liked making her happy, seeing her smile.

"I'm being serious. Do you like them?"

"I don't *dis*like them. We had several at the ranch when I was growing up. But they were always more of my mother's thing."

She frowned. "Oh."

"Why do you ask?"

"The shelter is filled beyond capacity, and I've never actually had a pet, so I thought maybe a kitten...but it sounds like it would be a bad idea."

"Why not a dog? I like dogs."

"Let's be honest. Neither of us has the time for a dog. Our schedules are just too busy."

He couldn't deny that. "You're right. But a cat?" He made a sour face. "They're so...sneaky."

"Never mind. Like I said, it was just a thought."

She sure didn't put up much of a fight.

He shrugged apologetically and said, "Sorry."

"No, it's okay," she said, forcing a smile. And not a very convincing one. "I've gone this long without one. When I get my own place I'll have to find a pet-friendly apartment this time."

Though he knew it was inevitable, the thought of her eventually moving out didn't sit well with him. He liked having her there, knowing that she was just across the hall if he needed her, or if she needed him. Though he would much rather she be a permanent addition to his bed, even if all they intended to do was sleep. He'd gently suggested on more than one occasion that she stay the night in his room, but she never would. Their wedding night had been the only exception.

"I'm used to sleeping alone," she'd explained, but he had the feeling it was more than that. He just wasn't sure what. He'd begun to wonder if this friends with benefits deal they had going was a little more complicated than either had expected. Aside from the sex, their relationship hadn't changed, so why did everything feel so…different? Was he falling in love with her? For real? And if he was, what next? Did he take the chance and tell her? If she didn't share those feelings, he knew it would only drive her away.

That wasn't a risk he was willing to take.

Twelve

Julie believed Amelia when she said she only wanted to talk to Luc, but she seemed to be the only one in town who did.

"Everyone hates me," she told Julie that Friday, while they shared lunch in the hospital cafeteria. When Tommy slept, which was quite often due to the heavy dose of pain meds that he was on, Amelia would sometimes sneak away and visit Julie. She was the only friend Amelia had in town, and though they were an unlikely pair all things considered, they had quite a bit in common.

"I'm sure no one hates you," Julie said, though she, too, noticed Amelia getting the cold shoulder and more than a few suspicious looks. "Luc is a respected member of the community. People are just very protective of him."

"I noticed," Amelia said, moving her food around her plate, but not really eating much. With her son's surgery scheduled soon she was understandably edgy. "I'm getting sick of hospital food, so I went to the diner last night. But I got so many dirty looks I had to leave. Even the waitress gave me the cold shoulder. I had them wrap my food up and I took it back to the hospital to eat."

Julie hated that people would treat her that way when they didn't even know the full story. Didn't even know Amelia. Did no one care that she had a sick child? Why couldn't they cut her a little slack? "If they knew you like I do, they wouldn't act that way."

"They don't want to know me," she said. "I can see now that coming here was a mistake. After the surgery, as soon as Tommy is stable enough to be moved, I'm going back to Houston. I'm as big a joke there as I am here, but at least there I don't get sneered at every time I walk down the street. They're kind enough to do it behind my back. The poor little debutante with the sick kid whose husband couldn't keep it in his pants."

Julie cringed. "Ouch."

"I know. And my parents hold me personally responsible for tarnishing our family reputation."

That was just wrong, but Julie knew from experience how unreasonable parents could be. "How is your husband cheating on you your fault?"

"Oh, they didn't care about the cheating. That's just what husbands do, apparently."

"According to who?"

"Houston high society."

"That's crazy," Julie said.

"At first Tom, my ex, was very discreet, but I knew something was up. He'd work lots of late nights and went on weekend business trips. I fooled myself into thinking that I was imagining things. I was used to men fawning all over me. I was young and beautiful and rich, and I knew it. It was a blow to my pride to think that my husband, the man who was supposed to worship the ground I walked on, would stray.

"I was sure that fatherhood would settle him down."

"Did it?"

She shook her head. "It only seemed to push him further away. Tom was never there for our son, not even when he was an infant. Even less after he was diagnosed. All the money and status in the world wasn't worth my baby being treated that way."

"What did you do?"

"I got really, really angry. Then I said enough is enough and divorced him."

Julie admired any woman who had the courage to stand up for herself in the face of adversity.

"For what it's worth, I never would have had the guts to do what you did," Julie said.

"Humiliation is one hell of a motivator."

Julie told Amelia about her abusive ex, and how long it took her to screw up the courage to walk away. "He completely shredded my self-esteem. I was weak and pathetic."

"You were doing the best you could with the skills you learned growing up."

"That's just the thing. I never learned how to defend myself."

"That's my point. You were totally ill equipped to deal with the situation, but you still got away. You prevailed."

"Not as soon as I should have."

"Julie, I stayed for over *four* years."

"But you were married with a son. There was nothing keeping me from leaving. Nothing but my own cowardice."

"Don't be so hard on yourself," Amelia said. "You're one of the bravest people I know."

For a second Julie was sure that she was joking. Brave? *Her?* "How could you possibly think that?"

"Look at all the extraordinary things you've done. You've traveled all over the world helping people. You ventured off on your own and turned a terrible situation into something really good. That takes guts."

Julie had never really thought of it like that before. "I guess so."

"As crazy as my parents drive me, my mother especially, the idea of completely cutting them from my life is terrifying. I think about it all the time, but I could never actually do it. Despite everything, their opinion still matters to me. You don't seem to let anyone else's opinions color your judgment. If you did, you sure wouldn't be sitting here with me. The town pariah. I thought talking to Luc's friends and the people in town might give me some insight into how to relate to him. To make him listen to me. Maybe find some common ground. All I've managed to do is make a whole bunch of enemies."

"What those people think shouldn't matter to you. You know your intentions were good. That's all that's important."

A frown furrowed her brow. "I guess."

After lunch Julie went back to her office, feeling bad for Amelia. She believed it would be in Amelia's and Luc's best interest to talk, to settle the past so they could both move forward, but if Luc refused, there wasn't much Julie could do about it.

Or could she?

She wasn't duplicitous by nature, but if the situation called for it, and she truly believed it could benefit Luc, even she could be a little creative.

* * *

A few hours later Julie's phone rang and she was surprised to see Elizabeth's number on the screen. Her first thought was that it was her nurse and something was terribly wrong. And if she was calling Julie, Luc must have been unreachable. But when she answered it was Elizabeth's voice, and she sounded just fine.

"Something arrived for you today," she told Julie. "Can you get away from work? You should probably come home and open it."

It was an odd request, to say the least. "Who is it from?"

"I'm not sure, but I think it might be perishable."

It was probably something from her sister, who had finally called Julie to congratulate her on her "pseudowedding"—Jennifer's exact words. She'd probably sent chocolates or a fruit basket. "Can't you just stick it in the fridge for now?"

"It wouldn't fit."

"Can you open it for me and tell me what it is?"

"I wouldn't feel right opening someone else's package," she said. "You should come home."

Julie looked at the pile of transcripts from the interviews she'd conducted with spinal patients, and had been hoping to review that afternoon, but for whatever reason her coming home now was important to Elizabeth, and that was good enough for her. "Let me finish up what I'm doing, then I'll come home. Give me thirty minutes."

"See you soon!"

That was a little strange, but, okay. She finished what she'd been working on and headed home, surprised to find Luc's Beamer in the garage next to his mother's van. What was he doing home so early?

Julie let herself into the house, hung her keys on the rack next to the door and called, "I'm home."

"In here!" Elizabeth called back from the vicinity of the living room. When Julie got there, she saw Elizabeth in her chair, and Luc sitting close by on the sofa. He was dressed casually in jeans and a polo shirt, and next to him on the cushion was a brown cardboard box. It was around eighteen square inches and from what she could see, unmarked. The top wasn't sealed, either. Nor did it look like it ever had been. It would have been pretty easy for anyone to peek inside.

"You're home early," she said.

"I am," he agreed, wearing what she could only describe as a sly smile. "I had a few things to take care of this afternoon."

There was a weird vibe in the room. A feeling of expectation. She looked from him to his mother. "Is everything okay?"

"Fine," he said. So why were they looking at her that way? As if something was about to happen.

"So is that it?" she asked, nodding to the box.

"That's it," Elizabeth said. "Open it."

Julie eyed it warily. Was something going to explode or jump out at her? Was this some sort of gag gift? Because it sure didn't look as if had been shipped there.

"Come on," Luc said, sliding the box closer to himself to give her room to sit. If it were something volatile he probably wouldn't do that. Right? Of course, if he were the type of man to give his wife a box of some volatile substance, she wouldn't be married to him.

She sat gingerly on the edge of the cushion. He slid

the box to her, and feeling a little nervous still, she reached for the top. She tested the weight of it, and it was definitely too light to be a fruit basket. Bracing herself, she lifted the flaps, sure she was in for a shock. And boy, did she get one when she looked inside. Curled up in the bottom of the box, on a hospital baby blanket, lay a sleeping ball of fluffy, snow-white fur with an itty-bitty pink nose and black tipped ears.

"Oh my gosh, it's a kitten!" she said, but by their smiles, it was clear that they both knew exactly what was inside the box. "Did you do this?" she asked Luc.

"My mom and I went to the shelter today."

"But...you said—"

"Did you honestly think I wouldn't let you have a cat?" he asked.

Actually, she had. He'd said no, and in her world, no meant no. "But I thought you didn't like cats."

"I said I didn't dislike them. Would I rather have a dog, yes, but as you said, we don't have the time."

"It would probably be best if I watch him for you while you both work," Elizabeth said. "Until he gets bigger and knows his way around the house."

"He?" Julie said, lifting him gently from the box. He was so small and fragile looking. As she cuddled him in her palms, he blinked his little eyes open and looked right at her, making a soft mewling sound, as if he was saying hello.

"He is a very special kitten," Luc said. "One that no one else wanted."

Who in their right mind wouldn't want this adorable little ball of fluff? "Is there something wrong with him? Is he sick?"

"He's blind," Luc said. He moved the box out of the

way so he could scoot closer. "I guess it's common in white cats. There were a dozen or so other kittens available, but Megan said the little ones go fast. I knew you would want an animal who really needed a good home. We looked at the older cats first, then Megan told me about this little guy. The second I saw him I knew he was perfect."

"He is perfect," Julie said, rubbing her cheek against the softness of his fur, and he started to purr. A surprisingly loud purr to be coming out of something so small. "He's just so tiny and sweet. I love him."

"There's the added bonus of him not jumping up on things," Luc said, rubbing the kitten under the chin with his index finger. "Since he wouldn't know where to jump."

"He really can't see anything?"

"Megan said he won't respond to visual stimulation. Otherwise he's perfectly healthy. He'll need shots eventually, but that's about it."

"How old is he?"

"Eight weeks."

He was wide-awake now and fussing to get free, so she set him down on her lap, but he didn't stay there long. He sniffed around the sofa cushions for a few seconds, then leaned way over the edge, and before she could grab him, toppled over and landed on his back on the rug.

"Oh no!" she said, reaching for him, thinking he might be hurt, but he got up on his feet, shook it off and started sniffing around the coffee table leg. "Resilient little thing, isn't he?"

"What will you name him?" Elizabeth asked.

"I'm not sure. I'd like to get to know him a little better before I give him a name."

The nurse came in the room looking for Elizabeth. "I'm sorry to interrupt, but it's time for your PT."

"Already?" Elizabeth said with a sigh. To keep the circulation moving in her legs she had a daily physical therapy session. "It can wait a while."

Luc shot her a look. *Mother.*

"Fine, fine, I'll go," she mumbled, wheeling her chair from the room.

"So you like him?" Luc asked, even though it was pretty darned obvious.

"He's adorable."

"His litter pan and food are in the utility room. I wasn't sure where you would want to keep them."

"In my room for now, I guess." She scooped the kitten up before he could get far, but he didn't want to be held and struggled to get free. She set him back on the floor and watched him sniff around. "This is the sweetest thing anyone has ever done for me."

"And I know just how you can thank me," he said his lips tipping up in a sly grin. She knew that look, and what it meant. And she was more than happy to oblige.

She leaned in and kissed him, and when he slid his hand behind her neck and under the root of her ponytail, cradling her head in his palm, she was toast. Luc knew just what to do to get her engine revving, and right now, her gas pedal was to the floor.

"Maybe we should take this upstairs," she said. "If you have time."

"I could be persuaded to take the rest of the day off. How about you?"

"I don't know, my boss is kind of a hard-ass."

Luc grinned. "I think he could make an exception just this— Ow!"

He winced in pain, and she looked down to see her sweet little kitten climbing his leg, nails out.

"Hey, you," she said, carefully extracting him from Luc's slacks, hoping that he hadn't ruined them. "Climbing up pant legs, not cool."

"Beth warned me that he can be very mischievous," Luc said. "She said that we have to keep a close eye on him until he's familiar with the layout of the house."

Considering how big the house was, that could take a while, and she could hardly imagine anything so small and sweet being mischievous. How much damage could one tiny kitten do?

It didn't take long to find out.

Thirteen

They took the kitten along up to Luc's bedroom, putting him on his blanket in his box on the floor by the bed. Luc had never been a cat person. As a kid he pretty much ignored the ones they had on the ranch. But he couldn't deny that this little guy was kinda cute.

When he first walked into the shelter he'd been overwhelmed by the volume of animals in need of homes, and picking one seemed a daunting task. He'd wandered the facility looking in cages. His mother had been no help at all. Had it been up to her they would have left the place with a couple dozen felines. It had been Megan who swayed him in the right direction.

He had been looking at the older cats, the ones who had been in the shelter the longest, when Megan suggested a kitten.

"I would think that kittens would be pretty easy to place," he'd said. "Julie would choose a cat no one else wants."

"I have just the thing," Megan had said, steering him to a cage in the kitten section. "Someone brought in a litter last week, and this little guy is the only one left."

The second he saw the little white fur ball he was

sure Julie would love him, and when Megan told him the kitten was blind, he knew it was fate.

Julie was so independent and capable, not to mention practical, it wasn't often that she let him do anything really nice for her. So when she asked him about getting a cat he lunged at the opportunity. Nothing meant more to him than making her happy.

And she seemed happy now. But they barely had a chance to get started in bed before the kitten climbed up the side to join them.

"Down you go," Luc said, scooping him up and setting him back in his box. "This is your bed."

They had just taken off their socks when he was up there with them again, so back in the box he went. And back up he climbed a few seconds later.

"This is not working," Luc said, dropping the kitten into his box again, this time not quite so gently. And back up he came like a spring, clawing his way up the comforter. "Do we have any packing tape?"

Julie shot him a look. "If you're thinking we're going to tape his box closed, think again."

Okay, bad idea. "We could lock him in the bathroom."

He got another look.

"Have you got a better idea?" Luc asked, putting the kitten on the floor this time. "Shoo. Go play."

When he didn't immediately spring back up, they both sat there waiting, watching the edge of the bed for his reappearance.

A minute or so passed and no kitty. "You think he got the hint?" Luc said.

"Seems that way," Julie said, then she looked behind them and started to laugh. "I take that back."

Luc turned to see that the kitten had come up the opposite side of the mattress this time and was sitting behind them. He yawned and licked his paws, content as could be.

Luc sighed and shook his head. "Ideas?"

"Let's wait a minute and see what he does. He's got to be tired from all the climbing."

They sat and watched while the kitten sniffed around the bed for several minutes, nearly toppling over the edge a few times. He made his way to the head of the bed, up onto Luc's pillow, where he curled up in a ball and promptly fell asleep.

"So now what?" Luc asked.

"It's a king-size mattress," Julie said. "There's room for everyone."

It was a little strange at first, making love with an audience, even if that audience was asleep, but eventually Luc forgot he was even there. They stayed on their side and the kitten stayed on his, while Julie "thanked" Luc.

Afterward, as they lay there together, Julie cuddled up against him, the kitten woke up, toddled over and joined them. He flopped down on his back, right on Luc's chest.

"This is the best gift anyone has ever given me," Julie said. She tickled the kitten's belly and he attacked her hand.

They played with the kitten for a while, and then Julie grabbed her phone from the bedside table to check the time.

"Are you getting hungry?" she asked Luc.

He eyed her warily. "When I said cats are delicious, I was kidding."

She laughed and gave him a playful nudge. "It's almost dinnertime. And it's Friday. We should do something."

"We still haven't had that romantic dinner out that I promised you. We could get dressed up and go somewhere nice, just the two of us."

"Or we could see if your mom would like to join us. We could go to the diner. And if she's feeling up to it afterward maybe we could take her to see a movie."

"Are you sure that's what you want?" he asked her.

"She's been stuck at home for almost two weeks now, and she's definitely well enough to leave the house. I would feel guilty going out and leaving her home alone."

Luc grinned and shook his head.

"Why are you looking at me like that?" she asked him.

"You're an extraordinary woman, Julie."

She blinked. "I am?"

He nodded.

"Why?"

"I offer to take you out to an expensive, candlelit dinner, and you would rather spend the evening with my mother."

"She's my friend. I want her to be happy. You know that it's only a matter of time before she gets another infection."

"I know," he said, his heart aching at the thought of losing her. "She's getting more and more fragile."

"So let's have fun with her while we still can."

"What are we going to do with him?" Luc nodded toward the kitten, who had curled up between them on the comforter and was sound asleep again.

"He can stay in here," she said. "As long as he has food and water and a litter pan he should be fine. And we keep the door closed. How much trouble could one tiny kitten get into?"

They had a nice dinner with Luc's mother, then took her to the theater to see the latest chick flick. Julie knew for a fact that Luc would have picked an action film any day of the week. Frankly, so would Julie, but his mother wanted to see a romantic comedy. It was after eleven when they finally got home.

"I'll help the nurse get her into bed," Luc told Julie. "You should probably go up and check on the fur ball."

She headed upstairs, opened the door to Luc's bedroom and switched on the light. "Here kitty, kitty. Mummy's home."

He wasn't on the bed sleeping, where she would have expected him to be, but then what did she know about having a cat? The most she'd ever had petwise was a caterpillar in a glass jar, until her father saw it there and flushed it down the toilet.

"Kitty, kitty," she called, checking all around the bedroom and the bathroom. "Come to Mummy."

She waited, but when he didn't come trotting out to greet her she frowned. "Where are you, you silly kitten?"

There was no sign of him so she got on all fours to look under the bed. From behind her she heard, "I don't know what you're doing, but I like the view."

She turned to see Luc standing behind her. "I can't find the kitten."

"He's got to be here somewhere," he said. "Did you try the closet?"

"Not yet."

Luc headed that way while Julie crawled over to check under the chest of drawers.

"Um, Julie? I found him."

"Oh thank goodness." She jumped up and darted to his closet door to join Luc. She looked inside and gasped. It was as if a hurricane had torn through. A dozen or so of Luc's clean, pressed dress shirts lay in piles all over the floor like an Egyptian cotton rainbow, while several others hung half on and half off the hanger. From the cuff of one, dangling a good two feet from the floor, hung the kitten, his claw snagged.

"Oh my gosh!" Julie dashed to his rescue, carefully unsnagging his nails and cuddling him to her chest. "You poor baby. How long were you hanging there?"

Luc just looked around, shaking his head. "What was that you asked? 'How much trouble could one tiny kitten get into?'" He spread his arms wide. "Here's your answer."

"He has been busy, hasn't he? On the bright side he'll probably sleep well tonight."

"So I guess I should have listened to Megan when she said that he's mischievous."

"I'm sorry. I hope he didn't ruin them."

"You'll make it up to me," Luc said, and she didn't have to ask what he meant. She helped him clean up the kitten's mess, then spent the next hour or so making it up to him, and what a hardship that turned out to be.

After making love again, he asked her to stay with him all night. She said no, he said please. She couldn't recall him using the word *please* any of the previous times he'd asked her and hearing the word spoken so earnestly, seeing the earnest look in his eyes...well, she just couldn't tell him no.

"Just this once," she said, settling back against the pillows. "But I'm used to sleeping alone, so I'll probably toss and turn most of the night. I apologize in advance if I keep you awake."

"It's a king-size bed, you won't even know I'm over here," he said, but nothing could be further from the truth. He never even made it onto his own side. He curled up behind her, his arm draped across her hip. And as if that wasn't crowded enough, the kitten, who was clearly exhausted after his adventure, curled up on the pillow above her head. She was annoyed, and utterly content at the same time. She closed her eyes, mentally preparing herself for a long restless night, and when she opened them again, it was morning. Not only had she not had a lousy night's sleep, she felt well rested and full of energy.

Luc was gone, but he'd left a note on the pillow. "Volunteering at the clinic until noon. How about lunch in the hospital cafeteria at 1:00?"

She looked at the clock, stunned to find that it was almost 10:30 a.m. She grabbed her phone off the bedside table and typed up a quick text.

Lunch sounds great, see you at 1:00.

He responded a few seconds later with a happy face icon.

She would have plenty of time to shower and make a trip to the pet supply store.

Speaking of pets...

She reached up over her head to pet the kitten only

to realize that he was gone. *Here we go again*, she thought. She pushed herself up out of bed and threw on the T-shirt and panties she'd been wearing the night before. She looked in the obvious places first. Under the bed, in the closet by his food dish, in the bathroom by his litter. But she couldn't find him anywhere. Had he snuck out when Luc left?

She checked everywhere, every corner and nook. She even checked under the covers, in case he'd been sleeping beside her when she flipped the blanket off.

Nothing. It was as if he'd vanished.

Where the hell could he have gone? she wondered, a feeling of panic building in her chest. How in the world would she find him? In a house this huge it could take days.

She was checking behind the curtains one last time, and was about to initiate a whole house search, when she heard a loud and very unhappy-sounding meow. But it seemed to be coming from above her head. She looked up to find the kitten clinging to the curtain valance on top of the rod, and now that she took a better look at the curtain panel, she could see teeny tiny holes where his claws had sunk in. The little imp had climbed all the way up, and apparently couldn't find his way back down. "You are mischievous," she said, getting up on her tiptoes to scoop him up. "Let's not go up here again."

She put the kitten in his box, grabbed the rest of her things and walked across the hall to her own room.

She set the box on the bed. "You stay here while I take a shower."

She didn't really expect him to obey, so it was no surprise when he escaped the box, tumbled down from the mattress onto the floor, got back on his feet and followed her into the bathroom where he started digging around in his litter. He may have been blind, but he had no trouble getting around.

Figuring he would be safe in there with her, she shut the bathroom door, locking him in. She undressed, turned on the water and stepped into the shower, leaving the door open an inch, so she could hear him if he got into trouble again. Though she wasn't sure what kind of trouble he could get into. There was really nothing for him to climb. The room was all tile and porcelain, which he couldn't get his claws into.

She was lathering her hair when she saw the shower door move, and looked down to see the kitten poking his head in. "You don't want to come in here," she said, but that was exactly what he wanted. He took a tentative step inside, and when the outer edge of the spray hit his fur, he stopped, looking confused. She thought for sure that he would turn tail and run; instead, he walked right under the spray, rubbing against her ankle with his soaked white fur, crossed to the opposite side, then sat down and started to clean himself.

What the heck? A cat who liked water?

She picked him up and set him on the bath mat, but before she could get the door closed, he was back in the shower. After one more failed attempt she managed to get him out of the shower and the door closed.

She finished, toweled them both off—which he didn't seem to appreciate much—then blow-dried her hair and got dressed. By the time she was finished, the cat had pulled another vanishing act. It took another few minutes of searching and this time she found him playing inside a canvas bag on her closet floor.

She carried him down to the kitchen where Elizabeth was sitting having her morning coffee and reading the newspaper. "Oh, there's the little guy!" she said, and Julie set the still-damp ball of fur in her lap.

"What happened to him?" Elizabeth asked, frowning up at Julie. "He's all wet."

"He took a shower with me."

Elizabeth's brows rose in disbelief. "Cat's don't like water."

"Someone forgot to tell him that."

Looking perplexed, she said, "That's odd."

Julie shrugged. "Maybe it has something to do with him being blind. Or maybe he's just weird."

"How was his first night home?"

Julie grappled for the right word. "It was…eventful."

She told Elizabeth about Luc's shirts, the curtain incident and finding him in her closet.

"He was probably bored," Elizabeth said. "Kittens need lots of stimulation."

"I'm going this morning to buy him some toys."

Looking excited, Elizabeth asked, "Would you like me to watch him for you while you're gone?"

"You don't mind?"

"Of course not. Take all the time you need."

"I do have several errands I'd like to run." He looked pretty harmless sitting there in Elizabeth's lap licking the water from his fur, but Julie knew what a little terror he could be. "But are you sure? He's a handful."

"I've had lots of cats. I'm sure I can handle it."

Julie hoped so. Shy of locking him in her room alone for the day, which seemed cruel, she really had no other choice. At least until he was bigger.

"Can we talk for a minute?" she asked Elizabeth, taking a seat at the kitchen table.

"Of course, honey. You can talk to me about anything, you know that."

She did, but this was different. "I need a favor. And it's a big one."

"As long as it doesn't involve me getting up and dancing," she joked. "Name it."

"Luc mentioned that you'll be at the hospital Monday for an iron infusion."

"That's right."

"Would you come to Amelia's son's room while you're there. Just for a few minutes."

She sighed. "Julie, I know you and she have become friends, and against my better judgment I've kept my opinions to myself, but—"

"I know you two didn't get along, and I know how Luc feels about her, but she really has changed. She knows she treated you badly and she'd only like the chance to apologize. She's been carrying around a lot of guilt—"

"Which was her own doing," Elizabeth said sharply.

"She doesn't deny that."

"Luc may be a grown man, but he'll always be my baby, and she hurt him deeply."

"She wants to make amends."

"Did she ask you to ask me?"

"No. But she's my friend and I want to help her. She asked Luc if she could visit you but he wouldn't allow it."

Up went Elizabeth's hackles, and in a cutting tone she said, "Who I do and don't see is not his choice."

Julie knew Elizabeth would feel that way, which is

why she'd brought it up. If she was going to persuade Luc to talk to Amelia, she would need Elizabeth on her team. Was it a little underhanded and sneaky? Maybe so, but Julie believed deep in her heart that Luc needed to settle things with Amelia, and this was the only way she could see to make that happen.

"If I didn't know better, I might think that you were trying to push the two of them together," Elizabeth said.

"If they're meant to be together, nothing I do or don't do will change that."

"That's very convenient for you."

Julie blinked. "What is that supposed to mean?"

"It's the perfect excuse to keep him at arm's length."

"It's not that," Julie said, though Elizabeth's words hit a little too close to home. "Whether he falls in love with Amelia, or some other woman, I just want him to be happy."

"Have you considered the possibility that Luc might be in love with *you*?"

She considered and dismissed it. But not to protect herself as Elizabeth implied. Julie was a realist. She knew that sex did not always equal love. Not the forever kind.

"I really feel that he needs this to move forward," Julie told the older woman. "With me or anyone else."

Elizabeth sighed. "I suppose you're right."

"So…you'll talk to her?" Julie said.

"I'll think about it," Elizabeth said. "But no promises."

That was all Julie could ask. "Thank you."

"I wouldn't do this for just anybody."

"I know."

"Even though you and Luc are married in name only, I think of you as my daughter."

"And I consider you one of my closest friends."

Elizabeth smiled.

"Well, I should get going. I'd like to stop by the hospital and check on Amelia. Her son's surgery is Tuesday and she's getting nervous."

"You really do like her," Elizabeth said, looking perplexed. "And you trust her?"

"I do. She just wants to make amends."

The older woman nodded slowly and said, "I'll keep that in mind."

Fourteen

Having never had an animal before, there had never been a need to patronize a pet supply store. The sheer volume of available products was mind-boggling. Julie stood in the cat food aisle for a good forty-five minutes reading labels and looking up online reviews on her phone. The litter aisle was a nightmare as well, and the toy aisle even worse. There were a bazillion choices of every shape and size. How was she supposed to know what a blind kitten would like to play with? Even something as simple as picking out a collar took forever.

She made her selections to the best of her ability, nearly having a stroke when the cashier rang it all up and gave her the total. No wonder the shelter was always desperate for donations. Everything was so expensive.

With the kitten taken care of, Julie drove to the hospital. She had a few spare minutes, so when she got there, she made a quick detour to Tommy's room. Amelia sat in a chair next to her son's bed reading to him. She smiled brightly when she saw Julie, but the dark smudges under her eyes said it had probably been a long night.

She patted her son's arm. "Wake up baby, look who's come to visit."

With effort, Tommy opened his eyes, flashed her a sleepy smile and said, "Hi, Julie," so softly she had to strain to hear him.

"How are you feeling today," she asked him, but he had already fallen back to sleep.

"They had to up his pain meds again," Amelia said, concern darkening her features as she gazed down at her son. "Thank God the surgery is Tuesday. I never thought I would hear myself say this, but I'm actually a little homesick."

"Understandable considering the way people have been treating you."

"It's lonely. Tommy sleeps most of the time, and no one else around here talks to me unless they have to."

Not only did she look exhausted, but she'd lost weight, meaning she probably wasn't eating properly. The last time they had lunch she'd only picked at her food. "Have you been sleeping?"

"As much as I can. The nurses come in at all hours of the night to check on Tommy and I'm a light sleeper, so they inevitably wake me up. I'm only able to catch an hour or two here and there. I could swear that sometimes they do it just to mess with me."

"You need some uninterrupted sleep," Julie told her. "In a *real* bed."

"I can't leave the hospital. I don't want Tommy to wake up alone."

"You're no good to Tommy if you don't take care of yourself."

Her expression said that she knew Julie was right.

"Are you working today?" Amelia asked her.

"Nope, I'm meeting Luc for lunch."

"Speak of the devil," Amelia said, looking past her to the door. Julie turned to find Luc entering the room.

"Am I late?" she asked with a smile, but he didn't smile back. Now what?

"I have the results of the blood test from this morning," he told Amelia in his "doctor" tone, and the grim look he wore made Julie's heart drop.

Amelia must have sensed that something was amiss, that it wasn't just Luc being his usual bitter self, because her face paled a shade and she asked, "Is something wrong?"

"Tommy's white count is up," he said.

"What does that mean?"

"It could mean that he has an infection somewhere."

"Which means what exactly?" Amelia asked him, and Julie could see that she was struggling to hold it together, to be strong for her son.

There was genuine compassion in Luc's tone when he said, "If it remains elevated we may have to postpone the surgery."

The devastation on Amelia's face made Julie's heart hurt for her. "How long?" she asked.

"It's hard to say until we know what we're dealing with. Days, a week. Maybe longer."

Amelia looked so pale and distraught Julie worried she might lose consciousness. Julie wasn't a hugger by nature, but she felt compelled to do something to ease her pain, and Amelia readily accepted her embrace.

"I'm so sorry," Julie said. "I know this is frustrating, but I'm sure he'll be better in no time."

Amelia clung to her for several seconds, then let go and blinked away the tears that hovered just inside her eyelids. She took a deep breath, pulled herself up by her bootstraps, lifted her chin and asked Luc, "What's our next move?"

"I'm going to start him on a round of broad spectrum antibiotics, and do more tests. See if we can pinpoint the problem."

"You think that will take care of it?"

He hesitated, then said, "I'm cautiously optimistic. But if you would like to get a second opinion—"

"No," she said firmly, shaking her head. "If I didn't trust your judgment we wouldn't be here. Do what you think is best."

A look passed between Luc and Amelia, and they both smiled. Was he finally coming around?

Julie felt as if a weight had lifted from her shoulders. For a few seconds anyway, before she felt a sudden and intense twinge of something unpleasant.

It was envy, she realized. She *wanted* the two of them to bury the hatchet, so why would she feel jealous?

Jules, you're being ridiculous.

She shoved the feeling deep down where it belonged.

"I'll stop by later this afternoon to check on Tommy," Luc told Amelia, and she flashed him a grateful, if not exhausted smile.

Amelia needed sleep. Badly.

"Can I see you alone for a minute?" Julie asked Luc, nodding toward the door, and he followed her into the hall. "Let's go down by the nurses' station."

When they were far enough away that Amelia wouldn't hear them, Julie turned to him. "In light of what just happened in there, I have a favor to ask."

He looked confused. "Something happened?"

"You and Amelia had a moment."

"We did? When?"

"Just a minute ago. You smiled at each other."

"I smile at a lot of people."

Now he was just being difficult. "There was a connection. Don't deny it."

He shrugged and said, "If you say so."

Did he seriously not see it?

"You mentioned a favor," he said, wiggling his brows at her. "Your office or mine?"

She couldn't help but laugh. "Not that kind of favor. I was hoping you could maybe say something to the nurses about the way they've been treating Amelia. I would, but I feel as if it's not my place to tell them how to do their jobs. But if you say something—"

"I'll talk to everyone," he said.

One less thing to worry about. "Thank you."

"We should get down to the cafeteria," Luc said.

"About lunch…" She looked from her watch to Tommy's room.

"Go," he said with a grin. "Amelia needs you. We'll have lunch another day."

"You're sure? Thanks for understanding."

He reached up and touched her cheek. "I hope Amelia realizes how lucky she is to have you as a friend."

Julie knew that she did. "How late are you working?"

Luc looked at his watch. "I should be home for dinner."

She pushed up on her toes to kiss him goodbye, aiming for his cheek, but Luc had other ideas. He cupped the back of her head and pulled her close, slanting his mouth over hers, and then kissed her in clear view of everyone at the nurses' station. And not a hospital hallway sort of kiss. This was a bona fide, just-wait-until-I get-you-home kiss.

Public displays of affection usually made her uncomfortable, but she could feel herself melting against him as he drew her closer. Until someone at the nurses' station wolf-whistled.

She pulled away and grinned up at him, her cheeks warm and her blood pumping. "That was nice. A little inappropriate considering where we are, but still nice."

"You're my wife. I can kiss you however and wherever I want."

"Is that how it works?"

"Damn straight." His eyes locked on hers, and the look he gave her was so supercharged with desire her heart skipped a beat. He was playing a role, that's all. They both were. But something in his eyes said he may have forgotten that.

"But I'm not really your wife," she reminded him.

He took her hand, grazing his thumb over her wedding band. "As long as this ring is on your finger, you're my wife. In every sense of the word."

He looked so serious, as if he really meant it, which was as confusing as it was terrifying. And yes, maybe a little exciting, too. Not to mention totally unrealistic. "Aren't we a little far into the game to be changing the rules."

"Maybe I don't like the rules anymore."

Her heart jerked violently, and then raced ahead double time. What the heck was he trying to say? Did this have something to do with her decision to sleep in his bed last night? Was she unknowingly leading him on? That had certainly never been her intention.

She took a step back and he let go of her hand. "I'd better go."

"Eventually we'll have to talk about this."

No they wouldn't, because they had already talked about it. It was a done deal. His friendship meant too much to her to risk losing over a misguided sexual relationship. Even if it was really fantastic sex. "I'll see you later."

Looking resigned, he said, "See you later."

She could feel his eyes boring into her back as she walked to Amelia's room, but she was too chicken to turn around and face him. She was terrified of what she might see. Maybe it would be wise to put a little distance between them. Perhaps Luc was becoming a little too comfortable with the physical aspect of their relationship.

Amelia stood next to her son's window, gazing blindly out the window, looking distraught.

"Everything will be okay," Julie said.

Amelia turned to her. "Deep down, I know that."

Amelia would feel so much better if she could get some uninterrupted sleep, and was able to take a long hot shower. Or better yet, soak in a hot bath with essence of lavender and lots of bubbles. Which Julie just so happened to have at her condo…

Before she could talk herself out of it, Julie pulled her key ring out and unhooked the key for her condo. She crossed the room and handed it to a confused Amelia.

"What is this for?" she asked Julie.

"My condo. I want you to use it as a home base while you're here in Royal."

She looked warily at her sleeping son. "You know

how I feel about leaving the hospital. What if Tommy wakes up…"

"He'll be fine. The nurses will take good care of him."

Amelia looked from her son to Julie, and back again. "I don't know…"

"Have you seen yourself in a mirror lately? You look terrible."

Amelia sighed, her shoulders sagging. "And I feel terrible. But he needs me here."

"Does he need you, or is it that *you* need *him*?"

Amelia frowned.

"Do you think Tommy doesn't notice how you look? He needs you to be strong for him. You can't do that if you're about to collapse."

Julie's words clearly hit home. "I guess I could sneak out for a little while."

Feeling relieved, Julie jotted down the address for Amelia, who typed it into the GPS on her smart phone.

"You know, you're going to be a great mom someday," Amelia told her.

It was meant as a compliment, but it made Julie's heart hurt. She wouldn't be a good mother, because she would never have children. If she couldn't set aside her fears and let her guard down for Luc, her best friend, there was little hope left of her ever finding Mr. Right.

Fifteen

Late that afternoon, when Luc pulled into the garage, Julie's car was gone. He felt both disappointed and relieved at the same time. They needed to talk, to figure this marriage out. Despite his best efforts to adhere to their "plan," to think with his head, his heart seemed to be calling the shots now. He wanted Julie, in every way a man could want a woman. But her unwillingness to even consider discussing it didn't bode well for him. And she was so insistent that he and Amelia settle their past, he couldn't help but feel that she was hoping that he and Amelia would fall back in love. That would certainly save Julie the task of confronting her feelings. The difficult ones, that she kept buried deep. Her heart was like a fortress, and he wasn't quite sure how he would tear the walls down.

Or if that was even possible.

Luc let himself into the house, and found his mother in the family room, by the window overlooking the garden, reading a book. On her lap, curled in a ball, slept the kitten.

"Babysitting?" he asked her with a grin. He'd suspected she would enjoy the kitten as much as Julie did.

"Houdini," his mother said, and in answer to his confused look, added, "That's the kitten's name."

"Why Houdini?"

"He's an escape artist, and once he gets away, finding him is almost impossible."

"He's white, how could you miss him?"

"You'll see. And when you're searching for him, do yourself a favor and look up. That's where he prefers to be."

"Up where?"

"Anywhere he can reach. If he can get his nails into it, he starts climbing and doesn't stop until he reaches the top."

"Like what?"

"A bed, curtains, a pant leg. A *bare* leg—and you can bet that my nurse wasn't happy about that. It doesn't matter as long as it takes him vertical."

Luc frowned. "He's blind. That could be very dangerous."

"I tried to explain that to him, but you know cats," she said with an exaggerated shrug, "they never listen to reason."

He shot her a look.

She smiled. "On the bright side he has a very hard head."

"And how do you know that?"

"Every now and then he gets overexcited, takes off running and slams headfirst into something. Usually a wall or a piece of furniture. I won't lie, it's hard not to laugh, but he just shakes it off and keeps going. Then, bam, he hits something else. He'll do that three or four times in one spot, until he learns the landscape. I think he's mapping out the house."

"With his head?"

His mother shrugged. "Whatever works, I guess."

Luc wondered if cats were capable of using that sort of logic. "I don't suppose you know where Julie is."

"She's sitting with Tommy while Amelia naps, so he won't wake up alone."

"Where is Amelia?"

"At Julie's condo. She insisted that Amelia go there and take a nap."

Julie's condo? Hadn't she given it up when she moved in with him? She'd never actually said she would, but he'd just assumed...

He sighed and shook his head. Wrong again.

"Dinner will be ready at seven," his mother told him, in a tone that said being late was unacceptable.

Which gave him just enough time for a couple of beers at the Texas Cattleman's Club.

He turned to leave, but she stopped him. "There's something I wanted to ask you."

"About what?"

"I'm having my blood transfusion tomorrow and Julie asked me to stop in and see Amelia while I'm there. She said Amelia wants to apologize to me."

"Will you let her?"

"That's what I'm not sure about. I feel as if forgiving her would mean being disloyal to you."

A week ago, he may have thought so, too. But this wasn't about him anymore. He was finally at peace with their past. Didn't Amelia deserve the same?

"You should talk to her," he said. "I didn't want to believe it either, but she really has changed."

His mother gasped softly. "Don't tell me you still have feelings for her."

The idea made him chuckle, because other than sympathy for her and her son, he didn't feel much of anything for her. "Not at all. And I wouldn't consider your speaking to her as disloyal. In fact, I think it would be good for both of you."

"She broke your heart."

"Only because I let her." And now it looked as if he might be in a similar situation with Julie. Would he chase her down, only to have her break his heart? He'd been patient these past weeks, but his patience was wearing very thin. Either she loved him or she didn't. He needed to know if they had a future together.

When he got to the club he took a seat at the bar, ordered a beer and settled in to watch the basketball game playing on the television. He'd had three beers when his phone rang. It was Julie. But he had no idea what to say to her.

He ignored the call, turned the ringer off on his phone and ordered a scotch

The bartender, who knew he normally didn't have more than a beer or two, regarded him with growing concern. "Everything okay?" he asked.

"I should think that's pretty obvious," Luc said, swirling the scotch in his glass. Then he drained it in one swallow, set the glass down a little too forcefully and tapped the bar for another.

"Not until you hand them over," the bartender said, holding out his hand.

Without argument Luc dug his keys out of his pocket and dropped them in his hand. He was no stranger to the end result of drinking and driving. He'd seen it far too many times to make the same mistake himself. If he had to he would walk home.

Everything was getting a bit fuzzy, so Luc wasn't sure how long he'd been sitting there or how many drinks he'd consumed when Drew sat down at the bar beside him.

"Hey," Drew said, gesturing to the bartender for a beer.

"Hey," Luc replied.

Drew took a long pull on his beer when it arrived, then set it down on the bar and asked Luc, "You want to talk about it?"

"About what?"

"Whichever sorrows you're drowning with that scotch."

Trying to drown, and failing miserably. In fact, Luc felt even worse than he had when he walked in the door.

"You gonna make me guess?" Drew asked.

"I'm in love with Julie." He'd never said that out loud before, and hearing those words come out of his own mouth was a little surreal. So he said it again. "I am in love with Julie."

"Are you trying to convince me or yourself?"

He laughed bitterly. "Drew, I would give anything to go back to way things were before, when I didn't know what I was missing. When being her best friend was enough. But being with her has changed me, and now I can't change back."

"What makes you think you have to?"

"She doesn't love me."

"I don't believe that for a second."

"Okay, she isn't *in love* with me."

"Have you told her that you're in love with her?"

"She won't give me the chance. I tried to talk to her about it today and she refused to listen. She wants things to stay just the way they are now. I'm worried that if I push her too hard, it will only drive her away." He used to believe that he could think his way out of any situation but this one had him stumped.

"So what are you going to do?"

"If I knew that, I wouldn't be sitting here. Maybe I shouldn't do anything yet. Maybe I should give her more time. Just keep doing what we've been doing. Everything was perfect until I brought it up today."

"It seems to me that if things were perfect, you wouldn't have had to bring it up."

He'd be damned if Drew wasn't spot on. As close as Luc and Julie were, emotionally and physically, he wanted more. Being Julie's friend just wasn't enough now. But was he willing to risk their friendship?

Maybe he didn't have a choice.

Looking thoughtful, Drew said, "Maybe what you need to do is shake her tree a little, see what falls out."

"I'm not sure what you mean."

"Nudge her out of her comfort zone. See what she does."

"And how would I do that?"

He shrugged. "She's your wife. You know her better than anyone. You'll think of something."

Luc thought he knew her. Now he wasn't so sure. Maybe all this time he'd only been letting her see what she wanted him to see.

Maybe deep down he didn't know her at all.

Sixteen

Sunday was supposed to be Julie and Luc's special day, but he spent the majority of it in bed nursing a hangover. They had planned to have breakfast at the diner, then check out the recently reopened organic produce store to buy fresh flowers. After their food settled they would take a long walk in the park. Then maybe they would head back home for some afternoon "exercise." Later he would take her to dinner, then it was back home to make love again.

Instead Luc spent Sunday in bed nursing a hangover. It didn't take a genius to know why Luc had gone out and gotten hammered.

She knew that sleeping in his bed had been a bad idea. She should have listened to her instincts. She'd given him the wrong impression, led him on. She'd made him fool himself into believing that he was in love with her. But men confused sex with love all of the time, right? Or was it the other way around?

Either way, she would be sleeping in her own bed from now on.

She and Luc barely said two words to each other all day. She slept in her own bed that night, though she didn't do all that much sleeping. Luc didn't even try to talk her into staying with him, and when she kissed him good-night his lips felt so cold. So passionless. She knew that in a day or two he would realize what a huge mistake he'd almost made thinking they should take their relationship to the next level. He would realize that they were better off as just friends, then everything would go back to normal. Everything would be okay.

The kind of baggage Julie carried around wasn't so easily shed. And the idea of opening those bags and rooting through the traumatic events of her childhood made her feel sick to her stomach.

Monday dragged by, and every time Julie tried to see or call Luc he was too busy to be disturbed. He was still upset. She got that, but he was going to have to let it go at some point, so they could get back to being best friends. One day of the silent treatment had taken its toll. She missed him. She just wanted things to go back to the way they used to be. Friends with benefits. Hell, if it meant restoring their friendship to its previous, uncomplicated manifestation, she would even be willing to end their physical relationship. Though that would seriously suck.

Tonight, she decided. After dinner she would take him aside and offer to have that talk he wanted. Now that he'd had a few days to think it over, she was positive he would agree that it was best for both of them if they just kept going the way they had been.

The only bright spot of the day was when she stopped in Tommy's room to find Amelia next to her sleeping son's bed, tears in her eyes.

Julie's heart sank. Was his infection worse? Would they be postponing the surgery? "What happened?"

Amelia turned to her and smiled. "His white count is back to normal. They're going ahead with the surgery tomorrow morning at seven a.m.!"

Julie was thrilled for Amelia and Tommy, but her happiness deflated like a balloon when she realized what that meant for her and Luc. With such a delicate surgery on his schedule, the last thing Luc needed was to be distracted by their marital issues. That conversation they were supposed to have would have to wait.

The day of Tommy's surgery, Julie left Houdini in Elizabeth's capable hands and drove to the hospital early, intending to spend her morning waiting with Amelia in her son's room.

She'd heard Luc getting ready for work, but stayed in her room until after he left. She didn't want to risk a confrontation on this very important morning. Besides, after having two whole days to think about it, he would come around. She knew he would. He just needed time to realize the mistake he'd made letting his heart overrule his head. Then they could go back to being best friends.

Julie stopped in the cafeteria for coffee and doughnuts on the way up, and by the time she got to Tommy's room they had already wheeled him out for surgery. Amelia was sitting cross-legged on her air mattress, looking surprisingly well-rested and calm.

Julie handed her one of the coffees and offered her a doughnut. "I figured you could use this. One cream, two sugars, right?"

"You're a goddess," Amelia said, taking them from her. "How are things going?"

Julie sat in the visitors chair by the window. "Good."

"Luc came in to see me a little while ago," Amelia told her, and at the mere mention of his name Julie's heart dropped. It had been doing that a lot—pretty much every time she thought of him or heard someone say his name. "He explained what will happen during the surgery, and what to expect when Tommy is out of recovery," Amelia was saying, and Julie struggled to stay focused, but all she could think about was her looming conversation with Luc. "I'm still nervous of course, but I know that Tommy is in good hands. I'm more concerned about the pain he'll be in afterward, and the physical therapy he'll go through."

Speaking of being nervous...

She and Luc had barely talked since Saturday. What if he'd had enough? Would he back out on their deal and ask her for a divorce?

Of course he wouldn't. But it didn't hurt to prepare herself for the worst. Everyone should have a backup plan.

How could things go from blissful perfection to so unbearably confusing so damned fast?

Julie left briefly to get them lunch from the cafeteria, and when she came back, Amelia was beaming.

"You just missed Luc."

Down her heart went into her stomach again.

"How did it go?" she asked, even though Amelia's relief was explanation enough.

"The surgery was a success and Tommy is in Recovery and doing great."

"That's wonderful news," she said, hugging Amelia. With the surgery over and declared a success, it was time to talk to Luc.

After Tommy had been returned to his room and

settled in, Julie went by Luc's office, almost hoping he wouldn't be there. But he was. He sat at his desk, chair turned toward the window, his back to her, hands folded in his lap.

It took all of her courage to step inside and close the door, and if Luc was aware of her presence, he didn't let on.

"Hey," she said, so nervous that her hands were trembling.

"Hey," he replied, not turning around. Not even moving.

"Can we talk?"

He swiveled around to face her. He wasn't smiling. He wasn't frowning, either. His features looked frozen in a nonexpression, his eyes blank. "About what?"

"This thing happening between us."

"You mean love?"

She cringed.

He shook his head, looking so disappointed. "You can't even stand to hear me say it, can you?"

"It's not that. I just..."

"Don't bother trying to explain. I know you well enough to recognize when you're running away."

She could understand why it might look that way. But she didn't want to *go* anywhere. "I'm not, I swear."

"You just don't trust me."

Why would he think that? After all they had been through. "That's not true."

"Isn't it? Then tell me why you kept your condo?"

She bit her lip, unsure of how to answer, to make him understand.

"Speechless?" he asked. "Always have a backup

plan. Isn't that what you've always told me? I just never imagined you would need a backup plan from me."

To deny it would be a lie. And it sounded horrible when he said it like that.

He leaned forward in his chair. "I know you better than you know yourself, Julie, and maybe that's the problem. I got too close and now you're running scared. You don't trust me."

"I do, it's just… Can't we just go back to the way things were before? When we were best friends?"

He sighed and sagged back into his chair. "We can't unring the bell. And I can't go on pretending that everything is okay. Because it's not."

She felt utterly sick inside. "I don't want to lose you. You mean more to me than anything."

"Just not enough to love me."

He was breaking her heart. "Luc—"

He held his hand up to stop her. "Sorry, that was a low blow. It was uncalled for. Like you said so many times before, you feel what you feel. Or don't feel. And the fact of the matter is that I love you and you don't feel the same about me."

"If we could just talk about this—"

"There's nothing to say. My mind is made up."

Her heart dropped so violently she could barely breathe. It wasn't supposed to be like this. He was supposed to agree with her. He'd always been on her side, but now, when she needed him most, he was just going to do what? Divorce her?

"W-what are you saying?" she asked, her voice so wobbly her words were barely understandable.

"We can't be together anymore," he told her. "Not like before."

"Are you saying you want a divorce?"

"I made you a promise, one I intend to keep. We can go on living like a married couple, but it would be best if we saw each other as little as possible. That will be much easier if you take the spare room downstairs."

She could hardly believe this was happening. He was ending their relationship, just like that? "So that's it? We're not even friends anymore?"

"That's it," he said, that damned blank look on his face. He could have the decency to show a little emotion, to feel angry or hurt. *Something*.

"What about work? Are you firing me?"

"No, but I think that after you establish your citizenship, you should consider looking for another position. It would be easier on everyone."

Then what reason did she even have to stay in Royal? She'd had such grand plans for making Royal her home, and suddenly now they were unraveling around her. Maybe she would be better off in South Africa after all. Maybe it would give her the chance to make a new start.

Julie was a nervous wreck for the next few days, praying she didn't run into Luc, then feeling so cold and empty inside when she didn't. Luc was really good at making himself scarce.

How was it that just a week ago everything was fine. She was happy, he was happy. Why did he have to go and ruin everything?

That wasn't fair and she knew it. This wasn't his fault. It was all her. But she missed him, in a way she had never missed anyone. She woke up lonely and went to bed feeling sick. When she was able to sleep, which wasn't often, he tormented her in her dreams.

He preoccupied her mind until she could barely think of anything else.

What the hell was wrong with her? Why was she such a mess?

She tried her best to keep her feelings to herself, to put on a good face, but she must not have been very convincing because Amelia confronted her Sunday afternoon at the hospital.

Tommy was working with his physical therapist and making impressive progress, so Julie and Amelia went down to the cafeteria for lunch.

"I am not going to miss this hospital food," Amelia said, glaring with contempt at her overcooked burger and soggy fries. Julie pushed her tuna salad around the plate but couldn't make herself take a bite.

"You've been unusually somber this last week," Amelia said.

So much for putting on a good face. She felt like an empty shell, as if losing Luc had sucked everything she loved about life right from her. The days seemed to have no point. Food lost its flavor and not even sleep was an escape from the harsh reality of how horribly she had screwed things up. Why hadn't she just told Luc that she loved him?

Because it would have been a lie, and no matter how much she missed him, he deserved someone who could love him with her whole heart. Someone who trusted him the way she never could.

"I thought I would give you time to work it through before offering an ear," Amelia said, "but we have to leave tomorrow. Could you at least assure me that you're okay?"

Julie put her fork down, feeling hollowed out and cold. A nonperson. "To be honest, I'm not sure if I am."

Amelia's brow knit with concern. "Do you want to talk about it?"

She hadn't intended to tell Amelia about her pretend marriage, but there was no way to explain the situation without telling her the whole truth. Besides, *not* telling her seemed dishonest somehow. "If I tell you a secret, do you promise not to say anything to anyone. And I mean no one."

"Of course."

She took a deep breath and said quietly, so no one else would hear, "Luc and I aren't really a couple. We only got married to keep me from getting deported."

Amelia sat back, looking stunned. "I have a hard time believing that."

"It's the truth."

"You two are Royal's 'it' couple. Everyone talks about you. You're the blueprint for the ideal marriage. The fairy tale come true."

She'd had no idea people viewed her and Luc's marriage that way. It looked as though they had successfully pulled the wool over everyone's eyes. Which only made her feel more depressed and vacant.

"So, if you're just friends, your relationship isn't physical?"

"Well, it was. But not anymore."

"Something happened?"

Unable to even look at her food, Julie pushed her tray away. "He told me that he's in love with me."

Amelia looked confused. "And that's a bad thing?"

"It's not part of the plan."

"The plan? Wow, sounds serious."

"We weren't supposed to fall in love, but he broke the rules and now our friendship is over."

Amelia sat a little straighter. "So, what are you saying—he's available?"

That was a strange question. "I suppose so."

"And you aren't in love with him."

She didn't like the direction this conversation was taking. "I tried. I just can't feel something that I don't."

"You're sure."

Julie blinked. "Of course I'm sure. If I were in love with someone, don't you think I would know it?"

Amelia was quiet for several seconds, mulling something over, her expression serious. "If I tell *you* a secret, do you promise not to tell anyone?"

"Of course."

She looked around and lowered her voice. "This is a little embarrassing, but when I made the decision to come here, I sort of had it in my mind that if Luc was still single, and there was still a spark…"

Julie's heart skipped a beat, then picked up triple time.

"When I thought he was a married man I backed off. But if your marriage is a fake, maybe I should re-think things."

"Maybe you should," Julie agreed.

"That wouldn't bother you? Not even a little? Because now that I know you're not really married, what reason would I have not to go after him myself? It wouldn't technically be cheating."

"No, but—"

"Hell, for all you know, he and I are already fooling around."

She could see what Amelia was doing, and it wasn't going to work. "But you're not."

"How do you know that when he's 'working late' he's not actually with me? I'm at the hospital 24/7 It would be really easy for us to fool around behind your back. Maybe use your condo for a quickie."

"But you wouldn't do that to a friend," Julie said.

"Are you sure? How well do you really know me? Maybe people hate me so much because they've seen Luc and I together. They know we're messing around."

Julie knew Amelia was only trying to make a point, but she felt unsettled nonetheless. "I'm sure someone would have mentioned it."

"You would think so, but all my friends—or should I say ex-friends—knew what Tom was doing and no one said a word to me about it. I didn't find out until after the divorce that he'd had sex with my maid of honor in the men's room at our wedding reception."

Julie gasped. "Did he really?"

"And what about the nurse I saw Luc take into his office the other day after his secretary left? What reason do you think he had to close and lock the door? Maybe you aren't the only friend he's sleeping with."

Julie felt a twinge of something unpleasant. "We are talking hypothetically."

"Are we? If I did see Luc with another woman would you want to know the truth? Would it even matter? If you're not really married—"

"Yes!" Julie said, much louder than she'd intended, causing the people around them to turn and look. She lowered her voice to a whisper. "Yes, I would want to know. And yes, it would matter."

"Why?"

She felt her coffee rising back up her throat.

"You're looking a little pale," Amelia said. "Something eating at you?"

"Is he really seeing someone else?"

"Why does it matter?"

She didn't know why. "It just does."

"Perhaps you're feeling a little jealous?" Amelia said.

Julie's first reaction was to deny it, but whoever the woman was, if there really was another woman, Julie wanted to claw her eyes out.

Oh God, she was jealous. And not just a little. The thought of Luc being intimate with someone besides her made her feel like barfing. "That doesn't mean I'm in love with him."

"Since you became friends, how many serious relationships have either of you been in?" Amelia asked her.

Julie frowned. "Well, I haven't been in any, and if Luc was seeing anyone seriously he never told me. But we're both very focused on our careers. We don't have time for serious relationships."

"Yet you manage to find time for each other."

She was right. Luc had always made time for her and she him. With the exception of the past few days, they'd barely gone twenty-four hours without talking to each other in six years. The day wouldn't feel complete if she didn't hear his voice at least once. And lately, with all the fantastic sex they'd been having...

She thought of him touching another woman the way he touched her, or even just holding another woman's hand, and felt sick inside. Before now she just hadn't let herself think about it. Now she could think of nothing else.

"Oh my God," she said, barely able to catch her breath as reality cracked her hard in the chops. "Oh my God."

She must have started turning blue, because Amelia gave her shoulder a nudge and said, "Breathe, Julie."

She sucked in a deep breath. "Oh my God. I'm in love with Luc."

Amelia was smiling. "Funny how it sneaks up on you."

How had this happened? *When* had it happened? Was she just so used to suppressing her feelings and guarding her heart that she hadn't *allowed* herself to see it?

Now that she had, it was almost overwhelming. She felt happy and excited and scared to death. But in a good way.

"I'm in love with Luc," she said again, the words rolling so naturally off her tongue it was as if they had been there all along, just waiting to be set free. "I. Am in love. With Luc."

In the midst of all those feelings she had another thought, one that sent the air hissing from her balloon of happiness.

"I know what you're thinking," Amelia said, her words startling Julie.

"What am I thinking?"

"You're afraid that it's too late, that you blew it. You're terrified that he's going to reject you."

She'd deny it if she could, but that would be a lie. And hadn't she been lying to herself for long enough? Wasn't it about time that she be honest not just to Luc, but to herself? She'd taken a lot of chances in her life, lived on the edge, but why was she so afraid to take a chance on Luc? And at this point, what did she have to lose?

"I think I need to talk to him," she told Amelia.

"I think you do, too."

Her hands began to shake and her heart went berserk in her chest. "What if it's too late?"

"Then, you can at least say that you tried."

Luc had the courage to put himself out there. To take a chance on her. And for his trouble, all he'd gotten was shot down. Now she needed to do the same for him.

"I have to go," she said. "I have to talk to him."

"Yes you do."

"What time are you leaving tomorrow?"

"As soon as Tommy is discharged. Probably around noon."

"I'll be back to say goodbye." They both stood and Julie hugged her hard. "Thank you so much."

"For what?"

"Making me see what an idiot I am."

"Well, we all act like idiots at one point or another."

If that was the case, Julie was queen of the idiots. She gave Amelia another squeeze, then set off to find Luc, hoping she wasn't too late.

"Are you going to mope around all day?"

Luc looked up from his computer screen, which he hadn't bothered to turn on yet, to find his mother in the doorway of his home office. "I'm not moping. I'm reflecting."

"She'll come around."

He hadn't said a word to his mother about the Julie situation, so either Julie had told her or she'd figured it out on her own.

He'd honestly believed that giving Julie an ultimatum, threatening their friendship, would make her see reason. Five days later he was still waiting.

Talk about a major fail.

Now he'd painted himself into a corner and he wasn't sure how to get back out. If this time apart had proved anything, it was how much he needed her in his life. Even if all she could be to him was a friend. He'd screwed up big-time and now he had to figure out a way to make it right. If that was even a viable option at this point. He had failed Julie in the worst possible way. She needed to know that he was there for her no matter what; instead he'd given up on her. He couldn't imagine a worse betrayal.

"I don't suppose you've seen Houdini."

Luc gestured behind him, to the window valance, where the kitten sat a good eight feet off the ground, happy as could be. Despite being blind, or maybe because of it, he was fearless. In the past few days he'd taken full run of the house, where there were virtually millions of places to disappear. But on the bright side, he was starting to learn his name, and would sometimes come when called. If all else failed, opening a can of cat food usually did the trick.

"Is there anything I can do?" his mother asked, and Luc shook his head. "I just hate to see you both so unhappy."

He swiveled his chair around and looked out the window. It was nearly April and the spring flowers were in full bloom. Yet he'd never felt more depressed and gloomy. "She made her choice."

She sighed. "You're making this so much more complicated than it has to be."

That was easy for her to say.

"She's right, you know."

At the sound of Julie's voice, he swiveled back around. She stood in the doorway behind his mother.

"Would you look at the time," his mother said, wheeling herself out the door. "I'm late for my physical therapy."

"Can we talk?" Julie asked him. She looked almost as bad as he felt. Her voice quivered and he could see that her hands were trembling. What now? Was she going to ask him for a divorce? Put an end to this charade before they caused any more damage?

"I guess that depends what you have to say."

"You can't even imagine how hard this is for me. Letting my guard down. Admitting how wrong I was. I screwed up. I was too scared to admit how I was really feeling. I couldn't even admit it to myself."

"And how are you *really* feeling?"

"I love you. I'm *in love* with you. This week apart has been awful."

He didn't want to appear too eager. After all, he did still have his pride to consider. But he was having a whole lot of trouble keeping his butt in the chair. He needed her in his arms. Needed to smell her hair and taste her lips. He just plain needed her.

Her voice shook when she said, "I know it's a lot to ask, and I probably don't deserve it, but if you could give me just one more chance."

"You're right, it is a lot to ask," he said. And if he didn't love her so much, he may have told her to take a hike. Luckily for them both, he just couldn't seem to live without her. "How do I know that you won't freak out and change your mind?"

"You don't know. And I have no clue how to convince you, if that's even possible. But I had to try."

He rose from his chair and though Julie looked terrified, she stood her ground. He walked over to her, until they were nearly toe to toe, and said, "We could start with a hug, and go from there."

He could see the instant she finally let go. The defenses dropped and she threw her arms around him, a quivering bundle. "I'm so sorry," she said.

He held her tight. This was right where she belonged. With him, forever. He wouldn't be letting her go again. "I'm the one who's sorry. My pride was bruised. I never should have given up on you."

She sighed, laying her cheek against his shirt. "You had to. It was the kick in the pants that I needed."

He cradled her face in his hands. There were tears in her eyes, but they were happy. "I love you, Julie."

"I love you, too," she said, "So much. I can't believe I almost blew it."

He grinned down at her, so relieved and happy it almost didn't seem real. "You didn't. I wouldn't have given up so easily."

"Amelia told me that everyone considers you and I the blueprint for the perfect marriage. The fairy tale come true."

"I guess they were right," he said.

"But we still have one thing left to do," she told him. "To make it official."

"What's that?"

She smiled and kissed him, with so much love in her eyes it almost hurt. "Live happily ever after."

* * * * *

"You want an heir?"

Jen heard her voice as if coming from someone else.

"Yes. An heir you'll give me."

The room started spinning. "I knew you'd have a price for helping me, but I never thought it would be that."

"What did you think it would be? Yourself?"

Yes, she'd thought he'd want an affair. But she wouldn't have considered that a price. It would have been a reward.

His brooding gaze captured her wandering eyes. "I never bargain for sexual favors."

"No, you'd just have to make your desire known and women would line up to give you your heir."

"I am making my desire known. To the only woman I ever considered for the role."

"Why me?"

He gathered her tighter against his incredible heat and hardness. "Because you're in my arms, within an hour of meeting. The attraction between us combusted the moment I saw you, and it's been raging higher ever since."

She wanted to wind herself around him, to forget everything and act on the need burning them up.

For the first time in her life she didn't have control. And she loved it.

* * *

Pregnant by the Sheikh
is part of The Billionaires of Black Castle series:
Only their dark pasts could lead these men to
the light of true love.

PREGNANT BY
THE SHEIKH

BY
OLIVIA GATES

Published in Great Britain 2015
by Mills & Boon, an imprint of Harlequin (UK) Limited,
Eton House, 18-24 Paradise Road, Richmond, Surrey, TW9 1SR

© 2015 Olivia Gates

ISBN: 978-0-263-25252-1

51-0315

Printed and bound in Spain
by CPI, Barcelona

Olivia Gates has always pursued creative passions such as singing and handicrafts. She still does, but only one of her passions grew gratifying enough, consuming enough, to become an ongoing career—writing.

She is most fulfilled when she is creating worlds and conflicts for her characters, then exploring and untangling them bit by bit, sharing her protagonists' every heart-wrenching heartache and hope, their every heart-pounding doubt and trial, until she leads them to an indisputably earned and gloriously satisfying happy ending.

When she's not writing, she is a doctor, a wife to her own alpha male and a mother to one brilliant girl and one demanding Angora cat. Visit Olivia at www.oliviagates.com.

To Kathryn Falk. Words aren't enough to describe what your unstinting support means to me, and how it has made what I feared might be impossible come true.

One

Jenan Aal Ghamdi watched the man she was getting engaged to flit among throngs of congratulators—and almost barfed. Again.

It never failed. Every time she looked at him, hell, every time she thought of him, nausea overpowered her. It was a testament to her self-control that she hadn't thrown up all over him yet.

The one thing stopping her from giving in to the compulsion was the stronger aversion to rejoining that tragic farce of an engagement celebration. It had taken her over an hour to escape the hordes of prying—and pitying—guests and take refuge at the far end of the massive ballroom. She'd managed to slink away unnoticed only because she'd refused to wear the getup her "fiancé" had sent her. He'd wanted to flaunt his newly massive wealth and drape his "acquisition" in an oppressively ornate costume complete with scaffolding. With the ton of clashing jewelry he'd provided, she would have glittered with the power of ten disco balls. As it was, in her most obscure and suitably mournful matte black evening gown, she now blended into the darkness of the ballroom's periphery. It was a minuscule victory, but with her expectations reduced to nil, anything counted now.

Retreating farther away from everyone's line of sight, she started breathing normally again. And a surreal sense of detachment descended on her yet again. It was as if none of this was really happening to her but to someone else. As if this was some ridiculous dream she was confident would fade into nothingness the moment she woke up.

The artificial serenity lasted only moments before the illusion splintered and reality crashed over her again, with another wave of queasiness.

She was really getting engaged to Hassan Aal Ghaanem!

The man who happened to be the king of Saraya, who held Zafrana, his neighboring desert kingdom and her homeland, hostage.

No, she wasn't getting engaged to the man, she was being bartered to him. Sold. Tonight felt like the beginning of the end of her life as she knew it. The end of her life, period. Whatever came after marrying him wouldn't be considered life. Not in her book.

But though this fate was inescapable, she'd still refused to have this reception in Saraya, or even in Zafrana. It had been another empty triumph when he'd relented and agreed to hold it here, in her New York City stomping grounds.

The city had been her home for the past twelve years. It would stop being so once she started serving her life sentence as Hassan's wife. But she'd refused to go back to that region to be buried there for the rest of her life a second before she absolutely had to. She'd fled, determined to never return, except for fleeting visits, which had been few and very brief.

But she'd been regretting her insistence since the moment she'd seen that man's over-the-top arrangements. If there was anything more abhorrent to her than Hassan himself right now, it was being the center of attention in such an extravagant, overexposed event.

If this party had been held in their homelands, it wouldn't have gotten any coverage, what with the privacy measures imposed by the ruling class. But in the heart of New York City and in such a venue with all those high-profile attendees, this engagement party would be all over the worldwide media. Which taught her not to struggle while sinking in quicksand. Her attempt to assert herself had only made her sink deeper in this mess.

But teaching her a lesson about defying him hadn't been Hassan's objective in arranging this spectacle. The man considered nothing but himself. And as the king of a recently prosperous kingdom—now that King Mohab Aal Ghaanem of Jareer was giving Saraya 30 percent of the new kingdom's massive oil wealth—Hassan Aal Ghaanem had been on a splurging spree after decades of being held back by his kingdom's limited finances.

So here they were, in the Terrace Room at The Plaza, where many a legendary celebrity had held prominent events. After all, Hassan considered himself on par with those people.

Any other time, she would have appreciated the almost five-thousand-square-foot ballroom that had been restored to its early 1900s grandeur. When she'd been here before, the painted ceilings, cathedral-like arches and elaborate pillars leading to its wraparound gallery had transported her to the Renaissance, while the original crystal chandeliers, wall paneling and carpeting had added a golden age refinement to the classical setting. Being here now, for this horrendous occasion, it felt like the setting of her life's worst nightmare. It literally was.

Tearing her gaze away from the five hundred guests that filled the ballroom to capacity, her eyes fell to her bare hands. She'd refused to accept the priceless pieces from Saraya's royal jewelry to be her *shabkah*—what literally meant "binding." She was damned if she'd wear his shackles for all to see...

"Are you sure about this, Jen?"

The soft voice, barely audible above the Sarayan celebratory songs blaring over the sound system, sent a spasm through her chest with its melancholy. Zeena, her baby half sister. If anyone was feeling as bad as she was about this whole thing, it was her.

She turned to her, her lips crooking in an attempt at lightness. "Oh, I am, Zee. I'm sure there's no other way out of the mess Father and Zafrana are in but for me to marry that old goat."

And that mess wasn't a recent development, but one with decades-long roots. It was also one she had an indirect hand in.

It had started when her father, Khalil Aal Ghamdi, had found himself on Zafrana's throne after King Zayd, his second cousin, had died, with him as his closest male relative. Pushed into a position he'd been unsuited for, her father, a dreamer and an artist, had been unable to become a man of state and had been led astray by many an unqualified or malicious counselor.

When she'd returned to Zafrana after graduating from Cornell University with degrees in economics and business administration, she'd seen how her father's imprudent policies had led to the kingdom's steady deterioration. She'd tried to guide him, but his entourage's opposition had been vicious. They'd undone everything she'd accomplished until she'd found herself with only two choices: dedicate her life to fighting that vicious cycle or withdraw from the battle and flee the whole region, where the very way of life was anathema to her. She'd chosen to give up and leave.

As a result of her withdrawal, Zafrana was now cripplingly in debt…to Saraya. And Hassan was now poised to annex the kingdom through a marriage of state. Which, her father had informed her, was the only way to save Zafrana. Knowing the depths of the debt, she believed him.

"But you can't marry him. He's—he's *old*!"

At Zeena's horrified lament, Jen huffed in bitter irony. "Yeah, I noticed. Hard to miss when your prospective groom is as old as your own father, and reprehensible to boot. Not to mention heinously boring. And to think when the marriage of state was first proposed, I point-blank refused to marry Najeeb."

Zeena's honey-brown eyes flared with hope. "Maybe it's not too late to take your refusal back! I know you love Najeeb like a brother, but if you have to marry anyone, at least he's a great guy. And a real hunk. You might end up loving him…*that* way!"

Jen regarded her seventeen-year-old stunning beauty of a sister and remembered again why she was doing this. She sighed. "You think I wouldn't have grabbed that option if it was still on the table? But Najeeb was as adamant in refusing to marry me just to serve his father's political ambitions. Then he left to places unknown on another of his globe-trotting humanitarian missions. That's why Hassan decided he'd marry me himself."

"Doesn't this man have a shred of decency? He's actually two years older than Father!"

"He actually considers he's done the noble thing, offering his oldest son and crown prince first, and that it was my and Najeeb's refusals that made him resort to this option. He feels quite righteous, I assure you."

Zeena looked on the verge of crying again. She'd been looking like that ever since she'd heard the news. But she was clearly past the shock phase and into the bargaining one.

"But if you really have to go through with it—" she paused to shudder "—maybe it won't be for long."

"You're hoping he'll soon drop dead and release me from my life sentence?" She shook her head at yet more proof of how young and naive her sister was. "Zee, darling, I know anyone over forty is ancient to you. Hell, I'm only thirty, and you make me feel old whenever you're shocked I do stuff you think reserved for only 'young' people. But Hassan is a very robust sixty-five, and I expect him to live another healthy, obnoxious thirty years."

Zeena clearly couldn't imagine that terrible fate, or could, and it horrified her. Her tears finally flowed, her voice breaking. "At least tell me it will only be for show."

Jen sighed again, not knowing what to tell her sister. Their father had mumbled such an assurance, but she figured it had to be what he'd told himself so he wouldn't feel even guiltier about sacrificing her. Hassan already had a chokehold over Zafrana's resources and assets, but in their region, blood mattered far more than money when it came to political power. This marriage had to produce an heir, one who'd become her father's, too, for Hassan to acquire all the power he wanted over Zafrana. Only through such an heir could Hassan rule Zafrana during her father's lifetime, then fully annex it in the event of his death, once his heir became king, and Hassan became regent until said heir came of age. Hassan sure had his ducks in a row. And she was the first one he had sitting just where he wanted her.

Zeena must have read the truth in her resigned eyes, as her tears flowed faster. But she still tried again. "If all he has over Father and Zafrana are debts, maybe we can find someone to pay them off. Like the other royals in the region. Surely great men and kings like King Kamal and King Mohab will help."

Jen shook her head, wanting to end this. "I approached everyone with power in the region myself, but all kings Kamal, Mohab, Amjad and Rashid could do was try to make Hassan relinquish those debts to them, and he refused. Without resorting to drastic measures, there's nothing they can do."

"Why won't they employ those measures? This *is* drastic!"

"It isn't as easy as that, Zee. These men owe it to their own kingdoms not to involve them in other nations' conflicts. And since the influx of oil money, Hassan now has major foreign allies whose interests lie with Saraya and who'd take exception if the other kingdoms enforced embargos on it, or initiated a bigger conflict with it. Also, with the tribal nature of the region, those kings have family alliances with Saraya, making things even more complicated."

She knew each king wanted to tear Hassan apart with his bare hands. But those hands were tied by so many protocols. They were forced to accept any form of peaceful resolution, even if they itched for something extreme. Said *peaceful resolution* was now her, and her hopefully fertile womb.

"So this is for real?" Zeena asked. "There's no way out?"

"No."

Her succinct response fell like a blow on Zeena, rocking her on her feet. The next second, Zeena's arms were convulsing around her, and her tears were wetting her bosom.

Jen's eyes filled, too. She hadn't shed tears since her mother's death when she was seven. But she'd never been able to bear her baby sisters' distress.

Apart from loving her most in the world, Zeena and Fayza looked up to her. Her every success had been a triumph to them. She'd been their role model, her life one they hoped to model theirs after. Zeena wasn't only weeping for Jen's derailed future, but for a loss of hope in her own.

But that was why Jen had agreed to this marriage. To protect her sisters' futures.

She'd only told Zeena there was no way out so she wouldn't compound her distress with guilt. For there certainly was a way out for Jen had she wanted to take it. She could have told her father and Hassan to take flying jumps off their respective kingdoms' tallest skyscraper. But she hadn't. For two reasons.

The first and lesser reason was that she couldn't stand aside and let their father be humiliated and hurt. She loved him, in spite of his weaknesses, felt even more protective of him because of them. She knew he shouldn't have become king, that it continued to be an unbearable burden. But fate had conspired to put him on the throne, and it had been the one thing that had appeased many a tribe at the time. He'd sacrificed his own desires for Zafrana's. This current mess was not solely his fault. In her pursuit of independence, her career and immigration to the United States, she'd stopped following the developments in Zafrana, until things had deteriorated beyond resolution. The internal situation was now so volatile, if the major tribes didn't get a solution soon and with their interests finally threatened by Saraya's impending takeover, civil war would erupt.

But the major reason she'd agreed to the marriage remained her sisters. Even if she'd been able to leave her father and her people to a doom they'd caused, she couldn't leave Zeena and Fayza to a fate they hadn't brought on themselves. If Hassan couldn't have her, he'd ask for one of her sisters. And their father would be forced to comply.

But they were nothing like her. They were too young, too sheltered and too inexperienced in life and with men. They didn't have the power of another nationality and the protection of personal wealth. If Jen left, neither of her sisters would be able to resist being shoved into this marriage. Zeena would crumble, and the two-years-older Fayza would do something drastic.

So it was up to her to protect them. She had to marry that power-grabbing old man and save them. And along with them, her whole family and kingdom.

She hugged the sobbing Zeena tighter, kissed the top of her head soothingly. "Don't worry about me, Zee. You know me. I'm a survivor, a winner, and I'll find a way to…to…"

Words and thoughts petered away. The whole scene in front of her blurred, then disappeared. Nothing remained but a man. The most magnificent male she'd ever laid eyes on…

"To what?"

Jen started at the question, blinked as if coming out of a trance. For seconds she couldn't remember where she was, why she and Zeena were sharing this fervent hug and why her baby sister was looking up at her with such entreaty.

Then noise and lights and movements and memories started to register again. But her senses remained trained on the man as he stood at the ballroom's wide-open doors, surveying it with all the somberness of a general studying a battlefield. He filled her awareness, the sheer force of his presence nullifying everything else. As if he had some kind of gravity well that nothing could resist or escape.

Then he moved, and the crowd parted for him, seemingly unable to withstand being in his path. It felt as if he had a spotlight trained on him, illuminating him even as he dipped in areas of shadow. What else explained why he looked more vivid, more in focus than anyone else who was dozens of feet closer?

"Who's *that*?"

She blinked again as she forced her eyes back to her sister. Zeena had followed her entranced gaze to the mystery man and was staring at him openmouthed. So he had the same effect on her. Of course he did. He had everyone around mesmerized.

It seemed so weird that she didn't know who he was, since she felt she…recognized him.

Exhaling at her inexplicable reactions and thoughts, she shrugged. "I have no idea."

An assessing expression came into Zeena's eyes as she let her go, before impishness suddenly replaced anguish on her face. "Want me to go find out?"

Jen raised one eyebrow. "And how would you do that?"

"I'll walk right up to him, introduce myself as the sister of the bride and just ask."

Jen winced at the word *bride*, but waved dismissively. "Thanks, darling, but you probably wouldn't be able to move, let alone speak, if you come within talking distance of him."

Zeena looked back at the man who kept coming closer to their hideout and sighed. "Yeah, I'd probably turn to stone if he even looked at me."

So even Zeena with her limited experience with the world in general and men in particular felt the impact of this man. As for herself, she'd been exposed to some of the most powerful men on earth in over a decade of studies, travels and public and private work, and she knew beyond a doubt that this man was exceptional among even those. More than that. He was one of a kind. The way he affected her was unprecedented. And that was from afar, when he was completely unaware of her.

Suddenly, knowing who he was became the most important thing to her. Before she led a mockery of a life dictated by everyone else's interests, she was due for one thing all her own. What better than to indulge her unstoppable curiosity about this man? After all, where did being perfectly responsible and in control lead her? But then, why should she even need a reason? She was just going to find out who he was, not have a fling with him.

Yeah, right, as if such a force of nature would look in her direction, even if he weren't here attending her engagement party.

But she would do this, for herself. Even if for some reason she felt the simple action of discovering his identity would have some unpredictable and serious consequences.

Straightening, she rolled her shoulders, as if readying herself for a fight. "I'll do it. I'll go investigate."

Before she strode away, Zeena's hand on her forearm stopped her. "Just be careful. This guy is radiating something fierce."

Jen's gaze went to him again, and she nodded. "That's called power. The unadulterated form."

"I guess. But he just feels—" Zeena looked suddenly uncomfortable "—dangerous."

Jen's lips curved as she repeated to her sister what she'd just been thinking. "Darling, I'm just going to find out who he is, not have a fling with him."

Zeena gave an embarrassed giggle as Jen swept her velvet cheek in one last reassuring caress before striding away.

As she rejoined the crowd, heading for the one most likely to know who that man was, Jen exhaled a ragged breath. For Zeena was so right.

She had no doubt this demigod was very dangerous. Deadly. But that only made her desire to find out everything about him even more overpowering.

She zeroed in on Jameel Aal Hashem, her five-years-younger maternal cousin, a walking encyclopedia of social gossip and celebrity news. She'd bet her mystery man hadn't escaped her cousin's all-encompassing curiosity.

And she was right. Before she could even ask Jameel, he pointed out the stranger in a fit of ecstatic excitement.

After gushing about how he couldn't believe *he* was here, Jameel told her who he was. Numair Al Aswad.

And how fitting that name was. He was indeed as majestic and sleek and powerful as his namesake. He *was* actually known by the English version of his name: the Black Panther of Black Castle Enterprises.

Now that she knew his name, she knew far more about him than Jameel possibly could. Since she'd become deeply involved in the world of business, anywhere she'd turned there it had been, the global corporation he'd founded that was shaping the market in every major field that made the world go round.

As the senior partner, Numair was a leader among the gods of science, finance and technology responsible for Black Castle Enterprises' staggering success, and one of the most individually rich and powerful men on the planet. And now she'd found out that he was also the sexiest thing to ever walk the earth.

But not much was known about his personal life. Only that he came from Damhoor, a kingdom in her region, but had immigrated to the United States in his childhood, and his parents were long dead. As far as she knew, he'd never been married.

Then at one point, as Jameel joined her in openly drooling over the man, Numair turned and looked straight at them.

At *her*.

His gaze slammed into her own with the force of a lightning bolt. Feeling as if it had fried her brain, nothing was left in her mind but alarm.

Had he felt her staring at him?

Before her stalled breathing could restart, people moved in front of her, severing the electrified visual contact.

Shaky with relief and disappointment at once, she murmured something to Jameel and hurried away, unable to risk being in Numair's crosshairs again.

Secure that Hassan hadn't bothered to look for her, she maneuvered around the few people who recognized her to rush back to her retreat. She wanted to continue watching Numair from its safety. The memory of savoring his magnificence would be what she'd remember from this wretched night.

As she reached her previous vantage point, another jolt hit her again. It was fiercer this time, making her stumble and drop her purse. Cursing when it opened on impact, spilling its contents, she crouched to retrieve them…and felt as if the place was plunged into darkness. The next second, she knew why. It was the massive figure towering over her, seeming to block out the whole world. She didn't need to look up to see who it was. The current that now mercilessly arced through her told her who it was.

Numair.

As her chest filled to bursting with erratic heartbeats, he dropped to his haunches before her. Before she could raise her eyes to his, his hands, cool and calloused, brushed hers and zapped her with another thousand volts as he took the purse from her limp grasp and put everything back in it, his every move the essence of control and elegance.

As he handed it back to her, she mustered enough volition and looked up…and lost what remained of her compromised balance. Only the hand that shot out to support her stopped her from flopping back on her ass.

Finding herself inches from him was as heart-stopping, literally, as finding herself face-to-face with his predator namesake. All that lethal power coiled and simmering under the polished, perfect veneer of savage beauty.

She now realized she'd gotten it wrong before. He was no demigod. This was a full-fledged god, one who ruled over a whole pantheon of deities. A desert god in specific, forged from its heat and harshness, from its mystery and moodiness and magnificence. He might not have lived long in her region, but his heritage was carved in his every line.

And *carved* was an accurate word. Every inch of him seemed to have been hewn by some divine force. His all-black formal silk suit and shirt clung to a body she had no doubt was solid, chiseled muscle. The clothes offered not an inch of padding to the breadth of his shoulders and chest, no accentuation to the hardness of his abdomen and thighs or the sparseness of his waist and hips. This was the full potential of the species realized, a powerhouse of virility and manliness.

And that was before she took in the details of his face. From a luxurious mane of raven silk that would reach almost to his shoulders when freed, to stunning emerald eyes that seemed to radiate a hypnosis, to sensual lips and polished teak–colored skin spread taut against a bone structure to tear heartstrings over, he was breathtaking.

Then he was pulling her up to her feet as he uncoiled to his full height, and for the first time ever she felt dwarfed. She stood six feet in three-inch heels, and he still towered over her by what appeared to be half a foot.

Then he did something that once again made her heart hammer as if it was trying to ram out of her chest. He raised a hand and swept back the swath of hair that had cascaded over her face, ensnaring one strand, rubbing it between his fingers.

"You hate being here."

No preliminaries. Just...*bam*. Of course he would follow no rules. It made it even worse that his voice was like darkest velvet gliding over her every nerve. Did he have to sound mouthwatering, too?

Without meaning to, she found herself responding, as if under the effect of a truth serum. "I do."

He nodded, as if he'd already been certain, but approved

her corroboration. "This—" he swept the whole scene in a disdainful flick "—is unworthy of your tolerance or your presence."

She had to force the mouth that kept dropping open closed. "Sometimes we're forced to put up with much, for the sake of what's more important than our own preferences or what we think we're worthy of."

His lips and eyes hardened, clearly disapproving. "Nothing is more important than your preferences. And your worth is not a matter of opinion. Only the best is good enough for you. The only thing you must always expect and get."

The heart that seemed to have taken permanent residence in her throat expanded at his praise. Even if it was empty hyperbole, it sounded fantastic coming from him.

"Uh, thanks...but you don't really know anything about me. And it's clear you have no idea who I am."

That dismissing wave again. "The moment I laid eyes on you, I knew everything I need to know about you. As for your identity, that makes no difference to who you really are, what you truly deserve."

"Oh, believe me, it does."

"Because you're Jenan Aal Ghamdi, and this is supposed to be your engagement party?"

He knew who she was. And it didn't seem to make a difference to him.

His next words made that clear beyond a doubt. "It's all quite irrelevant to me. And should be to you, too. You don't want to be here. But you want to be with me."

"I—I do?"

"Yes. As much as I want to be with you." His words were dripping in arrogant certainty. From another man, it would have been offensive. She'd handed other men their asses over *way* less. From him, though, it was just right. He had a right to such supreme self-assurance.

His eyes flared in the dimness as they caressed her half-open lips before settling back on her no doubt shell-shocked eyes. "Let me take you away from this farce. I'm the only one who can give you everything you need."

She gaped up at him. Was she so traumatized by the idea of marrying Hassan that she was having a wish-fulfillment hallucination? Creating this god of a man and making it so she'd had the same instant, inexorable effect on him that he'd had on her?

But nothing she could conjure could be as outlandishly incredible as him. No, he was real. He had really followed her here, and he really was offering…offering…

She didn't know exactly what he was offering. But anything coming from him sounded better than any fantasy she'd ever had. And more impossible.

Her situation might be irrelevant to him, but to her…

Suddenly, everything inside her hit Pause. In seconds, an urge took her over. A plan. It was rash, probably crazy, but it was all she could think of anymore.

This man was even more powerful than the monarchs she'd approached for help. His power was also unbridled by any of their tribal and political shackles, and it was more than enough to resolve Zafrana's crisis without her sacrificing herself to this barbaric ritual of an arranged marriage. Of course, a man like him wouldn't help out of the goodness of his heart.

She had a feeling he didn't have one.

But if he was as interested in her as he seemed to be, they might come to an understanding.

Even if she couldn't imagine he was that interested, he'd help with something that major. As a businesswoman, she was used to taking risks. The worst that could happen was he'd decline and just walk away. But since the stakes were so high and he was that tempting, she'd risk far more than his mere rejection.

Before she could think again, she said it out loud, making it too late to back down. "There *is* something I need."

"Anything."

His instant, unqualified statement gave her the last shove of courage she needed to make her request.

"I need you to get me out of marrying Hassan."

Two

"Done."

Numair watched the impact of his one-word answer widening Jenan Aal Ghamdi's magnificent eyes, spreading a deeper peach blush across the sculpted elegance of her cheekbones.

He was again almost overwhelmed by the need to trace that delectable color that kept surging across her face, the testament to his effect on this irresistible creature. And to luxuriate in every line of her masterpiece features, then drag her to him and taste each one before settling on her lush, dewy lips and devouring them.

It again baffled him, his response to her, the intensity, the immediacy of it. This was unprecedented, inexplicable. Yet it was most opportune. He'd come here for her after all.

He'd come knowing everything about her from the day she'd been born to the moment before he'd seen her. He'd compiled a dossier on her thicker than any he'd ever had on a quarry. From photographs, he'd noted her esthetic symmetry, but he hadn't had any response to it, as usual.

Then he'd seen her in the flesh, and all thoughts of swallowing the bitter pill of necessity had been decimated by the thunderbolt of his response to her. Compulsions he'd never even imagined had taken him over the moment he'd laid eyes on her across the distance.

No. They'd done so even before he had. He'd *felt* her first.

Not that he'd realized what it had been he'd felt when a charge of energy had zapped him as soon as he'd entered this ballroom. He'd told himself it must have been a surge of resolve, obliterating any aversion to being here, to launching his mission. Those sensations had strengthened with each step he'd taken until he'd become certain it wasn't internal, but a response to another person. A woman. Though he'd never felt anything like that toward one, the awareness he'd felt had been definitely...sensual.

Once sure of that, he hadn't wanted to find the source of the disturbance. It would have been self-sabotaging to make contact with someone who'd triggered such an aberrant reaction in him when he was here in pursuit of a specific woman.

Then that beacon of sensations had moved, and before he could rein himself in, his gaze had been dragged toward it. And he'd found himself looking straight into her eyes. The heart that never faltered and barely sped under extreme conditions, that he almost never felt at all, had dropped a few beats before it had started thundering. It continued to do so.

As their gazes had meshed, so much had collided inside him. Disbelief, wonder, elation and a dozen other things. His target was the same woman who'd had this inexplicable influence on him. He hadn't even thought what his mission would be like, but had been bound on seeing it through regardless. But this presented what he hadn't even considered a possibility. That it would be enjoyable, even pleasurable.

Then he'd followed her, no longer out of calculation but compulsion. Everything he'd said and done since had been spontaneous. And real. One thing had been driving him, the one thing he was certain of.

He wanted her.

Then she'd shocked him yet again when she'd given him the means to the very thing he was here to achieve. Stopping her marriage to Hassan Aal Ghaanem.

But since he'd let go of all premeditation, he hadn't even hesitated. His response had been instantaneous.

The moment it had left his lips, he'd wished it back. This wasn't how he'd intended this to go. He'd intended to maneuver her, to reel her in slowly, to spoil Hassan's marriage arrangement by seducing his bride-to-be and claiming her for himself. What he'd just offered wouldn't serve his purpose.

But he couldn't take it back. Not when she'd looked up at him with such hope and entreaty as she'd made her request.

Nothing remained on her face now but shock. She must have expected him to say just about anything else but his succinct promise.

He watched the smooth column of her throat working, and he hardened all over as he imagined his lips soothing the convulsive movement, swallowing her moans at their origin.

Then in that velvety voice that strummed every male fiber in his body, her husky question validated his assessment of her incredulity. "Just…done?"

That was his cue to add some qualification, to drive his own bargain. But he couldn't bear to think of interrupting the unrehearsed progression of events.

Deciding to let this play out and adjust his direction later, he nodded. "I did say I'd do anything for you. I intend to."

And the strangest thing was, he did. Apart from what he had to gain by intervening, what drove him now was the need to wipe this trapped expression from her face. He'd come here thinking she'd agreed to marry Hassan to have access to his bottomless oil-money resources. While her history painted a picture of an independent, successful woman, he'd known of many such women who preferred being subsidized once the opportunity presented itself. That she'd refused to marry Najeeb, then consented to marry his father had made him think she'd preferred the older man who'd make far less demands, and who'd be far easier to manipulate.

But one look at her had told him that she found Hassan and the idea of marrying him abhorrent on all levels. How she was being forced to enter that marriage, he had no idea yet, but he didn't doubt that she was, and that she was seething with futile rage at having no choice. A choice he would now give her.

Not that she believed he could, not as easily as he'd implied. He saw the flare of hope in her eyes dim with the gloom of reality. "Intentions are one thing, executions are another."

"Not to me. Anything I intend, I execute."

At the certainty in his words, her gaze flickered again. "But surely not *anything*."

He shrugged. "I can do anything I put my mind to. I always have. And I always will."

Her edible lips hung open for moments before a breathy chuckle escaped them. Her every expression and sound inflamed him. Her every inch, even in that unflattering dress, seemed to be exerting an inexorable gravity on his every cell and sense.

She shook her head in dazed humor, and the silky waves of her hair undulated around her shoulders. "You know what? I believe you can. The universe must bend over backward to accommodate you." Her eyes turned serious, and he wished to fast-forward in time to when she'd look up at him with eyes blazing with passion as he rode her to ecstasy. "But don't you want to know what this is all about before you make such a commitment?"

He shrugged again. "All I need to know is that you en-listed my help in escaping a fate I believe is worse than death to you. Whatever needs to be done, I'll do it."

"But you still need to know details, so you can decide what needs to be done."

And he gave in to the urge. He reached out and cupped her face, groaned as her firm softness filled his palm, as her flesh singed him with that perfect storm of chemistry that had erupted between them.

He barely stopped himself from swooping to claim the lips that spilled such an intoxicating gasp at his touch. He groaned. "You can tell me everything you want…in my suite."

His hand melted down her neck and shoulder before it closed over a resilient arm as he turned toward the French doors to lead her outside.

At her rooted unresponsiveness, he frowned. "You do know who I am?"

She had to. She wouldn't have asked what she had from someone else. For who else could she think could thwart a king?

But he was suddenly uncertain she knew. After all, nothing so far had followed any logical projections.

She silently nodded, her eyes still filled with that shell-shocked expression.

He pressed. "You're not sure you can trust me?"

She shook her head, then squeezed her eyes shut. When

she opened them again, they blasted him in an even hotter wave of unconscious sensuality. He barely suppressed a shudder.

But her color had become hectic and her breathing erratic. She swayed unsteadily in his grip.

Suddenly anxious, he asked, "Are you all right?"

She nodded again, then groaned. "Hell, I keep nodding and shaking my head as if I've forgotten how to speak."

His eyes assessed her as he took his hand reluctantly away. "Maybe you don't want to speak to me anymore."

Her cough was incredulous. "You're kidding, right?"

"You tell me. It's clear I'm...agitating you."

"Oh, you are. But it has nothing to do with not trusting you. I *do* trust you."

He surveyed her expression, not sure if he was reading it right. Because even knowing who he was, such conviction should be premature. And she didn't strike him as someone given to making such serious claims lightly.

He gritted his teeth. "You don't need to say what you don't feel to placate me or to be polite. You have no reason to trust me. Yet. But I will give you any guarantees you demand so you'll feel safe with me."

A chuckle burst from her lips. "Oh, you have much to learn about me. When I'm not in my professional mode as a multinational business consultant, I lead with my real opinions first and don't bother asking questions later."

This did feel like the truth. This attitude suited her, and everything he felt from her.

His lips relaxed in response to her infectious smile. "I would have nothing less than the whole truth from you."

"Well, you've come to the right person for that."

"I'll count on it. I have no tolerance for empty etiquette and pulling punches, either."

"Yeah, I noticed. You tell it as it is, in the most shockingly direct way possible. Welcome to the club." She grinned up at him, and he again wondered how he didn't have her pressed into that column at her back and was all over her. She made his condition even worse when she sighed, the sound caressing his every nerve. "But I do trust you. I just know you'd never harm me in any way. And don't ask me how I know that. It has nothing to do with anything I know about you. I just do."

"Then why were you so alarmed about coming to my suite if it didn't occur to you I'd take advantage of you?"

Again that unfettered chuckle. "As if. I bet you bound over women who pursue you begging to be taken advantage of."

"You're not *women*. You're you."

"Even if you consider me different…"

"Not different. Unique."

Her color heightened again with pleasure at what should have been an exaggeration but was anything but. "Even if you do consider me that, I can't imagine other men's weaknesses ever applying to you. You wouldn't prey on anyone weaker."

Her opinion of him had something searingly pleasurable swelling inside him. Yet…"I *felt* your anxiety, your distress. I still feel them."

Something soft and even more hard-hitting than all her previous expressions came into her eyes as she cocked her head at him, her lips quirking. "Hello? You do realize you're the most overwhelming man alive, right? As if that wasn't enough, we broke every rule of personal interaction. Heck, we've already progressed to discussing wedding-busting plans. Excuse me if I'm rattled to my core."

"You don't need to be. I care nothing about rules. Between us those don't exist. And you know it."

"You think I know anything right now? I'm not even sure this is really happening or that you really exist. I only know that nothing has ever come close to hitting me this hard."

"Another thing we share, then. Even before I saw you, you hit me harder than anything ever had."

She scrunched her nose at him in adorable teasing. "Don't *you* say what you don't mean to try to tickle my ego."

His lips twisted, admitting his condition to himself even as he did to her. "I do mean it. Your ego has every right to be rolling on the ground laughing." Her chuckle tinkled like crystal with such genuine pleasure, he had to fist his hands to keep them from grabbing her. But he also needed to resolve this issue. "So were you just surprised I asked you back to my suite?"

That delightful lopsided grin flashed wider again. "Surprised is the understatement of the century. But seriously, I just needed a moment for a reality check. And to breathe. You, sir, are more breath depleting than the most insane roller-coaster ride."

Just then another unprecedented thing happened. His own lips spread with a combination of emotions he didn't recognize. If forced to name them, he'd guess they most approximated delight, indulgence, even tenderness.

His smile had an equal and opposite reaction on her. While everything about her made him hard as steel, she melted against the support of the column at her back.

Her gaze poured hot, glazed reproach over him, making him start to ache, throb. "You should be banned by law from doing that. Everything about you is already overkill. A smile, and *that* kind, too, can cause widespread damage."

His smile only widened as triumph revved inside his chest. "No danger of that, as I have no smiles of any kind for anyone. This is exclusively for you."

"So I'm a target group of one, huh?"

Something tightened in his chest as he heard the word *target* on her lips. What she'd been to him before he'd seen her. Now it suddenly felt wrong.

Oblivious to his thoughts, she gazed up at him with what he now believed *was* trust and...was that admiration, too? "I came here tonight thinking I'd run out of luck for life, but because I met you and you've offered what you have, no matter what the outcome will be, I'd already revised my opinion. But to be the sole recipient of your smile? Talk about my luck making a total turnaround."

Giving in to his compulsion, he tugged her to his side. "I'm willing to talk about anything. Just not here. Come with me?"

She nodded, shyness tingeing her gaze, affecting him more because he knew only he elicited such a reaction from her, and it was genuine, like everything else about her. "Just promise me a chance every now and then to catch my breath."

"Although it's the last thing I want, I'll give you all the time you need to feel at total ease with me."

Her eyes twinkled impishly at him. "I don't think it's humanly possible to feel relaxed around you."

After that first smile, another came easier to him. "Tension works, too. As long as it's the delicious kind."

She sighed dramatically. "I don't know about that. What you provoke is too scalding to be called anything so benign."

Her ready confessions of his effect on her surged through him again with such unstoppable desire. Unable to wait any longer, he swept her outside.

As he had her rushing to keep up with his eager steps, she melted into him, as if she needed his support. Then as he steered her toward the elevators, he felt her tensing against him.

This tightness in his chest returned. "Worried again?"

Her smile brightened once more, becoming whimsical as she shook her head. "You'd never be a threat to me, Sheikh Numair. If I have anything to worry about, it's what an overpowering temptation you are."

Something twisted in his gut when she called him *sheikh*. It sounded...so right.

His arm tightened around her, as if in thanks. "It's only fair, since you're that, and more, to me."

Sharing a smile of expectation with her, feeling as if everything he'd ever wanted was within his grasp, he took her into the elevator.

As Numair held the door open for her, Jen walked past him on legs that at once had the consistency of steel and jelly.

She was really here. In his suite.

Trying to focus on anything besides the feel of him at her back, his scent and heat flooding her senses, she tried to look around.

Though she'd stayed at The Plaza before, it had never been in such a room. The one-of-a-kind Royal Plaza Suite was on a level of magnificence that equaled Zafrana's royal palace. Though with the hard times her homeland had fallen on, the state of the two places couldn't be compared. This suite that sprawled over almost five thousand square feet in the most private area of the legendary hotel, overlooking the most prized views in Manhattan—Fifth Avenue and the Pulitzer Fountain—was impeccably maintained. With its rich decorations, sumptuous textiles and exquisite furnishings, all inspired by the ambiance of the royal court of Louis XV, it was the ultimate in luxury. While Zafrana's royal palace, where she'd grown up, was on its way to becoming dilapidated.

Her gaze strayed back to Numair, and she found herself wondering what his home looked like.

Not that she'd ever find out. Whatever was happening here, whatever he was offering, whatever he wanted in return, she had no illusions it would be anything but transient.

Which she was okay with. Anything she'd have with him, anything he could do for her, would be far more than anything she'd dared dream of an hour ago.

Ya Ullah, had it been only an hour? She felt she'd known him, had been in this state of agitated excitement in his company, forever. It felt like days ago when she'd made her reckless request.

She'd more than half expected he'd shrug and move on. His immediate and unequivocal response had been the last thing she'd expected. And it had shocked the hell out of her.

But what else was new? Everything from the moment she'd laid eyes on him had been one shock after another. And here she was. In his suite. What she'd never done with any man. Not even the man she'd once married. She'd always met any man on her turf. She'd dictated the pace, the rules.

She hadn't even thought of trying to impose those on Numair. Even when he'd made it clear he'd accommodate her every wish. It wasn't because she needed his help or because he'd promised it. He was just…overriding. And for the first time in her life, she loved being swept away, not being in control of herself or the situation. Numair made what should have been a disconcerting experience, to someone as obsessive about autonomy as herself, exhilarating.

His hand once again burned her waist through her dress as he guided her through a succession of vestibules to a massive space hosting a sumptuous ten-seat dining table and a luxurious sitting area.

Stepping away from his electrifying touch, she sought the refuge of the grand piano at the far corner. Once behind it and taking in the whole scene with him at its center, she felt herself stumble out of the surreal state she'd plunged into.

Numair might have admitted her equal effect on him, but would he consider it equally her right to follow her instincts as it was his? She did trust him not to make any move she didn't invite, but she suddenly didn't trust he'd view this whole thing as she did. Could he be so progressive he wouldn't hold it against her and change his treatment of her?

Well, if he wasn't, it would be his loss, and she'd be well rid of him. As she had been of her ex.

Striving for an even tone, she asked, "Are you in New York to attend the reception?"

Those amazing emerald-like eyes of his glittered. "I wasn't invited, no."

"So you heard royals from your region were having an engagement celebration at your hotel and you simply decided to investigate?"

"Something like that."

She'd have to be satisfied with that, because he didn't seem about to elaborate. Not that it mattered why he happened to be there. What mattered was whether he could truly help her.

Before she could reintroduce the subject, he came around the piano. "I detect a severe drop in temperature since we entered the suite. Having second thoughts after all?"

His voice had deepened, calmed, as if soothing a skittish mare. He reached for her hand that lay fisted on the black, polished surface of the piano. His hand was big enough to lose hers in, tough enough it could pulverize brick. Yet the gentleness with which he coaxed her hand open, the consideration in his eyes as he surveyed her no doubt tense face, suddenly made her ashamed of her surge of doubt.

Squeezing her eyes in contrition, she groaned, "I guess I got a bit paranoid."

He frowned. "Were you worried that your trust in me was unsubstantiated, and I'd do something against your will once I got you here?"

She shook her head vigorously, needing him to know this was something she'd never suspect. "Not that. I just worried you'd change your...attitude."

"Like men usually do, once they think they've gotten their objectives and no longer need to hide their nasty natures and double-standard convictions?"

From the way his gorgeous lips thinned, she knew if such men crossed his path, they'd regret it for life. He did have that protector/punisher vibe going.

She wished he'd let this go but knew he wouldn't. This man needed to know everything, to have a tight handle on every situation. He'd probe until she spilled everything that had crossed her mind in those moments of unease.

She sighed. "Men are like that to one degree or another in my experience, but mainly men from my region, yes."

One dauntingly arched eyebrow rose. "Are all men chauvinists there?"

"Double standards *are* the general stance, perpetrated by women even more than men. Anyone, especially a woman, who dares flaunt cultural rules and restrictions becomes stigmatized, no matter how modern everyone looks on the surface."

"Why did you fear I'd be like them? I was born in your region, but I was not raised there."

"Indoctrination happens at a very early age. It takes very progressive families and especially mothers not to imprint their children with the worst of the culture. In general, men there are raised to have very cruel opinions of women whom they perceive as 'loose.'"

"And you thought my early programming would resurface, and I'd judge you for coming up here with me?"

"It was a passing thought, okay? An ingrained reaction that really has nothing to do with you."

"But it wasn't ingrained in you because of the general state of affairs in your homeland. It was out of personal experience, wasn't it?"

She'd been right. He wouldn't rest until he had the whole truth. She sighed again. "How much do you know about me? You clearly investigated me before crashing the reception."

He guided her to the nearest couch, pulled her down on it with him. "Investigations provide only broad lines that can be interpreted in different ways that can all turn out to be wrong. You tell me what's accurate."

Shuddering as his power and warmth encompassed her, she leaned against the dark brown velvet couch. She hoped she didn't look as swooning as she felt as she gazed up at him.

"I am the very definition of *loose* in my region. From leaving my family at eighteen to live in another country, to supporting myself ever since, to making success and autonomy my life goal, to being a divorcée who hasn't returned home in penance, seeking the shelter of her family and the forgiveness of society, I'm the cautionary tale mothers tell their little daughters. Anything bad that ever befell me is advertised as punishment for my sins."

His expression hardened with her every word, until his face seemed to be hewn from granite. "Everything you just mentioned, everything you achieved and are, makes you only enterprising and powerful, a role model all women in and out of your region should aspire to emulate."

She let loose an incredulous laugh. At his imperiously

questioning look she explained, "It's just funny to hear you say what my baby sisters always do. But *they* are incapable of being impartial when it comes to me."

"I'm totally partial when it comes to you. I also happen to be absolutely right."

She again barely stopped herself from doing something impulsive. That was, more so than coming up to this suite. Something like throwing herself against his massive chest and smothering him in kisses. Which she might end up doing soon. Exposure to him was chipping away at any control she had left.

Watching her with that intensity that compromised her will, he said, "Your sisters are astute young ladies for making you their role model. You're the perfect one."

She waved his words away. "Let's not exaggerate, okay? I'd just die if they followed in some of my footsteps."

"Why? You're not proud of your achievements?"

"Those I'm proud of. I'm not proud of my mistakes."

"What are those? A failed, short-lived marriage? You think that disqualifies you as an inspiration?"

"Catastrophic choices certainly do. In my bid for freedom and independence, I made more than one. Like marrying the first man who seemed to be the opposite of the chauvinistic men I was used to, and finding out very soon he had equally objectionable traits, only on the other side of the spectrum. But whether I deserved it or not, I *was* their role model, and I strove to fill my position. The one thing I mourned most about being forced to marry Hassan was that I could no longer be that to them."

"You'll always be what your sisters look up to." He loomed over her as he sat up, his gaze seething with something she could only think was affront on her behalf. "Now tell me exactly how Hassan is forcing you into marriage. Leave out nothing."

Taking a huge breath, she started explaining everything.

He listened, his focus on her so total, it made it hard to speak. But she did, and she left nothing out as he'd demanded.

His expression grew almost scary as he listened, but he remained silent even after she finished, until she started to vibrate with tension. What if, now that he knew the extent of Zafrana's debts, he realized he couldn't do anything for her and apologized for giving her false hope?

Then he finally spoke, his voice a blade. "I knew about the debts, but I didn't know they were that crippling, or that the internal situation in Zafrana was that volatile."

"Father wouldn't have thought of asking me to do this for anything less."

He raised his hand, his jaw muscles bunching. "Nothing is worth imposing on you in any way, let alone sacrificing you. He should have sacrificed himself."

"He would have if it would have solved the problem."

"He should have considered any measures but bartering you to that old goat."

She burst out laughing. At his grim frown, she spluttered, "That's exactly what I called him earlier this evening to Zeena." At the growing thundercloud that gripped his face, she sobered. "What would you have done?"

"You don't want to know."

She gasped, for those five words painted a clear picture. This man was as deadly as she'd thought earlier, and not figuratively. He was no stranger to eliminating enemies. Even with his own hands.

Before she could process what kind of disaster she might have instigated by seeking his intervention, he demanded, "I need the specifics of those debts."

She latched on to the relatively innocuous subject. "Of course. You need to know everything before deciding whether you can help, or even if you'd want to."

He shot her one of those authoritatively reprimanding

glances. "Those specifics have no bearing on my decision. That was final since the moment I gave you my word. They are only for devising the most effective attack."

She shot up straight. "Attack?"

His eyes became icy emeralds. "There will be extreme measures employed in releasing Zafrana from Saraya's shackles."

Her heart hammered in dismay. "Define *extreme*."

"Eliminating the problem at the source."

"And how would you do that?"

"That's my business."

"Actually, it's mine, too. Mine, mainly. I'm the one who asked for this, and if you're going to do anything to…to hurt Hassan, I'd have to withdraw my request."

"You care what happens to him?"

"No, but I don't want him to meet with an unnatural end, either. For Saraya. For Najeeb. For peace's sake."

She thought his eyes flared at Najeeb's mention, but he only said, "Peace is always achieved after a war. A war always comes with heavy losses."

"I don't want freedom that comes at such a price."

"You think I'd kill him, don't you?"

"You sure made it sound like that."

"His demise *can* be easily arranged." As she started to splutter in alarm, his lips twisted in a lethal smile. "But it just happens I'm not considering liquidating him. Just his chokehold over Zafrana, and with it, most of his assets."

She held his gaze until she decided he was telling the truth, then collapsed back in relief. "For a moment there I thought I'd just signed Hassan's death warrant."

"It *is* the preferable, cleaner solution." As her heart pounded again, he added, "But I won't let him off that easy. Hassan's actions deserve protracted punishment before I even consider granting him reprieve."

"You still make it sound as if you'll end up offing him!"

When he only shrugged, she sat up again and threw her hands up in the air. "*Ya Ullah*...I can't believe we're sitting here haggling over the pros and cons of assassinating Hassan."

"To off him or not to off him, that is the question."

That, and his bedeviling expression, made her burst out laughing. "You fiend! You had me going there." Melting back again, she grinned. "So what do you intend to do, for real?"

"Which part of *that's my business* don't you get? You made the demand, now sit back while I take care of it as I see fit."

"Beggars can't be choosers, huh?"

"You'd never be anything but what you are, a princess whose demands must always be met."

His over-the-top statements kept leaving her breathless, her lips tingling with the need to taste them at the origin.

But she still had to make sure of one thing. "If my requests are that important to you, promise you won't go overboard. Just do enough to set me free, and hopefully set Zafrana back on the road to economic independence. I don't want any fallout to hit my father or Zafrana. Or Saraya."

He inclined his magnificent head, making her again wish he'd release his raven's-wing silk from its imprisoning band. "I promise I will be surgical. My excisions will leave the whole region healthier. Just for you."

Breath left her on a choppy exhalation. "You're really going to do this." She shook her head dazedly. "Wow... just give me a second to get my head around all of this."

"Take all the time you need." He did this heart-melting gesture again, reaching for a lock of her hair and rubbing it in utmost enjoyment between his fingers. "But you can start celebrating your restored freedom right now."

Moved to the brink of tears, she squeezed her eyes shut.

When she finally opened them, they'd filled her eyes, soaked her voice. "I need to apologize."

He frowned. "Never apologize, not to me. But what do you think you should apologize for?"

"For what I thought when I first thought of asking you for this."

"What did you think?"

"That you'd never do anything out of the goodness of your heart. That you don't have one."

A mirthless huff escaped him. "You were right. I don't have one. Not in any humanly accepted sense."

"From where I'm sitting, you have something better. I thought you'd never do anything for anyone without something of equal or more value in it for you, and I was wrong."

"Maybe you should withdraw your apology. Since you weren't wrong. I do want something."

Her heart forgot to beat. "You do?"

"Yes." He held her gaze in the snare of his. "An heir."

Three

"An heir."

Jen heard her voice as if coming from someone else. Reaching her ears from the end of a vortex of incomprehension.

The hypnosis in Numair's gaze only intensified, as if he was compelling her to say what he wanted her to say.

Good luck with that. It was a miracle she'd been able to produce sound at all, to parrot him. After the agitated excitement of meeting him, the soaring hope that he'd restore her freedom, the release of all tension when she'd made sure he would, it hadn't shocked her when he'd said that he had a price. What had flabbergasted her was the price itself. She couldn't even process it.

He couldn't have *really* said... "An heir?"

At her croaking question, without any change in his expression, he inclined his head. "Yes. An heir you'll give me."

Ya Ullah, he'd said it again. And this time he left no doubt who would provide him with said heir.

The expansive room started spinning, and the sick sensations that earlier had her in their grip crashed back on her. She pressed her head into the headrest, as if to stop the churning. "You're not joking."

"I've never been more serious."

Feeling as if she'd fallen into a trap, nausea almost blinded her. "Why are you doing this?"

In response, he covered the space between them. Before she could think of scooting away, she found herself half draped over his great body, stunned by his sheer strength.

"Doing what?" His whisper fanned her face, and the fragrant, virile scent of his breath and flesh only made the room spin harder. She tried to fidget out of his embrace, but he had her head cradled in the nook of his arm, supported by his muscle-laden shoulder, and her face tilted to look up at him. "Being truthful about what I want? I thought you appreciated total honesty."

"When did you decide you wanted it?" she whispered. "You can't have come up with it when I asked you to help me." She tried to shake her head and only felt the world spin again. He secured her tighter and her queasiness quieted. She moaned, in relief this time. "I thought you would have a price, but I never thought it could be something like that."

"What did you think it would be? Yourself?"

Now that he'd said it out loud, it felt presumptuous for the idea to have crossed her mind. But given his apparent interest in her, it had been the only thing she could think of.

She'd thought the most he'd want would be a short affair, maybe only while he passed through New York this time. But she wouldn't have considered that a price. It would have been a reward to be with the first and only man she'd wanted breathlessly on sight. In any other circumstances, she would have given anything to be with him, no matter how fleetingly. To have both him and her freedom would have been the most incredible opportunity of her life.

But it was clear she'd read the situation all wrong. No, she couldn't read it at all.

This was totally incomprehensible.

A gentle finger below her chin tilted her face up to him, his brooding gaze capturing her wandering eyes. "I never bargain for sexual favors, and I certainly would never take advantage of a woman's need in any other way."

Now that he put it that way, she again felt silly for thinking what she had. This was a man who must have his pick of the rare beauties and celebrities of the world, and there was no way he'd ever paid for his pleasures. She couldn't see a woman alive who wouldn't react to him like she had, wouldn't want him at any cost.

He went on. "I also never stomached passing liaisons, but I never had any desire for anything more. My life revolved around work and amassing wealth and power. Those were everything I wanted for as long as I can remember. Then recently, everything changed."

Curiosity, and something poignant and more powerful— empathy—dragged her out of her confused dismay.

Had he suffered some recent life-changing crisis that made him take stock of his life, forced him to reassess his lifestyle?

She realized he was waiting for her to ask before he elaborated. So she forced her constricted throat to release the question. "What happened?"

"I hit forty, and it made me feel I need to rearrange my priorities and adjust my path. It never bothered me before that I have no family, and no one to leave my fortune and legacy to. Now it does."

She gaped at him. This was again the last thing she'd expected he'd say. She'd expected a reason as unique and earth-shattering as he was. He was the last person on earth she would have believed could have a midlife crisis.

Maybe she'd read him wrong all along. Just like she'd been way off the mark in assessing what he'd want in return for helping her. But she still could think of no reason that he'd want an heir from her, of all women.

She put her bewilderment into words. "So you decided to join the human race after a lifetime of just dominating it. But now you feel the urge to perpetuate your genes. If you make your desire known, women would form lines spanning the globe for a chance to be the one to give you your heir."

"I *am* making my desire known. To the only woman I ever considered for the role."

Her confusion deepened. "Why would you consider me at all, let alone have me on a short list of one?"

"To borrow your earlier words, you're kidding, right?"

"To borrow yours, I've never been more serious."

He caught her chin between those powerful, roughened fingers. "How can you be? You're here with me—" he gathered her tighter against his incredible heat and hardness, making her senses whirl harder, her every muscle liquefy even more "—in my arms, within an hour of meeting. You would have been there within minutes had we been in different circumstances. The attraction between us combusted the moment I stepped into that ballroom, and it's been raging higher ever since."

She still couldn't believe she affected him as intensely as he did her. Even if she did, that wasn't an acceptable explanation. "I can understand this would make you want me in your bed—"

He interrupted her. "And you would have considered that a fair price in return for my services?"

"Your *services* would have been circumstantial, since

I would have come to your bed anyway, if you wanted me there."

At her admission, his eyes simmered with a triumphant glow. Which was weird, really. Didn't he already know any woman would throw herself at his feet, if only he would let her?

But it was clear her words didn't only please him, they stoked his lust. The heat emanating from him rose, igniting her own higher, and the hardness below her became a steel shaft of discomfort digging into her thigh. Her core throbbed with an empty ache she'd only ever felt since he'd touched her.

She wanted to wind herself around him, to tell him to forget everything—her need for his *services* and his for an heir—and act on the need burning them up.

Instead, she said, "As I was saying, even if you wanted me on sight, that still doesn't translate to considering me for the role of mother of your heir. From my vast experience with the obscenely rich and powerful, sexual desire is not even among the prerequisites in choosing who to procreate with. I'm sure a man like you has strict criteria for said role, and countless other women who're better candidates for it than me."

"I may be obscenely rich and powerful, but I already told you I care nothing about anyone's rules. I make and follow my own." Sensual appreciation weighed down his lids, filled his lips as his hand painted her from shoulders to buttocks in luxurious caresses. "But I do have extremely strict criteria in the mother of my heir. That's why only you will do."

"Why? Do I somehow fulfill more criteria than others?"

"You fulfill every single one, and others I didn't even have till I met you." He cupped her cheek hungrily, his gaze devouring her. "I want my heir to be born of the perfect woman."

This made her snort. "Boy, are you barking up the wrong woman. I'm so far from perfect I'm in another galaxy."

His fingers sank into her hair, gave a pleasurable tug at her nape. "You are perfect to me. Just like I, with all of my glaring flaws, am perfect to you."

Her snort was more indelicate this time. "What glaring flaws? You *are* perfect, and would be so in anyone's eyes."

"Would I? That's news to me, since both allies and foes consider me a monster." Before she could object, he pressed on. "From what you know of the business world, you must know what it took to rise to my current status and to maintain it. You know I must be ruthless and remorseless, and that I don't give a damn what the world thinks of me, and that nothing is beyond me. From our interactions so far, you must realize I'm dangerous, even deadly, and I can destroy anyone I decide deserves it, even kill them, without turning a hair."

She stared at him. He'd put everything she'd felt about him in her bones into words. Everything that made him even more perfect to her.

She nodded slowly. "Instinctively, and logically, I know you're all that."

His lips spread in satisfaction. "All that makes me the opposite of perfect to everyone. Except for my partners, I'm someone to dread, or at most to appease, either in the hope of winning my favor or avoiding my danger. As for the women who pursue me, most risk it for the lure of said obscene power and wealth, and a few for the misguided fantasy of attempting to tame the most dangerous predator there is. But all fear me, and none trust me." His arms squeezed her tighter into his containment, his eyes growing more possessive. "You're the only one to ever see me for what I am, scales and claws and fangs and all, and instead of putting you off, everything about me is exactly what appeals to you. As you say in your region, I'm the one to *yemla ainek*—the one to 'fill your eye.'"

It was as if he was reading her mind. More, her deepest, most private beliefs and yearnings.

Again she nodded, not even thinking of contesting his verdict. "I left naiveté and idealism behind when I was seven, grew up in the cutthroat worlds of highest-level politics and business. I've long since learned that the best men need to have a lot of monster in them to be merciless enough to make the painful decisions, cunning enough to beat evil at its game, strong enough to enforce harsh changes for the better and resilient enough to be the one left standing after a war and doing as much good as possible in this crazy world."

His eyes darkened with her every word, until those fathomless black pupils engulfed the glowing emerald. She felt as if she was watching a panther in the seconds before he pounced. And she couldn't wait for him to. Even when she knew she might not survive his ferocity.

Then he did. Growling deep in his gut like his namesake, he brought her fully over him, making her feel she was no more than a twenty-pound baby. It should have been terrifying to realize just how much stronger than her he was. But his roughness was infused with such care, it only sent all her senses soaring.

She tumbled over him, the skirt of her dress riding up as he splayed her thighs wide, had her straddling him. The moment she felt him fully against her, between her legs, she almost fainted with the spike of arousal. Then his lips opened over her neck, and she did swoon. Her head fell back, giving him fuller access, surrendering to his pleasuring.

She needed this, needed him, come what may.

"You feel and taste even better than I imagined. Jenan…"

She jerked as if at the sting of a lash when he said her

name. She'd never liked her full name. Now it inflamed her to hear it on his lips, in that voracious growl. But he was sending her out of her mind with everything he did. The way he moved against her, breathed her in, touched and kneaded and suckled her... It was all too much.

And too little. She needed more. Everything. His mouth and hands all over her, his potency inside her.

"Numair..."

At hearing her moaning his name, the same desperation she felt reverberating inside her seemed to emanate from his body in shock waves. Then he swept her around and brought her under him on the couch, then bore down on her.

The world disappeared again, nothing remaining in her awareness but his greed and urgency and lust dominating her.

Spreading her thighs around his hips, he pressed between them, his hardness grinding against her entrance through their clothes. Her back arched deeply to accommodate him, a cry tearing from her very recesses at the feel of him, the sight of him above her.

"Jenan." His growl sounded pained as he surveyed her for one last second. Then his lips claimed hers, branding them. She opened wide to his invasion, and his tongue thrust deep, singeing her with pleasure, breaching her with need, draining her of reason.

Pressure built—behind her eyes, inside her chest, deep in her loins. Her hands convulsed on his arms, digging into his muscles, everything inside her surging, gushing, needing anything and everything he'd do to her. His fingers and tongue and teeth exploiting her every secret, his manhood filling that distressing void he'd created inside her...

Something buzzed against her thigh, made her lurch beneath him. After moments it stopped. Then it started again until it finally made him stiffen above her. Then he was cursing viciously as he rose off her.

The moment she lost his anchoring, she whimpered. His tempestuous glance told her he was feeling exactly the same. Wild with hunger and frustration.

He whipped out his phone in barely controlled fury. He only bit off a few phrases before ending the call. She vaguely understood it was one of his Black Castle partners. It figured only one of them would warrant Numair interrupting their first kiss.

As she finished the thought, she found herself snickering. First kiss indeed. First ravishing more like.

Numair's grimace filled with mock reproach and a too-real self-deprecation as he surveyed her still boneless condition. "I'm glad one of us is not in agony, and can still laugh."

"I'm not laughing… I'm snickering."

His huff sounded genuinely amused, not to mention surprised. "Thanks for the correction. Care to share the source of your merriment? I can use something to take my mind off the urge to hunt Antonio down for interrupting us. Or to pounce back on you and finish what I started."

Before she blurted out for him to just do the latter, she remembered they'd been in the middle of a game-changing conversation. And they hadn't reached a resolution yet. There might not be even one to reach.

Dismay finally made her pull herself up from her flagrant surrender. Numair remained towering over her as she sat up, like some all-powerful genie from a fable. The searing sensuality of his scowl made it almost impossible for her not to pull him back over her. Only the "heir" thing stopped her.

Before she could reintroduce the subject, Numair suddenly came down beside her again and, with shocking ease, pulled her back onto his lap.

After sealing her gasping lips in a kiss that robbed her of volition, he pulled back, his eyes smoldering, explicit with what he'd do to her once she stopped arguing.

"Do you still have any questions why I chose you?" He took a hand to his lips, nibbled on it in lieu of her mouth and had her gasping and squirming in pleasure. "It's because I don't want my heir to only be born of the perfect woman, but of perfect pleasure. And it is perfection between us. The way we make each other feel is magical. And I will accept nothing less. I will have nothing else."

She had no more arguments about that. It was magic. At least for her. But if he said it was the same for him, she had to believe him. He had no reason to lie or even exaggerate.

Almost all men in her experience had reason to do both. They thought all desert kingdoms swam in oil money, didn't believe her when she'd said Zafrana didn't. Even those who did believe her still thought she was talking relative poverty in the millions instead of billions. She'd had too many imposters try to land the loaded princess they'd thought she was. Her ex had been one of those.

But Numair was far richer and more powerful than her whole kingdom put together, with Saraya thrown in for good measure. She could only believe what he said, and that the desire he displayed was 100 percent real.

But he'd spoiled it all with that heir talk.

He was now suckling her fingers, each pull a stab of pleasure in her core. It was almost painful to stop him, to relinquish the delight, but she had to make him realize how preposterous she found his demand.

"Numair...I do want you, completely, even mindlessly." He growled and pressed her harder into his erection, dragging another moan from her depths. "But no matter how much I want you, I can't act on my desire when I know your sole purpose of sleeping with me is so I'd give you a baby."

He gave the finger he'd been suckling a sharp nip, heightening her distress. "It's far from my sole purpose. It's actually the product of my *only* purpose now. Untold pleasure. Which I will give, and take, as often as you can stand."

She squirmed over his lap, making both their conditions worse. "What if it turned out to be a disappointment instead? What if all those initial fireworks fizzled out, and we turned out to be incompatible in bed?"

His lip curl was dismissal itself. "We will be incendiary. The moment you say yes, I'll demonstrate."

Feeling squeezed into a tighter corner as his every word decimated her arguments, she still asked, "When you say heir, you mean a male child, right? What if I agree to your insane proposition, and I get pregnant with a girl? Or I can't get pregnant? Or you can't father children?"

His smile became more forbearing, as if he considered her what-ifs ridiculous, and her adorable as she worked herself up in a lather.

"Finished enumerating your worst-case scenarios?" He shrugged a shoulder, making everything she'd said irrelevant. "You only have to say yes and I'll take care of the rest."

She had to laugh. "I did think you were a god when I laid eyes on you, but you clearly think you are literally one, if you think you can make fate bow to your desires like that."

He gave another nonchalant shrug. "I always create my fate to my specifications. As I'm doing right now. I recognized you as the one tailored to my every need and demand. Once I have you, I'll fulfill every major milestone I have left in my life's master plan."

That made her sit up on his lap. "Okay, time out. I know you're master of all you survey and all, but even you must know how crazy you just sounded. I hate to break it to you, but there is stuff in life that is outside your control."

"We can and do control our destinies. You can either relinquish control over yours by considering others who'd never truly appreciate your sacrifice or even fully benefit from it, or you can say yes to me and take control of your fate."

"How would being an instrument in *your* so-called master plan make me mistress of my own fate?"

"Because contrary to everyone else in your life, I will never threaten your autonomy. At your demand, I will only boost your powers, support your plans and remove obstacles from your path. You will *choose* to say yes to me, because you'll weigh all pros and cons, and the pros will crash heavily in my favor. Once you do, we'll become lovers. I'll give you anything you've ever wished for, in and out of bed."

"When you say pros and cons, getting rid of Hassan is among the pros, right? You *are* making this quid pro quo."

"No. I promised I'd rid you and Zafrana of Hassan, and I will, no matter what happens between us. You can immediately tell your father you've found a solution for all your problems and are sending Hassan to hell." He nibbled the fleshy side of her hand, and she involuntarily pressed harder into him in response. "You will become my lover and bear my heir because of a dozen other reasons, all borne of your free will. The foremost one is because you can't wait to be in my bed, taken and mastered, serviced and pleasured."

He punctuated his last words with suckles and nips that had every cell in her body clamoring for everything he'd just tantalized her with.

"What free will?" she moaned, deep and long. "*Ya Ullah*, Numair, now I know what it feels like to be swept along on a deluge. You *are* one."

"I will sweep you into a realm neither of us has ever entered, one of pure pleasure. Then when you become pregnant, we'll marry."

She choked. She coughed until she felt as if her life force would be expelled. As Numair realized her distress, his efforts to end her paroxysm only made things worse.

When the shock-induced attack finally came to an end, she looked up at him through eyes that felt inflamed. "Why can't you be like other men and just do the obvious thing? I ask you for a huge favor, and you ask for one in return and be done with it? You had to go demand an heir, and now marriage? Who said marriage was an option at all?"

His face became implacable. "I do. And it wouldn't be an option. It would be a must."

This made her push out of his arms, needing to put some breathable space between them. "Thanks, but no thanks. I was married once, and it isn't for me. The most I fantasized about was a hot affair with a sex god who had the power to get my kingdom out of its worst historical bind. I'm not up for becoming a wife. Certainly not to a man who, when all is said and done, considers me the best specimen to procreate with."

His lips pursed disapprovingly as he watched her scooting away from him. "Apart from the blatant inaccuracy of this last statement, you've already discussed having a child with me, which means you were considering it. What did you expect you would do once you were carrying my child? That you'd have it in secret, give it to me and disappear? Or that you'd have it out of wedlock, a princess from your region of all places? Or did you think you'd have it here and cut all ties with your kingdom? And where did you figure I'd be in all this? On the sidelines, content to see my child once every blue moon? Sending checks and not taking any role in its upbringing?" Before she could think of a response to his barrage, he declared, "We *will* get married as soon as you become pregnant."

Bombarded by his inexorable will, she felt as if she'd choke again. Before she succumbed once more, she fumbled for the purse she'd dropped on the coffee table, then stood up unsteadily.

Once she'd taken a few air-filled steps away from him, she said, "I need time to think."

Then, on trembling legs, she strode out. He let her walk away.

As she opened the main door of the suite, she almost crumpled to the ground with fright when he caught her back.

She could *swear* she'd walked here all alone!

As he turned her, she started spluttering, "How...?"

He drowned her in a kiss that ended any possibility for independent thought or movement.

It was him who finally released her, only the storms in his eyes betraying his state of emotional and physical arousal.

Before he let her spill out the door, he said, "I'm giving you till tomorrow evening, then I will send my right hand for you. Tomorrow night, you sleep in my arms."

Four

Numair watched Jenan receding down the corridor as if she was escaping a widening chasm.

Every step taking her away from him had him vibrating with dread that he'd just committed the biggest mistakes of his life. Letting her go, and before that, introducing the subject of heir and marriage so prematurely.

What if, in spite of the unstoppable desire that had exploded into existence between them, he'd come on too strong, and she'd run away thinking it the better fate to marry Hassan, a man she'd find far easier to handle?

Expending the last of what he'd previously thought was limitless willpower, he squashed the urge to stalk her, haul her back inside, lock every door and simply overpower her reluctance and misgivings. He might have decreed he'd take her tomorrow night, but everything in him was roaring for him to claim her right now.

But he'd already cornered himself, making it impossible

to do anything but watch her go. Anything he did now to override her would only make things worse.

He didn't recognize himself in this condition, as he'd never been almost out of control. He'd never been unable to project the consequences of his actions, had never acted on impulse or taken a step without premeditation. His brothers had always said he was the epitome of what it meant to be Machiavellian.

But everything he'd done since he'd seen Jenan hadn't even been actions but reactions, all unpremeditated and uncalculated. He was suffering from something he'd never experienced. A form of insanity.

And it was because of her. Jenan. He was beginning to think she was truly her name. At least one meaning of it.

The meaning he was sure her parents had meant was the plural of *jennah*—garden, what the ancients called paradise. That meaning was apt, too. But it was the colloquial meaning of the word that was relevant to his condition, what he now suspected she could induce. Madness.

But even in his state, he wasn't so far gone he didn't realize she was returning to her Tribeca apartment in lower Manhattan alone. Whether by cab or her own car, it was still a fifteen-minute drive and it was now—he flicked a glance at his watch—2:00 a.m. Time had really flown with her.

But it would compound his self-sabotaging behavior to follow her now. To ensure her safety without further damages, he would have to settle for having her followed.

The moment she disappeared around the corner, he whipped out his phone, called Ameen, sent him a photo of her from the digital file he had on her, ordered him to tail her home then report to him.

Afterward, he stared at the photo. It superficially resembled the woman he'd spent the past six hours with. It was like a lookalike, the mask she presented to the world, hiding her true nature. The charisma that leaped in her eyes, the wit and whimsy that played on her lips and the sheer impact she'd had on his senses in reality were absent. Even so, heat spread inside him just looking at the photo, when before meeting her, he'd surveyed it with the utmost clinical coldness.

Finally closing the door, he went back inside, homing in on the spot where he'd almost made love to her.

Sitting down, he caressed the place where she'd sat, feeling her warmth, even when there was no way it was still detectable. But then her feel was imprinted on his hands, permeating his senses. Her breath still filled his lungs, and her taste still tingled on his tongue.

Jenan. Mind-twisting, will-warping madness.

He'd wanted to possess her every second of the hours he'd spent with her. But he'd managed to hold back, to do what he'd thought more vital—negotiate the terms of future, limitless intimacies. Then she'd revealed her convictions, so serious and unwavering as she lay soft and surrendering in his embrace. She'd exposed the indomitable realist who'd smashed cultural and gender restraints, who didn't have a smidge of silliness or squeamishness in her expectations, who'd taken on the world and won.

Everything she was explained why she'd hit him that hard. The infallible instincts that had steered him throughout a nightmarish existence, had made him not only survive but triumph over everything and everyone, had recognized her. She had been made to understand him, to withstand him, to appreciate the monster inside him when it sent everyone else cowering.

Rationing his response had ceased to be an option.

He would have taken her, and she would have let him if not for the interruption. Now frustration ate through him. Not that having her would have quenched this blazing need. It would have only left him hungrier for her. He'd never known such ferocious desire existed, or that he of all people could be victim to it. But everything with her had been the most exhilarating thing that had ever happened to him. The attraction that had arced between them had been the most invigorating thing he'd ever experienced.

It was also the most dangerous.

It had messed up his fine-tuned conquering methods, pulverized his impregnable rules. It had reduced him to a reactive, starving man who didn't follow plans and didn't have brakes. He'd never once considered the possibility that he wouldn't get everything he wanted. He'd always gotten his every planned result because he'd never cared what anyone thought of him. People had always been most welcome to hate or despise him as long as they bowed to him. How they bowed had never been a concern. In fact, he'd always preferred to force them to their knees.

But he couldn't afford—no, couldn't *contemplate*— that Jenan would feel any aversion, or even reluctance toward him. He had to have her early eagerness back. He had to have that total trust and admiration lighting up her face again.

He had to have *her*.

And to think he'd come tonight bent on systematically seducing Khalil Aal Ghamdi's daughter to obtain his vital heir. But what he'd planned in cold blood had turned into a consuming need. Now instead of gritting his teeth and mating with a woman he'd been certain wouldn't arouse his most basic urge, he would burn in the raging flames of his desire for Jenan. If their brief time of delirium was anything to go by, he was in for the untold pleasure he'd promised her. More. He was in for the first true pleasure of his life.

If only Antonio hadn't called when he had. He would have been inside her now, taking her to the first peak of many. But it was a paramount rule of the Black Castle brotherhood, a rule *he'd* made, to immediately respond to any communication from a brother. With their lethal pasts and perilous presents, no one knew when it might be a matter of life or death.

But Antonio hadn't been in danger. For some reason he didn't give a damn about, he'd picked then of all times to recommend a few more hypnotherapy sessions for Numair.

Cursing vehemently, he reached for his phone, then paused. Though Antonio had called him barely half an hour ago, he could now be asleep.

Once their brotherhood's field surgeon in their years as the slaves of The Organization, Antonio had become Black Castle Enterprise's resident medical genius, the creator and director of their avant-garde and booming medical R&D business, and a surgeon who was one of the world's most brilliant and unorthodox. He kept hours as extreme and unpredictable as everything about him. He was also known to sleep at will, to charge his batteries whenever possible for the grueling days he maintained in his lab, the OR and the boardroom. Numair had seen him fall asleep sitting up, in under thirty seconds. It was very possible he'd fallen asleep immediately after his fateful phone call.

But so what? He hoped Antonio was in deep, blissful sleep after months of severe deprivation, or on the verge of orgasm with a woman he'd been panting after for years. He'd love to return the favor.

He almost drove his finger through Antonio's speed-dial number. By the third ring, Numair was ready to storm out, raid Antonio's Fifth Avenue penthouse and punch him awake.

Then the line clicked open, and Antonio's calmly teasing voice came on. "I thought you wanted to kill me when I called earlier."

"I did," Numair bit off. "I still do."

"I interrupted something major, huh?"

"You interrupted *the* major something. And you weren't even dying."

"So this is a courtesy call for our history's sake, before you come make sure I rectify my oversight?"

Any man would have been worried if he'd inadvertently cost Numair what Antonio had tonight. But having faced death on an almost daily basis together, and defended each other with their lives for over fifteen years, Antonio had reason not to fear Numair's retaliation. Not that he feared anything. Antonio was the most imperturbable being who'd ever lived. Even more than any of them. Numair wouldn't be surprised if his nerves were made of actual steel.

He finally asked, "Why the hell did you call, Bones?"

"I told you why, Phantom."

They always reverted to those code names, what they'd known each other by in The Organization. Those who remembered their names had been forbidden to use them. Numair hadn't remembered his, Phantom being the one name he'd known most of his life.

He'd been among hundreds of boys who'd been plucked from all over the world and taken to that isolated installation in the Balkans and turned into mercenaries. He'd been too young when he'd been taken but had still been "broken in," punished if he mentioned anything from his previous life. He'd first been conditioned to respond to a number. The name Phantom had come much later. He'd forgotten everything about his past. All that had remained of his memories before he'd come to what he'd later called Black Castle had been the name of his panther toy, Numair, and what he'd much later realized were the names of desert kingdoms, Saraya and Zafrana. And the memory of drowning.

He'd spent over twenty-five years of his forty in Black Castle before he'd orchestrated his and his brothers' escape ten years ago. He'd spent most of those in frustration, unable to build an investigation into his origins on the sparse memories he had. Not knowing who he was had remained a gaping hole in his being.

Then Antonio had finally developed a method of aggressive hypnosis tailored to Numair's condition and character. He'd thought it would be effective, but warned it could be dangerous. But Numair would have risked anything to find out the truth. He'd been certain someone had been responsible for his decades-long ordeal, and he wouldn't rest until he'd found them and made them pay.

Antonio's efforts had seemed to be another dead end, but he'd already expected that initial failure, since Numair was resistant to hypnosis. He'd never expected it to be anything but a long-term therapy as they'd been excavating memories Numair had before he'd been four.

But long-term was what Numair was all about. He'd started planning his escape from The Organization when he hadn't even been ten. He'd put it into action twenty years later.

In captivity, Numair had grown up fast, toughening into steel and developing an undetectable cunning that had enabled him to navigate his ruthless environment and manipulate his monstrous jailors. By ten he'd already carved a place for himself as the establishment's most valuable acquisition and future asset. Based on his uncanny abilities in every skill it took to make the best spy, they'd changed his name from a four-digit number to Phantom, beginning a trend of calling boys by names that symbolized them.

But he'd known he wouldn't be able to escape alone. He had to have help. And in turn, help others escape. Recognizing six boys, all younger than himself, as kindred spirits who had superior abilities complementing his own, he'd manipulated their captors into making them his team. He'd made each swear a blood oath to live for their brotherhood and for one goal—to one day escape and destroy The Organization, saving other children from their fate.

They had implemented his convoluted plan, and after they'd escaped, they'd built new identities and created Black Castle Enterprises, using their unique skills. That was, all but Cypher. He'd left their brotherhood after an explosive falling out. He'd pledged they'd never see him again. They hadn't.

Though Cypher's loss remained an open wound in their brotherhood, they'd compensated by focusing on their original pact, dismantling The Organization from the outside in, methodically and undetectably.

Meanwhile, each also pursued his personal quest, for the family he'd been taken from, the heritage he'd been stripped of or for a new purpose and direction. Their bigger quest was sometimes forced to the background until more pressing personal issues were resolved, as it had during Rafael's quest for vengeance and Raiden's quest to reclaim his heritage. Both men had achieved their purposes, and unexpectedly found wives, too. Now it was his turn.

Four months ago, Antonio's hypnosis had borne fruit, and he'd remembered enough to finally piece together his history. He'd found out how he'd ended up in The Organization's grasp. And who he really was.

So what had the damned Antonio been thinking when he'd called earlier?

He again flayed Antonio with his exasperation. "Why in hell did you suddenly think I need more sessions? Their objective has already been achieved."

Antonio switched to doctor mode, this frustrating, all-knowing attitude. "That's what you decided, not me. Your memories were so deeply buried and so partially formed in the first place, then so fractured by trauma and suppression, I was forced to pull back constantly. I had to spread out the sessions, dig over a longer period or risk damaging your psyche and sanity."

That was news to Numair. "You mean you could have forced memories to the surface faster? You took all those years intentionally?"

"Didn't you hear the part where I said *or risk damaging your psyche and sanity*?"

"You actually think I have anything inside my head that could be damaged?"

"As my mentor and slave driver, I would have said your head is made of solid steel. But as your doctor, I've touched a few deeply hidden and relatively softer spots. The consistency of rock, granted, but under enough pressure even steel can snap and rock can be pulverized."

"Where is this leading exactly?"

"You remember—no pun intended—the key memory that was the basis of your investigations into your origins?"

He remembered nothing more. Once the memory had exploded in his mind, he'd felt as if he'd been reliving it. It had been so real he'd almost drowned before Antonio had pulled him out of the hypnotic state.

That memory was of him on a yacht with his father when men, who looked like monsters in his memories, had boarded them. His father had been struck unconscious then thrown overboard. Numair had no doubt he'd drowned immediately. Then the men had tossed him after his father.

He should have drowned, too. And he'd always remembered the sensations of drowning, what had spawned an unreasoning hatred of swimming, even as he'd been forced to excel in it. More probing had unearthed memories of swimming lessons since he'd been born. Investigations had revealed he'd managed to swim to shore in Turkey, where he'd been taken to an orphanage. Over a year later, an Organization recruiter had taken him. And his real ordeal had begun.

Analyzing the history of the whole region at the time, he'd found out that his father had been Hisham Aal Ghaanem, the then Crown Prince of Saraya. And he'd been his father's heir. He'd concluded that his father's assassination had been orchestrated by his brother, Saraya's current king, Hassan. Getting rid of him, too, had spared his uncle from being only regent until he came of age.

"I'd like to revisit that memory."

Antonio's demand ended his musings. "Why?"

"Humor me."

"No."

"Just no?"

"Yes, as long as you won't give me a reason beside wanting to strap me down and poke around in my head again."

"As if I want to poke around that dungeon you call a head. It's filled with rotting corpses and dismembered remains."

"As if your head isn't."

"It's my head, so I have to live with it. Infesting it with the contents of your far more nightmarish skull is up there in my priorities with contracting an incurable STD." Numair started to growl, and Antonio raised his voice, drowning his. "But I feel there are more fragments still stuck in there, like shrapnel. I'm worried if they surface on their own they'd cause uncharted damage. Before you scoff, just imagine yourself with the balance that keeps you precariously on the side of the angels shattered. With your power and intellect, you'd be a full-blown monster. So I'm really worried about the world here."

Numair hated to admit it, but in The Organization, he'd seen the kind of widespread mayhem caused by those who'd been irrevocably damaged by his kind of life— even when they were nowhere near his caliber.

He exhaled. "What memories could be more damaging than remembering my father's murder and my own near drowning?"

"I don't know. But I've been reviewing the videos and notes of our last sessions, and I'm convinced what you now know isn't the whole story."

"It's the relevant part of it."

"Why are you being so pigheaded? I thought you want to find everything about your past."

"I know enough."

It was Antonio's turn to exhale in exasperation. "As long as you understand you're ignoring my medical recommendation. And you run the risk of having those memories resurface and tear through whatever is keeping you from going berserk."

"I understand. Anything else?"

Antonio's huff was self-deprecating. "I should have implanted a posthypnotic suggestion in that impenetrable skull of yours when I had the chance."

"But you didn't." He infused his voice with the older brother's and leader's criticism his brothers had grown up with. "I always said your moral afflictions stop you from maximizing your opportunities."

"Yeah." Antonio sounded vexed, then he suddenly brightened. "But I can always hit you with a tranq dart and have my way with you."

"As if I wouldn't see you coming a mile away."

Antonio chuckled. "Go ahead, underestimate me. I'll have you on my table again yet, Phantom."

"Dream on, Bones."

Then as it was their way, with the conversation over, they just terminated the call with no lingering goodbyes.

Afterward, he sat there staring ahead, his conversation with Antonio forgotten, his mind again full of Jenan and how he'd come to meet her.

She was part of the other side of his heritage. His mother

was Safeyah Aal Ghamdi, a princess of the royal family in Zafrana, a cousin of the late king, Zayd Aal Ghamdi, and Jenan's distant relative. His mother had left the region after her husband and son had been presumed dead thirty-seven years ago and had never come back. She'd never remarried, and had died four years ago in England.

Then when Zafrana's king had died twenty-two years ago, the throne had gone to his closest male relative, his cousin Khalil, Jenan's father.

His plan coming here had been simple. To reclaim his heritage, and punish the monster who'd murdered his father and caused Numair to rot in hell for a quarter of a century.

He was still working on providing irrefutable proof of his identity. With his father being dead almost four decades, it was hard to find anything with his DNA. Proof positive was to find his remains, so he was scouring the Mediterranean where his father's yacht had sunk.

Once he found it, he'd reclaim his true identity. He didn't fear exposure, like Rafael Salazar, who'd been abducted from his parents. No one in The Organization knew who Numair really was, having obtained him as an anonymous child from an orphanage in a faraway country. And he'd make his story work perfectly with the meticulous history he'd created for his Numair Al Aswad persona.

Once he decided to announce his real identity, he'd reveal the part where he'd survived the assassination attempt. His story would diverge from the truth when he'd claim he'd been found by a fishing fleet on the shores of Damhoor, a neighboring kingdom to Saraya, and taken to an orphanage there. A couple who'd been working there had adopted him almost immediately, but had never announced it since adoption was forbidden there, taking him to the States as their biological son. They'd told him he was adopted only when he'd been in his late teens.

The other truth he'd say was that it had taken him all that time to investigate his origins.

Until he proved them, he planned to prepare the playing field. And to punish Hassan. Before he exposed him for the murderer he was and throw him in a dungeon for life, he'd first disgrace and destroy him a bit at a time. Everyone should be happy with that, since all monarchs in the region wished he'd abdicate the throne to one worthy of it. But that wouldn't be Hassan's crown prince and his cousin, the much-loved Najeeb, but Numair himself.

If his cousins contested his right to the throne, which he fully expected they would, he had the power to curb them and any allies whose help they enlisted, and the finances to buy them all a few times over. If not, he could escalate to whatever level of conflict it took to make them bow down to him. He had no problem taking the throne in a coup. Or starting a war to claim what was his. It wouldn't be the first time he'd instigated an armed conflict.

The other part of his plan had been to claim the other side of his heritage.

He'd come here bound on taking Zafrana's throne, too, and saving his other homeland from its inept king. The only way to do this was through blood. Khalil's blood. Through one of his daughters. Jenan had been the obvious choice, since her half sisters were so young. Then Hassan had made a bid for her, unintentionally trying to beat him to Zafrana with his same plan.

That had posed little change in his plan. Instead of claiming Jenan directly, he had to pulverize Hassan's bid first. He'd intended to seduce her, impregnate her then marry her, becoming Zafrana's de facto ruler during Khalil's life through the marriage alliance. After Khalil's death, when the throne became his child's, he'd intended to rule as regent until his child came of age.

Then in mere hours, everything had changed. His one

objective was now Jenan. Not because she was strategic to his plans, but because he had to have her.

Now he feared his marauding ways had alienated her.

He heaved up to his feet, his every muscle bunched as if in preparation for the fight of his life.

Not having her wasn't an option. He wouldn't retreat and change his approach. He'd escalate his attack, besiege her, leave her nowhere to run and hide.

Tomorrow night, Jenan *would* be his.

"You are my hero!"

Jen winced as Zeena launched herself at her the moment she opened the door for her and Fayza the next morning.

Fayza, her ball-of-energy nineteen-year-old sister, zipped around her and inside her apartment, excitement radiating from her eyes and spilling from her lips. "When they realized you disappeared from your own engagement party, Father and Hassan almost had strokes. Father with worry and Hassan with outrage. It was *so* funny."

Though her sisters were in such good cheer, she still worried. "Is Father okay?"

"Yeah." Fayza threw herself down on Jen's huge floral couch in the living room. "His blood pressure is just through the roof."

Jen groaned at what Fayza considered okay. "*Ya Ullah,* Fay, the way you take nothing seriously will one day give *me* a stroke! Please tell me you gave him his medication!"

"Yeah, yeah." Fayza rolled her hands, in a hurry to attack the next topic. "I bet it didn't work until we called him on the way up here to tell you you're okay."

But she wasn't okay, might never be okay again.

Since she'd left Numair, she'd been unable to sleep or even sit, pacing holes in her wall-to-wall carpeting, her stomach eating itself with tension and hunger, yet unable to

tolerate even a sip of water. Every inch of her buzzed with
excess electricity, every nerve so taut she felt they'd snap.

"You know, sis…" Fayza stretched out, her knee-length
raven hair a sharp contrast to the pastel print sofa, her gold
eyes glittering with mischief, her face the very sight of
admiration and smugness. "We always thought you were
a wonder woman, but that stunt you pulled last night?
That qualifies you for an all-time record in sticking your
tongue out to our collective region, culture and history."
She guffawed, drummed her heels on the couch. "I would
have given anything to see Hassan's face the moment he
realized you'd just up and left." She jumped up onto her
knees as Jen approached, draped herself over the couch's
back like an inquisitive cat. "So what did you do instead
of attending that funeral? Caught a movie? Went roller-
skating? Or came back here, ordered pizza, watched Will
and Grace reruns and did your toenails?"

"She left with a hunk from some Arabian Nights fable."

Zeena's enthusiastic declaration was followed by total
silence as Fayza's irrepressible chatter came to an abrupt
end. For three seconds. Then she exploded.

"*What?* And you didn't tell me? Zee, I'll kill you!"

Jen grimaced at her sister's loudness as Zeena spluttered, "Tell you what? All I know is that this genie seemed
to appear out of nowhere, materialized beside Jen and then
poof, they were both gone."

Jen had to laugh. As ridiculous as that account was, it
sounded more plausible than what had actually happened.

Fayza turned excited eyes to Jen. "Spill!"

Knowing it was pointless to avoid their questions, Jen
told them everything, with some key elements left out. Like
Numair almost making love to her, and his pregnancy-to-
marriage demand.

It was late in the day before Zeena and Fayza left, during which they did order pizza, watched Will and Grace reruns and did their nails—hands and feet.

The two girls floated away, buoyed by delight that their big sister wouldn't barter herself for their kingdom's peace and economic salvation, and that a knight in shining armor had charged to her rescue.

Jen closed the door behind them, slumped against it and let the smile she'd pinned on for their benefit crumble. If only they knew her knight was a black-as-sin marauder, and as unstoppable as a hurricane...

Though she still couldn't bring herself to do as he'd demanded—tell her father everything would be taken care of—she did believe Numair when he'd said she didn't have to say yes to his proposition in return for his help. That wasn't why she was in such turmoil.

It was his demand itself. Becoming his lover, sleeping in his arms, sharing every intimacy sounded deliriously fantastic. Since he'd touched her, she'd been aching with need for him. She felt certain he was the man who'd show her what sex could really be like, what passion and satisfaction were.

Yet getting pregnant by him? It sounded terrifying.

But what was her alternative? She could continue to live alone, work, succeed, exercise, volunteer... Rinse and repeat. Sure, that was great, and it had been good enough—before him. But she'd had the hope that she'd one day find a man and fall in love, at least in lust. But now she knew no other man would ever compare to Numair. She'd never look at another man twice, let alone share her body with him. So if she didn't indulge her feminine urges with Numair, she'd have to put them in deep freeze for life. That sounded as horrible as a lifelong prison sentence. Living in hope, even if it never came to pass, was one thing; knowing there was no hope was another.

As for having a baby, she'd always thought she'd one

day have one. But since she'd given up on marriage, and no one had tempted her to have sex with him, she'd thought she'd seek out a donor. But after Numair, that didn't feel like an option anymore. Now that she knew he existed, that she could want a man that much, that he wanted her as fiercely, how could she contemplate having a child not born of this *perfection*, as he'd said?

To have a child with this wonder *would* be incredible. And once she got pregnant, if they married as he'd insisted, he'd certainly never be a needy, clingy, exploitative partner, like her ex had been, so she had nothing to worry about in that arena. He'd also promised he'd never smother her. Realistically speaking, with a man like him, who was so preoccupied with burdens the magnitude of which she probably couldn't imagine, the opposite would probably be true. He'd probably have little time for her, giving her all the space she needed and then some.

His ardor would probably cool off gradually, too. And hers as well, no doubt, especially with a child changing the essence of her existence. Once things settled, she'd end up having everything she had now, plus a child and the best possible partner in raising it.

Though Numair felt as if he was missing human components, she had a feeling he would make a good father. That protector vibe told her he would. She knew in her bones she'd be safe with him, and so would a child.

In fact, the more she thought of it, the more it sounded too good to be true. She couldn't even imagine why all this was happening to her, of all women. It sounded like too much of a coincidence, too much the answer to her every fantasy. Everything about him, everything he'd said and done, was the best thing she could have hoped for. So was it what it appeared to be? Or was there somehow more to it?

She had a thousand questions. And worries. This man was the most unfathomable quantity she'd ever met. She knew there was *far* more to him than even she could imagine. And for some reason she couldn't even begin to explain, she felt there was far more to this whole thing…

The bell rang right at her back. She jumped as if at a close-range gunshot, blasted out of her reverie.

Her eyes tore to the clock on the wall. It was 7:00 p.m. This had to be Numair's right-hand man.

Heart hammering, she squared her shoulders. She *would* go to Numair. To ask him to have a long, rational talk.

She'd ask her questions, demand her terms—her safeguards, more like. Once he'd given her satisfactory answers and they had a roadmap of sorts, she'd tear his clothes off and demand he show her no mercy.

Inhaling a bolstering breath, she opened the door with the smile she'd patented for strangers. The next second her lungs almost burst in shock.

Numair. On her doorstep.

Before she could draw another breath, she was swept up as if she was made of cotton candy, in arms that defined power, looking up into a face that was mastery incarnate.

Kicking the door closed behind him, he looked down at her with a voracity that turned her body from solid to molten. And that was before his deep, devouring words hit her.

"I realized I've been remiss. I spoke of the untold pleasure I have in store for you if you say yes, but gave you no true sample of my claims. I'm here to rectify my oversight."

Five

A high-pitched alarm kept clanging in the distance.

Jen vaguely recognized it was logic, reminding her that she hadn't asked her questions, stated her terms or obtained her safeguards.

She let it clamor, then tuned it out. Everything it was yelling about suddenly felt irrelevant. Anything would be when you were drowning. As she was. In Numair.

And he hadn't yet done anything but sweep her up in his arms and claim her lips. If she felt taken, possessed, devoured already, what would she feel like when he fully made love to her?

For the first time in her life, self-preservation wasn't her foremost consideration. She wanted him more than she wanted to be safe. It was insanity and she knew it. She never knowingly did insane stuff. But for him, she'd do anything. With him, she wanted everything.

Suddenly the world gave way beneath her, and she felt she was plummeting. He'd only put her back on her feet.

The only reason she didn't heap to the ground at his feet was because he kept one muscled arm around her waist. It tightened, pulling her against him fully, her toes barely touching the ground. She was totally in his power, loving it and delighting in every hard inch of him that was imprinting her trembling flesh. She moaned when his other hand rose to cup her cheek.

"I spent all night and all day in agony. Tell me you did, too." She could only nod, but her muteness seemed to satisfy him. "And as I suffered, I planned everything I'd do to you, all the ways I'd assuage the hunger, slowly, thoroughly."

She was all for *thoroughly*. But didn't know if she could withstand slowly. The plea to hurry and take her would have spilled from her lips if they weren't trembling out of control with anticipation.

He made it worse, rubbing his thumb against them, his breathing becoming audible, each draw into his endless chest chafing inside her own. "I never knew wanting like this, or anything like you, existed. I thought the ferocity of my desire scared you, that it sent you running away."

She forced words out. "It scared me how much *I* wanted you. I was terrified I was out of my mind."

"You were. As I was. As I still am. As I will remain." His thumb stilled. "Are you still afraid?"

She rubbed her lips against his hard flesh, begging him to continue. "Only that my heart might stop."

Triumph and lust blasted her as he pressed her harder into his length. "I *will* stop your heart. With pleasure."

She nodded, closed her eyes to savor the sensations that emanated from her deepest recesses. She moaned as she caught his tormenting thumb in a nip.

His sharp intake of breath sliced away more of the leashes of her inhibition. She grazed her teeth along his skin, the skin of a seasoned warrior, hardened in battle, scarred in ordeals, healed with limitless stamina and now impervious. She again wondered what kind of life he'd really led. As if tasting him would explain it to her, she suckled him, and his texture and taste only had more moist heat surging in her core.

A fiercer inhalation expanded his chest, crushing her swollen breasts against it. He rubbed against them until she felt they'd burst, the abrasion of his hardness and their clothes turning her nipples into pinpoints of agony. A scalding growl rumbled from his depths as he tugged her thigh around his hips, the hand at her waist securing her there as he ground his erection against her melting core.

She whimpered as he started thrusting against her, at the same time ravaging her neck in suckles she knew would leave their mark. Pleasure hurtled through her blood, making her lightheaded. Her knee buckled, and he picked her up, had her wrapping her other trembling leg around him, letting him have all her weight, making him crush her to him even tighter.

She felt as if her very existence depended on him, his body and breath, his hands and mouth, as he tasted her flesh and took over her will. She was no longer herself, but a mass of need open to him, his to exploit and plunder. There was nothing more to hear but his voracious growls and her thundering blood as he stroked her up and down his body, had her ride his erection through their clothing.

The throbbing between her legs escalated into pounding, and she cried out his name. His torment only increased until she nipped at his lip in her desperation.

"You've got it all wrong." His bass tone made her eyes snap open. "I'm the one who's going to feast on you tonight, wring your magnificent body of every pleasure it's capable of experiencing."

She nodded, her breathing becoming ragged, her lungs

starting to burn. She'd agree to anything he wanted to do to her.

He rested his forehead against hers. "This is unparalleled. Agonizing but sublime."

"Yes," she whispered.

Nothing she'd ever experienced had prepared her for this. For him. She was disintegrating with need, yet she knew this protracted inflammation of their senses would make his eventual lovemaking far more satisfying than a frenzied coupling would have been.

He separated from her, making her cry out again with his loss, but he did so only to press her against the wall. He slid down her body, then, in torturous slowness, rubbed up over her again as he bunched her stretchy dress on the way up. His visual embrace was only interrupted for the seconds it took to sweep the garment over her head.

He set every inch his lips and hands touched on fire before going to her bra's clasp, snapping it undone. She gasped as its constriction eased, then louder at the spike of ferocity in his gaze as he monitored her reaction. He drew more gasps as he caressed her bra loose, then in one silky sweep, he freed her from its bond.

Suddenly, shyness hit her out of nowhere. This man she'd met only last night was here, in her home, just inside her door, and he had her almost naked as he stood fully clothed. It was crazy. It was insanely arousing. And it was the best thing that had ever happened to her. And the most overwhelming.

Before she could snap her arms over her nakedness, he dropped to his knees.

Seeing him kneeling before her, looking up at her with what looked like wonder, her lips dropped open with unbearable stimulation, but no words came out.

It was him who talked. "I thought I knew what I'd find

beneath that dress you hid behind. I was wrong. You're a goddess, Jenan."

This made words of incredulity escape her. "Look who's talking."

"I'm done talking." He tugged her hard to him, rumbling, "Now I worship you."

She would have keeled over him if his shoulders hadn't stopped her forward pitch. He added to her imbalance as he fulfilled his pledge. She whimpered at each kneading of her buttocks, lurched with every tongue thrust into her navel, shook at each drag of teeth across her breasts. Her moans sharpened as he clamped her nipple, until a cry rushed out at his first hard suckle.

"Numair...*please*."

In answer, his thumbs hooked into the top of her panties, peeling them down her shaking legs.

In seconds she was standing in nothing but her sandals, her clothes discarded at her feet. Numair's eyes roamed her every inch as if he would gobble her up.

Everything spun. This was really happening. Numair was really here, and he had her naked. He would take her. And she would let him.

Let him? She wasn't begging him to only because she could barely breathe.

She watched him as if from another realm as his hands closed over each leg in turn and his lips melted down her flesh, kissing and fondling from foot to thigh. Her consciousness flickered like a bulb about to short out.

"The feel of you, the taste and scent of you are perfection, magic. Madness. *Enti jenan ann jadd*."

She gasped. He'd just spoken in her mother tongue. Said that she was truly madness. She'd always hated it when people attributed this meaning to her name. Which they did a lot, as they deemed most of her actions since she'd turned eighteen to be deranged. But the way he said it, the way he meant it… Like everything else, when it was from him, she loved it.

By the time he'd explored her every inch, she'd become a literal puddle. She could feel her arousal running down her thighs, could scent it, and she knew he saw and smelled it, too, from the wildness she felt emanating from him. Then something scalding rumbled from his depths, and he pressed her back, slid her up against the wall, opened her thighs and draped them over his shoulders.

Before she could register his intention, he nudged the lips of her femininity with his nose, rumbling again as he inhaled her deeply, and those rugged fingers caressed them apart, sliding through her molten need. She keened, lurched with jolts of sensation almost too much to bear. Oral sex had left her repulsed or numb before, but not now. With Numair she ached for it. As he dipped a long, powerful finger inside her, each slow inch made her feel how empty she'd been all her life. How only having him inside her would fill the void.

But she wanted *him*, and she tried to tell him by tightening her legs around his head, pulling his hair out of its confinement and dragging him up by it. He only opened her fully and burned her to the core in his ragged hunger.

She malfunctioned completely as his tongue and teeth scorched the heart of her femininity, slowly, thoroughly, as he'd promised. The sight of his magnificent head between her thighs, the knowledge of what he was doing to her was almost more incapacitating than the physical maelstrom.

Through the delirium, she watched him cosset her, strum her, drink her, revel in her need and pleasure. He seemed unable to have enough, and yet to know when she had.

"Now let me see how much I pleasure you."

Just by his demand, by the exact pressure and speed he seemed to know would unravel her, her body heaved in a chain reaction of searing ecstasy. He held her eyes all through it, watching her greedily.

After he'd wrung her of everything her body had to give, she went down like a demolished building all over him. A rough sound of gratification rolled from his gut as he received her collapsing weight effortlessly and stood up.

She flopped in his arms like a rag doll until he whispered in her ear, "Wrap yourself around me, *ya jenani*."

His words injected power into her limp muscles, made her clasp her arms around his shoulders, her thighs around his hips. She would give him anything he wanted.

It was indescribable, being draped around all his power, feeling everything he was encased within her limbs. She now knew she'd been empty and anchorless all her life, would remain so if she couldn't enfold him, hang on to him like this. The thought should have scared the hell out of her, this dependence she was developing unknown to her. It only felt amazing now.

She rested her head against his shoulder as he strode with her clasped tight across her two-room apartment, as if he knew exactly where her bedroom was. Which she wouldn't put past him, to have already obtained the blueprint of this whole building and its unit models. This was a man who was always in the know, about everything and everyone.

She felt as if she was gliding through a dream, her body echoing with the hum of pleasure he'd just given her. And it was as if she was seeing everything for the first time. Everything with him felt new, painted in wonder, infused with magic. And madness. He'd been so absolutely right about that.

As he crossed into her bedroom, she was roused from her delicious lethargy again. Numair had entered her most private place. And she suddenly wished she'd installed so many more lights, so she could revel in every single detail of his perfect body when he finally let her see it. As it was, there were only her bedside lamps and two lamp stands in the opposite corners. But she suddenly noticed something else.

Her bold decor in gradations of teaks and greens with accents of ebony seemed to echo his coloring.

Raising her gaze to him as he closed the door, as if he was making sure he had her locked away with him from the world, she melted a caress down his chiseled cheek. "See this place? My inner sanctum?"

His smile was scalding. "It's all you."

"Actually, it's all *you*." His hands tightened on her back and buttocks, his pupils flaring in surprise. She elaborated. "Every color here is yours. Your skin, your eyes, your hair. It's as if I've picked every one to suit you, as a tribute to your beauty. Seems my preference for the color scheme was some kind of prophecy."

His eyes went supernova as he bore down on her against the door he'd just closed. "Everything you say, everything you do, everything about you, sends me out of my mind. Your bill is getting heavier. And I will exact payment in full, *ya galbi*."

She shuddered at the impact of his sensual threat, the sensory overload of being sandwiched between his heat and the cool door, of feeling the steel of his erection nudging her oversensitized intimate flesh.

But it was hearing him call her "my heart" in her mother tongue that tore a sob from her depths, made her drag his head down and crash those cruelly arousing lips down on hers.

When he pulled away, his face had transformed into that of a total predator. "I wasn't exaggerating before. You *are* tampering with my sanity, Jenan. I've never even imagined being out of control. But I am now. So don't touch me again, don't hurry me, don't say a *thing*, if you don't want to have a raving lunatic all over you."

She giggled. "If this is you out of control, I'd hate to see you in it. You'd probably kill me with frustration—"

His lips crashed on hers, swallowing her words.

She'd imagined being kissed since she was old enough to know what kisses were. She'd tried many, many kisses before. It turned out she shouldn't have bothered imagining or trying.

This was a kiss. From those lips. This man. A kiss from now on could only be his, each sweep and thrust burying her under an avalanche of sensations.

Then she was flat on her back, and he was on top of her, like last night. But she was now fully naked and on her bed. And she combusted. She undulated beneath him, writhed, whimpered for him to please, please hurry. But he subdued her, took his time. He held her arms above her head as his other hand flowed down her face, her shoulder, ending up squeezing the aching heaviness of one breast.

His eyes were vehement with warning. "You can't implore me to hurry. You can only moan in pleasure. That's as much as I can endure."

"Let me see you," she moaned.

"You're already breaking the rules."

"You're unfair," she lamented.

"It's your beauty that's unfair."

She tried to free her hands, needing them on any part of him without the barrier of clothes.

He only immobilized her, then, growling deep like a feasting predator, he continued owning her body.

He took her to the brink so many times, until tears slid down the sides of her face and wet her hair. Only then did he come up to straddle her.

He kneaded her breasts, grazed her nipples. "I've never seen or tasted anything so beautiful."

Her hands shook on his belt. "I want to see you—I want you filling me. Please, Numair, please, *now*."

He escaped her flailing efforts, tore off his shoes and socks, then surged up to stand on the bed over her, his endless legs like pillars of a great statue on both sides of her. Then he started stripping, exposing his glory.

She rose to her elbows, gaping at his proportionate perfection, all that rippling power encased in polished teak, accentuated with dark silk. But her heart fisted until it emptied at the evidence of violence he'd suffered. She'd expected he'd led a life full of danger, what had led to his current expertise. But his body painted a far harsher life than she'd even imagined.

A cry spilled from her as she surged up, hands and lips trembling over his scars. Once she'd reached the one just beside his heart, she felt pain echoing what he must have once felt, and tears filled her eyes.

His hand closed over both of hers over his heart. "It was long ago, in another life."

Her tears flowed. "You must have suffered so much…"

"I survived, and it made me stronger." He came down on his knees, dragged her up and crushed her to his length, his lips scorching her face. "And it all brought me here, to this point in time, to you."

What he said was so poignant, the spasm in her chest intensified.

He raised her face to his. "Do my scars repel you?"

That turned off her distress like a tap. "*No*. Like those harsh, merciless things I felt in your nature, these marks of suffering and endurance make you even more unbearably arousing to me. They make me want to devour you even more. Numair—" she moaned between kisses all over him, reaching for the briefs that did nothing to imprison his erection "—you're more beautiful than I even imagined. I want to worship each inch of you."

With a groan of relief, he dodged her groping lips and hands and tore off his briefs in barely leashed ferocity. "Later, *ya hayati*, much later."

Hearing him use another of the lavish endearments used in her region, "my life" this time, made her collapse back on the bed, shaking with anticipation, but also intimidation. She'd never seen anything approaching his girth and length and hardness.

He came down over her again, threaded his fingers through her hair. "Now I take you. And you take me."

Though she doubted she could take him, she arched up into him, held out her trembling arms. "Yes."

He impacted her with his full weight, made her cry out, reveling in how her softness cushioned his hardness.

Perfect. No, sublime. Just like he'd said.

She opened her legs wider, and he guided them over his waist. Then he stilled over her.

Squeezing his eyes, he rose off her to reach for his pants, produced a condom from its back pocket. Tearing the foil with his teeth, he rose on his knees between her splayed thighs and started to roll it over his erection.

His actions finally registered. He was protecting her. He was giving her the choice. And she made it.

Her hand shot out, convulsing over his, stopping his action.

His eyes spewed surprise. "Are you protected?"

She shook her head.

The triumph that flared in his eyes almost knocked her out. "You're saying yes."

She nodded, tears beginning to flow again. She was saying yes to everything. She wanted him to claim her fully, wanted his seed inside her, knowing it would probably take root, hoping with everything in her that it would.

"You don't want to wait? Until after I demonstrate why you should say yes?"

"I had all the demonstrations I need the moment I saw you standing on that threshold last night."

His face seized with such pride and possessiveness, it would have made her run screaming before, but it was exactly what she needed from him now.

Her surrender deepened as he cupped her hips in a huge hand, tilting her, prostrating her. Holding her gaze, he dragged it down to where he held his erection with the other hand. He made her watch as he nudged his scorching crown against the knot where her nerves converged. She rose off the bed on a shrill cry of ecstasy. He slid up and down, circling her quivering bud as he bathed himself in her readiness, until she writhed, her gasps fracturing. Once he'd made sure he'd taken her back to the edge of insanity, he positioned himself at her entrance. Then he plunged inside her, feeling like a newly forged sword just out of the fire.

She screamed at the pain and shock of his invasion.

Even after she'd seen how big he was, she'd hoped it wouldn't hurt too much, since she'd had sex before and she was so ready. But it seemed she couldn't have been ready for him. Nothing would have made her withstand that first thrust. She doubted nothing ever would, that he'd always hurt her at first. And he'd give her unimaginable pleasure in contrast afterward. Even though the pleasure hadn't come yet, she knew it would. And it would be devastating.

On the second thrust, he seemed to realize her pain.

He froze above her, his voice a bass rasp. "Weren't you married before?"

His question elicited an amused huff. "I thought so. Seems I wasn't."

"You're so tight, as if your body was never tried."

"It wasn't. Not by you." She shuddered beneath him, the pain receding, tremors of deep delight starting to seep into the flesh clenched around him. "I do feel it's my first time."

Her actual first time had been nothing like this. It had been a disappointment wrapped in a vague ache. It had been on her wedding night. If it had been before, the marriage itself wouldn't have happened.

"I hurt you." He sounded more distressed than she did.

"Yes." He cursed, tried to pull out of her, but she clung to him inside and out. "You're hurting me so good. The pain is nothing compared to how you feel inside me. I want it to hurt. I want you to brand me."

She clamped his hips in her quaking legs and pulled him deeper. With the action he grew even bigger inside her. Caring nothing that it burned, she thrust her hips upward, engulfing more of him. It was overwhelming, being stretched by him, being filled by him beyond her capacity.

"Give me all of you." She confessed what she'd been thinking right before he came. "Show me no mercy."

"You *do* want a raving lunatic all over you."

"Oh, yes, please."

Instead, he withdrew, and she cried out with his loss, urging him to sink back into her. He resisted her squirming pleas, his shaft resting at her entrance for a moment before he sank slowly back inside her.

On a gust of passion, she opened wider for him. He watched her, gauging her reactions, adjusting his movements to her every gasp and grimace, waiting for the pleasure to submerge the pain before he let her really have all of him, before he showed her no mercy.

"Glorious, *ya galbi*, inside and out." He braced over her on outstretched arms, his muscles bulging, the tendons standing out in his powerful neck. Everything about him confessed his equally agonized pleasure. "So tight, so hot… Jenan…you're burning me."

His face clenched in what did look like suffering as he started pounding into her, forging farther inside her with each plunge.

Then he angled her and sank in her to the hilt. "Burn me, *ya jenani*, consume me as I invade you, take all of me, all the way to the heart of you."

She arched beneath him, thinking he'd reached her heart for real. And he had—the heart of her femininity, her womb. That intimate nudge was beyond anything she'd dreamed of. She'd been resigned to live alone, to never know true intimacy. But now, as he'd promised, every spark of sensation she was capable of feeling gathered into one pinpoint of absolute being, with Numair. Then it exploded.

A stifled shriek tore from her as she shattered around his invasion. She reformed only to splinter again and again around his pounding thickness. Her screams filled her head, accompanying the ecstasy razing her body.

Then his roar drowned everything out as she felt him stiffen in her clutching arms, ramming her deeper than ever before as he spilled into her, his seed filling her.

He was the only man she'd ever let take his full pleasure inside her. But he'd also been the one to give her far more than pleasure. Her first true intimacy.

Her cries stifled as it all finally overwhelmed her, loosened her grip on consciousness...

A sweep of delight cascaded down her back and buttocks then up. Again and again.

Jenan rose slowly from the depths of bliss to the realization that she was being stroked like a feline. And she was lying on top of a great one, who seemed to be purring a deep, deep rumble that vibrated in her bones. The sound was one of absolute satisfaction.

Yeah. She knew exactly how he was feeling. She felt satiated in ways she couldn't have imagined, in perfect peace for the first time in her life.

His lips moved against her forehead. "I trust your two-hour sleep was recharging?"

"Two hours!" She struggled to prop herself over his chest, her hair raining down on it.

His own hair was fanned around his head over a pillow the exact same color of his eyes, making him look like a black-maned lion instead of the sleek, gleaming panther he usually was. She almost collapsed on top of him again.

"Anything to add, besides incredulity at the length of time you were asleep? Although you already said yes, I'm still anxious to know if I delivered on my big promises."

She pulled a face at him, combing her fingers through the luxury of his hair. "If you'd delivered any more, I would have expired. I did for those two hours."

"I did, too."

"You did?"

"I lasted long enough to not crush you beneath me, then all I know is I woke up ten minutes ago to find two hours have passed. Another all-time first."

"This never happened to you?"

"You're the first thing to ever knock me out. And without even trying. I'm starting to worry what you'll do to me when you do try." He shifted, brought her to her side facing him, kissed her deeply, leisurely, then whispered into her lips, "This was, hands down, the best thing that has ever happened to me. *You* are."

She suckled the tongue rubbing against hers, caressed the muscled back rippling with mind-boggling power beneath her fingers, disbelief still reverberating inside her. That she'd found him. That he'd wanted her. That they'd shared all this, a lifetime's worth of events and emotions, in only twenty-four hours. Dare she expect more and even better in the days and weeks to come?

She smiled into his kiss. "Same here. Word for word."

He pulled back to look at her, his own smile bliss and

bedevilment at once as he pressed her flush against him, driving his intact arousal between her thighs. "Not letter for letter?"

"You're too greedy, sir."

"I'm not." As her eyebrow rose in challenge, he kept a straight face as he elaborated, "I'm insatiable."

She laughed. It was such a delight to be exposed once again to that unexpected and unusual sense of humor that was the exact thing to tickle hers.

She wiggled against his erection. "I have rock-solid proof to this claim."

He turned her on her back with a growl before he suddenly stopped. "Have you told your father everything?"

"Since I had no details, I preferred to say nothing."

"So you disappeared from your so-called engagement party, let them all go insane wondering what happened to you, without a word of explanation?"

"Yep, that's it in a nutshell."

His lips suddenly spread into one of those smiles that gave her severe arrhythmia. "I said you were perfection."

She grinned back. "I'm not going to keep saying *look who's talking*. I'll record it so you can play it back whenever needed."

He guffawed, his first full-fledged laugh that she'd heard. Or it might be his first ever, since he looked very surprised, as if it had never happened before.

Yeah, right. He'd lived forty years without laughing from the heart even once?

No matter what, he was laughing from the heart now. She adored the ease and humor that flowed between them, when in her experience, postsex had always been tense and almost hostile. But that had been post–disappointing sex. She'd never known what post-earth-shattering sex was like. Till now.

Before he continued his earlier thought that had been

interrupted, she held him off for one more question. "You haven't told me what you do intend."

He rose on extended arms. Seriousness replaced the mischievous passion in his eyes. "Tell your father to say nothing to Hassan and fly back to Zafrana. We'll meet him there, where I'll convene with him and his cabinet to get the details of the kingdom's problems and debts. I have an idea already, since I spent the past night and day investigating the situation. I expect to set things in motion immediately. Once I do, we'll go to Saraya and disabuse Hassan of his having the upper hand and the title of your fiancé."

Her heart tightening, she stared at him in dismay.

Seeming to realize her distress, his gaze filled with concern. "Are you okay? Are you feeling any pain?"

She shook her head, bit her lip. "Don't get me wrong. I appreciate what you're doing beyond words. I really want this mess over with and Zafrana out of danger. But I really hoped I didn't have to go back again."

His expression cleared then heated, seduction in one lethal package. "But it won't be the same when you go this time." He bore down on her. "This time you'll be with me."

"You expect to carry on our…affair there? You want to kick up a region-wide scandal?"

"I care nothing what others think, as you know, but for your and your family's sake, there won't be a whiff of scandal. I know how to keep a secret."

Still worried, she murmured, "I bet you can."

"Leave everything to me and just concentrate on being totally free, on taking everything you want with me."

When he put it that way, how could she object?

He stabbed his fingers into the hair at her nape, tethering her to the mattress by it, making her gasp then open wide for him, lips and legs. "Say yes, *ya jenani.*"

Unable and unwilling to say anything else, she cried out, "Yes!" as he plunged inside her.

And all through the night, she said an inordinate amount of yeses to just about everything, every apprehension evaporating in the conflagration that consumed her body and soul.

Six

"Are your sisters to be trusted?"

Jen watched Numair's lips move, and the constant urge to capture them, lose herself in their pleasure and possession, almost overwhelmed her again.

She *had* heard him, understood the individual words, yet couldn't come up with a collective meaning for his question. Her mind's processing powers were busy catapulting back in time to what those lips had been doing to her for the past three days. Day and night and in between. Up till fifteen minutes ago when her sisters had come on board his private jet now sitting on the tarmac.

After that first night in her apartment, he'd taken her back to his suite at The Plaza, and they hadn't left it. They'd done nothing but feast on each other, each time better than the one before it. They'd made love in so many ways she'd never known possible, ways she hadn't dreamed of or thought would be pleasurable. Not until she'd done them with him. She'd been right beyond her wildest dreams.

The incredible being known as Numair was the one man to teach her all there was to know about passion, the one who could plumb her sensual potential. And then some.

He was standing before her, perfection and beyond in a casual black suit and a shirt one hue darker than his eyes. She'd picked it for him, loving how it made his eyes even more incandescent. He was exuding vitality and virility and that all-out hunger that only seemed to increase in his eyes, in his vibe. It made her feel wanted, cherished, limitless.

He now quirked a dense eyebrow as if to prod her... The eyebrow she'd indulged in tracing with her lips and fingers and nibbling with her teeth...

"Jenan?"

"Huh?" was all she finally said.

"I was asking if I can do this..." He cast a quick glance over her head, then scooped her up into the bedroom of his plane, closing the door and pressing her against it. He bore down on her with his bulk and arousal, sank onto her lips. When he raised his head, she was wound around him, arms and legs. His gaze was satisfaction itself as he viewed her blatant arousal and completed his question. "In front of them, and trust them not to out us to the whole world?"

Landing with a thud from euphoria back to reality, she unclamped him from her limbs and found ground again. "I would usually say *el serr fe beir*, or 'the secret is in a well' with them. But then nothing is usual about you. Or us. You are such a huge deal, they've had their jaws on the floor since they've seen you in close quarters. They're bursting at the seams with curiosity about the nature of our relationship and they've already asked me the same question in a hundred different ways, and none of my half-truths have satisfied them. I expect they're going to work on you now in their quest for the truth."

After taking another brief kiss as if he couldn't stop

himself, he said, "How about we appease them, take them into our confidence?"

She licked his lingering taste off her lips before chewing on her lower one. "I usually trust them with anything, but then I never had any secrets for them to keep. They're so used to flaunting my news in everyone's face. I'm sure they'll want to brag about you, and I don't want to put them to such a test. Even if they promise to keep our secret and mean it, you, as you very well know, are too much. You would make anyone break their rules and do things that are totally out of character."

"Anyone, but not you."

She giggled. "You're kidding, right?"

"I'm doing no such thing. You're following every rule you forged for yourself, taking what you believe is right for you without consideration of society's restrictions. Everything you're doing with me is perfectly in character for you. You're enterprising, direct, fearless and a precise judge of character. You knew at once I'm the one for you, and you didn't waste time in empty maneuvers, just took what you want and need."

"When you put it that way, you almost make it sound as if I knew what I was doing."

"You did. You do." After another deep, drowning kiss, he raised his head, ran a coveting finger from her cheek down to the cleavage hidden by her demure, floor-length russet dress. "So will we or won't we?"

"Now that I think of it, with the way they both live online, if we don't want this shared with a few million of their close friends on social media, you won't only be unable to haul me and devour me like you just did, you'll also have to keep your hands to yourself completely."

A thundercloud of a frown came over his face. "Fifteen hours without touching you at all? That's not even a possibility. I only *look* like a superman."

She poked him playfully, found his usually rock-hard abs the consistency of steel. "Relax, or you might snap something. Consider it a chance to find out if abstinence is as good for the soul as it's always advertised."

"Who says I have one?"

She laughed, gave him an exuberant hug. "Since it's something most people are supposed to have, you probably don't, since you can't possibly have something so mundane. Come to think of it, if you don't have a soul, it must be superfluous, since you're perfect just the way you are."

Before he could pounce on her again, she slid through his arms, opened the door and rushed out of the bedroom.

All she wanted was to drag him down on that king-size bed and continue their intimacies. But she half expected her sisters to barge in looking for them. And for answers to their burning curiosities.

In truth, she wished she could tell them, to have it all out in the open. But it was unheard of for a woman from her region to announce that she had a lover. The only accepted relationship was marriage, or the engagement leading to it. Anything else had to be done in secret and never admitted, or it had to look like the accepted cultural format. Her society took hypocrisy so far that it accepted that people who wanted to have a one-night stand or were even paying for sexual favors to resort to *katb el ketab*, or literally "writing the book of matrimony," then divorcing as soon as the next day. *That* was all right with the so-called conservative society. But adults who wanted to be together without social subterfuge? They were punished and persecuted.

No wonder she'd never wanted to come back.

But then if it ever came to a worst-case scenario, she figured Numair was so powerful that even the collective venom of society wouldn't be able to touch her, or her family. He wouldn't let it. Not that she wanted to let it come to that.

He followed her, his tension bombarding her back. It heightened to full blast when Fayza and Zeena's voices rose from the conference/entertainment area they'd been exploring with the flight attendants since coming on board.

She tossed him a teasing smile over her shoulder. "Think of the appetite we'll work up by the time we arrive in Zafrana. I can't wait to see the hideaway you've arranged for us there."

His lips compressed in a severe line. "I'll tell your sisters we're not taking them with us, that another of my jets will fly them back to Zafrana."

Her smile widened before it faltered then disappeared. "You're serious!"

"Fifteen hours without touching you is beyond serious."

She gaped at him. "What excuse could you possibly give for not taking them with us now?"

"That we've had a change of plans and will make long layovers for business purposes in places where they can't go sightseeing or shopping. I'll make them grab gratefully for the direct flight home I'll offer."

"Are you always ready with a convincing story like that?"

His stony scowl told her his mind was made up and wouldn't budge. She still had to try to budge it.

She exhaled. "I really want you to have some time with my sisters, as I doubt you'll see them again alone for any length of time. Put up with the no touching for a few hours, and I'm sure they'll fall asleep at one point. You know I'll race you to bed then. We'll have your flight attendants standing sentry to alert us when they wake up."

His gorgeous lips twisted. "Then what? You'll explode from my arms, jump into your clothes and rush out to pretend you've been out here all along?"

"No, you'll do that." She met his returning scowl with a devilish grin. "You'll pretend you volunteered your room to me."

"You want me to tear myself from your arms because of your sisters, and go out to them? Aren't you afraid I'll eat them?"

She whooped with laughter. "Nah, they're too skinny and cute, and you're used to crunching overfed monsters. You're drafted into service because you can dress far faster than me."

"Only if you're okay with me going out to them in only my pants."

"I sure am not," she exclaimed, her insides tightening yet again at envisioning the sight of him half-naked. "I want their ovaries intact!"

"What ovaries? They're kids."

It again delighted her that he continued to prove he was nothing like other men. She'd seen how men of all ages looked at her gorgeous sisters, caring nothing that they were lusting after girls still in their teens, the age of their daughters or even granddaughters. No matter how they attempted to mask their sexual assessment and coveting, it was always there in their eyes, especially on that first exposure to her sisters' intense natural beauty.

There'd been nothing but neutrality in Numair's eyes and vibe. He considered them just people, who happened to be females, very, very young ones. And it wasn't because he could be old enough to be their father.

Numair didn't define himself according to such trivialities as age, but rather experience, abilities, impact. And in those, he'd sure amassed far more than dozens of successful, influential men his age. He was a man who'd seen and done and fought and triumphed over so much, his soul, or whatever he had that stood for one, was jaded and ancient.

And it made him the be-all and end-all of her fantasies, those she already had or was still forming.

She sighed, running her hands down the chest she'd just imagined naked. "Oh, Numair, you'd endanger any female alive, age notwithstanding. But we will fly my sisters home, and you will not scare them now, nor storm out half-naked and eat them because they woke up and interrupted us."

"How about we get our sentries to stall them until both of us can go out and play this charade for their benefit?"

Intensely pleased he'd started negotiating, she shook her head. "It has to be only you for a very obvious reason. Being made of steel, you don't show the aftereffects of our lovemaking. Apart from not turning into a swollen mass like I do, your hair just falls into this silky swathe no matter how much I mess it up. I need ten minutes minimum to get my hair into a semblance of order."

"Or maybe I can just lace your sisters' food with a sedative and have them sleep throughout the flight."

She guffawed. "Don't mess with such stuff. I might be the one who ends up ingesting the sleeping curse, and then where would you be?"

"In Frustrationland." He exhaled heavily. "Fine. We'll do it your way. But if they don't sleep…"

"They will, they will. They spend half their lives sleeping like cats." At his resigned mutter, she took one of his hands to her lips before placing it on her heart. "Cheer up. This will work beautifully, you'll see."

That incredible emerald of his eyes, what she could look into forever, seemed to catch fire. "Anything with you works beyond beautifully. It's why I'm in such a state."

Scalding joy surged from her depths to drench every nerve ending. It was beyond incredible that he felt as uncontrollably passionate about her as she did about him. Those early days of exquisite intensity were indescribable. And though she didn't hope things would remain on this level, this time of pure passion was worth anything. It would be unforgettable, and she'd cherish it forever.

He gathered her to his hard length, as if he really couldn't withstand not touching her for more than minutes. "I want more of you constantly. I feel vicious toward anything that can deprive me of you even temporarily."

"Think happy thoughts. At least nothing vicious. Zee and Fay can't withstand a drop of your aggression."

"Zee and Fay, eh? You don't expect me to call them that?"

"Why not? And I'm Jen, by the way."

"No. You're Jenan."

Her smile widened at his proprietorial attitude as she again wondered how she adored things from him that she'd abhorred from others. "All my life, when anyone called me Jenan, always meaning madness, they regretted it."

"You're *my* Jenan. *My* madness. Anyone else who trifles with your name and that meaning of it *will* regret it."

"Don't go all Terminator on me, or I will end up without relatives."

"Relatives who provoke you and sneer at your name and character? They certainly deserve terminating."

"Let me fight my own battles, okay?"

His ominous expression eased as he bowed his head in concession. "Until you call on my intervention."

She rewarded his newfound flexibility with a loving nip of his chin. As he groaned, tried to deepen the intimacy, she pulled away with a sigh of regret.

"About Zee and Fay... Since they were babies, they adored that I came up with abbreviations for their names. Especially Fayza. She hates her name even more than I do mine."

"You're more a mother to them than an older sister."

It was a statement. A very astute one. Though the girls'

mother—her stepmother—was alive and well, she wasn't maternal in the least, and she'd left both girls to the care of relatives and hired help from birth. Jen had intervened early, making them her responsibility. Even after she'd left for the States, she'd had them with her there every summer and holiday possible. She sure had the lion's share in raising the girls.

She sighed. "They're my girls. I'm the one who'd do anything at all for them."

Something…enormous flared in his eyes.

She was thinking she'd only guess at its significance, unable to trespass on what felt like an intensely personal reaction, when he ended any speculation.

"I feel the same way about my brothers."

She blinked. "I thought you were an only child."

"I am. Those brothers are ones of my choosing, our bond not one of blood, but forged in trials of fire."

"Your Black Castle partners."

She wasn't asking, just stating. He nodded. She wished he'd elaborate about them, about how he'd chosen them, about their trials.

But she was never one for probing such deep privacies. He'd tell her when and if he wished.

"So Fay and Zee? Will you call them that? For me?"

"For you. You've invoked the binding spell that makes me do anything." Indulgence and self-deprecation twitched on his lips. "No one has ever made me change my mind once it's made up. You're seriously messing with it, *ya jenani*."

Her heart hitched again. "Only fair, since you're scrambling mine big-time."

He opened his mouth to object, and she rose on tiptoes and closed it with an ardent kiss.

Before he deepened it, she stepped away, giggling. "You probably don't have to worry about them anyway. I bet being exposed to you will excite them so much, they'll be exhausted in a couple of hours."

That lethal smile of his dawned again. "In that case, let's go get those girls of yours, and let me proceed to knock them out of our way."

Giggling again, feeling as though she was perpetually a few inches above ground, she called out to her sisters.

In a minute, Fayza and Zeena came sauntering in, their eyes widening again as they fell on Numair, no doubt stunned all over again by his sheer physical presence.

She understood the feeling exactly. Every single time she looked at him, it was a total shock to her system. Just like that first time. Even more each time.

Numair invited them all to take their seats, then gave the order to take off. Little was said until the jet was done climbing and was cruising almost imperceptibly.

Then Fayza turned to him. "So you're the 'undisclosed businessman' this jet was sold to a couple of months ago."

Numair turned his focus on her, and Jen felt that Fayza regretted inviting it, struggled under its impact.

"I think you have it mistaken with another plane."

"I saw a hundred-million-dollar high-tech customized Boeing 737 in an aviation exhibition in Shanghai, China, unveiled three months ago that looked a lot like it. They said they made a replica for an undisclosed businessman."

Numair gave a slight nod. "I've heard about it, but this jet is two years old, and is a Black Castle Enterprises production."

"You mean your business makes planes, too?" Fayza's eyes widened. "But how does that fit with being one of the world's most important contractors in military intelligence and counterterrorism?"

Numair's gaze sought Jen's, communicating so much in the brief visual embrace. It assured her he was "thinking happy thoughts," as she'd recommended. It also expressed approval of Fay's curiosity and intelligence, but above all appreciation of Jen's efforts in raising her sisters.

Turning his gaze back to Fayza, he said, "You've done your homework, I see."

Fayza looked at Zeena, and the two grinned conspiringly at each other.

It was Zeena who said, "We've been doing Google searches on you since Jen told us you'd be taking us all back to Zafrana on your jet."

"Very efficient of you."

After that kudos, Numair's expression turned enigmatic. Jen couldn't help thinking it made him even more menacing than usual. This man did have something inside him that wasn't a soul. Some spirit of vengeance, maybe.

"But now you know what I am," he drawled. "Weren't you worried about coming to the panther's lair alone?"

"We're not alone," Zee blurted out. "Jen is here."

"You think Jenan can protect you?"

Zee nodded vigorously. "She always has. She'd never let anything bad happen to us."

"Even if you turn out to be some nut," Fayza said. "Jen can take on anyone. She's a black belt in kickboxing."

"Is she, now?" He turned to Jen, his gaze cascading down the body he had an inch-by-inch knowledge of, inspecting the memory of every muscle, sending her hairs standing on end so hard they almost shot out of their roots.

"No, *she* isn't anymore," Jen groaned. "My competing days are long gone. I now kickbox to stave off the march of pounds."

"You're still the best!" Zeena protested.

"She is!" Fayza chorused, looking as if she'd die of chagrin now that Jen had shot down her bragging.

"I'm sure she is," Numair placated them smoothly, before turning back to her again. "I would pay anything for a demonstration of your skills."

Fayza quirked her lips smugly. "You can get one for free. Just make an inappropriate move."

"That's a pity, as I don't make those. My moves are all preemptive."

Zeena giggled. "Those would probably also qualify you for a demonstration."

He turned his burning gaze to Jen. "Would they?"

She pulled a mock challenging face. "Why don't you try one on me and see?"

He shook his head. "I bet you reserve your demonstrations for defending others. A satisfactory one would only be on the girls' behalf, I suspect." He turned his gaze to them, and they visibly shrank back and huddled together like two cornered cats. Suddenly, he laughed. "Relax, Fay, Zee. I promised your big sister I won't eat you."

As the girls' faces brightened at his amusement, she rushed to alleviate the rest of their alarm. "Don't listen to him, girls. He won't abstain from eating you because he promised, but because you're not his staple diet."

Numair's nod was seriousness itself. "It's true. To my species little girls are grass, while we're meat eaters, blood drinkers and bone crushers."

For a moment or two the girls appeared unsure whether he was serious, then they must have decided he was really funny because they burst out laughing.

She noticed that something came into Numair's eyes as he watched them splutter. Like what came into his eyes when she said something that particularly appealed to him or surprised him. It was indulgence—minus the heavily sensual undercurrent, of course. The protector vibe was back full-on.

"Grass!" Fayza howled. "We're grass!"

Numair's lips quirked in response to their hilarity. "Yes. So watch out for the hares and the sheep of this world. They're the real danger."

Which was absolutely right, come to think of it. Ed had definitely been a cross between the two creatures. She still couldn't believe she'd married him. Sure, she'd been rebelling. At Fayza's age, she'd been looking for the opposite of her kingdom's chauvinistic men. But still, Ed? She'd put up with him for six whole months before she'd kicked him out on his ear. She must have had a severe judgment blackout at the time.

"But we're not little girls!" Zeena protested belatedly.

Numair's faint smile was all forbearing. "Oh, yes, you are. You're so little I can barely see you. But you'll soon grow bigger and bigger, and your worries and burdens and responsibilities will grow with you. Being little is good. Savor it for as long as you can."

Her throat tightening with emotion at the direction the conversation had taken, Jen interjected, "They'll always be little, as long as they have their big sister."

"Having a big sister like you is a sure way to remain protected, to never face the world alone."

His eyes held *such* warmth. She'd seen them in every temperature, but that was the hardest hitting yet.

"Were *you* ever little?" Fayza asked, her expression filled with curiosity.

He shrugged. "I didn't get the chance to be."

Jen's throat closed completely at the world of pain hidden behind his words. She'd thought he'd acquired his scars as an adult. But had he? A history of early abuse didn't coincide with what was known of his past. But was it his real past? A man like him could rewrite his history with utmost ease. So had he? And what was his real story? Would he ever tell her?

Seeming unwilling to discuss his past, he said, "About your earlier question, Black Castle Enterprises has companies and businesses that produce everything from screws to planes. We produce all our methods of communication and transportation from start to finish. This way, we get everything done to our specs, and it slashes our cost by two-thirds or more, not to mention it puts us in control of our electronic security and personal safety."

The girls looked even more impressed, if that was possible, as Zeena asked, "So how much did this plane end up costing you?"

"Around fifty million," he said. "It's still a lot, but if I'd bought it at this level, it would have cost a hundred and fifty. It's paid for itself in the past two years with the amount of commuting I did with hundreds of people who are key to my businesses. It seats up to thirty people, and I fly up to two hundred times a year, not to mention the other benefits I reap from it. I didn't get to become a billionaire by splurging on things that cost far more than they're worth and aren't an investment that will pay back in spades for the effort, time and money I put into them."

Fayza chuckled. "Fifty million is pocket change compared to the whopping half a billion one of our region's royals recently paid for his latest private jet."

Numair raised one eyebrow. "I will have to hunt him down and rid the world of his excesses."

Jen covered her forehead theatrically. "Don't give him ideas, girls. If you don't want to get rid of someone for good, don't bring them to Numair's attention."

After the girls laughed, thinking that was an excellent joke, Fayza pursued her line of questioning. "So what's the specs of this jet?"

Numair's answer was immediate, and involved. "It's between a Boeing 737 and 777 in size, but you're excused in thinking it was the first, since seeing the interior without the usual seating doesn't give you an accurate estimate of its size, and it's also a twin jet. It flies seven thousand nautical miles at point eight Mach uninterrupted, or roughly sixteen hours of nonstop flight, before it needs refueling.

It has three sleeping areas, and the meeting area has an internet signal booster, so it's the best place to talk on your smartphones, play on your tablets or work on your computers online. You've seen the entertainment/conferencing system. In case you want to hold a party in the air, just let me know."

Both girls' jaws dropped.

Then Fayza exclaimed, "God, you mean it?"

"Ask Jenan. I never say anything I don't mean."

Jen nodded sagely. "He means it."

The girls squealed with delight, deluged Numair in thanks. Even though they were the daughters of a king, the girls hadn't grown up in anywhere near that level of luxury. Their father would have indulged them even with Zafrana's deteriorating economic conditions, but Jen had made sure he didn't, so they didn't grow up spoiled and desensitized from excess.

But now a little indulging from someone who could so afford it was okay. And how they appreciated it. Numair, on the other hand, didn't seem at ease under the bombardment of their gratitude.

To end the subject, Numair asked Fayza, "So how do you know about that other plane you thought this one was? I didn't realize following the news of aviation exhibitions was among the things a girl your age would be interested in."

Fayza sat forward eagerly. "I want to be a pilot, and I'm interested in everything man-made that flies."

And Jen was doing everything to make sure Fayza realized her dreams and soared as high as she could.

The next second, her heart scattered its beats at his feet as Numair said something to the same effect. "Whatever you need to realize your ambition, I'm at your service."

When the girls realized he indeed meant it, and what it meant for someone of his power to help open closed doors or level road bumps for them wherever they needed, Fayza and Zeena again buried him in delight and gratitude.

Intervening this time, Jen began to interact with the trio more instead of only watching them and contributing to their exchange at key points. Then over an exquisite lunch, the conversation and banter flowed more fluently with every passing second.

The girls of course kept trying to get to the truth of *why* Numair was helping Jen, and by association, them, what was in it for him and what exactly had happened in the past four days. Numair deflected their persistence, gave them answers that were at once true, yet said absolutely nothing of the truth. It was uncanny.

But what most delighted Jen was how Numair, for all his widely known misanthropy and his initial reluctance to have her sisters on board, treated them much like she did, with care and indulgence, albeit with his own version of overwhelming authority and firmness. He acted as she'd always imagined a magnificent older brother would be with them. She knew she was getting way ahead of herself, but she'd stopped worrying about anything that would happen down the road. She'd just enjoy the incredible present.

With that in mind, she threw herself into being with the three people she loved being with most in the world…and hoped her sisters would go to sleep soon.

Numair stood at the top of the stairs of his jet and looked over the land he hadn't set foot on since he was a child. Zafrana. Half of his heritage.

Suddenly, all his senses revved, and he turned to the one who had total dominion over them now. Jenan looked even more breathtaking than ever as she approached him. Together they'd step onto the land she'd relinquished by choice and he'd lost by treachery. He would now reclaim it for himself, and make it a place where she could be happy and fulfilled, a home that deserved her.

Her eyes were full of all the wonders they'd experienced together. But for appearances' sake, so they wouldn't invite people's interference into their new and vital bond, she kept to herself the hands that had sent him mad with desire and ecstasy for four straight days.

He luxuriated in how refreshed and satiated she looked. For the girls *had* slept. They'd woken up only during descent. He'd had Jenan in his arms, under him, all around him, for ten straight hours. Half of the time had been consuming pleasure, and the rest rejuvenating slumber.

When her two sisters stepped out behind them, he turned to look at them. It had surprised him to find himself liking them, needing to please and defend them, and not only because they were her family. They smiled at him with that growing fondness and admiration that so affected him as they all descended the stairs to the limo waiting to take them to the VIP arrivals lounge.

As they entered the lounge, the girls rushed to their friends, who'd come to inspect Numair's jet for the promised in-the-air party. He was exchanging an amused intimate smile with Jenan when a deep voice boomed behind them.

"Jenan."

As they swung around, a man, almost as tall and big as him, was striding toward them, his face tinged with an anxious, angry fire. Numair recognized him at once.

Najeeb Aal Ghaanem. Saraya's crown prince. His cousin and the oldest son of his murderous uncle.

Then Numair's head almost exploded with aggression. Najeeb had reached for Jenan, took her by the shoulders in an urgent grip.

"I cut short my tour as soon as I heard. I went to New York last night but couldn't find you or anyone, couldn't get any reliable account of what happened. I called King Khalil, who told me you were returning home, so I flew here to wait for you." His teeth gritted. "My father has crossed every line this time. I can't apologize enough to you, but you don't need to worry. I'll put a stop to this."

Unable to bear it anymore, Numair clamped his hand around Jenan's arm and pulled her into his side. "*I'll* put a stop to this."

Najeeb blinked, as if it was the first time he'd realized Jenan wasn't alone.

As he made eye contact with him, Numair barely held back from knocking him out. From doing far more. He'd killed many men with one blow when he'd felt none of the blind rage he felt now.

The damn man was not only handsome, he also looked noble, sophisticated, his highborn nature oozing from every pore. And he had this…warmth about him, this heroic vibe to boot.

Everything about him was the very opposite of his own savagery and rawness and coldness. Their radically different lives, what Najeeb's father had been responsible for, were written all over them. And he hated him for it.

But he didn't contemplate killing him for that. It was for daring to lay a hand on her, for calling her Jenan. But most of all, for existing and for suiting her far more than he ever could.

Najeeb's surprise abated, righteous anger flooding over his face in its place. "Who the hell are you?"

Though he knew everything about Najeeb, he growled back, "I ask the questions here. Who the hell are *you*?"

As Najeeb bared his teeth and Numair took a step forward to meet his confrontation head-on, suddenly Jenan stepped between them.

Placing one flat palm on each of their chests, she calmly gave each a firm shove. The action itself, more than the power of it, made each of them stumble a step back, severing the chain reaction of aggression.

Looking from Numair to Najeeb, she smiled with mock demure sweetness. "Let this little, helpless, has-no-say woman make the introductions. Numair, meet Najeeb Aal Ghaanem, Saraya's crown prince and my fiancé's oldest son. Najeeb, meet Numair Al Aswad, mega intelligence and counterterrorism mogul…and my lover."

Seven

Jen looked coolly between the two towering hunks who flanked her as they relinquished their visual and verbal duel and turned to gape at her.

Yep. She'd sure managed to shock them out of the impending explosion that had almost ignited out of nowhere.

Anyone might think she was insane, insisting on hiding the truth from her sisters, then blurting it out like that to Najeeb on sight. But though she hadn't really given it any thought before doing it, she did think with Najeeb, the secret would certainly be in a bottomless well.

Najeeb was the most honorable person she'd ever known. Since she'd been a child, she'd always looked up to him, wished they could be closer. For he was exactly the older brother she'd always wished she'd had.

That was why she knew she could tell him anything. Najeeb was the material the knights of old had been made of. Those who would lay down their lives for you once you had their alliance.

Not that she wanted anything anywhere near that drastic from him. She just wanted to come clean to someone about her and Numair. Najeeb was the only one she could think of whom she could tell anything to and trust he'd never expose it at whatever price to himself.

Najeeb, surprisingly, was the first to recover from her bombshell. His gaze couldn't decide what to be—stunned or amused. "Okay, Jenan, you achieved your purpose. You stopped me in my tracks. Very efficiently. I'm sorry I flew off the handle, but I was livid since I heard what my father made you agree to. I was ready to strike out at anything—" he flicked a withering glance at Numair "—or anyone in my path."

Great. Najeeb had jumped right into denial, while Numair was over his surprise and seemed to grow bigger with Najeeb's every word. The danger levels emanating from him entered a critical stage.

She sighed. "I did want to shock you into stopping, and that's why I resorted to the truth. It's always more shocking than any fabrication."

Najeeb looked disbelieving for a few more moments, before he choked, "You're not joking?"

"To borrow a favorite line from someone who's standing right here, I've never been more serious."

"How...?" He paused then realization dawned like a fireball in his sunlit eyes. He looked back at Numair with hostility turning to horror. "You're Numair Al Aswad!"

"So now you recognize me."

"Now I wish I don't." Najeeb turned to Jen in dismay. "How on earth did you get mixed up with a man like him?"

Something scary rolled from Numair's gut. "You have questions, you have anything to say, you talk to me."

Jen raised her hands. "Boys, please, hold your testosterone missiles. I'm standing right in the middle, and your aggression is literally turning my stomach."

Both men apologized simultaneously, stopped, glared at each other, started again, overlapped each other's words again, then fell silent. They stood there seething with frustration as they summed each other up. And she saw something she hadn't realized before.

They looked *so* much alike.

If she'd been meeting them for the first time, she would have thought they were blood relatives, even brothers.

Apart from Najeeb having hazel eyes and close-cropped hair, what really distinguished them wasn't genetic, but the result of their radically different characters and paths in life. Najeeb lacked the harshness that etched Numair's features, the ruthless shrewdness that emanated from him. And while both men were almost the same breadth and height, their bodies displayed the difference between the supremely fit and powerful man that Najeeb was and the lethal juggernaut that Numair was.

But those differences only made them feel more kindred. She couldn't explain why she felt that, but she did. And suddenly this whole situation became untenable.

As the men started arguing again, she clamped each by his arm. "Will you stop alarming everyone in a mile's radius?" She looked from one to the other as they brooded down at her. "Can we now go have this out somewhere private, or do we need some internationally sanctioned neutral ground and peacekeeping forces to keep you two in line?"

They ended up in Numair's place.

The "hideaway" he'd prepared for them. With no roads leading to it, the only transportation was by helicopter.

Though she'd lived in a royal palace, this place still stunned her. She couldn't believe she hadn't even known it existed in her own homeland.

Contributing to the uniqueness of this resort-size property was its seclusion. For a hundred square miles she saw nothing but desert conservation land all around.

Once they'd entered through the semifinished palm wood and bronze gates into this desert paradise, she felt they hadn't only left city life behind, but modern life altogether, too. The understated luxury was so at one with the environment, the villa lacked any trace of the artificial elements that had always put her off in the opulent places she'd been in in Zafrana, from the palace to the houses of the nobility and big businessmen. While all those places strived to belong to an era in architecture and decoration, this place had a timelessness about it.

It was made of the desert, its materials, its color palette, of its majesty and tranquility. Of the many things that took her breath away were the free-roaming oryx and gazelles just outside the gates, and the incredible infinity pool at the back of the sprawling villa. It looked like a swimming pool at its near end, with mosaic walls, steps and ledges in blues and greens, but on its far end it looked like a spring, like those found in major oases, its edge seeming to abruptly disappear into another realm. A mile-long barricade of palm trees separated the back of the property from the rest of the desert that stretched in gently undulating dunes all the way to the Anshar mountains on the horizon.

Inside the villa, spaces flowed onto each other; balcony doors opened to all directions. Every surface was made of stone, colored glass and bronze, and all the furniture and upholstery handmade, everything in warm earth tones, with russets and reds adding splashes of vividness. The whole place felt like an escape into a mystical retreat of solitude.

Numair had somehow read her every preference, even those she'd never fully formulated. He'd known what would most delight her. And in those short days while he'd been always with her, he'd searched for it, found it and acquired it. She didn't think this property was a lease. He moved around here with the assurance of someone who owned the place, even though it was his first time here. The one who'd flown here to close the deal, who now showed them around, was his right-hand man, Ameen. But then, Numair entered any place and owned it, and the people in it.

She couldn't wait to be alone here with him. But for now she had to resolve this issue with Najeeb. Most important, she had to give it her best shot to fix that inexplicably catastrophic first impression between him and Numair.

Now Ameen left their trio in the great space that had many sitting areas, a dining room and four stone fireplaces. Numair handed her down on one of the divans strewn in pillows covered in hand-woven wool in colorful, geometric Zafranian designs. She tried to catch his eyes, exchange the intimacy they'd been reveling in since their first night together. But his focus was trained on Najeeb.

It was beyond clear he abhorred having Najeeb around. And he wasn't thrilled with her, either, right now. He'd bowed to her wishes when she'd invoked what he called her binding spell, suppressing his aversion and inviting Najeeb here. But he wasn't about to pretend he was okay with it.

It baffled her that his vexation with Najeeb hadn't only persisted but seemed to be intensifying.

The two men had gotten off on the wrong foot, both of them having been in a volatile state. Najeeb had already been outraged and easily triggered by a strange man's contention. And Numair, in the acute stage of excessive passion, had his territorial instincts at high alert. With both of their alpha-male levels at the maximum, a locking of horns had been inevitable, and the situation had shot to the danger zone with a few aggressive words.

But while Najeeb had reverted to his usual self-possession and equanimity, Numair's hostility was still building.

Not that he displayed any aggression. On the surface he

was even more neutral than Najeeb, coldly assessing. But she now had a direct line to his inner feelings. She felt a volcano seething inside him.

As soon as they were all seated, with her facing both men, Najeeb left the visual wrestling match with Numair and turned to her. "I'm all ears."

Filling her lungs with air, she let it all out in a long exhalation. "What do you want to hear?"

"The truth."

"I told you that right off the bat. But if you want it in chronological order, here's a rundown of how things happened. You refused to be bundled with me in a marriage of state to serve your father's expansion plans, and disappeared. He decided he'd do what you wouldn't and marry me himself. He cornered my father, and my father in turn threw the ball in my court. I had to pick up the ball, since I knew if I didn't, one of my sisters would be forced to. Then came that fateful evening five days ago, and I met Numair. The rest I already told you."

"*Ya Ullah*, I leave for a couple of weeks, and this happens." Najeeb seemed to struggle to process the events his father had set in motion, his fury again rising. Then suddenly his face turned into a mask of righteous rage. "Back in the airport, he said he'd put a stop to this. Is this what he promised you in return for becoming his lover? Is this how he forced you into his bed so soon?"

Before she could say anything, Numair said in a seething tone, "*He* doesn't coerce women into sex. And suggesting that I have is an insult to Jenan. She would never be coerced into anything like that for any reason."

Najeeb turned his wrath on Numair. "Jenan is a hero, and would pay any price to save her loved ones. She *was* being coerced to marry my father for their sakes."

"*She* is sitting right here." Jen exhaled. "How about we talk *to* each other?" She looked at Najeeb. "I am with Numair because I want to be, because I want him. I hope this answers your questions and closes this subject."

Najeeb stared at her, evidently still stunned that she was talking so openly about her affair with Numair, that dangerous stranger he seemed to know even more about than she did. They'd never talked about anything that even neared such candor and sensitivity.

But he was one of the most flexible, progressive people she'd ever met, and she'd always known that if she needed, she'd be able to talk to him about anything.

He finally nodded. "You're one of the most enterprising and advanced people I know, Jenan." A huff of surprise escaped her. Good to know they held each other in equal regard. Without inquiring about her amusement, he went on, "For a woman from our region to achieve what you have, you had to be far more powerful than a man who achieves the same things. I always admired your strength and will, how you escaped the shackles of your status and stood in the face of our culture's condemnation and our society's persecution. I'm proud of everything you've achieved, and I am proud that your decisions and actions have always proved to be the best thing for you. I also always thought you a most astute judge of character. But I won't lie and say I'm not skeptical this time."

"You think I don't know what I'm doing, huh?" She shrugged. "It's your prerogative to feel any way you want about this, and it's mine to do as I want—and being with Numair is certainly what I want. I only ask that you keep what I divulged to you to yourself, until further notice."

"If you don't want others to know, maybe it's an indication that you feel it might be wrong."

"C'mon, Najeeb, you know better than that. In our region it's best to hide anything you truly care about. People have no concept of boundaries, and they swarm over anything that's made public knowledge, thinking it their right to poke and prod, to interpret it according to their own set of narrow-minded values, to cheapen and sabotage it. You know that when it comes to me alone, I care nothing about what people think, that I always announced all of my tradition-busting decisions before, but this time—"

Najeeb raised his hand. "You don't need to convince me of anything, or to even ask me to keep what you told me a secret. There was never a possibility I'd share anything you told me or anything I find out about you on my own."

Her lips spread. "Why do you think I told you in the first place when I didn't even tell my sisters?"

Alarm spread over his painstakingly sculpted face. "Don't even think of telling them. They and their friends must be speculating enough as it is just seeing you with him. Don't add fuel to the fire by any confirmations."

She chuckled. "Just what I thought, and that's why only you know."

He exhaled heavily. "*Aih.* Only I know. *Ya Ullah, ya Jenan*… I only hope you won't live to regret this, and it won't come at as big a price as I fear."

She felt another wave of aggression blast from Numair, but when he spoke his voice was chillingly calm. "So you've changed your strategy. Now that you failed to shame her or make her doubt her decision, you're trying to plant fear of me in her heart."

Najeeb regarded him with the same arctic composure. "If she doesn't fear you, then she doesn't know what you really are. You, Mr. Al Aswad, are a man to be dreaded. A man to avoid at all costs."

Numair inclined his head. "You're absolutely right, Prince Aal Ghaanem. I am far more than that. With anyone but Jenan."

It was clear Najeeb got Numair's message loud and clear, that he was foremost among the *anyones* who should dread and avoid him. From Najeeb's nonchalance, he was answering with his own unspoken "Anyone but me, buster."

Out loud he said, "You're saying you're changing your ways for her? Or that you're different with her?" Najeeb turned to her, his eyes reproachful. "And you fell for that?"

In one of those imperceptible moves, Numair was sitting on the edge of his seat, like a crouched panther seconds from a neck-gouging attack. "I said you talk to me. I won't say it again."

"How about you keep your threats to anyone who might actually give a damn about them, Mr. Al Aswad?"

"If you don't, Prince Aal Ghaanem, then you don't know what I really am as well as you think you do."

"And it's clear you know nothing about me if you think you can get away with threatening me."

Having heard enough, Jen surged to her feet. "Okay, my neck is really starting to hurt watching your delightful volleys." She planted her fists at her waist. "May I interject with a tiny reminder that you gentlemen are on the same side?"

Numair and Najeeb turned to her in surprise and not a little affront at her suggestion.

An incredulous chuckle burst from her. "*Ya Ullah*, you're both so busy posturing and being macho and trying to wrestle each other under the table that you didn't stop to realize that." At their darkening scowls, she sighed. "I hate to break it to you, but you are. You both want to stop Hassan's nefarious plot and help Zafrana get out from under his thumb. And most important, you both want what's best for me." At their stubborn irresponsiveness, she prodded. "You do both want what's best for me, right?"

"You know that I…"

"You know that I…"

As soon as both men realized they were chorusing their response, they flung each other furious glances.

And she burst out laughing. "See? You not only want the same thing, you're saying the exact same thing, too." At their continued belligerence, she sighed again. "If you both do want my best, promise me you'll stop making me worry you'll tear each other apart the moment I turn my back. Do I have your words?"

Najeeb again surprised her, being the one who nodded first. She'd expected it would be Numair who'd rush to give her what she wanted. It seemed his antipathy toward Najeeb was messing with his priorities. Weird.

But he at last nodded, his voice bottomless, his gaze filled with unfathomable things as he said, "For you."

His response was still disturbing in every way possible, but it was enough for her current purposes. She knew he'd abide by whatever word he gave her.

She looked at each of them. "Since I'm the one with the most at stake here, in every way possible, how about you let me steer this conversation?" They both nodded at once this time. Her heart lifted at the progress. Wishing those two would realize they should be allies, she grinned from one man to the other. "I know both of you planned to be the one to resolve this crisis, so how about we discuss how you intended to do that? Maybe you can jointly devise an even more efficient way?"

"My plan doesn't need any boosts in efficiency," Najeeb said. "I'll force my father to back down."

Numair looked at Najeeb, his lips twisting in irony. "What a coincidence. That is exactly my plan."

Jen's laugh rang out again. "See? You two are so alike, you're almost twins." As their faces darkened again at her assertion, she placated them. "Not that either of you can see or admit it now, but one day you'll realize I'm right. And boy, will I enjoy saying I told you so. But since we have more pressing issues at hand, and you at least admitted you share a common goal, how about you share the specifics of your plans to force Hassan to back down?"

Neither man ended up sharing the specifics of his plan. Or made any promise to work with the other, either.

But at least the hostility that had erupted between them had subsided.

At least it had on Najeeb's side. As for Numair, it seemed as if an impenetrable shield had come down around him, stopping her from reading his thoughts or sensing his feelings, leaving her wondering what their truths were. But she couldn't ask. Not because Najeeb was around, but because she'd never probe into private stuff Numair didn't volunteer.

Najeeb, on the other hand, was a totally different matter. She'd insisted he stay and share their dinner, and he'd accepted her invitation, gradually relaxing in their company. Shedding his confrontational attitude, he'd asked Numair informed, in-depth questions about his work, seeming genuinely interested, then impressed. He had even ended up asking if Numair could use his unique experience and influence to collaborate with him in his humanitarian efforts. Numair had seemed reluctant to give any answer. She felt it was not because he didn't want to help, but because it would involve him with Najeeb. But Najeeb was a master negotiator and had somehow managed to extract a promise from him.

By the time she'd seen Najeeb out alone, as Numair had taken an important and long call, Najeeb had given her his verdict on Numair.

He was big enough to admit he'd been wrong. Both his opinion of Numair and their relationship had changed radically. He'd said he knew men, could sense any sign of sleaze, exploitation or mistreatment a mile away. And he'd seen and sensed only respect and consideration in

Numair's treatment of her. He'd also felt how passionate Numair was about her, and how protective.

Before he'd crossed to the massive clearance where the helicopter had been waiting to take him back to the airport, Najeeb had laughingly said it looked like the Black Panther of Black Castle had finally found the one to tame him. He'd always heard that the most dangerous predators, once tamed, made the best lap cats.

"I thought he'd never leave."

Jen yelped in delight as Numair did this incredible thing he always did. He appeared out of thin air and snatched her off her feet with the utmost ease, then drowned her in the staggering, cherishing power of his embrace.

She clung to him with everything in her as he strode eagerly with her across this unique place, nuzzling her face and lips into the power of his warm neck. At the villa's far end, they entered the most stunning bedroom suite she'd ever seen. Though they were totally alone now, Numair still kicked the door closed, as he always did.

As he crossed to the king-size bed, she took in the tasteful decorations in what looked like authentic Zafranian antiques and handcrafted furnishings. Painted glass and copper lanterns hung from heavy chains, while complementing sconces hung on the walls. Bedouin jars and vases in varying sizes lay on shelves and tables and stood beside the heavy mahogany doors leading to the suite's bathroom and dressing rooms. A braided-wood-and-straw chest sat at the end of the bed, while sofas with the same design and materials and ornate stone-and-bronze tables filled the sitting area facing the balcony doors. All over the floors and even on select places on the walls were hand-woven carpets in the deepest reds, honeys and browns, the same hues of the whole villa. And she suddenly realized.

All the colors in this place were hers!

She'd at first thought he'd bought this place furnished.

But this was too specific to be a coincidence. He had to have done this for her, an answer to her bedroom in New York. But she couldn't even imagine how and when he'd managed to order it done, and no doubt to oversee its realization to his precise vision. It was another proof that Numair was even more powerful than she could imagine.

But he'd taken it beyond matching her coloring. There were other incredible touches. For instance, binoculars on one table and a telescope by the balcony doors, to watch the animals in the morning and the stars at night. But what touched her to her core, had tears surging in her eyes, was an easel with every kind of canvas and paper and art material neatly stacked next to it.

She painted, and he must have noticed that most of the paintings hanging in her Tribeca apartment were desert landscapes. Anticipating that being here would stir her creativity again, he'd provided her with the means to indulge it whenever the mood struck.

Before she could thank him for being so unbelievably thoughtful, he passed the bed, opened the balcony doors and stepped outside to a wooden deck overlooking another, smaller infinity pool. By day the pool would spill out into a never-ending vista of the dramatic desert views. It was now a glittering turquoise splash in a night lit only by a nascent crescent moon and an explosion of sparkling stars. Numair wanted to make love out in the open, with only the canopy of sky and stars for cover.

In the middle of the expansive deck, a gigantic mattress was spread in covers the same deep mahogany red of her hair. He kneeled on it with her still securely held in his arms and tore the covers away before placing her down on the crisp cream sheets and coming down on top of her.

Crying out with the overload of emotions and sensations, she wrapped her arms and legs around him, her breath hitching, her body trembling, molten. It had been twelve hours since he'd made love to her, but with the way her senses were clamoring, ready and on the verge of combusting with his every touch, it felt like twelve days.

His hands alone possessed the ability to dissolve her shackles and release her potential, to expose her to his transfiguring appreciation. In a few hammering heartbeats, he had her open to his desire, making her all-powerful with it. Then his lips and tongue and teeth were all over her, making her feel as he always did, savored and worshipped and devoured.

Then he rose to expose himself to her hunger. She lay there unable to move with craving, her night-adjusted vision luxuriating in his star-silvered perfection.

He kneeled before her and she reached to caress his manhood. Hard and engorged, it felt as if it had been chiseled by virility gods and gifted with endless stamina and discipline. As her hands failed to span his incredible girth and length, the now-accustomed-to thrill of intimidation rattled through her. It again awed her that her hunger was so vast it enabled her to contain that much demand.

In response to her ministrations, his fingers shook in her hair and his formidable body trembled over hers. Her heart expanded. Loss of control wouldn't mean a thing from anyone else. But from Numair, with his supreme sufficiency and restraint, such a demonstration of dependence, such a confession of need, was profound.

What she felt was no longer about hunger, if it had ever been. The need had become all about him and being merged with him.

She cried out her desperation. "Numair, fill me…"

By the golden lights coming from the bedroom and the silver of the moon and stars, she saw the sequence of emotions unspooling across his face as her plea shattered him. He bore down on her, opened her wide around his hips, raised hers off the bed. He held her in one hand, the other supporting himself as he rose halfway on both knees. Then he plunged inside her.

Her scream at his abrupt invasion didn't alarm him now. For he knew that she was yearning for the full power of his flesh in hers, the mutual domination and captivation. And he gave it all to her. He slammed into her, and she screamed for more, knowing he had more, as long as she could survive.

Then too soon, the tidal wave was cresting. Feeling her mounting distress, he rose on extended arms over her. Her gaze clung to his as he burned her with his greed for her total surrender and pleasure. When she started pleading, he angled his thrusts and sent her over the top.

Orgasms crashed through her, over and over, ebbing and cresting again and again. His mouth milked hers for each last stifled scream as she bucked and heaved beneath him, his growls that of the predator he was. On the jet, after their last explosive coupling, he'd said he'd end up dying in her arms of a pleasure overdose. Every time with him felt as if his prophecy would come to pass. What an ecstatic end that would be.

Once she subsided beneath him, he stopped for a while then started again, building his rhythm and her desperation until she pleaded for him to plunge with her this time into the abyss of ecstasy.

Growling with satisfaction at her resurrected hunger, then with his own desperation for release, he let himself go and climaxed inside her. His buttocks tightened hard as he lodged himself into her womb and let loose the jets of completion, roaring his pleasure, his surrender to this overpowering need between them.

The sensation of his release inside her, the intimacy of it, the hope that it would implant the miracle of a life they both wanted to make together... Everything overloaded her system into another orgasm. One more power-ful than the last.

She surrendered to the ultimate pleasure, and the world faded away, as usual, nothing remaining in existence but him and being merged with him...

When she stirred from blissful oblivion, she found her-self over him, beneath thick covers, with the balmy desert night sifting through her hair.

Without moving, she pressed her lips over his heart. "Thank you."

A deep chuckle reverberated beneath her ear. "Thanks are certainly mutual here."

"I'm not thanking you for driving me out of my mind with pleasure. Mere *thanks* doesn't do justice to what you do to me."

He turned her on her side so he could look down at her. "Then what are you thanking me for?"

"You should be asking, what *not* for." At his uncom-prehending frown, she nipped his rugged jaw, delighting in how his beard bristled against her teeth. He'd shaved before they'd disembarked from his jet, but a dark stubble had grown out again. "You really have to work on being able to accept gratitude and take your dues."

"Whatever you think I did..."

Her kiss sealed his lips, stopped his argument. "What you keep doing is not a matter of opinion, but facts as solid and as wonderful as every inch of you."

His groan filled her lungs as she ran her hands down every one of those inches she had access to. "Anything I do for you is my absolute privilege and my intense pleasure."

Her passion-swollen lips spread into a grin. "Fine, but I still get the privilege and pleasure of thanking you, all the time, so get used to it."

He looked down at her thoughtfully. "I thought you

didn't have much to thank me for today. You evidently consider Najeeb a dear and valued friend, and I jumped down his throat, and I didn't warm to him for the hours he stayed here. I was a lousy host."

"I already knew you don't do warm, Numair, and are not one for social graces."

The power and bulk pressed to her turned to steel. "Like Najeeb, you mean? The perfect gentleman? The living, breathing epitome of the knight in shining armor?"

Her eyes widened as realization suddenly hit her. "Was that what this was all about? You were jealous?"

His eyes blazed into hers. "Insanely." He raised a brow at her. "Perhaps even murderously."

Her mouth dropped open before she exclaimed, "But we're like brother and sister. We refused to even consider marrying each other, triggering this whole mess."

"I knew that, on a logical level. But there was no reasoning with the beast who could only see that his mate was so at ease with someone else." As she shuddered in delight at the word *mate*, he wrapped her hair around his hand and took it to his lips, caressing it as he would her mouth. "I could *feel* your history, your long years of knowledge and understanding, and I suddenly felt like an outsider."

Was that insecurity that came into his eyes? Numair? Was it even possible?

Unable to bear that he'd feel anything bad on her account, she pulled him closer. "My brief days with you mean far more to me than all the years I've had with most people in my life put together. I've come closer to you than I have to anyone I've known my whole life. And I never wanted a gentleman or a knight in shining armor. I want you, the man I knew from the first glance was a ruthless marauder in darkest armor."

His chest expanded, pressing into her sensitive nipples, his darkened eyes brightening again. "So you're not disappointed with me for being the cold bastard that I was with your friend?"

"You can't help what you feel, but you did what I asked. You stopped antagonizing him, invited him here to your place, even when you wanted me here alone this first time—"

He swept her to her back and loomed over her. "And every time. From now on, Ameen will only come when we leave, to clean and maintain the place. But while we're together, no one else will ever set foot here. And it's *our* place, not mine. In fact, since I acquired this place for you, it's yours."

She blinked. "What do you mean acquired it for me?"

"I mean I wrote it in your name."

She jackknifed, sitting up. "What?"

He leaned back on one elbow, indulgence playing on his lips. "I have a copy of the deed here, and another has been sent to your legal representative. This place is all yours, all you. All I ask for is the privilege and pleasure of sharing it with you."

Unable to wrap her mind around the enormity of his gesture, she could only stammer, "But…but…"

He pushed her down again, pressed his lips to hers in a silencing, drowning kiss.

By the time he raised his head, hers was spinning, with everything he was, everything he'd been doing to her and for her. Then his next words made the whole world spin.

"Tomorrow I go resolve your father's and your kingdom's crisis. Now sleep with me under the stars, in this paradise where only we exist, *ya habibati*."

She surrendered to him as he adjusted their position for comfort, secured the covers over them and fell silent. In a minute she was certain he'd fallen asleep.

But there was no way she could, too. Every time she

replayed his last words in her mind, she could barely breathe.

He'd said *ya habibati.*

When he wasn't in the throes of passion.

My darling. My love.

Eight

"**Y**ou should have told me I'd meet you on a *One Thousand and One Nights* set. I would have come in costume."

Numair stared at the man who approached him as he stood at the top of the stairs facing the helipad. The last man on earth he'd ever thought would come to his assistance. Richard Graves.

The Englishman had waited until the helicopter's rotors had stopped before he talked to make sure Numair heard his mockery. As if Numair didn't already know it was his default in general, and with him in specific.

Only two years older than himself, Richard had been Cobra to him for the sixteen years he'd known him in the prison of The Organization.

But he wasn't one of his brothers. He'd been one of his jailers. He'd long been his nemesis. He was now his partner. It was…complicated.

Richard was now looking around the expansive desert vista surrounding Numair's home.

Yes, his home. That was what this place had become in the past six weeks. His first home. Anywhere Jenan was with him, even part-time like now—when she spent most of the days with him, making love, conducting their businesses remotely, just being together, but spent the nights in the royal palace for appearances' sake—would now always be home to him.

She was home.

"So you've finally found your roots, eh? Happy now?" Richard drawled as he came to stand eye to eye with him. He was the only one who'd ever matched him in strength, in power, in danger and ruthlessness.

Numair glared at the man he'd loathed for the past twenty-five years. The man who'd once been his best friend.

Not that they'd ever mentioned this brief period when they'd been the most important person to each other. Not between themselves, and certainly not to others. All his Black Castle brothers knew was that they were sworn enemies. His brothers had spent the past two decades wondering and asking why. But neither he nor Richard had ever volunteered an explanation. What had happened between him and Richard had been before he'd made the others his team. And it had been unforgivable. Richard should be grateful Numair hadn't killed him the moment he could.

And he would have if not for Rafael Salazar, his youngest brother. Richard had been Rafael's handler, and Rafael had formed an unbreakable bond with him, considered him his mentor, his older brother, even. When Richard had left The Organization and caught up with them by tracing Rafael, Numair and the rest had unanimously decided to eliminate him. They'd considered him the enemy, and a lethal threat to their new identities. Exposure as the agents who'd escaped The Organization would have meant their certain deaths. Or at least being forced to relinquish the identities they'd gone to so much trouble to create.

It had been a simple equation. Richard or them.

But Rafael had put himself between them, insisted he trusted Richard with his life and theirs, that if they got rid of Richard, they had to get rid of him, too.

Rafael's adamant position had forced them to trust his judgment as they always had, and to back down. Not that Richard had made that easy. He'd taunted them, warning them that in a confrontation between all of them and only him, they would be the ones in danger.

Rafael seemed to have called it right, since Richard hadn't exposed them. But Numair suspected it had only been because Richard considered Rafael his younger brother, had killed and would die for him and wouldn't risk him being taken down with them. Numair had wanted nothing more to do with that bastard. But he'd soon found himself forced to collaborate with him in building Black Castle Enterprises.

Being pragmatic, he'd known only Richard had the knowledge, skills and power he needed to construct something impregnable. His own field was military intelligence, espionage and counterterrorism, putting him in position to deal with the huge political and criminal issues that faced a corporation of their size and reach. But Richard was the one who was an incomparable security specialist, who dealt with the everyday dangers, the security issues in the real and cyber worlds that could bring any business down.

So they'd become, for all intents and purposes, partners. Not that this had changed their personal position. They would always remain antagonists.

Richard's lips twisted as he returned his antipathy, just with his usual sarcasm. "I should have known you came from such a land, where vendettas are inherited and cherished as the source of honor and glory. You can't help what you are, it seems. It's in your genes."

Usually, he engaged Richard in the rituals of their on-going cold war. But Numair couldn't afford to do that now. Not when that damned snake had something he needed.

Knowing that, and determined to make the most of Numair's inability to react as he wished to, Richard smiled like the serpent he was.

Pushing the jacket of his handmade sand-colored suit out of the way, he shoved one hand into his pants' pocket, with the other one still holding the briefcase he was here to deliver. Without attempting to give it to him, he looked around like someone assessing a pawned property he'd come to acquire in lieu of an unpaid debt.

"So I see you installed yourself in a setting appropriate to your future lofty status, until you take over Saraya's royal palace." Richard gave him a baiting glance, one of the staple methods of interaction between them. "You even acquired yourself a local princess."

Numair bristled but forced himself not to flay Richard alive. He wanted that briefcase with a minimum of fuss.

Obviously, Richard had other plans, as his goading intensified. "At first I thought you were stringing her along to spoil Hassan's marriage plans. I thought you'd asked me for help with the release of Zafrana's financial assets to deprive him of his power over Zafrana, to contribute to crippling him before you struck him down. But then you continued carrying on with her, and I realized your actions have all been directed to making *her* and her father indebted to you, and dependent on you. You don't only want Saraya's throne, you want Zafrana's, too. And she's your ticket to it."

This made Numair relinquish any thoughts of restraint. He grabbed Richard's arm with a force that had broken lesser men's arms. "Keep your realizations and theories to yourself, Cobra, and don't even *think* of Jenan again."

Richard's eyes widened, with surprise not pain, the caustic derision disappearing from his expression, contemplative scrutiny descending in its place.

Then he grimaced. "By God, not you, too, Phantom."

Numair knew exactly what Richard meant. Two of Numair's brothers had already succumbed to what they'd all previously considered an ailment none of them was susceptible to. Love. Rafael had married the daughter of the man he'd thought had sold him to The Organization, and Raiden had married the woman who'd once been sent by his former handler to expose him.

But if there was anyone they'd all thought was 100 percent impervious to any emotions, let alone love, it was Numair. And his current companion, of course.

Richard said exactly that. "Besides me, you're the literal last man on earth I expected to fall in love."

If Richard expected him to deny it, to consider it a weakness he wouldn't admit to anyone, most of all to his lifelong nemesis, he had another think coming. The moment he could, he'd shout it from the rooftops if need be. He'd made his peace with the life-changing realization.

He *had* fallen in love with Jenan.

But even that statement wasn't accurate. He'd far more than fallen in love with her. He felt as if she'd become an extension of his being, the most vital part that he'd perish without. Dependence on someone else had been unimaginable before; absolute self-sufficiency had been the basic fact on which he'd built his whole life. Even the brothers, who were integral to his life and self, he'd depended on for survival and practical matters, never emotionally. He'd never felt he'd die if he lost them. He felt that about her, and more. He could live only with her.

This profound dependence had started from their first

meeting. Right then his fundamental being had recognized hers as the only one to mesh with it, to complete his missing parts. The feeling had taken root during the night he'd first claimed her, as she'd claimed him right back. Every day since, those roots had been growing deeper, becoming entangled, encompassing everything inside him.

Their intimacy, in and out of bed, had been growing exponentially, and she'd been totally open about what he made her feel. But she hadn't made a straight declaration of her love. He hadn't, either, but he had been calling her "my love" and "my heart" and "my soul" and meaning every word. She hadn't reciprocated.

But just before Richard arrived, something terrible had occurred to him. He couldn't believe it hadn't before. Being with her did tamper with his every mental function.

He'd realized he should hope she wouldn't declare her love. Not yet. Not before he settled his mission, and could tell her the whole truth...

"Seriously?" Richard's scoff yanked him out of his oppressive musings. "You're going to be one of those men who zones out when they even picture their beloved?"

He forced his focus back on Richard. "I said Jenan is off-limits. To discussion. To speculation. To thoughts."

"Thoughts, eh? You have a way of enforcing that ban?"

"If you value your family jewels, you'll shut up, give me that briefcase and get the hell out of here."

"Leave?" Richard feigned a shocked face. "Without taking a tour of this *Arabian Nights* reproduction?"

"I can take the briefcase from your dead body, Cobra."

Richard laughed, true amusement in the lethal rumble. "I'll die another day, thank you, Phantom." He swung the briefcase up, hugged it to his chest, provocation set on maximum. "I flew fifteen hours straight to come here. Doesn't this warrant that you offer me a drink, at least?"

"No, it doesn't. Now give me the damned documents."

"Just like that? I get nothing in return."

"You do. I owe you one. Collect it anytime."

"I'll collect it right now. I want that drink."

Numair seethed with frustration. He could always beat Richard to a pulp. Problem was, Richard would inflict as much damage on him. They were each other's match. And he couldn't have Jenan arriving to find him torn and bloody. His scars continued to hurt her, and he couldn't bear disturbing her anymore if he could help it. Which meant he couldn't vent his aggression. Ever again.

As he was about to take that insufferable creature to force-feed him that drink, Richard added, "And I want to meet that mythical being who brought you to your knees."

Numair rounded on him, snarling, "You can ask for anything of equal value to what you're giving me. *Anything* involving Jenan is invaluable, and will never be an option, for you or anyone else. But now you've dared to ask that, I wouldn't offer you a sip of water if you were dying of thirst, so you might as well give up and go the hell away."

Richard transferred the briefcase behind his back. "You know I never give up. And I'm going nowhere. So what will you do? Kill me like you've wanted to for the past twenty-five years?"

"If that's what it takes to get rid of you."

Richard's devil eyes flared with challenge, and Numair's body bunched in preparation for that climactic fight he'd been burning for since he'd been fifteen. But a deep sound doused his aggression.

The helicopter bringing Jenan to him.

As he relinquished his confrontation with Richard and rushed down the stairs to the helipad, Richard huffed a laugh.

"Saved by the copter." Numair turned his fed-up gaze to him, and Richard wiggled an eyebrow. "You were."

He stopped where he always waited for her, watching the helicopter landing, and Richard appeared beside him.

"I expect this is your beloved. What opportune timing. I'll get to meet her after all."

Suspicion exploded inside Numair's mind. "You timed your arrival so you'd intercept her."

Richard's eyebrows shot up in what looked like genuine incredulity. "Bloody hell, Phantom, you're in a far worse condition than I thought. How would I have known when she comes to visit? Or if she comes at fixed times at all?"

"You know anything you want to know."

"True. But that's only if I wanted to know. And a few minutes ago I didn't even realize that woman's significance to you. Why would I have tried to *intercept* her?"

That made sense to Numair. It was possible he was just being paranoid.

But he'd learned it always paid to be that and more. And with someone like Richard, nothing was ever at face value. Richard might have long realized his true feelings toward Jenan and was here to do some kind of mischief. He couldn't afford that. He had enough worries where she was concerned. He couldn't add a whiff of trouble to them. And Richard was trouble in its most concentrated form.

He grabbed Richard by his lapels, hauled him closer until their noses almost touched. "Listen, Cobra, if you think I was ever your enemy, it's nothing to what I'll be if you step a millimeter out of line. I'm indebted to you for acquiring the original signed documents releasing the last of Zafrana's stocks and bonds, but you're here only because you insisted they were too crucial to be entrusted to a messenger. I should have known you didn't come because you cared about the documents or my plans."

"No? If I don't care, why did I even help you in the first place? I could have just told you to sod off."

"Are you telling me you care now? If I live or die? This is you and me, Cobra, remember?"

Richard gave a gruff exhalation. "As if you ever let me forget. But I also remember we were once best friends."

"Yes, until you reported that I was planning to escape so you could gain your superiors' favor. My body still bears the scars of the sixty days straight they tortured me within an inch of my life in punishment."

There. He'd gotten it out in the open at last.

Richard stared at him for a long, charged moment. Then he exhaled. "Did you ever wonder why I did it?"

"No. Because I already knew why. You were a monster by choice and preference, Cobra. You still are."

After holding his eyes for another moment with an inexplicable expression filling his own, Richard finally shrugged. "As are you. Or at least, as you were, until Princess Aal Ghamdi."

Numair looked back as the helicopter landed, seething with urgency. "Don't think my feelings for her tame me, Cobra. A predator with a mate is even more deadly."

"But more vulnerable."

Before he could snarl a response, the copter's door was flung open and Jenan jumped out, hitting the ground running as usual. Forgetting Richard within a heartbeat, he swung around and rushed to meet her halfway.

Watching her run to him was, as always, an agonizing joy. Her hair caught the declining rays of the sun and reflected it into tones of fire and ruby. Her eyes rivaled its golden heat. Her smile was everything he lived to see anymore, her body everything he lived to feel and her whole being everything that embodied his reasons for existence.

Suddenly her expression sobered, and her steps faltered. Something sharp stabbed him in the gut at the loss of her eagerness, even when he realized it was on account of Richard's presence. She'd only just noticed that hulk. And it doused her spontaneity. Another thing for which to wish Richard an eternity in the deepest abyss.

As he covered the remaining distance and took her in his arms, Jenan asked, "Who is that?"

He gritted his teeth over the expletives on the tip of his tongue. "Richard Graves. My associate."

"Not one of your Black Castle brothers, is he?"

Numair's heart fired. Every time she mentioned his brothers or made a comment that correctly diagnosed a truth he hid, the need to tell her everything almost over-powered him. With those uncanny instincts of hers, she'd realized there was far more to him than what he'd made known.

But she accepted the darkest parts she knew of his man-ufactured history without reservations, with even admi-ration for what he'd become. It made him hope that when he was able to divulge the whole truth, it wouldn't shock her, wouldn't alienate her.

He now only said, "No, he's not."

"I thought Black Castle was exclusively a partnership between you and those men you consider brothers."

"Richard, regretfully, is the exception."

"Regretfully, huh?" She suddenly chuckled. "And he's still in one piece and living and unavoidably in your life, too? He is certainly a man worth meeting. Introduce me?"

Grinding his teeth again, he knew he had to comply. At least he'd made Richard realize he *would* kill him this time if he messed this up with Jenan. He hoped, for her sake, that Richard behaved. He'd rather not kill him in front of her.

Entwining her arm with his, he took her to meet Richard.

Deep into the night, Numair woke up with a start.

He subsided when he felt Jenan draped over him, every inch of her warm, firm, precious flesh plastered to his.

They'd made love for hours after Richard left. To his shock, Richard had behaved with perfect gallantry in Jenan's presence. And Jenan had been her usual spontaneous self with him. Numair, however, still wanted to kill him. He clearly had serious insecurity issues, even when he knew he had no reason to.

But he did have a reason, he corrected himself. A huge one. And it had nothing to do with jealousy.

During the past weeks, while everything had fallen into place according to his methodical plans, with him releasing Jenan from Hassan, then forcing him to relinquish Zafrana's debts one at a time, with the last ones being what Richard had brought him today, he'd kept realizing that nothing was going as he'd envisioned.

The cousins he'd come here intending to engage in a vicious fight were nothing he'd thought they were. They were all admirable men and women. Even worse, he liked Najeeb more every time he saw him. His plan to wrest the throne from him after condemning his father for a murderer and destroying his family honor no longer seemed feasible. For how could he deal with Najeeb with as much cold blood as he'd always dealt with adversaries when he no longer considered him one?

But that was only his secondary worry. His main one was focused on Jenan. The foreboding that had been building inside him had crystallized during Richard's visit.

At first, he hadn't thought a day would come when he'd regret not being honest about why he'd wanted an heir.

But if he put the rest of his plan into action, she'd realize his early purpose. He had no doubt the totally honest woman that she was, who'd accepted his declared reasons in good faith, would feel betrayed and used. Now he didn't know how to rectify his initial mistake.

His only hope was that she wasn't already pregnant.

Which was probably too much to hope for after their weeks of unprotected lovemaking.

But she must have been checking regularly, and if she'd said nothing, it was possible she wasn't yet pregnant. If she wasn't, he didn't want her to get pregnant anymore. He didn't want a child to complicate matters between them more than they already were, to make her more prone to being vulnerable and inconsolable when the truth came out.

But he wouldn't know where to go from here until he asked her, knew for certain if she was or wasn't pregnant.

Coming to that conclusion, he closed his eyes again and did something he'd never done before.

He prayed. To whatever was out there and might listen. He prayed that she wasn't pregnant, that he'd be granted a second chance to make this right.

Jen watched Numair prowling toward her in the mirror as she brushed her hair in long, leisurely strokes, imagining herself stroking his magnificent body.

Not that she needed imagining. He'd given her absolute freedom to do whatever she wished to him and she'd been losing her mind all over him, doing everything she'd ever dreamed of with that body of his. And he'd been doing everything she'd known about, and many, many things she hadn't known about, with hers. To both their complete and supreme ecstasy.

He now came to tower over her from behind, his eyes flaring and subsiding like glowing emeralds, snaring her eyes in their reflection. In her mind she only saw a sequence of events that had happened so many times during the past six delirious weeks. Numair picking her up, making her feel weightless, thrilling her yet again with all the power this man of hers possessed. And how he used it all to worship and pleasure her!

Then his hands descended on her shoulders, and she

shuddered in anticipation, though she knew she shouldn't be inviting another session of passion. She'd told her father she'd be back in the palace in an hour to give him proof Zafrana's debts, and his mess, had been wiped clean. Thanks to Numair.

But surely her father could wait a few hours longer…

"Have you…checked?"

Numair's quiet question felt like a slap of icy water across her heated body and fantasies.

There wasn't any use wondering what he was asking about. His meaning was totally clear. And her instant mortification had an equally known origin.

For she hadn't checked.

She'd been avoiding doing so. She hadn't wanted to make sure if she was pregnant, even now that her period was late. He might have insisted that wanting her had come first, and still did, but she feared that becoming pregnant would destroy their intimacy, not solidify it.

She also believed he'd insisted on marriage early on in order to give his heir the legitimacy she now suspected he'd never had. He'd always avoided talking much about his past, but she was now convinced the facts he made known were nothing but a fabrication, that he'd never had a family, and that his childhood had been too terrible to share.

She wanted to do anything at all to make it up to him, to give him everything he wanted and needed, yet she couldn't bear that he'd marry her for any other reason but for her.

And there was another concern. Though he'd been deluging her in his passion and consideration, she still felt him holding back…*so* much. Not knowing what he was hiding of himself, of his past, she couldn't chart the future.

That was why she dreaded changing the present. And her pregnancy would blow that up big-time.

Instead of saying she hadn't checked, she said, "There's nothing yet."

And it was as if a dagger drove into her heart.

That flare in his eyes. That convulsive squeeze of her shoulders. That shudder that emanated from his body and reverberated in her own.

He was *relieved*.

That she *wasn't* pregnant.

The magnitude of his relief had almost rocked him off his feet. If he hadn't grabbed her shoulders so hard, she thought he might have even slumped to his knees.

His reaction was so startling, so incongruous with everything she'd believed up till this point, about him and about what he wanted. She felt beyond shocked.

And there was only one explanation she could find.

He'd changed his mind.

He no longer wanted to have an heir.

Not from her.

Numair didn't know how it was possible, after all he'd done in his life, that he'd deserved a second chance.

Yet he'd somehow gotten it.

Jenan wasn't pregnant yet.

The news had almost buckled his knees when bullets had failed to do so. Relief still so enervated him, he hadn't been able to do anything since she'd left for Zafrana's royal palace an hour ago.

This development bought him the most precious commodity—time to resolve everything. This way he could let it be her choice to give him a child after she knew everything about him, and everything that had brought him into her life. He wanted nothing but for her to have the dignity, the freedom and self-determination to decide to be with him, to share her life and child with him, after full disclosure.

This was everything he wanted now. He no longer cared about taking over Zafrana's throne or even Saraya's. He no longer even cared about punishing his uncle or avenging his father or himself. All the ugliness and horrors and suffering suddenly felt as though they had happened in someone else's past, someone he no longer was.

He was now a new man, a man who loved Jenan with all the heart she'd created inside him. He cared only that she forgave him his initial deception and gave him her trust, her love, forever. Nothing else but her mattered.

As for resolving the other matters he'd come here for, his plans had radically changed. He still had to depose Hassan, as this was no longer just about him, but because he couldn't let such a criminal continue ruling his homeland. He now just had to find a way that wouldn't hurt or disgrace the rest of Hassan's family…and his own. Then he'd be able to confess everything to Jenan.

Suddenly, another realization burst in his mind.

He couldn't make love to her anymore!

Though there was a possibility he couldn't impregnate her since he hadn't yet—which he also realized didn't matter at all—he couldn't continue making love to her without protection, in case they finally succeeded in creating a child before he resolved everything. And he couldn't suddenly start using protection, either, not without explaining why.

His only way out was to not make love to her at all. It felt like the most mutilating sentence he'd ever had inflicted on him. But it was a price he had to pay for his mistakes, until he fixed them and told her the truth.

He could only pray to whoever or whatever had answered his first prayer, that when he did, she'd still want him and would give him a second chance.

The second chance his life depended on.

"Is Numair coming today?"

At Fayza's eager question, Jen turned from staring

numbly at her reflection in her bedroom mirror. She found both her sisters with their heads poking around her suite's door, their long hair cascading like waterfalls of mahogany and ebony. They were now the one thing that made being back in Zafrana's royal palace, in Zafrana at all, in this whole life, bearable.

She had one response for them. "No, he isn't coming."

And she feared he never would again.

"But we want to ask him if we can have another party on board his jet," Zeena lamented.

"Can we call him?" Fayza zoomed inside, bombarding her with questions. "We don't have his phone number. Does he even answer if it's a number he doesn't know? Or does he know our numbers? Would you call him for us?"

"Don't you think we've taken enough from Sheikh Numair?"

Jen's heart squeezed at their father's weary voice. He now followed the girls into her suite at a much slower pace, as if it hurt to walk.

Forcing a smile, she rose to greet him, and he took her in arms that trembled and kissed the top of her head.

It felt as if her father had grown smaller in the past months, had aged far beyond his sixty-three years. Being helpless to solve his kingdom's problems, and the shame of having to sacrifice his eldest daughter as their only solution had taken their toll. Even now that it was over, it seemed the ordeal still echoed its distress and defeat inside him. It probably would for the rest of his life.

She pulled back, wanting to soothe him, even when she had nothing but dread and pain inside her own soul, and he looked at her with a world of contrition in his eyes.

"When you first came to me with Numair and told me he'd resolve Zafrana's debts, I couldn't believe he'd do that without asking for something even bigger in return. I didn't even know if he could do it. Then Hassan called everything off, and I knew Numair had fulfilled his promise. A week ago, I got back everything I signed away, just because Numair willed it. Now I find myself in an even bigger debt than what bound me in servitude to Hassan. This time to Numair. The debt of the restoration of your freedom, of our kingdom's stability and of my dignity. And it's a debt I have no idea how I will ever repay."

Swallowing the knot in her throat, she tried to keep the tremors of anguish from her voice. "Numair doesn't want, or expect, anything in return."

Numair didn't want anything anymore. Not from her.

"Are you certain, *ya b'nayti*?" She winced at how her father called her "my daughter," as his eyes, so much like hers, probed her in hope. "I thought you were the prize he had his heart set on."

Unable to utter another word without succumbing to the desolate weeping that had overcome her so many times in the past week, she just shook her head.

That hit her family hard, made them cut their visit short. They'd all come with everything they'd wanted to say or hoped for involving Numair. They'd had their hearts set on Numair ending up with her.

As she'd believed he would. Until that day she'd told him she wasn't pregnant.

Since that day, he'd been finding excuses not to meet her, and if he had to, he made sure it wasn't in their place or anywhere private. Every instance of pointed distance had solidified her suspicions. He *had* been relieved she hadn't become pregnant, and he wasn't risking she might become so. But it was far worse than she'd at first thought. It wasn't the heir he'd changed his mind about.

It was her. He no longer wanted her.

It had taken her seven weeks to fall irrevocably in love with him, to become unable to think how she'd lived before him, or to imagine a life without him. It had taken him the same time to have enough of her.

Who was she fooling? It hadn't taken her that long to fall for him. She'd done so on sight. Every day since had only driven her deeper into dependence.

And while his desire for her had seemed to intensify, too, it had just come to an abrupt end that day. Ever since, he'd been pretending to still want her, but he escaped any intimacy under a dozen pretexts. He might think he was letting her down gradually, but she couldn't bear that. If he no longer wanted her, she wanted it over. Now.

Waga'a sa'aa wala kol sa'aa. The pain of an hour rather than that of every hour.

The adage was true. But she knew this pain would only grow until it consumed her. For this was worse than anything she'd feared. Just before her family had come, she'd succumbed and…checked. The two pink lines had appeared instantaneously. It was as she'd feared for some time now.

She *was* pregnant.

Knowing for sure that she carried the baby of the only man she could ever love—when he no longer wanted that child or her—was pure, unremitting agony.

Now she wanted, *needed*, to look him in the eye and get the closure of hearing him say it.

That he no longer wanted a child. Or her. That he'd never really wanted her, not as she wanted him.

That it was over.

Nine

Numair stood aside and let Najeeb pass inside what he and Jenan had come to call *Malaz*, or Sanctuary. Their home.

The home he'd contrived not to let her come to for a whole week now. He'd known if she came, he'd succumb to his need, and more, to hers. The questions, the uncertainty in her eyes every time he'd seen her at the palace or elsewhere with others around during the past week had been killing him. But he hoped, after Najeeb's visit, the separation he'd enforced on them would be over forever.

He'd invited Najeeb here to face him with the truth.

Najeeb regarded him with confusion as Numair invited him to sit down where he had the first time he'd come here. Their relationship had changed radically over the past weeks since that hostile first meeting. But their interactions had remained with Jenan at their core. No doubt Najeeb couldn't understand what they had to discuss in her absence.

Najeeb asked at once, "Is this about Jenan?"

Numair sat down on the armchair facing him. "Everything is ultimately about Jenan. But this is about you. And me. And our family."

Najeeb went still, his face freezing. "*Our* family?"

"Yes." He leaned forward, pushed toward him the dossier with all the evidence of his identity.

The teams he'd had scouring the Mediterranean with Black Castle patented equipment and technology had found the sunken yacht. And the remains. A DNA test had proved his memories without a doubt. The remains were incontrovertibly of Hisham Aal Ghaanem. Hassan's brother. And Numair's father.

Najeeb went through each document, mounting shock an expanding sweep emanating from him.

Then Najeeb raised his eyes, and there was something there that shocked Numair in turn. The last thing he'd expected Najeeb to feel. Delight.

"You're my cousin!"

Numair's throat closed. Najeeb's reaction rocked him to his core. He'd been bracing for Najeeb's disbelief, suspicion, dismay and a dozen other things that would be natural reactions when faced with a revelation of this magnitude. But this—the unmistakable acceptance and instant eagerness—hadn't even been reactions he'd imagined. Najeeb continued to decimate his every expectation. And if he'd already been wondering how to become his antagonist and rival for the throne, he now wondered if he could be.

Najeeb sat forward, every line in his body explicit with his excitement. "*Ya Ullah*, after all these years! What happened? How did you find out? Did you just find out? *B'Ellahi*, this is incredible, amazing! Wait till Haroon and Jawad and my other siblings find out about this! The girls especially will go ballistic. They've been swooning over you, and now they'll have premium bragging rights. But we'll have to make it clear right off the bat to every other lady in our family and acquaintance that you're the exclusive property of Jenan—"

Hating to do it, Numair had to interrupt his zeal. "I got you in private because I don't want anyone but you to know. You'll realize why when I tell you the whole story."

Numair couldn't believe how it dismayed him to see the spontaneity in the other man's eyes dimming. He'd no doubt extinguish it completely if he declared his right to the throne.

For now, he told him the story he'd already decided to tell him. The attack, his father's murder and how he'd been left for dead, and the fictional parts about being rescued then adopted, then back to the truth of retrieving his memories of the incident after years of hypnotherapy.

Najeeb looked more moved with every word. Then he let out a ragged exhalation. "But this means you knew your true identity when we first met. Why didn't you tell me then?"

"Because I was still searching for the proof you have in your hands now."

"You thought I wouldn't believe you without evidence?" Najeeb seemed stunned that Numair had considered such a thing.

"Wouldn't you?"

"To borrow your and Jenan's favorite catchphrase, you're kidding, right? After my initial hostility, which was all concern for Jenan, I felt a kindred link to you that I couldn't explain. I would have believed you without any proof beyond those of my instincts." Suddenly, he laughed. "But it's your lady's instincts that are uncanny. She's the one who saw through it all from the first moment, who kept saying we felt as close as brothers. As we are."

"As we are," Numair repeated, something hot and overriding stirring in his chest.

He had his brothers, and they were an essential part of his being. But the tug of blood between him and Najeeb was something he'd never experienced, or expected to. Since the last trace of worry he could rival him for Jenan's affection had been erased, and now that Najeeb accepted him so readily, he let it sweep him.

He hated to spoil those moments of closeness, to tarnish the purity of Najeeb's goodwill. But he had to tell him the rest.

"Making contact with my long-lost family wasn't why I went to your father's reception. Or why I came here."

That again stunned Najeeb. "What else did you want?"

"To reclaim my birthright. And to exact vengeance."

The light in Najeeb's eyes went out. "Vengeance?"

"I believed your father had mine killed."

To say Najeeb was shocked was like saying Numair slightly liked Jenan. Numair could feel his statement tearing through the other man's very foundations.

Then shock gave way to adamant rejection, and Najeeb just said, "No."

Before Numair could respond, a sound emptied his mind. That of the helicopter that had been bringing him Jenan for the past weeks. All but this last one.

He heaved up to his feet. "We'll discuss this at length, Najeeb. But for now just stay here and wait for me."

Before Najeeb could even blink, Numair ran out.

He had no idea how he'd send Jenan away without explaining why, but he couldn't have her see Najeeb. The can of worms had been opened, but nothing had yet been resolved.

By the time he crossed the villa, she was already opening the front door. He rushed to intercept her, and she raised her gaze to him. What he saw in her eyes made him almost stumble.

She looked...bereft.

Forcing his legs to work, he reached her as she closed the door, and pulled her into his arms. "Is everyone all right?"

She nodded, but pushed out of his arms when she always clung.

At a loss what to make of her disturbing disposition, he said, "You didn't tell me you were coming."

Her eyes again rose to his, and they looked so wounded, foreboding pierced his heart. "You would have only found a way to escape seeing me. But don't worry, I won't stay where I'm no longer welcome."

He gaped at her. "What?"

"You should have told me the truth the moment you realized it."

Everything inside him stilled. Had she somehow found out the truth and it was too late to be the one to tell her? Was that the reaction he'd been dreading?

He finally choked out, "What truth?"

"That you no longer want me."

This was literally the last thing he'd expected her to say. It hit him so hard, everything in his mind fractured.

"Jenan, this is insane…"

"Yes, it seems my name is quite apt. I must be insane to feel crushed now when you already told me what you wanted from the get-go. But you don't want it from me anymore, and I'm here to tell you it's your right to change your mind. But it isn't your right to drag this out, to not just release me. If you think evading me is letting me down easy, it's far more painful than if you'd just looked me in the eye and told me it's over."

Every word fell on him like a sledgehammer.

He'd been so consumed in his worries and efforts to put things right, he'd made things catastrophically worse. He hadn't even thought how his evasions would seem to her, but she'd found them so inexplicable, so hurtful, she'd reached the worst possible conclusion.

Before he could think of anything to say, she strode past him, heading toward where Najeeb was seated.

He pounced to stop her. "Where are you going?"

The spasm of pain that twisted her face almost tore his heart apart. "I said not to worry. I won't try to stay or to impose on you. I'll just get some stuff I need. You can send the rest later. Or just throw it away."

He wanted to blurt out a thousand protests, but only one thing made it out of the churning mess in his mind. "This is *your* place."

Her forlorn expression deepened, widening the wound her pain had gouged in his being. "I only considered it mine when I thought you were, too, when we were together. But you're not, and we won't be again. Tomorrow I'll send you the papers reverting the ownership to you." She tried to move again, and his hand tightened convulsively on her arm with horror at the terrible things she believed. And suspicion blossomed like an ink stain in her eyes. "You have someone inside?"

Shocked all over again at her horrific assumption, more evidence of how disastrously he'd messed up, he could only stare at her helplessly.

And everything in her eyes died. It felt far worse than anything he'd endured in captivity, seeing that look in her eyes.

"Jenan, please…"

Tears arrowed down her cheeks, drowning her words and his. "I never expected you to love me as I loved you. I only ever wanted you to be honest with me."

Hearing her for the first time say she loved him—only for her to make it in the past tense—was unbearable. Like knowing he could have saved someone's life, and out of his own negligence, he'd arrived just moments too late.

This time he didn't let her resist him, but crushed her in his arms. "Jenan, Jenan, what have I done to you, to us? I damaged your trust in me so much you think I have a woman in there?" A tear splashed over his chest, corroding its way through to his heart as she shook all over and struggled to escape his embrace. He crushed her to him harder, groaned between feverish kisses all over her face. "Everything you think is the absolute opposite of the truth. It agonizes me to know I made you think it. But it's true I don't love you like you love me." At her lurching sob, he squeezed her tighter, as if he'd merge her into his body. "After all I've suffered in my life, I love you far more than you can ever love me."

This time when she struggled, it was to look up.

Her eyes looked so fragile and inflamed she had to have been weeping long before she'd come. But that dreadful grief was giving way to hope. His heart swelled with impending relief only to shrivel the next second.

"It's true he doesn't have a woman in there. The secrets he's been hiding are far, far worse than that."

Both he and Jenan swung around at the dark drawl.

Numair's arms loosened around Jenan with dismay, letting her go as her face went slack with surprise. "Najeeb."

He couldn't have them both here now. It might cause a chain reaction he wouldn't be able to control.

Numair turned urgently to Jenan. "I do have secrets, but they have nothing to do with us, with what I feel for you. I also have reasons for the way I've been behaving, and I'll explain everything, only later. Please, *ya habibati*, just go now, let me conclude this with Najeeb and trust that everything I do is for you, for us."

As Jenan's eyes softened with such relief and tension left her body, Najeeb's harsh sarcasm washed over them once more, stiffening her all over again.

"Your powers of manipulation border on magic, don't

they, Numair?" Najeeb's steps were measured, his face as hard as stone, his eyes simmering with rage. Then he turned his gaze to Jenan. "When I heard your anguish as I approached, I thought he'd told you everything." His gaze swung back to Numair. "But then I realized you were still playing her. What I felt the moment I saw you *was* right. There are far darker things to you, and colder, more terrible motives to your being with her than even I feared. But you realized I was on to you, and you poured on the pretense, conned me like you conned her from the start."

"I might have hidden some truths—"

"Some truths?" Najeeb scoffed. "You hid every truth. All the time we've been dealing with a total fabrication."

"This *is* the real me. I only had to settle things with you first before I told her everything."

"About that." Najeeb flicked him a contemptuous look. "I sat in there wondering why you revealed your truth now, and I realized it's because you've reached the point in your meticulous plans when it suited you to do so, when you were ready to strike. But when you looked so shaken by Jenan's arrival, and so anxiously asked me to stay inside, I realized this was one thing you didn't account for. For us to meet at this delicate point, exposing everything to her prematurely. According to your plans, she would have been the last to know the truth, right? When it was too late for her to do anything about it."

Unable to act on his rising dread and aggression, Numair said, "You have this all wrong, Najeeb."

Until this moment, Jenan had been mutely gaping at them. Now she came between them, her voice a brittle tremolo. "What plans? What truth?"

Before Numair could try to mollify her again, Najeeb ended any hope for containing this disaster.

"That his name isn't Numair, but ironically, a synonym

of that, what I'm sure he meant. It's Fahad. Fahad Aal Ghaanem."

After seconds of nonreaction, the widening of Jenan's eyes said that she recognized the name. The confusion that flooded them right after said she couldn't process, or believe, the connotations of that name.

Najeeb ended her uncertainty. "Yes, *that* Fahad Aal Ghaanem. The cousin we all thought long dead."

It took frozen moments before Jenan shook her head, her bewilderment deepening, not lessening. "How?"

In answer, Najeeb succinctly recounted the story he'd told him. As he spoke, Jenan's eyes were riveted to Numair, as if struggling to superimpose the new truths on what she'd known of him, what she'd had with him, till now.

When Najeeb fell silent, she asked shakily, "Why didn't you tell me?"

It was Najeeb who answered again. "This was another thing I sat in there trying to understand. Then I worked it all out. You see, right before you arrived, Numair—or should I say Fahad—told me he was here to exact revenge. On my father, whom he accused of having his father killed. The other reason he mentioned was to reclaim his *birth-right*. And it all became clear. He had a convoluted plan to come here, hurt my father as much as possible until he had solid proof of his lineage. Once he did, he'd accuse my father of murder, deposing him in a scandal and of course getting rid of me as the current crown prince, and claiming the throne for himself." Najeeb turned to Numair, arctic challenge in those eyes that had been all warmth such a short while ago. "Did I miss anything?"

"It's not like that anymore…"

"What about me?"

Jenan's voice, so smothered in trepidation, drove a jagged edge in his gut, cutting short his protestations.

"Jenan, I said I'll explain everything later…"

"Will you?" Najeeb's words cut through his entreaty like a knife. "Why not do it now? She's asking a very simple question after all. Why did you approach her in the first place? Or should we say, target her? That was the other thing I sat in there trying to figure out, until I finally realized that your *heritage* isn't only in Saraya, but Zafrana. Your mother was Princess Safeyah Aal Ghamdi, and half of your blood is royal Zafranian blood. Being the power-monger that you are, and with the state the kingdom is in, you must consider you're the one who has both the right and the power to rule it. But since you don't have a direct claim to the throne as you do in Saraya, you concocted a more convoluted plan. You weren't *saving* Jenan from my father, or even trying to hurt him by decimating his power over Zafrana and the massive resources he'd expended to gain it. You wanted Jenan only to use her in the exact same way he intended to." Najeeb turned his pained gaze to Jenan. "Claiming you, having an heir from you, would make him control Zafrana's throne during your father's life, then after his death, until his heir, your father's heir, comes of age."

Jenan turned her gaze toward Numair. There was no shock or pain or accusation in there. Just emptiness.

As everything collided inside him, the vacuum in her eyes intensified, as if her essence had totally departed his body. A body that had nothing more to prop it up, and collapsed to the ground in a boneless mass.

"Jenan!"

Lightning-fast reflexes honed through decades of merciless training kicked in, fighting off the paralysis. He caught her before she hit the ground. But Najeeb had also charged to save her.

Finding Najeeb's hands crowding his on Jenan's inert body almost made his head burst with rage.

As soon as he laid her down with trembling care on the ground, he flung Najeeb away and tackled him there.

Najeeb was so stunned by his attack, Numair got a few jaw-cracking punches in before Najeeb pulled himself together enough to retaliate. At the first blow that connected with Numair's own jaw, something crashed in place inside him, rousing him from his blind wrath.

Najeeb was a powerful man, could hold his own with anyone else, but he wasn't a violent man, and certainly not a killer. But Numair was. Najeeb was no match for him. If he didn't curb himself, he would kill him.

Flinging himself off him and rebounding to his feet, he watched Najeeb rise to his, rubbing his already swelling jaw as if to make sure it was still hinged. Numair *had* pulled his punches, or it would have been pulverized now.

Looking at him as if at a horrific monster, Najeeb rasped with obvious difficulty, "What *are* you?"

"Something you can't even imagine in your worst nightmares. Consider yourself lucky. I have destroyed men for causing me far, far less than the incalculable damage you just caused me with Jenan."

As Numair moved, Najeeb's body stiffened in readiness for confrontation. "Stay where you are, you maniac."

Numair shot him a baleful glance as he rushed back to Jenan, scooped her unconscious form up and took her to their bed, where he'd missed having her like he'd miss a vital organ. She was warm, breathing easily. It seemed her nervous system had sought the refuge of oblivion to protect her from the brunt of Najeeb's revelations.

After minutes of trying to rouse her and failing, but knowing she was in no danger, he rose and turned to Najeeb, who'd followed him, as if not trusting him with Jenan now.

"I'm over my murderous fury, which thanks to your punch—" he rubbed his own jaw; Najeeb's punch would have felled any other man "—I realized was directed at myself. You only exposed the truth about what I once intended."

Najeeb tried a bitter laugh, and it came out a pained groan. "You know where you went wrong? If you'd come clean to me, to Jenan, if you weren't a cold, manipulative bastard, we would have gladly given you everything you wanted. I would have recognized your right to the throne, would have made my father relinquish it to you." He nodded toward Jenan. "And she would have loved you. Of her own free will, and would have considered you the one who deserves Zafrana's throne. Now I wouldn't entrust the fate of a heap of dirt to you, let alone that of my kingdom. And if you spread your vicious lies about my father and try to destroy my family, I'll fight you till my dying breath. As for her, don't hold *your* breath you'll be able to con her again."

Numair exhaled. "Though you might not believe it now, I got you here so I can resolve this with minimum damage to everyone. But you didn't let me finish what I had to say, and now anything you think is irrelevant. Fixing things with you will have to wait until I deal with this disaster you've caused me with Jenan."

Najeeb's antipathy wavered, before his gaze panned to Jenan and it turned to steel again. "You can try. But this woman would have died for you. If I know anything about her, she'd now rather die than let you near her again."

Turning to Najeeb fully, he let him see the monster he had inside him, and that he could no longer harness it. "You better pray that your prediction doesn't come to pass. If I lose her, I will have nothing else to lose in this world. Not even I can predict what I'd do then."

Najeeb must have realized it was dangerous to continue antagonizing him, and was clearly uncertain if he even should, because with a last glance full of confusion, he turned and walked out.

He fell off Numair's radar at once as he swooped down to Jenan, wrapping himself around her.

He wasn't losing her. Najeeb underestimated the power of what they had. She'd listen to him, and she'd understand, and she'd believe him again, trust him again.

Love him again.

Something hot and hard spread over Jenan, as smothering and inescapable as a shroud of burning steel.

Panic flooded her as she started to struggle, even when she knew there could be no escape. Sobs tore from her depths, gurgled to the surface.

"Shh, shh, *ya hayati*, calm down, everything is all right, you're safe. I'm here, and I'm yours."

That voice… Numair's voice. It had been the one thing she wanted to hear, the one thing to make her feel invincible. But now it made her suffocate with betrayal and misery.

The surge of memories tore her from the abyss she'd plummeted into and catapulted her into the far more horrible reality.

But she couldn't hide within oblivion anymore. She had to open her eyes and face him. Face the fact that her life would be nothing like she'd hoped or planned, but rather like everything she'd dreaded in other women's lives. Having the child of a man who cared nothing for her, suffering the perpetual heartaches and conflicts of being tied to him through that child for life.

But it was even worse in her condition. For even after finding out the truth, she knew she'd never stop yearning for him. For the Numair she'd loved. The Numair who didn't exist.

She opened her eyes and found him there, like dozens

of times before, wrapped around her, looking down at her as if only she mattered to him. When she now knew she never did at all.

"He's no longer here."

If desolation had a sound, this had to be it. The bleeding whisper that issued from her.

He blinked. "Yes, Najeeb left…"

"Numair." When she said his name, he sat up carefully, uncertain what she meant. She left him in doubt. "He was never here. He was a phantom."

He started at her description, looked stricken. "Jenan…"

She spoke over his ragged protest. "Everything I shared with him was a lie." She looked him in the eyes, and it almost ruptured her heart that they still looked like those of the Numair she adored, still uncannily hid the true nature of the malicious manipulator she now knew him to be. "I was a means to your ends. A chess piece you used and would have sacrificed as soon as you achieved your goal. But when you discovered you could do so now rather than later, you just cut me off."

His fingers sank into her shoulders, his eyes raging like infernos. "Don't even think that. None of that is true. Let me explain what Najeeb—"

"Najeeb only told me who you really are." She removed his hands from her flesh and pulled herself away from him. "I worked out the rest. For Najeeb doesn't know what I do. That you no longer have to marry me, or impregnate me to rule Zafrana, that you do have a direct claim to its throne, just like you do to Saraya's."

The need became desperation to escape the distress of his nearness and of being in the bed where he'd given her her life's only true and total pleasures, and then ruined her for life. She rose as if she'd been smashed and put back together with a precarious glue.

As he rose after her, she went on, "It's no wonder it took

you a while to find out. It was almost four decades ago, and most people in Zafrana don't know about it. Those who do probably don't remember it."

"Remember what? Jenan, *habibati*, just let me——"

"But I remember." Her choking whisper again silenced him. "How my father always lamented that he shouldn't have been king, that if not for a fluke accident, he wouldn't have been the rightful heir. He told me so many times when I was growing up that the late King Zayd had an heir who was tragically lost as an infant. The son of Princess Safeyah, a distant relative to the king by blood, but his sister in nursing, his mother having nursed her when her mother died in childbirth. This relationship superseded the much closer link of blood between him and my father, making her son his closest male relative, and his heir. You."

Silence and stillness expanded at her back as his surprise buffeted her. He hadn't realized that she knew.

But she did. And it explained all her questions about him, her incredulities about his coming into her life and her confusions about his recent turnabout.

Suddenly, his hands fell on her shoulders, feeling like twin bolts of torment that almost reduced her to ashes, his groan ragged. "Jenan, you have to believe me, I didn't know that."

She tore his hands off before they burned her through to the bone, then turned on him. "You didn't know that until you wasted too much time on me. But the moment you did, you tossed me aside." Another suspicion hit her, becoming a new terrible reality within a heartbeat. "But if you're trying to coax me again now, it means you know."

"I'm only trying to tell you the truth. I didn't know any of what you just said. And——" He suddenly stopped as her last words registered. Then he rasped, "Know what?"

"That I'm pregnant."

His instantaneous reaction was one of such consternation, it felt as if the heart hanging inside her by tattered strings was torn out completely and hurled on the ground.

The storm of misery that had been building inside her for the past week broke over her like a hurricane, destroying her soul and sanity.

She wept so hard, her tears became a downpour, draining her of everything that powered her being. Her hopes, her faith, her love...her soul.

She writhed weakly in his arms as he groaned and begged and tried to contain her in the now-oppressive circle of his arms, the embrace of deceit and cruelty.

Sobs hacked her insides and her words. "Now you know...your heir exists...you want to have it with the least conflict with the one who's regretfully carrying it...and what better way...than to con me again? The stupid, trusting, lovesick mark...you played from the first moment."

"No, Jenan, no, you have to listen to me."

"No...you listen. I loved Numair...I would have died for him, but now it's worse than if I'd simply lost him. Now I know that he never existed."

"I not only exist, and would die for you, but I only came fully into existence when I loved you. Before you, I never truly lived... Jenan, *habibati*, believe me..."

Unable to bear the scorching agony of his touch, she fought him frantically until he let her go.

She ended up against the door, sobs stabbing in her chest like skewers. He towered over her, a tempest of frustration and agitation raging on his face, knotting his every muscle. No doubt because things were no longer going his way.

But as everything in her clamored for him—the man who'd been as close to her as her very heart—another wave of desolation crashed on her. For she now knew.

She'd never rid her essence of the need for him. She'd never drain the poison of yearning from her blood without draining her very life with it. She'd never truly live again. Instead, she was doomed to just survive. For others. And without the man she'd loved, the man who'd turned out to be an illusion.

Once the conviction struck her, her weeping turned off abruptly. The suffering and desperation were too vast for tears. All that was left to feel was the resignation.

A deadened rasp issued from a throat that felt cut by thorns. "If you'd told me the truth, I would have realized you were the one powerful enough to save Zafrana. And if you'd wanted me at all, for real, I would have taken what I could with you even knowing you'd never feel for me what I feel for you. When you got enough of me, I would have at least remained intact. You could have gotten everything you wanted without destroying me."

She opened the door and spilled outside. Finding the helicopter still there was like finding a means of escape out of a flooding tunnel.

Before she stumbled to her salvation, he caught her back, his entreaties incessant.

Unable to endure one more touch or word, she wrenched herself from his arms with the last of her strength. "Don't you get it? You don't need to act anymore. I'm the one who's at your nonexistent mercy, who'll beg you not to deprive me of my baby. You won. Your plans worked. You'll have everything. Everything but me. But that won't matter to you, since I'm the only thing you never wanted."

Ten

So this was helplessness. This was desperation.

After a life of unimaginable ordeals, Numair had finally learned what these were. He'd been abused in every way, tortured to within a breath of his life, and he hadn't known anything like the sanity-destroying dread of the letdown, the desolation, the *end*, in Jenan's eyes.

And he couldn't do anything about it. Still, every cell in his body now fused with the manic urge to rampage after her, bring her back and keep her prisoner until he made her listen, made her believe him again.

But his every attempt to pull her away from the edge had only hurled her deeper into the abyss of distrust and betrayal. Anything more would only make things worse. She was in shock, and it would only intensify before it lessened. He had no idea when she'd be ready to listen to him. If she ever would again.

Suddenly, the sound of a helicopter approaching almost

made his heart detonate with hope. He found himself outside without even realizing he'd moved.

Then everything inside him shriveled again.

It wasn't her. It was Najeeb.

He stood there as the helicopter landed, as Najeeb jumped off, and hoped the man wasn't back to antagonize him again. He couldn't trust himself to pull back this time.

The signs of his earlier attack were becoming more evident by the second in the swelling and discoloration of Najeeb's face. But there was something new in the depths of his eyes. Not the early antipathy or the fleeting warmth or the recent bitterness. He looked troubled, anxious.

Najeeb started talking before he stopped before Numair. "When you said that my father had yours murdered, was that what you intended to say to shove both him and me from your path to the throne, or is it what you really believe?"

Needing to get rid of him fast, Numair gave him the short version of the truth. "It is what I believe."

"And you still got me here to seek a resolution?"

Najeeb answered his nod with a curt one, as if he now believed him. "Will you give me a chance to investigate this? I can't even begin to consider that my father is capable of such a crime."

He shook his head. "Listen, Najeeb—"

"No, you listen." Najeeb's agitation was no longer aggressive but entreating. "I'm not proud of my father. I know he's vain, imprudent and sometimes unethical, but I *know* him. He's not evil. And it would have taken unimaginable evil to have his own brother killed for the sake of the throne. He might appear power hungry, but he isn't. He's just a proud man who found himself in a role much larger than himself. He's done a decent job considering he inherited the kingdom in terrible shape from my grandfather. But unable to do better, and not having the best counselors, he turned to expansion to sustain the kingdom, like his bid to reannex Jareer, and once that failed, turning to Zafrana.

"But he never wanted the throne. Everyone who was around at the time would tell you how distraught he was after his brother's disappearance, how obsessively he searched for him, that even after being forced to abandon the search, he wouldn't sit on the throne until a year later, and didn't attempt to rule for yet another year, hoping his brother would return. But his cabinet eventually shamed and provoked him into taking his unexpected role seriously, and here we are today. Saraya, even with my father's mistakes, is a better kingdom than the one he'd inherited."

He ran a trembling hand over his close-cropped hair and blew out a heavy breath. "But not only am I convinced he isn't capable of having anyone murdered, let alone the older brother he worshipped, I'm also certain he would step down once he realizes who you are. In fact, he might even be relieved to finally relinquish the throne to its true heir."

Numair stared at Najeeb as he fell silent. He had heard everything Najeeb had said, but there was nothing inside him but the need to go after Jenan. Still, he had to say something to Najeeb.

All that came out when he opened his mouth was "I'm sorry I hit you, Najeeb."

Najeeb waved away his apology. "I was halfway back to Saraya when I realized no matter how you started with Jenan, you now truly love her. And that I caused a major breach between you and deserved a few broken bones—what I realize you could have easily given me, not just this lockjaw and black eyes in progress."

Needing this over now, Numair said, "I'm the one who gave Jenan every reason to suspect me. And I now believe Saraya's true heir is you. You're the one who lived there most of your life, who knows the country, who the people believe in and love. You're also the one who ameliorated your father's mistakes. Whatever Saraya is today, it's because of you, not him. But all this has nothing to do with what I believe about your father."

After a moment of total surprise, Najeeb's wariness was back full force. "So you still believe he had your father killed and you will still expose him?"

"No. I can't do that to you or to your siblings. This was what I got you here to tell you. That I'll force him to step down so you can take his place, not me."

This seemed to horrify Najeeb. "*B'Ellahi*...don't. I'm not ready to relinquish my freedom. But if you want what's best for the kingdom, we can work together behind the scenes to straighten things out without either of us being trapped in such a lofty position. You might think the throne is something to want, but believe me, what we now have is perfect. Power and the ability to do everything we want with it without being the ones everyone looks to for answers and solutions, the ones who are responsible and accountable for everything that goes on in their land."

Numair shook his head, suffocating with urgency. "I haven't made up my mind. I've just called you here to vet things out. I'm just telling you what I've come to believe lately."

"If you're still revising your stance, I hope you'll reconsider your belief about my father's guilt. I know I have no proof. I have nothing but my instincts and my lifelong knowledge of him. But if you've come to value me, I hope you'll value my judgment, too."

"Any resolution has to wait for another time, Najeeb."

"Just promise me you won't take any steps against him before we have unequivocal proof."

"I will do nothing until I get Jenan back. Only she matters to me now. Only she matters, period."

Knowing this was the most he'd get from Numair for now, Najeeb nodded. After a moment's hesitation, he extended his hand. "I'm sorry I made things worse. I hope you forgive me. I will do anything to rectify my mistake."

Even with a tornado of anxiety tearing everything up inside him, he took the proffered hand. "I was the one who started this, and I'll be the one to end it. At any price."

Before Numair withdrew his hand, Najeeb tightened his grip and dragged him closer, his eyes ablaze with sincerity. "I didn't mean what I said about Jenan earlier. She loves you, and if you love her as much, she'll believe you and in you again. She will take you back."

Numair said nothing as Najeeb turned to leave. For he'd felt how hurt Jenan had been, how pregnancy had multiplied her feeling of betrayal by a factor of a thousand. As he'd feared it would. Getting her back now felt like an impossibility.

But if he couldn't get her back, he would still pay his very life to restore her peace.

Two hours later, Numair couldn't wait anymore. One more second of inaction and he would suffer a stroke.

So he rushed to Zafrana's royal palace, all the way preparing his explanations. But he didn't find her there. The last time her family had heard from her was when she'd gone to him earlier that day.

Knowing she wouldn't answer him, he had her sisters try every method of communication. She answered none.

Out of his mind with anxiety, he sounded the general alarm to his brothers as he tore off to the States to search for her. But she seemed to have disappeared the moment she'd landed in New York, where all flights out of Zafrana landed in the States. During his flight, the men he'd sent looking for her couldn't find her anywhere she used to frequent, or couldn't even trace her steps after she left the airport.

His desperation burgeoned with every dead end, every second feeling like wading deeper in a waking nightmare.

Somewhere along the way, the nightmare metamorphosed into his old one.

But this time it was different.

Instead of men boarding his father's boat, it was tossed by waves as tall as skyscrapers. His father wrestled with a huge sail as he shouted for him to get back belowdecks before losing control of the sail that whacked him violently on the head and knocked him overboard. Then the boat capsized, tossing Numair after him.

Wrestling to the surface of the water, of the dream, his whole body discharging with sick electricity, he called Antonio and demanded that his brother meet him as soon as he landed in New York.

Antonio was there as agreed, in the limo that waited for him outside the airport. As soon as Ameen opened the door for him and he got in, Numair began to recount the searingly vivid vision.

Antonio's cool blue eyes regarded him calmly before the man exhaled. "That's what I've been hoping for, though I didn't think it a possibility it would happen spontaneously."

"What the hell do you mean?"

"I knew it would take an even more profound terror than the one you suffered when you saw your father drown and almost drowned yourself to drag more memories to the surface. When I asked for more sessions, I was going to try plunging you into an artificial panic state to dig deeper into your psyche. But since you fear nothing, I didn't know if I could even do it. But something did manage to scare you more than all the horrors in your life. Your fear for Jenan's safety and your dread you might even lose her. Those fears finally managed to jog your memories free."

"You think those were memories?"

"Not just any memories. I think these are finally your *real* memories."

"But I remembered a very different version before."

Antonio pursed his lips. "I did tell you I felt there was more to what you remembered. In hypnosis, subjects frequently take a kernel of a memory and dress it in confabulations that suit their emotional and psychological needs. You wanted someone to be responsible for your father's death, for your years of enslavement, so you invented the attackers, then used circumstantial evidence to form a perfect conspiracy that validated your alleged memories. We can do more sessions to make sure, but I'm fairly confident this is the truth at last."

Numair stared at Antonio, but saw only his realizations. He *had* needed an enemy to hold responsible, to vanquish, to pay for everything he'd lost and suffered.

But this *was* the reality at last. This was what had happened.

"I'm sorry, Phantom." Antonio looked serious when he almost never did. "As unsatisfying and unfair as I know this feels to you, it seems your father's death and your ordeal were only due to an accident."

At Antonio's unaccustomed sympathy, Numair roused himself from his musings. "No, no, it's okay."

Unconvinced by Numair's preoccupied response, Antonio pressed, "I think you should be relieved it was. This brings you closure, and rests your father in peace."

Numair nodded distractedly. Antonio *was* talking sense. But now that he'd given him a plausible explanation for the disturbing visions, the whole thing ceased to matter to him. All that mattered was that he found Jenan.

Antonio went on, "This even gives you the possibility of a family without the ugliness such a crime would have visited on all of you for generations to come."

The word *generations* hit Numair like a hammer to the

temple. For there would be a coming generation for him. It had been something he'd never truly visualized, even when there'd been every chance Jenan would get pregnant. And now she was.

But she no longer wanted to be. Not with his child.

"Phantom? Are you okay?"

At Antonio's nudging, Numair realized the rumbling sound he heard had been issuing from himself. It was a moan of agony, of regret and dread. "No, I'm not. I injured Jenan irreparably."

Antonio shrugged. "Prostrate yourself at her feet— which I'd love to see, by the way—and she'll forgive you."

"Even if she forgives me, she'll never trust me again. Or love me."

Before Antonio could respond, Numair's phone rang. A feverish glance at the caller ID made him growl as if with a kick in the gut. Richard.

The moment the line clicked, Richard's deep taunt poured into his brain. "After meeting your runaway princess, I'm considering doing her the favor of a lifetime and not telling you where she is."

Apoplectic fury took him over. Rabid threats, torrents of them, burst out of him like rapid fire.

Richard only chuckled. "Not only won't you flay me alive and all the other lovely sentiments you just expressed, you also now owe me another favor. No, scratch that. I now practically own you."

"Hang up, Richard." Numair's growl was so harsh it scraped his throat raw. "I'll find her on my own."

"Will you survive until then? And if you don't care about your suffering, would you leave her with disillusion preying on her a moment longer if you can help it?"

"Dammit, Cobra, *where is she*?" His roar made Antonio lurch and wince and Ameen almost lose control of the wheel.

"Don't give yourself a stroke, Phantom. You need your nervous system intact for crawling at her feet." Threats hurtled from Numair again before Richard interrupted. "I want a promise before I send you her location."

"What the *hell* do you want?"

"Nothing. Now. But when the time comes and I want to collect, I want one of those binding promises of yours that you'll do it without question."

"Do what?"

"Whatever I ask."

Though his head was about to explode with rage, Numair was ready to sign an actual contract that made him Richard's slave in return for immediate knowledge of Jenan's whereabouts.

"I pledge it. But say another word that isn't Jenan's location and I *will* flay you."

Richard hadn't said another word. He'd just chuckled and ended the call. The next second Numair's phone had buzzed with a text message with Jenan's address.

After dumping Antonio on the nearest curb, Numair had Ameen tearing back to his jet. He was now flying cross-country to California.

According to Richard, she'd rented a place in the desert. A year's contract had been signed. It seemed she'd wanted to escape her old life and anything that reminded her of him.

The seven and a half hours it took him to be standing on the doorstep of her rented condo in Rancho Mirage finished the last reserves of his endurance.

She opened the door, puffy eyed and precious and everything he wanted in life. He would have fallen to his knees before her if she hadn't immediately turned around, leaving him to follow her inside.

Clearly not surprised that he'd found her, she started

immediately. "I already told you you'd get what you want. You don't have to mollify me so I'd be easier to handle. I won't give you any trouble. I know no one can stop you, certainly not me, so I won't even initiate a losing fight."

"Jenan…please…"

Her deadened tone cut him off more effectively than if she'd screamed. "I'm pragmatic enough to know that whatever I wanted for my life no longer matters, and any plans or hopes I ever had are over. I have no one to blame for this but myself. I'm the one who disregarded every caution and plunged headfirst into your trap, and the result is an innocent baby, who's now the one thing that matters. I don't expect you'd be involved in its life as a regular father would, but you'll have whatever role you wish. Because I can't stop you, but mainly because I won't have the baby suffering the consequences of my folly in making you its father. I won't compound this disaster by turning its life into a battlefield over it.

"Now that you'll take over Zafrana and Saraya, you'll be there most of the time. But since you know my position on living there, we'll negotiate a schedule when I'll come periodically, so you can see your child. As long as you stay away from me, everything will be exactly as you want."

His every fiber shrieked for him to grab her, drag her back from the void of estrangement and into his heart. He could only stand before her, helpless for the first time since he was ten.

"I want nothing but for you to give me a chance to explain. What Najeeb said—"

"—is just what you told him." She spoke over him again, her lifelessness another blow to his shriveled heart. "But it isn't the truth still. I can feel it. I *always* felt you were hiding major stuff, but I deluded myself into thinking it was because they were such intensely personal and painful matters, they were unspeakable to you. I thought it would hurt you all over again if you ever had to relate them to someone. I couldn't think of trespassing on your private agonies, but I was stupid enough to keep hoping you'd one day feel enough for me, and trust me enough, to unburden yourself to me."

Suddenly, her mask of numbness started to splinter, tremors of anguish breaking through, eclipsing her fragile eyes, shaking her swollen features. "Now I know you were just hiding your identity and intentions. You never told me any truth. And you're still lying now."

With the first tear that escaped the trembling pool filling her reddened eyes, he staggered back, unable to bear the brunt of her disillusion and alienation.

"You're right. I was still lying. But no more. Though I would have given anything to never have you know the whole truth about me, I owe it to you to tell you everything."

She stumbled back, too, as if from the path of a bullet. "I'm sure you have some story you think will make me slide back into trusting you, or at least make me sympathize with your motivations and understand why you did what you did. But it's too late for that. Too late for anything."

The finality of her words felt like a mortal blow. How he remained standing, or even breathing, he had no idea.

"You already do understand why I did what I did. I wanted what I believed to be my birthright, and I always do whatever it takes to get what I want. As for making you sympathetic, there's no chance for that. The story I have to tell you—all the things you sensed me hiding—will only horrify you."

That stony distance in her eyes shredded his insides with regret. She'd once looked at him as if he was the only thing she wanted to see. Now a part of him was growing inside her, a miracle made of their essences and passion, and he was the one thing she'd rather never see again.

Exposing everything about his past—things not even his brothers knew in full—was something he'd never considered before. But he couldn't hide anything from her again. He owed her everything. The absolute truth was just the first thing among countless others that included the heart he'd grown to love her with, and the life that now meant nothing without her.

Feeling as though he was ending his own life, he told her everything. *Everything.*

It could have taken hours or only minutes to relate the horrors that had happened to him at The Organization, what he'd been forced to do, to endure, what had been done to him, what he'd been guilty of since that day he'd lost his father to what he now knew had been an accident. With every word he said, absolute shock mushroomed in her eyes.

Then he had no more horrors to relate and finally exhaled a resigned breath. "So whatever you thought I was, you now realize I'm so much worse. Far worse than anything you could even imagine."

By the time he fell silent, her body and face were shaking as if with a devastating earthquake. But it was the horror in her eyes that told him everything he'd ever feared had come to pass.

He'd scared and repelled her so completely, she'd probably risk whatever she now knew he was capable of to keep herself, and their child, away from him.

He squeezed his eyes shut on the alien feeling of defeat burning in his gut.

Knowing there was nothing to fear for or to lose anymore, he confessed what lurked in the darkest corner of his being. "I did anything I had to do to survive, and once I was free, I thought I could only remain free by destroying and conquering anyone in my path. I came here believing I'd decimate anyone who stood in the way to what I considered mine. I did intend to claim the unknown daughter of the king of Zafrana, and to use her in the same way Hassan intended to. I never considered things wouldn't go my way. I never took into account that I'd develop any feelings for you since I believed I was unequipped to feel any. Then you…happened to me.

"Everything else but you disappeared. Only you remained in my universe, a new one I never knew could exist. You melted the steel vault I built around myself. Now I am unable to seek its refuge again. I would die of exposure without you."

He finally opened his eyes and saw his devastation reflected in hers. "But you are right to reject me. Not because I betrayed you, since I didn't, but because I am what I am. You have every right to deprive me of yourself, of your love. Of our child. You should, for both of your sakes. I'm a monster. And I proved it when I hurt you—the only one who ever loved me, the only one I'll ever love."

Jenan had felt she'd known true agony when she'd thought she'd been nothing but a pawn to Numair.

But what she'd felt for her own injuries was a mere twinge compared to what she felt now for his.

Every scar on his body was the evidence of what should have broken him. But he'd only grown invincible, indomitable.

There was no doubt left in her. That was finally the whole mutilating truth. The answer to her every question and doubt.

He'd truly thought Hassan had been responsible for his father's death, for his enslavement. If anyone had ever had reason to employ subterfuge to gain his ends, it was Numair.

But there was no trace of subterfuge anymore. She just

knew it. This was everything he'd hidden from her. And she no longer had any doubt that what they'd shared had never been among the deceptions.

It had all been real.

As unthinkable as everything else had been, he loved her. As deeply and completely as she loved him. No. Far more, just as he'd said. Her love had been so fickle, she hadn't even given him the benefit of the doubt.

A lung-tearing sob of shame ripped through her.

And in the next instant she was in the haven of his arms, his feverish, trembling lips all over her face and head. Every sob that shook her seemed to rack him in agony.

"Don't do this to yourself," he whispered. "I'm not worth it."

She struggled out of his embrace, and his arms fell to his sides with a look of absolute despair. He thought she was rejecting him still.

And she pounced on him, squeezed him until she felt her arms would snap. Her tears were a deluge on his chest. "You're worth *everything*. The world isn't enough to do you justice."

It was his turn to push away so he could gape at her, incomprehension on his face. "But I thought..."

"Whatever you thought was wrong. I was only hurt because I didn't know the truth. If only you'd told me..." She stopped, wiped furiously at the flood of tears, remorse submerging her. "No, I had no excuse to behave as I did. I am the guilty one here, not you, since you had every right to keep your secret. What happened to you is so enormous, I'll live my life unable to fully grasp it all. But I loved you, and at the very first test of that love, I failed you."

He stared at her, stunned, everything inside him on full display for the first time.

Then he choked, "Loved? In the past tense."

"*Ya Ullah, no.* Every single moment in time. Even when

I thought I'd never be with you again, I knew I'd never stop loving you, yearning for you. I loved you from the first moment, and I'll love you till my very last breath."

A single tear escaped one of his eyes that had turned dark jade as he stared at her, almost panting as hard as she was. As if still afraid to let himself believe, to allow himself relief.

Then he reached out an unsteady hand to cup her cheek. "I need you to understand one thing. Then you can make this declaration again once you've heard it. I wasn't exaggerating. After a lifetime of emotional deep freeze, you've decimated all my barriers and hurled me into an inferno, one I need to burn in for the rest of my life. I will love you single-mindedly, *ferociously*...till *my* very last breath."

She hurled herself at him again, rained tears and kisses all over every part of him she could reach. "Yes, yes, please, love me just like that. It's how I love you..." Her heart twisted again. "Even though I don't deserve you."

He hauled her off the ground and crashed his lips over hers, swallowing her contrition and self-blame.

By the time he raised his head, hers was spinning, her body racked with the wildfire of reclamation and her soul with the grief of agony and guilt.

"Never shed any more tears for anything if you love me, *ya hayati, ya galbi*. You are my life and my heart. When I thought I lost you, I thought my life was over. But it has all turned out for the best. This way we've found each other in spite of everything, making what we have all that more unique and unstoppable. It was even my despair over your rejection then disappearance that drove me to finally remember the vital memory that exonerated Hassan and put my demons to rest at last."

She pulled him down to her for another frenzied kiss before she could reply, "So you really do believe it was an accident."

"Yes." His gorgeous lips suddenly quirked. "Now after I was about to puree Hassan, I might even tolerate him for Najeeb and his siblings' sake. You see, because of you I've learned how to compromise. Now that will allow us to have an extended family for our baby."

The way he said *our baby* skewered through her heart with poignancy, made her legs give out.

He cursed and swung her up in his arms, homing in, unerringly as always, on her bedroom.

What followed felt like a resurrection. A surrender of everything she was. And a possession of everything he was. A merging.

Then it was next evening, and he was starting to rocket her to the most decadent reaches of ecstasy again when she finally stopped his fondling hands, needing to say something coherent for a change.

"Numair, about the baby…"

He immediately frowned, his eyes turning wary once more. She was suddenly quivering with uncertainty again.

"You said you wanted an heir…but I have a feeling it's a girl. Don't ask me how I know—"

His lips stopped her agitated words. "I wish it *is* a girl. I lived all my life among rough, gruff XY creatures, and now I want to spend the rest of my life wallowing in the delights of female companionship."

"Really?"

"Really. I will only ever tell you the whole truth from now on."

She grimaced. "Uh…sometimes the truth isn't such a great thing to hear. Like when my nose blows up to double its current size with pregnancy hormones."

He tugged lovingly on a thick tress as he suckled a breast ripening more every day with those hormones. She was still deliciously sore from his nightlong ministrations.

"Don't they believe in the region this only happens when you're carrying a boy?"

"You've done your homework *very* thoroughly." She moaned with pleasure, then stabbed her fingers in his now loose hair, making him relinquish her nipple before she lost whatever was left of her mind again. She needed to say something else. "About Zafrana's throne…"

He lowered his mouth to her flesh again, skimmed his way up to her lips, his smile filling her with joy. "I have no more desire to take over my heritage. The only thing I care about now is the future we'll make together for our children."

"Children!"

"Only as many—or as few—as you like," he rushed to assure her. "This baby is all I need. *You* are all I need."

She groaned with yet another surge of emotion. "You are all I need, too. And I want everything possible with you, and as many children as you want. But let's just take one child at a time. Let me work on this one first."

He laughed and hugged her exuberantly. "We'll work on this one, and everything else, together."

As he lowered his head and began ridding her of her last shreds of sanity, she squirmed, making him stop again. "But you *have* to claim your heritage. It would be the best thing to ever happen to Zafrana and Saraya if you merged them and sat on their combined throne."

Nipping her lower lip, he murmured, "I only want to be on the throne of your heart."

"You've been there from day one," she moaned. "And you're now stuck there."

His chuckle filled her every cell with well-being as he slid his body over hers, setting her every nerve on renewed fire. "Now to make sure I am *fused* there."

Crying out as he entered her, merged them, she again

tugged on his hair before everything but him and those carnally emotional moments ceased to matter.

"Numair...please..." Drowning in sensation, she clamped her legs around his muscled hips to stop him from tipping her into oblivion. "Promise me you will. You'll make the best king for our region as well as for my heart."

He rose above her, his eyes a conflagration of love and devotion. "I might reconsider...if you do something for me."

She nodded frantically, losing the fight, starting to undulate beneath him, the pleasure so intense it was nearly blinding. "Anything. I'll do anything for you. I'll spend my life trying to erase everything you suffered."

The ferocity he'd promised her blazed in his eyes as he thrust hard, impaling her to her very center. "You already have. Just being you, just loving me against all odds. And now you have to promise me you'll make up for the fright and desperation you caused me when you disappeared."

"Whatever you want, it's yours."

"I want you to forever let me shower you and our family with my pampering and protection, my devotion and adoration."

She arched into him as he punctuated each phrase with a thrust until he splintered her into a soul-searing orgasm.

Long after he'd joined her in the depths of bliss, she belatedly and euphorically murmured, "Done."

* * * * *